A Bit Of A Do

David Nobbs's first break as a comedy writer came on the iconic satire show *That Was The Week, That Was*, hosted by David Frost. Later he wrote for *The Frost Report* and The Two Ronnies and provided material for many top comedians including Les Dawson, Ken Dodd, Tommy Cooper, Frankie Howerd and Dick Emery.

Apart from his nineteen novels, David is best known for his two hit TV series *A Bit of a Do* and *The Fall and Rise of Reginald Perrin*.

His new radio series *With Nobbs On* aired on Radio 4 in 2012.

Also by David Nobbs

DAVID NOBBS

A Bit Of A Do

A Story in Six Place Settings

HARPER

The names, characters and incidents portrayed in it are
the work of the author's imagination. Any resemblance to
actual persons, living or dead, events or localities is
entirely coincidental.

Harper
An imprint of HarperCollins*Publishers*
77–85 Fulham Palace Road,
Hammersmith, London W6 8JB

www.harpercollins.co.uk

This paperback edition 2012
1

First published in Great Britain by
Methuen London 1986

Copyright © David Nobbs 1986

David Nobbs asserts the moral right to
be identified as the author of this work

A catalogue record for this book is
available from the British Library

ISBN: 978-0-00-750577-7

Find out more about HarperCollins and the environment at
www.harpercollins.co.uk/green

For many good friends in the fair city and county of Hereford

Contents

First Do

August:
The White Wedding

The doors at the back of the abbey church creaked open, and the radiant bride appeared on the arm of her noticeably less radiant father.

Jenny Rodenhurst looked stunning in her wedding dress, which had achieved that elegance of simplicity which only money can buy. It was entirely white, and successfully combined traditionalism with modernity. Her accessories were extremely spare, in view of all the suffering in the Third World. Her lengthy train was held by two bridesmaids. One of them was very young, and the other one was very fat.

Her father, Laurence Rodenhurst, was as perfectly dressed as it is possible for a man to be without ceasing to look like a dentist.

Leslie Horton, water bailiff and organist, who hated to be called Les, launched himself into a hefty rendition of 'Here Comes The Bride'; and a brief burst of sunlight poured through the memorial stained-glass window dedicated to the King's Own Yorkshire Light Infantry, on whose side God had been in two world wars, though this hadn't prevented them suffering heavy casualties.

The sizeable congregation craned their necks with varying degrees of shameless curiosity to watch the bridal procession, as it moved slowly past the stall of devotional literature, past the red arrow that indicated the distressingly slow progress of the Tower Appeal Fund, past the empty back pews and massive columns of the austere Norman nave, towards the less fearsome, more decorated beauty of the Early English chancel. Now the bride and her father were level with the least important of the guests, the third cousins twice removed, the employees who just couldn't not be invited, and the funny little man with the big ears who turned up unbidden at all the weddings.

Rita Simcock, mother of the groom and wife of the town's

premier maker of toasting forks, was painfully aware that there were more people on the bride's side than on theirs, that the people on the bride's side were better dressed and more stylish. She was painfully aware that her younger son, Paul, the groom, was unemployed, and hadn't had the haircut that he had promised, and looked a mess. She was painfully aware that her elder son, the cynical Elvis, although he had a philosophy degree from the University of Keele, was also unemployed, there being no vacancies for philosophers at the Job Centre just then, and looked almost as great a mess as Paul.

Liz Rodenhurst, mother of the lovely bride, a year older than Rita but looking ten years younger, was aware of all these things too, but her main emotion as she watched the slow procession was one of irritation with her daughter for having had her beautiful hair cropped short before this day of all days. It emphasized the slight heaviness of her jaw. How perverse the young were. But then it was perverse of Jenny to marry Paul at all. 'If only I'd had the sense not to advise against it,' she thought.

The procession had reached the more important guests, first cousins twice removed, second cousins once removed, friends, uncles, aunts with unsuitable hats, Rita's slightly glazed parents, brothers, mothers, one wishing her son's hair was shorter, the other wishing her daughter's hair was longer – was nobody happy on this happy day? Certainly not the Reverend J. D. Thoroughgood. Hardly a genuine churchgoer among the whole caboosh.

As Laurence came level with Liz, he gave her a brief glance. 'What kind of a dash am I cutting?' it asked.

In reply Liz smiled, a brief demonstration of a smile, indicating to her husband that he was to remember to look happy.

Laurence nodded imperceptibly, then smiled bravely, though not entirely successfully. He was a tall, slim man with cool eyes, handsome in a rather theoretical way, like a drawing of a good-looking man. His hair was receding quietly, sensibly, with impeccable manners. Men considered him a fine figure of a man. Women didn't.

Ted Simcock nudged Paul, who stepped forward, almost tripping. At the sight of Paul, Laurence's smile flickered, then fluttered bravely, like an upside-down Union Jack in a stiff, biting, easterly wind. And the sunlight disappeared brutally, as if it had

12

been switched off.

Paul Simcock, the badly groomed groom, was twenty-one, and very nervous. His face seemed to be trying to hide beneath all that hair. His tie was very loosely tied – a compromise which pleased nobody. His inexpensive suit had almost been fashionable teenage wear when he had bought it. Five years later it was a museum piece. He had filled out in those five years, and it barely met around his groin, buttocks, chest and shoulders. He felt as if it had put *him* on in a great hurry. Buttons would burst and the zip fly open if he so much as gazed at a hard-boiled egg and Danish caviare canapé, and a pint of Theakston's Best would be out of the question. How he wished now that he hadn't been so stubborn in refusing his father's offer of a new suit.

How he wished he hadn't chosen the uncouth Neil Hodgson as best man.

The organ music ceased. 'Dearly beloved,' said the Reverend J. D. Thoroughgood rather severely, as if hinting that they would be more dearly beloved if more regularly seen at church. 'We are gathered here together in the sight of God . . .'

'I don't believe in Him,' thought Jenny. 'I wish we'd done it in a registry office.'

'. . . woman in Holy Matrimony, which is an honourable estate,' continued the vicar, whose own daughter had run off to London seventeen years ago and had never been seen again. Some said he retained the old words in all his services because for him time had stopped at that moment. '. . . instituted of God in the time of man's innocency . . .'

Liz Rodenhurst looked round at exactly the same time as Ted Simcock. Her eyes glinted, and Ted, father of the groom, spurned offerer of new suits, turned away hastily and hung on the vicar's words with exaggerated attention.

Liz smiled.

'. . . and therefore is not by any to be enterprized, nor taken in hand, unadvisedly, lightly, or wantonly, to satisfy men's carnal lusts and appetites.'

'No mention of women's carnal lusts and appetites, I notice,' thought Liz.

'. . . but reverently, discreetly, advisedly, soberly . . .'

'Oh I hope so,' thought Rodney Sillitoe, managing director of

Cock-A-Doodle Chickens and close friend of the groom's parents. 'I'll be watching her.'

'I'll be watching him,' thought his wife Betty, who was over-dressed as usual. 'If he lets the side down today . . .'

'. . . for which Matrimony was ordained,' continued the vicar in his strong, steady, undramatic Yorkshire voice, so unlike those comedy vicars on television which his wife always switched off, though they amused him as evidence of the media's tiny minds – not that either of them watched comedy or indeed television much, especially since time had stopped. 'First it was ordained for the procreation of children . . .'

'Yes, well,' said Paul Simcock silently, but half expecting to be heard by God, because under the powerful influence of the devotional atmosphere it seemed possible that He might exist after all. 'I'm afraid we jumped the gun a bit there.'

'. . . the Lord, and to the praise of his Holy Name.' The Reverend J. D. Thoroughgood's voice brought a touch of the hard limestone country into this town of the softer plains. 'Secondly, it was ordained for a remedy against sin, and to avoid fornication.'

'Sorry,' said Ted Simcock to his maker, and to his horror it almost came out aloud. His face, always slightly red, as if he overdid things, went even redder. He was a broad, bulky man, with slightly coarse features and fierce shaggy brows. His thick black hair was turning grey. Men didn't consider him much of a figure of a man. Women did.

'. . . that such persons as have not the gift of continency . . .'

'All right?' whispered Rita's mother, the seventy-six-year-old Clarrie Spragg.

'Oh aye.' Percy Spragg's answering whisper was much too loud, and Rita turned to give her father a frantic, warning glare.

'. . . themselves undefiled members of Christ's body. Thirdly . . .'

This time it was Ted's eyes that were drawn to Liz's fractionally before she gave him an unmistakeably meaningful glance. Laurence turned and saw Ted looking in his wife's direction, and Ted developed a sudden interest in the magnificent hammer-beam roof. Another burst of sunlight was streaming into the huge old church. The day was improving.

'Therefore, if any man can shew any just cause why they may

not lawfully be joined together, let him now speak, or else hereafter for ever hold his peace.'

The Reverend J. D. Thoroughgood paused dramatically, and swept a severe gaze over the congregation. The sunshine seemed very far away, in another world.

'Make somebody say something, please, oh Lord,' prayed Laurence with a fervour that surprised him. 'Save my daughter from this unsuitable marriage.'

'I require and charge you both,' said the vicar, damping Laurence's brief hope, and the church darkened again as the summer's day played grim meteorological jests with their emotions, 'as ye will answer at the dreadful day of judgement . . .'

'I don't dread it,' thought Rita. 'That's the day I come into my own.'

'. . . know any impediment, why ye may not be lawfully joined together in Matrimony, ye do now confess it. For be ye well assured, that so many as are coupled together otherwise than God's Word doth allow are not joined together by God; neither is their Matrimony lawful.'

Paul and Jenny smiled at each other a little uneasily, long-haired cheap-suited groom beside close-cropped, beautifully gowned bride, but united in their youth, their vulnerability and their love. They joined hands, and gave each other a little squeeze, and held their peace. Afterwards, both admitted that they had felt shivers and goose pimples at that moment.

'Wilt thou have this woman to thy wedded wife, to live together . . .?'

'He promised me he'd have a haircut,' said Rita to herself. 'He promised.' She had achieved, with her bottle-green two-piece suit and pink hat, the difficult feat of looking puritanical and over-dressed at the same time. Her austere hair style and natural air of worry made her look older than her forty-seven years. She had a hunched appearance, as if she were trying not to take up too much space.

'. . . and in health, and forsaking all other, keep thee only unto her, so long as ye both shall live?'

'Oh Jane!' called out the immaculate Neville Badger silently from the bride's side of the church, and this dapper doyen of the town's lawyers also had a moment of horror when he thought that everyone must have heard, so loud did his agonized private cry seem to him: 'Oh, Jane! Do you remember our wedding in this church?'

'I will,' whispered Paul, after a moment when it seemed that he would never speak.

The Reverend J. D. Thoroughgood turned to Jenny. Was it possible that he didn't think of his own daughter at this moment?

'Wilt thou have this man to thy wedded . . .?'

'Look happy, Laurence,' Laurence told himself. 'If you look happy long enough, you may even start to feel happy.'

'. . . keep thee only unto him, so long as ye both shall live?'

'Oh Lord,' prayed the immaculate Neville Badger. 'Why did you take her from me?'

'I will,' said Jenny clearly, with an outward confidence that contrasted sharply with Paul's delivery and made her parents feel that the money they had spent on her education had not been entirely wasted.

There was a slight commotion towards the back of the congregation. A second cousin twice removed had been overcome by emotion, and had to be removed. Rita was painfully conscious that it was on their side of the church.

Outside, in the bustling summer streets, people were peering at details of skiing holidays which they couldn't afford, gawping at dresses which they would never wear, and slowly reading the meagre lists of unappetizing catering vacancies in the Job Centre. To the town's seventy thousand inhabitants, the abbey church was so familiar as to be almost invisible.

The ancient market town had expanded rapidly with a mixture of light industry and heavy engineering, which were both now declining. A combination of ignorant councillors, apathetic citizens and ruthless property developers had removed almost all traces of its ancient heritage, except for the abbey church and the street names. Few tourists stopped off on their way to York, Durham and Edinburgh.

It wasn't surprising, therefore, that at the moment when the great West Door creaked open, nobody was looking at the abbey, except for a visiting Greek-Cypriot builder who was staring open-mouthed at the scaffolding which encased the massive tower.

Then suddenly the assertive strains of Leslie Horton, water bailiff and organist, who hated to be called Les, were mingling with the hum of the Saturday afternoon traffic. Now people stopped and stared, eager to see the lovely bride, the lucky groom, the proud parents, the hats and dresses of the aunts and cousins.

Six bachelor philatelists, on their way to an exhibition in the annexe of the Alderman Cartwright Memorial Museum (entrance by the side door, in West Riding Passage), watched from the top deck of a bright yellow corporation bus as the wedding guests filtered slowly under the four beautifully carved recessed arches of the Norman doorway. The philatelists were in a good mood, being as yet unaware that the exhibition of wildlife stamps had closed at one, due to local government cutbacks. One of them said, 'They haven't got too bad a day for it,' and the other five were not disposed to argue. For the paths were almost dry now after the last brief shower, and there was almost as much blue in the sky as cloud.

The wedding guests stood around in uneasy knots, not quite knowing what to do with themselves, while the funny little man with big ears who turned up unbidden at all the weddings hurried off to the Baptist Chapel, where a promising event was scheduled for three o'clock.

'Did you see Paul's hair?' said Rita Simcock in a low voice.

'I could hardly miss it,' said Ted rather less softly. 'It was on the top of his head, as usual.'

'S'ssh!' she hissed. 'He promised he'd have it cut, Ted. He promised. I mean . . . what *will* they think? They already think we're not good enough for them.'

'He's a dentist, Rita, not First Lord of the Admiralty,' said Ted.

'S'ssh! Here they come,' whispered Rita urgently. 'Look happy!' She turned to face the Rodenhurst parents, who were approaching with the immaculate Neville Badger. 'Didn't it go off well?' she said, giving a radiant smile that had no radiance in it.

'Very well,' said Liz.

'You must be very happy,' said Neville Badger. He was in his early fifties, but his recent grief seemed to set him apart as a member of the previous generation. 'Jenny looked a picture,' he said, turning to Liz and Laurence. 'A picture. I think she's putting on a bit of weight. It suits her.'

17

'Do you all know each other?' said Laurence. 'No? Ah! Neville Badger, a very old friend. Paul's parents, Ted and Rita Simcock.'

Neville Badger shook hands with Ted and Rita. Ted said, 'I own the Jupiter Foundry. I expect you've heard of us.' Rita frowned at him. Neville Badger didn't hear him, because of a passing motorcyclist with a faulty silencer and a hang-up about his virility; and when Ted repeated his statement, Neville Badger said, 'Actually, no.'

'Oh,' said Ted. 'Well, we . . . er . . . we make fire irons, companion sets, door knockers, toasting forks . . .'

'Are you a dentist, Mr Badger?' said Rita, breaking in hastily before Ted gave the whole of his firm's sales list, and smiling excessively.

'Oh no! No!' said Neville Badger too vehemently. He gave Laurence an uneasy, apologetic glance. 'No. I'm with Badger, Badger, Fox and Badger.'

'Taxidermists?' asked Ted.

'Solicitors!' said Rita frantically. She flashed him an angry glare, then switched on another nervously ingratiating smile for Neville. The sky was dotted with small white clouds, and in another remarkable meteorological coincidence . . . or celestial joke . . . the sun was popping in and out in ironical counterpoint to Rita's expressions. The sun shone when she frowned. The skies darkened when she smiled.

'I love a good wedding, don't you, Mr Badger?' she said.

'Yes, I . . . I do . . . I . . . excuse me.'

Neville Badger moved off abruptly. Rita stared after him in horrified astonishment, and the sun came out.

'His wife died six weeks ago,' explained Liz.

Two bright pink spots appeared on Rita's cheeks, and Ted gave her a look which said, 'You've done it again.'

Rodney and Betty Sillitoe were approaching. Rodney was forty-eight, Betty fifty-one, but she looked the younger. Rodney Sillitoe was wearing a very good suit, but it looked as if he had fallen asleep in a chicken coop while wearing it. Betty Sillitoe was so enthusiastically overdressed that she almost carried it off. Her dyed blonde hair peeped cheerfully out at the world round the edges of a yellow hat which wouldn't have been out of place in the Royal Enclosure at Ascot. Betty was always the first to draw attention to her dark roots. She dyed her hair to sparkle, not deceive.

'Well, that all went off splendidly;' she said.

Ted made the introductions. Rita wished he'd tried to hide the pride in his voice when he added, 'Rodney's the big wheel behind Cock-A-Doodle Chickens,' as if he were a prize salmon Ted had caught, and she knew that Liz had picked this up. Why else should she have exclaimed, as she shook hands with Rodney and gazed into his grizzled, lined face, 'Ah! A man of power!'

'Your girl looks a picture,' the big wheel behind Cock-A-Doodle Chickens told her. 'A picture.'

Rita tried to hide her irritation at all this praise of Jenny, and then found that she had a far greater irritation to hide. Her parents were hobbling painfully towards them.

Percy Spragg was a bow-legged, barrel-chested old man who appeared to be wearing a demob suit. Clarrie Spragg was a bow-legged, barrel-chested old woman whose face had set over the years into a fearsome and entirely misleading hardness in repose. She looked as if she had bought her clothes at a 1940s jumble sale at which she had arrived late. They looked to Rita as they bore down upon her like two pill boxes left over from our wartime coastal defences.

'Well, that were grand,' said Clarrie Spragg.

'Grand,' echoed Percy Spragg.

Ted effected the introductions reluctantly.

'By 'eck, your daughter's a belter,' Percy Spragg told the Rodenhursts, who flinched and smiled at the same time. Rita glared at her father, and Clarrie Spragg wasn't too pleased either.

Clarrie managed to force herself in between Percy and the group. She whispered grimly, 'Just you mind your Ps and Qs, Percy Spragg.' Her expression softened. 'All right?' she whispered.

'Oh aye,' said Percy Spragg much too loudly, and a playful gust sent his words streaming out over the gravestones which surrounded the abbey church. 'I've only been once since breakfast.'

Rita glared, and Ted hurried over to remove a Co-op carrier bag which was being drummed against one of the gravestones by the wind. As he bent to pick it up, another gust lifted Liz's dress and revealed an achingly tempting knee. He looked away hastily.

'Right, everybody,' said Nigel Thick, the carefully classless

19

young photographer from Marwoods of Moor Street. 'We're all set. Let's have the happy couple.'

There was a murmur of conversation and excitement, a communal release from tension like an echo of a distant mass orgasm, as the guests found that they had a definite role to play once more. They were watchers, admirers, murmurers of 'aaaah!' at appropriate moments. The uneasy knots broke up and reformed in a homogeneous mass. Except for Elvis Simcock, who prowled on the edges looking cynical, as befitted a young man who had studied the great philosophers and knew how weak-minded mass sentimentality is.

Paul and Jenny stood framed against the magnificent West Doorway of the old abbey church. A low-flying military aircraft struck a discordant note.

'I feel awful,' whispered Jenny, smiling rather desperately.

'Why?' whispered her husband of ten minutes.

'Right! Big smiles! Radiance pouring from every pore!' commanded the classless Nigel Thick. He thought that the taking of wedding photos was beneath him, but he was clever enough not to show this. He came out with all the right words, delivered with automated enthusiasm.

Radiance poured somewhat stickily from every pore, and froze on the cool breeze.

'Great! Terrific!' lied Nigel Thick.

'Wearing white,' whispered Jenny, free to answer Paul's question at last. 'Hypocrisy's the national disease, and we've started to build our marriage on hypocritical foundations.'

'Jenny!' whispered Paul.

'OK,' said the young photographer classlessly. 'Now a nice dreamy one. Two lovebirds gazing into each other's eyes.'

Two extremely embarrassed and shy lovebirds gazed into each other's eyes.

'Aaaaah!' went the uncles and aunts and cousins.

'Great!' said Nigel Thick, who intended to change his name to Barry Precious and become famous. 'Tremendous. Fabulous.'

'The cost of my dress could feed an African family for twenty years,' whispered Jenny.

'Jenny! Forget all that just for today,' whispered Paul.

'OK,' said Nigel Thick. 'Now a real sexy one.'

The happy couple made a brave stab at a real sexy one, and Jenny blushed prettily.

'Nice!' said Nigel Thick. 'Very nice.' Nice was the least complimentary of all his adjectives. He only used it when he meant 'Really awful!' but the massed ranks of the guests didn't seem to feel that it was awful. Another satisfied communal 'Aaaah!' drifted away across the town's jumbled-up skyline towards the foetid River Gadd.

'If our child grows up selfish and deceitful, it'll be our fault,' said Jenny. She didn't need to whisper, as a police siren was blaring.

'Jenny!' said Paul.

'OK,' shouted Nigel Thick, in competition with the siren. 'Let's go for something a bit more informal. Right? OK.'

'Is that all the man I've committed myself to for life can say – "Jenny!"?' said Jenny.

'Jenny!'

Jenny laughed and gave Paul a quick, spontaneous kiss. She had almost forgotten the watching throng.

'Good,' said Nigel Thick. 'Great. Terrific. Fantabulous.'

'"Committed for life!"' whispered Paul, as the siren faded into the western suburbs. 'It sounds like a prison sentence.'

'Oh Paul, you don't think that, do you?'

'No! Love! 'Course I don't.'

They kissed.

'Aaaah!' went the crowd.

'Ugh!' went the cynical Elvis Simcock.

'Very good!' went the classless Nigel Thick. 'Terrific! Nice one! Tremendous!'

Jenny and Paul disengaged in some confusion, as self-consciousness returned.

'OK,' said Nigel Thick. 'Happy couple out. Four proud parents in.' One day these people would have coffee-table books of his photographs. His mother still called them his 'snaps'. He was sure she did it deliberately.

The four proud parents took up their positions, Simcocks together, Rodenhursts together.

'Anything you ever want in the ironmongery line, Laurence,' said Ted. 'Custom-built door knockers, personalized coal scuttles, you name it, I'll give it at cost price.'

'Well well!' said Laurence. 'It seems that this union can be of great benefit to our family, Liz!'

Liz and Ted both gave Laurence sharp looks. Rita gave Ted a furious look. Laurence's smooth face remained innocent of expression.

'OK,' said Nigel Thick. 'Big smiles. Happiest day of your life.'

They all smiled, with varying degrees of artificiality and success.

'Terrific,' lied Nigel Thick.

'In fact, Ted,' said Liz, 'we already have one of your companion sets in our drawing room.'

'Oh! In your "drawing room"! Well well!' said Ted. He added, somewhat archly: 'I trust it's giving satisfactory service.'

'Actually the tongs have buckled,' said Laurence.

'OK,' said Nigel Thick. 'Nice dignified one. Nice and solemn. Four pillars of local society, linked by wedlock.'

They found being dignified and solemn easier than smiling.

'Great! Tremendous! Magnificent!'

'I'll bring you a replacement,' said Ted. 'Gratis. Have no fear.'

'Ted!' hissed Rita. 'Don't talk business at functions. Mr Roden-hurst doesn't talk about dental appointments at functions.'

'OK,' said the future Barry Precious classlessly. 'Now change partners. Symbolize that you're all one big happy family.'

The two couples changed places.

'Actually, I think you're both due for a check-up,' said Laurence smoothly, his face a mask. 'I'll get my girl to send you one of our cards.'

'OK,' said Nigel Thick. 'Arms round each other. Nice and friendly. No inhibitions.'

Liz's arm went round Ted, and he felt his bottom being stroked. Had he imagined it? No! There it was again, and a quick playful nip. He was terrified. Of course his bottom, by its very nature, was round the back, out of sight of people he was facing, but still . . .! Liz's arm was round his waist now. One finger stroked him very gently. It was too small a gesture to be seen by the assembled guests. But still . . .! He could feel the sweat running down his back.

Laurence put his arm round Rita with fastidious distaste. He looked like the leader of a nation embracing the wife of a hated rival at the end of a conference at which only a meaningless, bland communiqué had been issued.

'Relax!' said Nigel Thick. 'Let it all hang out.'

Laurence regarded this phrase with extreme distaste. He found it impossible to comply but, for the sake of Jenny and social decorum, he did manage to make a bit of it almost hang out. Rita smiled like the Queen being offered sheeps' eyes at a Bedouin banquet. Ted and Liz were more successful.

'Great! Terrific! Fantabulous! Marvellous! OK. Happy couple back in, with the two brothers.'

A robin watched beadily from its vantage point on a nearby gravestone as the four proud parents moved away. Ted gave Liz a warning look. Laurence noticed it, but Rita didn't. She was too busy indicating to Elvis that he was to smile. He made a wry face at her.

Elvis Simcock was twenty-four. He was taller, more self-possessed and wilder than his brother, and he was the only man at the wedding not wearing a suit, though he could have looked quite smart in his red cord jacket and tight brown trousers if he'd wanted to.

Simon Rodenhurst, Jenny's older brother, who was twenty-three, was well dressed in a rather anonymous way, a provincial professional young man who had never felt any urge to rebel. He worked for the estate agents, Trellis, Trellis, Openshaw and Finch. His face had an immature, unformed look, as if it were waiting for his personality to be delivered.

'Elvis?' said Jenny. 'Have you met my brother Simon?'

'No. That's one of the many pleasures I've missed out on so far,' said Elvis Simcock, and his 'hello' to Simon Rodenhurst was barely more than a grunt.

'OK. Big smiles. Bags of brotherly love,' said Nigel Thick.

Paul's and Jenny's smiles were a bit strained. Simon's was perfectly judged. The cynical Elvis's was grotesque, way over the top, a grinning fiend.

'Amazing!' said Nigel Thick, with more than his customary accuracy. He took pictures of the four proud parents with the happy couple, of the happy couple with the two bridesmaids, of the two bridesmaids together, of the very young bridesmaid on her own and therefore also inevitably of the very fat bridesmaid on her own, of the bride on her own and therefore also inevitably of the groom on his own, of the proud parents and the happy couple with Rita's parents. Ted's parents and Laurence's parents were dead, and Liz's widowed mother had remarried, lived in South Africa, and had been advised by her doctor not to travel.

Finally, Nigel Thick took pictures of all the guests, clustered round the great doorway in an amorphous throng. This picture offended his artistic sensibilities, but pleased his commercial instincts. It was ghastly, but everyone in it would buy a copy.

'Right,' he said. 'Say cheese.'

'Cheese,' said everybody except Laurence and Ted. Laurence said nothing. Ted said 'fromage'. There was a little laughter, but not enough.

'Great!' said the carefully classless Nigel Thick. 'Tremendous. Terrific. Marvellous. Fantastic. Fantabulous.'

The less-favoured guests began to move away, through narrow, unlovely streets of domestic brick, municipal stone and financial concrete, towards the drizzle-stained multistorey car park, which sat on the town like a stranded, truncated liner. On their left, in the bus station, laden shoppers clambered onto local buses bound for Bradeley Bottom, Upper Mill and Knapperley. Servicemen and girls with green hair sat in half-empty buses bound for York, Leeds, Wakefield, Goole, Doncaster, Wetherby, Selby and Hull. Beyond the bus station, in the cattle market, the last few cattle were waiting to be sold, like unattractive boy evacuees left till last in church halls. Old chip bags and empty packets of salt and vinegar-flavoured crisps bowled along the pavements in the fresh breeze. The town smelt of salt and vinegar and stale beer. The wedding guests felt out of place, and hurried to their cars.

The close relatives drifted slowly along the broad path between the graves, towards Tannergate, where shoppers gawped, and the beribboned limousines waited.

'Made an assignation with him yet?' said Laurence Rodenhurst under his breath.

'What?' said his wife Liz. 'With whom?'

'"With whom?" she says, grammatical even under attack. With the toasting fork tycoon. The knight of the companion set. Well, he's your type, isn't he? He has that rough, coarse quality that you regularly mistake for manly strength. I saw you looking at him!

Just don't let me catch you doing anything more than look at him, that's all.'

'Oh dear! What would you do if I did? Tear up a paper napkin?'

And, equally sotto voce, as they too walked away between the graves, the Simcock parents sparred.

'Why did you have to say "fromage"?'

'People laughed.'

'Out of pity and embarrassment. Why do you have to ruin the greatest day of my life?'

'I thought our wedding was supposed to be the greatest day of your life.'

'It was supposed to be.'

After walking away from Ted in anger, Rita found herself on her own. That was bad. Then Laurence approached her. That was worse.

There was absolutely nothing to say.

'How old is your father?' said Laurence at last.

'Seventy-eight.'

'Is he really?' He paused. 'Is he really? Well done.' Another pause. 'Well done indeed.'

Meaningless social noises. Nervous spasms expressed in words. Then silence.

Ted and Liz were following more slowly. Their words were overflowing with meaning.

'I want you,' said Liz in a low voice.

'I beg your pardon?' said Ted.

'I ache for your body.'

'Oh heck.'

'We'll see you at the hotel, then,' said Paul, when all four parents had at last arrived at the cars.

Ted kissed the radiant bride. 'You look a picture, love,' he said. 'A picture.'

This time, Rita found it impossible to hide her irritation.

The reception was held in the Garden Room of the Clissold Lodge

Hotel. There were two three-star hotels in the town. The Clissold Lodge belonged to Superior Hotels Ltd, who stood for quality. The Angel belonged to Quality Hotels Ltd, who stood for almost anything. The Clissold Lodge was therefore, at least until the Grand Universal opened, the best hotel in town. It was a late Georgian pile of no great beauty, a forbidding mass of darkening red brick, set in its own spacious grounds on the northern edge of the town. It had been erected by Amos Clissold, who made a fortune out of glue. His advertising slogan 'Ee! Buy gum! Buy Clissold's' hadn't changed for a hundred and twenty years. But after four generations of glue tycoons the dynasty had dissolved, other men had taken over the glue factory, and the Estate had sold the house.

The Garden Room was round the back. It was pleasant, spacious, dignified. French windows led out into its own private, walled garden, so that, when the sun shone, functions could be held indoors and out. And now the sun was shining quite warmly. Well, it would for the Rodenhursts, thought Ted.

There was a splendid-looking buffet down one wall, with a turreted three-tiered cake, and at the far end from the French windows there was another table with champagne bottles and glasses. The two waitresses wore smart black-and-white outfits. Paul and Jenny wondered how much, or rather how little, they were being paid.

Ted's plate was laden with pork pie, tiny sausage rolls, hard-boiled egg with Danish lump-fish roe, potato salad, Russian salad, tuna fish vol-au-vents, quiche lorraine, pilchard mousse, cottage cheese and anchovy savoury, and a frozen prawn and tinned asparagus tartlet. The buffet was perhaps not quite as magnificent as it looked, he thought, with gastronomic sorrow and social pleasure. He approached the immaculate Neville Badger, who was looking somewhat lost as he wrestled with a glass of champagne, a plate of canapés, and his grief.

'I . . . er . . . I do hope my wife didn't upset you earlier,' said Ted.

'No! Not at all!' said Neville Badger.

'I mean . . . she isn't the greatest one in the world for saying the right thing.'

'No, no. I assure you. No problem.'

'Are there many Badgers left at Badger, Badger, Fox and Badger?'

'No. Only me. My brother's in finance in Leeds, and . . .' Neville stopped, as if either the subject, or he, or perhaps both were exhausted.

'Your own children haven't followed you?' Ted asked.

'No . . . I . . . we couldn't have children. Oh Lord. Excuse me.'

Neville Badger hurried off. Liz Rodenhurst approached the dumbfounded Ted.

'You look so lost, so uncouth,' she said admiringly.

'Well . . . thank you.' Ted accepted the compliment doubtfully. 'She's beautiful,' he said, as Jenny walked radiantly past them, bearing plates of food for a group of friends by the French windows.

'No,' said Liz. 'She's attractive. That's very different. But not beautiful. Except perhaps today.'

'I can see where she gets it from,' said Ted. 'Being attractive, I mean, not being not beautiful.'

'Thank you. I think.'

'Liz!' Ted paused until the Reverend J. D. Thoroughgood had passed rather fiercely by, en route to do his duty by talking to Rita's parents, who were perched on chairs beside the fire extinguisher like wallflowers at a dance. Ted didn't want the Reverend J. D. Thoroughgood to hear what he had to say. On the other hand, he didn't want to delay too long, in case Rita came in from the garden. 'Liz? What you said earlier. I mean, wasn't it? A bit naughty. I mean . . . words . . . they needn't mean much, but they can be . . . you know . . . I mean, can't they? . . . Disturbing. Dangerous.'

'Do you really think my words don't mean much?' said Liz. 'Surely they aren't a total surprise?'

'Well . . . no . . . I suppose I've realized for quite a while that you were . . . er . . .'

'. . . aflame with sexual hunger.'

'Yes. No!!! I mean . . . Liz! . . . really!' He glanced round the crowded, buzzing room. Nobody seemed to be listening to them. 'I knew you were . . . not unattracted. I sensed you didn't find me repulsive.'

'I sense you don't find me repulsive either.'

'Well . . . no . . . I don't. Of course I don't. I mean . . . you aren't. Have you tried the tuna fish vol-au-vents? They're delicious.'

. Ted thrust his plate in front of Liz's nose – her exquisite nose, with those delicately flared nostrils that troubled him so deeply. As a diversion, the plate was a failure. 'Don't you want me?' said Liz, spurning the proffered delicacies.

'Of course I do,' he said. 'Of course I do, Liz. But.'

He turned abruptly, wriggling to get away with all the desperation of one of the nice, fat roach that he hoped to catch in the autumn competition on the so-called Wisbech trip, when they actually fished the straight, flat Ouse, miles from anywhere. How he wished it was the Wisbech trip today. The long coach ride south, to the flat, fertile Fens. The long, silent hours by the Ouse, under the wide sky. The long coach ride home. Good company. Good fishing. Good ale. Good singing on the coach. He even wished he were at home, at the sink, washing up. Washing up was an underrated pleasure. Not as exciting as sex, but infinitely safer.

He hadn't shaken Liz off. Realizing that she was following him, realizing how revealing that would be to anybody who suspected, he felt that he had no alternative but to pretend that he hadn't been trying to get away. He turned to face his tormentor.

'What do you mean, "but"?' said Liz. 'You can't just say "but" and walk off. It's unacceptable behaviour both socially and grammatically.'

'I suppose I meant . . . oh heck . . . that this is awful.'

'Awful? It's exciting. It's wonderful. I'm alive again.'

'Oh yes, I agree. Absolutely. It's very exciting. It's absolutely wonderful. But.'

'. . . it's awful?'

'Exactly.'

'Oh dear. Poor Ted. Poor poor Ted.'

Liz walked away, leaving him stranded. He bit altogether too ambitiously into a hard-boiled egg, and almost choked.

'But you promised, Paul. And I mean . . . what must they think?'

'That's it, isn't it? Never mind the greatest emotional commitment I'll ever make in my life. Just the parrot-cry of the narrow-minded. "What must they think?"'

They were seated, Paul and his mother, in an alcove in the man-made walled garden. It was a pleasant place of bricked paths and patios, studded with benches and urns. In the centre there was a small, round pond, in which silver carp held an eternal buffet among the water lilies, bladderwort and floating hyacinths. There were arches across which climbing roses had been trained. The clematis were in flower, and in a sheltered corner there was a fig tree, spreading its branches widely but producing only tiny fruit, most of which would drop off before they ripened. Perhaps it was no wonder, in this northern climate hostile to ripening figs, if Rita's emotional juices had dried out as her hair thinned and grew lifeless, and the worry lines deepened. The peace and calm of this garden couldn't reach her. It was always November, now, in Rita's garden.

'You don't understand the way their minds work,' she said. 'They look down on us. We're trade. They're professions. In his own mind, he's practically on a par with doctors, that one.'

'In Bolivia, Mum, they have sixty-five per cent infant mortality,' said the lucky groom with restrained fury. 'The average life expectancy of the tin miners is thirty-seven. The typical diet is boiled maize, followed, if they're very lucky, by more boiled maize. Extra boiled maize as a treat at Christmas. So I honestly don't think my having my hair cut matters very much.'

'Exactly!' Rita was briefly triumphant. 'So it's not much to ask to have it done, then, is it?'

'Bloody hell!' said Paul, leaping to his feet. 'All right, then. See you later.'

'Where are you going?'

'That new unisex place in Newbaldgate.'

'Paul! Not now! You're the groom.'

'So?'

'Nobody goes for a haircut during their wedding reception.'

'Then it's time to break the mould of British social behaviour. I mean I pay my mother the compliment of assuming that she wouldn't set out to spoil my wedding reception unless she felt that it wasn't too late to do something about it. So, I shall have a haircut. I don't want to start me honeymoon riddled with guilt. It might make me impotent. Then they will laugh at me.'

'There's no need to be disgusting!'

But Paul had gone in, through the French windows. He walked straight through his wedding reception, through the public rooms of the Clissold Lodge Hotel, down the wide steps, along the semicircular drive, past the rhododendrons and the cawing rooks in the long, narrow wood that screened the grounds from the Tadcaster Road, and out onto the surprisingly warm pavements of the outside world. He hopped onto a number eight bus, and was at the unisex hairdresser's before the last of his anger had drained away, and he began to wish that he hadn't gone there.

Ted didn't see his son pass. His eyes were on Liz, who was approaching him again in a manner that made him feel excited and nervous.

'You're absolutely right,' she said, raising her eyes and her glass of champagne to him. 'Words are too easy.'

'Absolutely.'

'Action's the thing.'

'Absolutely. Pardon?'

'Meet me in room 108 in five minutes.'

'I beg your pardon?'

'I've booked room 108. For them to change in before they go away. For me to do my hair in if it was blown to bits in the churchyard. Meet me there in five minutes.'

Ted looked round nervously. The hum of conversation was so loud that Kim Philby could have passed secrets to the Russians in the middle of the room without anybody noticing. But he was still nervous.

'Liz!'

'Don't you want to?'

'Well . . . yes . . . of course. Of course I do. But.'

'Oh! "But" again. But what?'

'I'm the groom's father. You're the bride's mother. It's their wedding day.'

'Is doing it any worse than wanting to do it?'

'No, but . . . I mean . . . they might come in themselves.'

'In the middle of their wedding reception? Besides, I have the key.'

'Yes, but . . . they'll be cutting the cake. There'll be the speeches.'

'We'll be back. Nobody'll miss us in this crush.'

'Yes, but . . . we're pillars of the local community. I mean . . . Liz! . . . they don't do things like that, pillars of the local community. They don't.'

'Yes, they do. They just don't get found out. As we won't. We'll never get a safer moment.' She moved closer towards him, so that briefly their bodies touched. He had to admit that the sensation beat washing up into a cocked hat. 'I thought you were a man of nerve,' she said.

'Oh heck,' riposted the man of nerve.

'We're off on holiday tomorrow. A month with Laurence! I want to remember you and me every day of that month, Ted. Give me something to remember.'

'Bloody hell. Bloody hell, Liz.'

'Room 108 in five minutes.'

And then she was gone.

'Oh heck,' said Ted. 'Oh utterly and confounded heck. Oh good God almighty.' Rita was approaching. 'Oh, it's you.'

'Can I have a word, Ted?' said Rita anxiously.

'Yes, if it doesn't take too long. I mean . . . oh God.'

'What?'

'Nothing.'

Rita chose an alcove on the other side of the garden, as far away as possible from the one in which she had talked to Paul. That was one recess she never wanted to see again!

The sun was high in a sky that was now almost entirely blue. Ted's bushy eyebrows asked the rather weary question, 'What is it this time?'

'It's Paul,' said Rita. 'He's gone.'

'Gone?' said Ted. 'They're never splitting up already! I know youngsters don't regard marriage as sacred, but . . .' He glanced at his watch. '. . . an hour and ten minutes!' He wished he hadn't looked at his watch. It reminded him that three of the five minutes had already gone.

'No! He's gone to have his hair cut.'

'Is he mad? Rita!! You've been on at him, haven't you?'

31

'I may have just touched on it.'

Rita began to cry. The immaculate Neville Badger approached them. He was adrift on the afternoon's unfamiliar currents, and was looking for somewhere to drop anchor. He saw that Rita was crying, and developed a sudden interest in silver carp.

'Love!' said Ted desperately. 'What's up, love?'

'Everybody says what a picture Jenny looks.'

'Well . . . she does.'

'Nobody says what a picture Paul looks.'

'Well . . . he doesn't.'

'Bolivian tin miners indeed!'

'You what?'

'She's changing him. He's never even mentioned Bolivia before. He's never even sent charity Christmas cards.'

'He's never sent any Christmas cards.'

'This is what I say. She's changing him.'

An airship was drifting slowly overhead. It had the name of a cigarette firm printed on it in huge letters, and was travelling towards the athletics meeting which the firm had sponsored in a moment of guilt. Did anybody look down from the airship? If so, could they have seen Ted glance surreptitiously at his watch? Five minutes and seventeen seconds. Zero hour plus seventeen. Oh good! Oh God!

He stood up.

'Don't leave me alone,' implored Rita. 'I hate functions. I feel so . . . dreary . . . drab . . . dull.'

'Don't be silly, love,' said Ted, trying desperately to encourage her, and swiftly. 'Don't be so self-conscious. I mean . . . nobody's looking at you.' He realized, even as he said it, that it was not the most felicitously expressed piece of encouragement in the history of the world.

'Exactly,' she said. 'I'm just a grey smudge.'

'Love!' he said. 'You aren't a grey smudge. You're not! I mean . . . love . . . I'm a man of discernment. A leader of industry. Would I have married a grey smudge? I mean . . . would I?'

'I wasn't a grey smudge when you married me!'

'Rita! Love! Look, I'm an Englishman. I'm a Yorkshireman. So, I can't come out with sweet nothings. I mean . . . I just can't. But . . . I promise you, love . . . you aren't . . . to me . . . in any way

. . . a grey smudge.' The die was cast. He knew that he couldn't not go to room 108, whether he wanted to or not. He would always feel that he should have gone. 'So . . . come on. Circulate. Mingle. We'll never establish our social equality with the Rodenhursts by sitting in corners and moping, will we?'

He led her in through the French windows, into a wall of talk.

Behind them, Neville Badger gloomily dropped a dollop of pilchard mousse into the pond. The silver carp fought for the privilege of devouring their distant relation.

'There's Laurence,' said Ted. 'Talk to him. Do your bit. Use your charm. Establish our social credibility.'

'Where are you going?' Rita was near to panic.

'If you must know,' said Ted, lowering his voice, 'I feel a pressing need to perform a certain natural function.' It wasn't a total lie.

'Ted!' said Rita, scandalized. 'You don't talk about that sort of function at this sort of function!'

'Well, you asked.' He steered her over to Laurence, who was moving away from the champagne table with a recharged glass. Ted carried straight on towards the doors which led into the bowels of the hotel.

Rita glared at him, then turned to Laurence and gave him what she hoped was a charming smile. It wasn't.

'It's a lovely buffet,' she drooled, hating her ingratiating voice. 'The tuna fish vol-au-vents are a revelation.'

'They have a good reputation here.'

'It's a lovely do altogether. I do like lovely dos.' Oh shut up, Rita. Listen to yourself. Unfortunately, Laurence had shut up as well. The seconds ticked by, and Rita felt that everyone in the room was gloating over her discomfiture. She felt absolutely enormous, and also about two inches high.

'Have you had your holidays yet?' she heard Laurence ask from what seemed like a great distance.

She heard herself start up again. 'No. We're going to the South of France with Rodney and Betty Sillitoe. You met them. He's the one who's the big wheel behind Cock-A-Doodle Chickens.' Oh God, Rita, why did you have to drag that in? 'We like France. Well, let's face it, it's a bit more sophisticated than Spain these days. We like something a bit out of the ordinary. Where are you going?'

'Peru.'

They would. They just ruddy well would.

Her parents hobbled painfully towards them, and her heart lurched in anticipation of further disasters.

'Hello!' said Laurence, glad of any interruption. 'And how are Mr and Mrs Twigg?'

'Spragg,' said the bow-legged Percy Spragg.

'Are you really?' said Laurence. 'That's grand! Jolly good! I love these old dialect words.'

'Dialect words?' said Percy Spragg, puzzled.

'Spragg.'

'That's my name.'

'Ah.'

Rita felt real fondness for her father then, for the first time in many years. It wasn't destined to last long.

'Well, how are you, anyway?' said Laurence.

'Grand,' said Percy Spragg. 'Just grand. By 'eck, Mr Rodenhurst, all them cars in t'car park. We've seen some changes in us lifetime, eh, Clarrie?'

'Oh aye,' said the barrel-chested Clarrie Spragg. 'We've seen a few changes all right, Perce.'

'I remember when it was all horses,' said Percy Spragg. 'Horse manure all over t' roads.'

'Percy!' said Clarrie.

'We used to shovel it up off t' roads when it were still steaming.'

'Dad!' said Rita.

'It were the 'alcyon age of rhubarb, never to return.'

'What a fascinating snippet of social history. Excuse me,' said Laurence, and he moved over to talk to his brother, who was held by many to be the leading gynaecologist in Crewe.

'Why do you have to show me up?' hissed Rita.

Her father's eyes glinted maliciously.

'Because you always think I'm going to show you up,' he said.

The afternoon sun streamed into room 108. Liz had pulled back the purple coverlet on the double bed. The sheets looked crisp and worldly.

Amos Clissold stared down at them sternly from the wall above the bed, as he did from the wall above every bed in the hotel. Ted wanted to turn the gum magnate's disapproving face to the wall. He wanted to put the Gideon Bible in the drawer of the bedside table. He didn't dare, for fear that Liz would laugh at him. As he slowly undid his shoes, he found himself wondering about hotel soap. What happened to all the unfinished cakes left by departing guests? Did the chambermaids take them home and recycle them, to supplement their meagre incomes? He tried to force his mind into more amorous channels. To no avail! Damn it, he could hear the hum of conversation and laughter from his son's wedding reception.

'Do you usually make love with your clothes on?' asked Liz.

'I can hear the reception.'

'They're chatting. They're laughing. They haven't missed us.'

'No, but . . . I mean . . . Liz . . . if we can hear them, maybe they'll hear us.'

'Above all that noise? That sounds promising!'

'Oh, Liz!'

'We're wasting time, and even I agree we shouldn't be away too long,' said Liz. 'Don't you want me?'

She removed the last of her clothes and stood before him, bronzed from her sun lamp, just a slight fleshiness about the thighs and stomach, maybe the breasts not quite as high as once they were, but he knew then that he would have wanted her if a hundred photos of the Archbishop of Canterbury had been staring down at him.

'Oh, yes! Oh Liz! Oh heck!' he said.

'Oh, Betty!'

Betty Sillitoe, who was over-perfumed as usual, was standing by the champagne table, sipping her drink. 'All a bit much?' she said.

'Dad talked to Laurence about horse manure.'

'Think yourself lucky he said manure.'

Rita poured herself half a glass of champagne. She had reached her limit. Any further crises would have to be met out of her own resources.

'You're the only person I feel close to,' she said. 'Not even the boys any more. What's happening to me? I want to scream, Betty.'

'Well . . . weddings.' Betty put an arm round Rita affectionately. 'I'm standing by the drink where I can keep an eye on Rodney and see he doesn't drink too much, bless him.' She sipped her drink and pointed towards her husband, smiling.

Rodney Sillitoe, the big wheel behind Cock-A-Doodle Chickens, was standing by one of the sash windows on the far side of the room. He was in earnest conversation with the radiant bride.

'Your dress is lovely, Jenny,' he was saying. 'Lovely.'

'Thank you.' She was holding her luxurious train over her arm. 'It's funny. You seem quite human.'

'I beg your pardon?'

'I'm sorry. I shouldn't have said that. Not today. Not when you're a guest at my wedding.'

'I didn't know it was rude to call somebody human,' said Rodney Sillitoe.

'No, but you know what I meant. You seem quite nice, but you run a kind of concentration camp for chickens. I'm sorry. I shouldn't have said that. Not today.'

'Yes, you should, because you mean it, and I admire you for it.'

'It's just that I think that if we think we have the right to exploit animals because we're superior to them, that makes us inferior to them because they never exploit us. Does that make me a crank?'

'No!'

'He can't resist an attractive young woman,' said Betty Sillitoe.

'Don't you ever feel jealous?' said Rita.

'Oh, he doesn't mean anything by it. He just likes being near attractive young women.'

'I envy you.'

'Rita! She does look a picture, I must say.'

'Must you?'

'Rita!'

'Chickens aren't like people, Jenny. They don't have the same feelings. They don't have the same expectations of life style.'

'I know. Fish have no nerves in their mouths, foxes enjoy being hunted, lobsters get a sexual thrill out of being boiled alive. I'm sorry. I shouldn't have said that. Not today.'

Jenny looked round the crowded room. She was searching for

help, but no help was at hand. She didn't want to go on with this conversation, on this day of all days, and yet she couldn't let it go.

'But how can you live with yourself?' she said, 'knowing how your chickens live.'

And Betty, from her strategic position beside the champagne, smiled indulgently as she watched their lips move.

'I love him for his foibles,' she said.

'You must feel envy sometimes,' said Rita.

'No. I wouldn't want anything in my life to be different from what it is.'

Rita closed her eyes, and swallowed her champagne as if it were medicine.

'I envy you,' she said.

'I don't look at it the same road as you, Jenny,' said Rodney. 'They're units. Costed items. I employ three hundred people in an area of high unemployment. I couldn't do that without my rationalized, cost-effective methods.'

The window could have afforded them a pleasant view over the park-like grounds. They could have seen peacocks strutting, song-thrushes holding their heads sideways as they listened for their afternoon tea, and a distant water tower, ringed by pines. Rodney and Jenny spurned these attractions.

'I suppose that's what people do,' Jenny said. 'Compartmentalize. I mean, they say Himmler was very fond of dogs. Or was it Goebbels?'

'It must have been dogs,' said Rodney. 'I don't think he was at all fond of Goebbels.'

'No! I meant . . . oh! How can you joke when I'm comparing you to . . . oh, not that I mean that you're really . . . sorry.'

'Bless you!' said Rodney Sillitoe, and he gave her an avuncular kiss which, like many avuncular kisses, held a distant echo of kisses less avuncular.

Jenny was angry. 'You're being patronizing now,' she said. 'You're forgiving me because I'm an attractive young thing. I don't want that. I hate that. I'm sorry. I shouldn't have said that. Not today.'

She kissed him.

37

'Bless them,' said Betty Sillitoe, watching the kiss.

'I envy you,' said Rita.

And in room 108, the father of the groom withdrew from the mother of the bride, in a moment of exquisite ambiguity, of relief and regret, of pride and shame, of ecstasy and horror. It was three minutes to four, and in the lounge and on the terrace the residents were ordering afternoon tea.

Exactly below the wet patch in the double bed in room 108 was the dry, happily innocent head of the bride's only brother, Simon Rodenhurst, of Trellis, Trellis, Openshaw and Finch. He was talking to Elvis Simcock, the groom's only brother.

'I'm sorry to hear you can't get a job, Elvis,' he said.

'Oh, that's all right, then, Simon,' said the cynical Elvis. 'That makes me feel much better about the total uselessness of my life.'

'I'm trying to be pleasant, Elvis,' said Simon.

'Effort, is it?' said Elvis.

'I just thought that as we're related by marriage it might be a good idea if we tried to get on with each other.'

'You're right,' said Elvis. 'I'll try. Sorry, Simon.'

Elvis gave Simon a semi-apologetic, semi-embarrassed hint of a smile, and they stood for a moment in a reasonably companionable silence as they searched for suitable topics of conversation.

'Were you named after . . .?' began Simon Rodenhurst.

'Of course I was, you stupid twit!' said Elvis Simcock, and he stormed out through the French windows.

And Rita, seeing this, said 'Oh dear' and sighed deeply.

'Rita!' said Betty Sillitoe, her blonde hair with its unashamedly dark roots mocking her friend's joylessly careful appearance. 'Rita! You can't take responsibility for how the whole of your family behaves, or you'll crack up. Relax. Have a drink.'

She poured half a glass of champagne for Rita, and topped up her own glass in order to be sociable.

'Thanks, but I've had enough,' said Rita. She put her glass down. Betty drank half her glass and refilled it from Rita's glass, so that Rita wouldn't feel guilty about the waste. You will crack up,

Rita, she thought. You're heading for a collapse, my girl, and where will we be then? What'll happen to our cosy foursome, our holiday in the South of France, our pleasant life together, our just reward for the modest wealth that we create for this community?

And Rita looked at the door and wondered why on earth Ted was taking so long. And she wondered how long Paul would be, and how they would explain his haircut. Where was her family when she needed them? Spread to the four winds. The panic came over her in waves, and she wanted to scream, and she mustn't.

Luckily, she hadn't realized, in all the crush and her self-obsessed panic, that Liz was also absent.

And Ted Simcock drifted into a half-sleep, vaguely conscious of Liz Rodenhurst's warm buttocks lodged in his crotch in the great warm tent of sensuality and satisfaction which was room 108 of the Clissold Lodge Ho . . .

The Clissold Lodge Hotel! He sat bold upright, every part of his body rigid, except one.

'Come on, Liz,' he said, leaping out of bed. 'We've got to get downstairs.'

As Simon Rodenhurst wandered out into the walled garden, determined to effect an improvement in his relationship with the cynical Elvis Simcock even if it ended with neither of them ever speaking to each other again, he passed the immaculate Neville Badger, drifting slowly into the Garden Room through the weeds of his Sargasso Sea.

Elvis Simcock was making faces at the carp. It was a one-sided game.

'I wish I was as thick as a fish,' he said.

'I'm sorry about . . . er . . .' said Simon. 'But you really shouldn't have a chip on your shoulder about something as unimportant as a name.'

'How would you like it, Simon, if you were called Garfunkel?'

'What did you read at university?'

'Dirty books mainly.'

'No. I meant . . .'

'I know what you meant. That was a little thing we Simcocks call "a joke". Philosophy.'

'Philosophy!'

'Don't sound so scornful. I've registered as a philosopher down the Job Centre. No luck yet. Although the way relations are between the two sides of industry in this country I'd have thought a bit of logical thought might come in handy.'

'Why don't you work for your father?'

'I have some pride. Our sort of people tend not to rely on that kind of privilege.'

They watched the carp in silence for a few moments, until that entertainment palled.

'What do *you* do?' Elvis made it seem more of an accusation than a question.

'I'm an estate agent.'

'Ah!'

'What do you mean – "ah!"?'

'I meant "Ah! I can't think of anything to say in response to something so incredibly boring, so I'll say 'Ah!'"'

'You can mock, but selling houses is a bit more useful than philosophy.'

'Well, I doubt if Bertrand Russell and Nietzsche would agree with that.'

'Bertrand, Russell and Neetcher? It rings a bell. Are they those big estate agents over at Beverley?'

'They are among the most famous philosophers in the history of Western thought, you ignoramus,' said the cynical Elvis Simcock.

'It was what we Rodenhursts call "a joke",' said Simon Rodenhurst of Trellis, Trellis, Openshaw and Finch.

And the carp swam round and round. Round and round.

Liz entered first, as casually and inconspicuously as she could.

Laurence detached himself without regret from a discussion about video recorders – his cousin Leonard was saying what a burden they were, all those programmes you'd recorded and never had time to watch, so you ended up getting up at seven on Sundays to catch up with them – and approached his wife. His eyes were cold.

'Where have you been?' he demanded.

'Having it off with the king of the door knockers.'

'What?? Liz!!' Laurence had turned quite white.

'I'm joking! Do you think I'd do a thing like that in the middle of my daughter's wedding reception? And, if I did, do you think I'd tell you?'

'Well, where have you been?'

'I needed some fresh air. In the immortal words that you have used to me so often, I have a headache.'

Liz moved on, towards Betty Sillitoe and Rita.

'Hello,' she said. 'I feel the need for some more champagne.'

'I'm practically a fixture in this corner,' said Betty, pouring a glass for Liz.

'Good idea,' said Liz. 'Best place to be.'

'Oh, not for the drink. To keep an eye on my wretched husband. He has been known to overindulge.'

'Haven't we all?'

'No,' said Rita, and she could feel the telltale pink spots appearing on her cheeks.

'What?'

'I know how much I like. I know how much is good for me. I won't change my ways just to please the so-called fashionable.'

'And why should you?' said Liz, pushing Rita's hostility round the post like any competent goalkeeper.

'I must say, Mrs Rodenhurst, it's a lovely do,' said Rita, accepting that her hostility hadn't landed on its target. 'The tuna fish vol-au-vents are quite an eye-opener.'

'"Mrs Rodenhurst"! Call me Liz! We're related now, Rita. Incidentally, where's that lovely husband of yours?'

'Well . . . er . . . Mrs . . . Liz . . . er . . .' Rita dropped her voice, and the pink spots blazed. 'I can't really say.'

'A mystery! How intriguing!'

'No. There's no mystery. He's . . .' The voice dropped to a whisper. 'He's answering an urgent call of nature.'

Liz seemed to find this amusing. She actually laughed. Really, there was no accounting for tastes.

'Oh, I see,' said Liz. 'Well, enjoy yourselves.' And she moved on.

'She hates me,' said Rita.

Ted felt that the casual air with which he returned to the reception was totally unconvincing. Everybody must be able to see

41

how furtive and nervous he felt.

Rita made a beeline for him.

'You took your time,' she said. It was a question in the form of a statement.

'Sorry,' he said. He lowered his voice to a near-whisper, and answered her statement. 'I've been really badly. I think it must be the tuna fish vol-au-vents.'

'They're delicious, Ted. They're different.'

'They're different all right. I happen to be allergic, that's all. Remember Sorrento.'

'Sorrento?'

'I had tuna fish then.'

'That was twenty-four years ago!'

'What difference does that make? It's lifelong, is an allergy.'

'Why did you eat them if you're allergic?'

'I didn't know I was allergic. I mean . . . love . . . I've only just discovered the common denominator.' Rita made no reply. 'Tuna fish.' Still Rita said nothing, and Ted realized that she was close to tears. 'What's wrong?'

'Sorrento,' she gasped.

'What?'

'We were happy then.'

'Rita!' He looked round desperately at the apparently happy and increasingly noisy throng. He had to stop her bursting into tears, here in the middle of the reception. He'd never live it down. 'Rita! We're happy now. I mean . . . we are. Aren't we?'

'I'm not. I'm absolutely miserable.'

But he knew then that she wouldn't cry. She had herself under control. Good old Rita. Oh God! What had he done? Well, he knew what he'd done. What he meant was, why had he done it? Well, he knew why he'd done it too. Oh God!

'Oh, Rita,' he said. 'Why? I'm happy. I am, love. I mean . . . reasonably. I mean . . . life's no picnic, but . . . I'm not *un*happy. So . . . I mean . . . why are you?' He had managed to steer her over to the champagne table during these tortured exchanges. 'Hello, Betty,' he said. He took a glass of champagne. Rita took it away from him immediately.

'You shouldn't drink champagne if you've been badly,' she said.

'Oh. No. True. Right.' Was she suspicious? Married twenty-

42

four years, and he didn't know. Oh God. Whether she was suspicious or not, he vowed to give Liz up. He would give up sex entirely and stick to marriage and washing up and fishing. He felt briefly better after making this decision. Then he remembered Paul's absence. He led Rita away from Betty Sillitoe and asked her if anybody had noticed that he was missing.

'No.'

'Oh good.'

'Good? It's a great tribute to our son's personality, isn't it? The first man in the history of the universe to go for a haircut in the middle of his wedding reception, and nobody even notices.'

'Oh, Rita! I hope they don't notice.'

'Don't you think they'll be a bit surprised when he comes in with a short back and sides?'

Jenny approached them, still holding her train. Her arm ached. What a palaver. If only they'd done it in a registry office.

'Have you seen Paul?' she asked, as if she had read their thoughts. 'Only I've just realized I haven't seen him for quite a while.'

'My word!' said Rita. 'Married for over an hour, and you're still so devoted to him.'

Jenny stared at Rita, thunderstruck, dismayed.

'Rita!' said Ted.

'I'm sorry,' said Rita. 'I'm on edge.'

Jenny touched Rita gently with her free arm. 'I want us to be good friends,' she said.

'So do I, Jenny,' said Rita. 'So do I.' She kissed her daughter-in-law on the cheek.

'Well, where is he?' said Jenny. 'I'm worried.'

'He's gone for a haircut,' said Ted.

'A haircut?? During his wedding reception??'

'It's probably my fault,' said Rita. 'He'd promised to get one, and I ticked him off about it.'

'Are you thinking of coming on the honeymoon?' said Jenny.

'What?' It was Rita's turn to look thunderstruck and dismayed.

'If he goes for a haircut during his reception because you tell him to, he may need you on the honeymoon to tell him what to do.'

Jenny blundered off in tears towards the door, and at that moment Paul entered, rather sheepishly. He hadn't had a haircut.

'Hello!' he said. 'I went for a walk. I was nervous.'

'That's not much of a haircut,' said Jenny. 'Was it worth it, I ask myself.' And she stormed out of the room.

'Oh heck,' said Paul.

Now it was a wonderful summer's afternoon, cloudless, windless. The buzzing hour. Light aircraft. Distant mowers. Imminent wasps. Whatever could buzz, did buzz. How lucky they would have been with the weather, if such considerations had still been important.

The residents having tea on the glass-roofed terrace watched the frantic groom chase the tearful bride along the hotel drive. The families on the putting green flinched as Jenny let her superb train trail along the gravel.

'Jenny! Come back!' yelled Paul.

'Why?' shouted Jenny, still running at full pelt. She'd been quite an athlete at school. In fact she could have played hockey for the county, if she hadn't found the atmosphere surrounding organized sport so reactionary.

'Because it's your wedding reception,' gasped Paul through bursting lungs. 'You'll always regret it if you spoil it.'

'That didn't stop you,' shouted Jenny. 'I'm surprised you didn't go to the pictures while you were out.'

She was fitter than him! He was making no impression on the gap between them. He felt that he was making no impression on the emotional gap either. 'Jenny!' he panted. 'I did it to stop her thinking she could get me to do what she wants any more.'

'By doing what she wanted? That's a funny way of showing it,' shouted Jenny over her shoulder, pounding on towards the Tadcaster Road.

She was drawing away from him! He felt a pang of sexist humiliation. He felt a pang of guilt at feeling a pang of sexist humiliation. He struggled on desperately. 'I never intended to have my hair cut,' he croaked. 'I just wanted to frighten her. That's all, love. Oh, Jenny, please! I love you! I love you!'

Paul's shouted endearments caused a sentimental chemist to miss a two-foot putt on the seventh hole. It also caused Jenny to turn and wait for him. She held out her arms, and he buried himself in her loveliness. They clung to each other, motionless.

44

Eva Blumenthal, a florist from Freiburg, watching their youthful embrace with delight and not a little envy, missed the teacup at which she was aiming and poured half a pot of scalding tea down the crotch of her husband Fritz, a corn chandler from the same ancient city. They play little further part in this tale, and sympathetic readers should be assured that they are happily married, with two boys, one daughter, a labrador and a BMW, and that they enjoyed their holiday, except for the ruining of a pair of Italian trousers and a Saturday night.

Paul and Jenny set off slowly back towards their reception, blissfully unaware that they were the object of so much attention.

'I don't want to lie to you,' said Paul. 'I did intend to have my hair cut.'

'Why didn't you?'

'There was a queue. Just as I got to the front a man barged in in front of me. Just because he had an appointment. I saw red and stormed out.'

'What a stormy day.'

'Well . . . I'm on edge. Weddings.'

'I know.'

'Come on,' said Paul, increasing his pace sharply. 'Everybody must be wondering where I am.'

'Yes,' said Jenny doubtfully.

'Anyway, it all ended up all right. I've taught her a lesson, and I haven't had the haircut she wanted.'

'I wish you would have a haircut,' said Jenny.

'What chance have they got?' said Rita, after the happy couple had returned and normality had been largely restored.

'They'll sort it out,' said Ted. 'You'll see.'

There were distinct signs of impending speeches. The best man, the uncouth Neil Hodgson, was sorting the tele-messages and looking sick.

'What does marriage mean these days?' said Rita.

'Love! Give them a chance.'

'What does our marriage mean?'

'Love! It means I love you, love.'

'Do you?'

'Love! I mean . . . really!'

'I'm frightened for them. I mean . . . what chance have they got if they haven't got any back-up?'

'Back-up?'

'Our two families making a real effort to be friendly to each other.'

'I'm doing my bit,' said Ted.

Laurence Rodenhurst made quite a good speech, which drew a few modest laughs from the guests. His Aunt Gladys from Oswestry described it as 'very appropriate'. She employed understatement in her choice of adjectives almost as much as the classless Nigel Thick used overstatement, and Laurence, a boy again, as always in her presence, blushed with pleasure at this high praise. 'At least the bridegroom was brief,' was her comment on Paul, but she couldn't bring this degree of enthusiasm to the uncouth Neil Hodgson's reading of the telegrams. She refused to call them tele-messages. And if 'Get Stuck In' was considered a suitable message from a teacher, it was no wonder that the nation was full of vandals and hooligans and drug addicts and sex maniacs and anarchists and businessmen who couldn't speak a word of Japanese.

Then there was the cutting of the cake. Soon that great three-tiered masterpiece, created by the Vale of York Bakery in Slaughterhouse Lane, would be travelling in tiny wedges in white boxes to distant, not-quite-forgotten relatives in Braemar, Vancouver and Alice Springs.

Now, as Laurence had arranged, the two waitresses took up permanent station at the champagne table, in the hope that this would deter all but the most unashamedly avid consumers of free booze. The waitresses couldn't afford to buy champagne, on their wages, and yet the smiles of this good-natured duo were a great deal less tired than their feet, even with people who treated them like automatic vending machines. Pam Halliday, the blonde, was dreaming of a big win on the Australian pools, and the ranch-style bungalow she would build for her parents. Janet Hicks, the redhead, was trying to forget her verruca. That night, in the public bar of the Crown and Walnut, she would drink pint for pint with Derek Wiggins, who drove a lorry for Jewson's, and after-wards . . . well, it would be nice to get the weight off that verruca.

She smiled deep in her eyes and got a rather startled look from Ted Simcock.

Ted sighed with instinctive envy of Janet's Saturday night, as he took his champagne out into the walled garden and approached his wife. There were quite a lot of people in the garden now, but Rita was just sitting there in a far, hidden corner, on a wrought-iron bench all on her own, not looking at anything. All was not well. In front of her there were two urns, in which geraniums, lobelia and begonias were flowering. Beside her there was a hydrangea. Rita had once said that, if she had been born a shrub, she would have been a hydrangea.

'Rita! What on earth are you doing?' he asked.

'Nothing.'

'Exactly. Come on, love. Please! Mingle!'

'Why? Nobody wants to talk to me. I see it in their eyes when I approach. "Oh God, here she comes."'

'Rita! Love! That's rubbish. I mean . . . it is. Absolute rubbish. Now come on! Make an effort, for Paul's sake. You can do it.'

'Just give me a minute.'

'Right.' He kissed her. 'Love!'

He entered the Garden Room, looking back to give her an encouraging 'see how easy it is' smile.

Ted's aim in entering the Garden Room was to summon up reinforcements to deal with Rita. It was family rally-round time. They must show her how much they loved her. Meeting Laurence was a nuisance.

'Reinforcements for Liz,' said Laurence, who was carrying two glasses of champagne.

'Ah.'

'I'm a lucky man, aren't I?'

'Pardon?'

'My wife's a very attractive woman.'

'Yes, I . . .' Ted looked briefly into Laurence's eyes, searching his intentions, wondering how much he knew. He found nothing, just two blue eyes searching his brown eyes. He hoped that Laurence was finding nothing except a pair of brown eyes searching his blue eyes. 'Yes, I . . . I suppose she is. I mean . . . I hadn't really . . . well, I mean, I had noticed, you couldn't not, it sticks out a . . . but . . . I mean . . . it hadn't exactly . . . if you see what I . . . Yes. Yes, I suppose she is. Yes, I suppose you are. Very. Yes.'

'I thought Paul made a good speech, considering.'

Ted wanted to say, 'What the hell do you mean – "considering"?' but actually said, 'Thank you. I thought he did very well.'

He approached Paul, who was talking with a group of his friends in front of the wrecked cake. 'Paul?' he said, and his tone made Paul move away from his friends. 'Paul? Your mother's in the garden on her own. She looks lost.'

'Oh heck. I shouldn't have gone off like that.'

'You're a good lad.'

At the other end of the buffet, the cynical Elvis Simcock was talking to Simon Rodenhurst, of Trellis, Trellis, Openshaw and Finch. Replenishments had ceased, and the buffet was now a pretty sad display. There were a few sausage rolls and slices of wet ham wrapped round cubes of pineapple, and quite a mound of tuna fish vol-au-vents, but many of the more popular plates were bare except for a few wisps of cress. Simon was shovelling sausage rolls into his mouth at a speed of which only nurses and people who have been to boarding schools are capable. 'Give up, Simon,' Elvis was saying. 'We've tried politics, religion, the royal family, the class system, sex, the nuclear holocaust, the meaning of life, estate agents' fees, blood sports, cars and Belgian beer, and we haven't found anything we agree about yet.'

'Sorry to interrupt,' said Ted.

'Please do,' mumbled Simon Rodenhurst, sending a thin spray of soggy pastry and suspiciously pink sausage meat over Ted's suit. 'Oh Lord,' he apologized, and his cheeks briefly matched the sausage meat.

Ted asked Elvis to go to the rescue of his mother. The great philosopher looked for a moment as if such a task were beneath him, then did a brief mime of the US cavalry. Ted didn't understand it, but assumed that it meant that he agreed.

'Hello, Mum,' said Paul. 'Are you all right?'

Rita tried a cheery smile. 'Fine,' she said.

High cloud was beginning to move in from the west, and the sun was more watery now. They'd been so lucky, considering.

48

'Mum?' he said. 'I'm sorry I went off like that.'

'I thought you were going to miss the cutting of the cake. What would they have thought?'

Elvis approached.

'Oh hello,' he said, with unwonted heartiness. 'I wondered where you were, our Mum.'

'Who sent you?' said Rita.

'What?'

'You've both come out to cheer me up. I thought for a moment it was spontaneous.'

'Surprisingly good speech, I thought, Paul,' said Elvis, ignoring this, 'but your friend Neil Hodgson was the worst best man I've ever come across. I couldn't make out whether he was drunk or dyslexic.'

'Dyslexia's a very serious condition, Elvis. You shouldn't make light of it.'

'Oh, I'm sorry.' Elvis was genuinely contrite. 'He is dyslexic, is he?'

'No, he's drunk, but he could have been.' Paul grinned triumphantly, then turned serious. 'It's yet another proof that this is not a caring society. I mean, fancy calling the condition of not being able to spell by a word nobody can spell.'

'All this caring about things, Paul,' said Rita, and Paul turned guiltily towards her. He had almost forgotten she was there. 'It worries me. You never used to care about things.'

Elvis looked up at a glider drifting peacefully towards Scummock Edge. He wondered how small they looked to the pilot. He wondered how small they really were.

'You never used to turn a hair about dyslexia among Bolivian tin miners,' said Rita, unheard by Elvis.

'They don't have that problem,' said Paul.

'Oh good.'

'They're illiterate.'

'She's changed you.'

'Yes. Until I met Jenny I was a great wet slob.'

'I loved that great wet slob. He was my son.' Rita burst into tears.

'Mum!' said Paul. 'Mum! What's wrong?'

'I've worn myself to a frazzle trying to lead a good life. A frazzle.

Ask Doctor Gillespie. Is it asking too much that there's somebody somewhere who likes me?'

'Mum!'

Paul put an arm round his mother, and even the cynical Elvis sat on the other side of her and put an arm round her too, and she couldn't remember when she'd last had any physical contact with Elvis.

'I like you, Mum,' said Paul, and he kissed her. 'I love you.'

'We both love you,' said Elvis, and he too kissed her. 'You just drive us up the wall, that's all.'

As soon as the lovely bride saw Paul's face, she detached herself from her friends and came to meet him. 'What on earth is it?' she said.

'Our two families. It really pisses me off. Mum's got the idea that they aren't hitting it off. And she's right, isn't she?'

'Oh God,' said Jenny. 'Bloody families.' She was still holding the train of her dress, even though it had been torn and stained during the chase along the hotel drive. 'It's supposed to be our great day and here we are having to hold a summit conference.' And indeed, as their reception swirled noisily around them, the young couple in the middle of the now untidily elegant Garden Room did look as if they were bowed down by the responsibilities of high office. 'We've got to do something about it, for our own sakes if not for theirs. I will *not* start my married life under a cloud. Look, you get my father to talk to your mum. I'll work on your dad and my mum.' Despite her politics, Jenny still found it difficult to refer to her father as 'dad', except to his face where she was encouraged by her knowledge of how much it irritated him.

'Right,' said Paul. He looked nervously across at Laurence, who was nodding and smiling at what looked like a very boring story. 'Oh heck.'

As soon as Laurence broke away – who else but his gynaecological brother would even know three jokes about hysterectomies, let alone tell all three, in swift succession, at a wedding reception? – Paul approached him, trying to think of an opening gambit.

'Hello,' he said, in the absence of any greater inspiration.

'Hello, Paul.'

No help there.

'Hello.' Pause. Can't go on saying 'hello' for ever. 'Er . . . will you do something for me?'

'Of course!' Unwise. Qualify it rapidly. 'If I can, that is. What . . . er . . . what is it you want me to do?'

'Mum.'

Total blankness.

'I beg your pardon?'

'Mum. She's a bit upset.'

'Oh. "Mum"! Upset?'

'Yes. You know, losing a son, all that. You know my mum. Well, no, you don't, but . . . you know.'

'You'd like me to have a little chat with her?'

'Well . . . yes . . . if you could. Now that we're related. She's . . . er . . . not always that good with people. You know. So, if you could sort of . . . you know . . . without her knowing that . . . you know . . . that'd be great.'

'Fine. Fine. Well . . . fine. Yes. I'll just top up my glass and . . . er . . . steam in. Yes.'

Jenny had to wait for her chance to talk to Ted. He was being buttonholed by Elvis. They were standing in front of the buffet, blocking access to the plate of tuna fish vol-au-vents, but nobody seemed to mind.

'Dad?' Elvis was saying. 'What would you do if I said that I'd like a job at the foundry? I mean, it's a hypothetical question.'

'Of course. Well, I'd say "Oh ho! We've changed our tune a bit, haven't we?"'

'Supposing I said, "Yes, I admit it. I have. I realize now that toasting forks have their place in the scheme of things. Mankind needs door knockers as well as linguistic analysis."'

'Well . . . I'd . . . I'd say the same thing as I said to our Paul. I'd say . . . "You'll respect yourself more if you can make your own way in the world." So, it's lucky the question's hypothetical, isn't it?'

'Yes. Yes, it is. Very lucky.'

Elvis went off to insult Simon Rodenhurst, but before Jenny could steam in, Ted had seen Neville Badger looking lost, and had steamed in on him.

'There's no need to bother with me, you know,' was Neville's encouraging opening gambit.

'I beg your pardon?'

'I shouldn't have come. People disappear when I approach them. They form groups to exclude me.'

'Surely not? This is England. This is Yorkshire.'

'Oh, I don't blame them. They aren't being callous. They just can't cope. Oh God, here comes poor Neville who talks about his dead wife and has tears in his eyes. You'd think a solicitor would know that grown men don't cry. It's so embarrassing.'

'Neville!'

'She'd have loved this day. She adored Jenny.'

'What can I say?'

'Precisely. Leave me be, Ted. I'm a ship without a rudder, drifting on a cold grey sea.'

'Exactly! So you're the very man.'

'What?'

'I know a harbour where there's a peeling old houseboat that could do with a lick of paint.'

'Peeling old houseboat?'

'My wife. She's in the garden. She's finding this difficult too. Would it be too much trouble for you to . . .?'

'. . . bring my charm to bear? Why not? There'll be some point in my existing for ten minutes or so.'

'Take her some tuna fish vol-au-vents. She loves them.'

'Right. I'll just top up my glass and . . . steam in.'

Neville Badger turned away to collect his cargo of vol-au-vents, and Jenny bore down on Ted.

'Hello, Jenny!' said Ted with an exclamation mark in his voice which meant, 'How lovely you still look.'

'I'd like to feel that our two families can be friends,' said Jenny.

'Oh, so would I. Very much so. Very much so.'

'Go and talk to Mum. I'd like you to get to know her better.'

'Bloody hell. I mean . . .'

'Please! She won't eat you.'

'Possibly not.'

'If only you'd give her a chance, I'm sure you'd get on. She isn't too bad.'

'No, I . . . er . . . I'm sure she . . . well . . . right . . . yes . . . OK . . . I'll . . . I'll give her a chance, Jenny.'

Jenny led Ted over to Liz, who was at one of the windows, admiring the peacocks with Laurence's Aunt Gladys from Oswestry.

'Such stylish birds,' Aunt Gladys was saying. 'They quite put some people to shame.'

'Do you mind if I borrow Mum, Auntie Gladys?' said Jenny.

'You may borrow your mother,' said Aunt Gladys. 'But I do hate to hear you call her "Mum".'

Aunt Gladys sailed away, an old tea-clipper, splendid and obsolete. She had found an artificial pearl in her portion of cake, and Liz had felt that her outrage was almost as much because it wasn't real as because it shouldn't have been there at all.

'Mum?' said Jenny. 'I want you and Ted to be friends.'

'Oh! Well, that's nice.' Liz's eyes met Ted's briefly. Neither dared hold the look for long. 'That's very nice. Well . . . I don't see why we shouldn't try to be friends, do you, Ted?'

'No. No, I don't. No . . . I don't see why we . . . er . . . shouldn't try and be friends at all.'

'Good.' Jenny moved off, with the satisfaction of a job well done.

'If she knew,' said Liz.

'I know. I feel terrible,' said Ted.

'Oh Lord. You don't suffer from post-coital depression, do you?'

'Liz! Please! I mean . . . really! Liz!'

'Do you want to forget it happened and make sure it doesn't happen again?'

'You know I don't.'

'Well, then. Nobody's suffered. Nobody knows.'

'I think Laurence suspects.'

'Well, yes, possibly. But Laurence and I have an arrangement. I do what I want, provided I'm reasonably discreet, and he doesn't do anything.'

Ted looked round nervously. Nobody was listening. 'Liz!' he said. 'I don't regard what we did today as reasonably discreet. I'm out of my depth.'

'You're going to find that you're a better swimmer than you ever believed,' said the bride's mother.

'Oh heck,' said her new lover, who had so recently promised himself that he would give her up.

The glider was barely more than a speck now, the same size as the kestrel that was hovering above the grounds in the gentle but freshening breeze.

Rita still sat in her corner, behind the urns, beside the hydrangea, protected from the breeze by the mellow brick wall, recently rather untidily repointed by employees of J. G. Frodsham and Nephew.

'Hello! There you are!' said Laurence, as if he'd been hunting for her for hours.

'Yes. Here I am. Hello.'

Rita made an effort, and smiled. Despite her smile, Laurence sat beside her and rested his arm on the bench behind her, as if to suggest that, had the back of the bench not been there, he would have embraced her actual flesh.

'You know, Rita, you and I have a lot in common,' he said.

'How do you make that out?'

'Well . . . I may seem to you to be the happy professional man . . . successful society dentist, lovely house, beautiful wife, two highly satisfactory children, suave, good-looking, confident. Actually I'm a seething mass of doubts and inadequacies.'

'Are you suggesting that I'm a seething mass of doubts and inadequacies?'

'No! Good heavens, no!'

'Well, why do you say we have a lot in common, then?'

The breeze brought the first faint smell of tomorrow's rain over the warm, walled garden, stirring the shrubs. The symmetrical elegance of the place was defiled by abandoned plates, with dollops of wasted pilchard mousse and mayonnaise.

'Why on earth should anybody think you aren't good with people?' said Laurence.

'Who told you that?' said Rita. 'Who sent you?'

'Oh Lord,' said Laurence. The faint gleam in Rita's eyes disconcerted him, and the knowledge that it was there surprised her. It was a faint indication that somewhere, beneath all the anxiety, there still remained vestiges of a sense of humour, that all might not yet be completely lost in the fragile, never-to-be-repeated adventure that was Rita Simcock's brief life on earth.

'People are being sent out in streams to see if I'm all right,' she said. 'It's very worrying.'

'Aren't you going to come in? It's cooling down.'

'In a minute. Now, please, Laurence, leave me alone.'

'Right. Right.'

And Laurence Rodenhurst returned to the Garden Room, not feeling quite as suave and confident as he had when he came out.

And Rita sighed with relief and stretched out her tense legs in her quiet arbour.

Enter the immaculate Neville Badger, bearing tuna fish vol-au-vents.

'Ah! There you are,' he said, as if he had been hunting for her for hours.

'All right,' said Rita. 'Who sent you?'

At the very moment when Rita said, 'Who sent you?' Eva Blumenthal, in room 109, was gently rubbing unsalted Welsh butter over the genitals of her husband Fritz, in an effort to alleviate the corn chandler's pain. In the Garden Room, exactly below this touching scene, Jenny was telling her young husband that she felt sick.

'I thought it was only in the mornings,' said Paul.

'It's the tension,' said Jenny. 'We've let the baby down, pretending it doesn't exist. Who knows what insecurities that may lead to? The science of the unborn baby is in its infancy.'

'Love!' said her husband of more than three hours. 'Love!'

'I think I might be going to *be* sick.'

'Well, walk out calmly. Look natural.'

'"What *will* they think?"'

'What?'

'They say as men get older they start to resemble their mothers.'

'That's a dreadful thing to say.'

Paul walked off in a huff, and immediately wished he hadn't.

Neville Badger entered from the garden, with his plate of tuna fish vol-au-vents. He saw Jenny walking slowly away from the buffet, trying to look calm and natural while feeling sick. Suddenly it became absurdly important to him that he shouldn't be entirely defeated in his efforts to get rid of the vol-au-vents. He hurried over to her.

'Jenny!' he said. 'Have a tuna fish vol-au-vent.'

She gasped, clasped her hand over her mouth, and rushed out. Neville Badger stared after her.

Paul rushed past.

'Paul! Have a . . .'

'Sorry,' said Paul, stopping briefly, out of politeness. 'It *was* a dreadful thing to say, but it was dreadful of me to say that it was a dreadful thing to say. I mean, in her condition. I mean, on her wedding day. Well, our wedding day.' Paul felt that this explanation discharged his social obligation to Neville Badger, and hurried off after Jenny.

Neville stared after him.

Ted approached. 'Any luck with Rita?' he enquired.

'No,' said Neville. 'Sorry. Have a tuna fish vol-au-vent.'

'Thanks.' Ted took a vol-au-vent.

'Tut tut!' said Laurence, hurrying forward to snatch the pastry case out of Ted's hand before he could put it in his mouth. 'Tut tut! You mustn't eat that. You're allergic.'

Laurence put the tired little delicacy back on Neville Badger's plate, and his eyes met Ted's.

How much had Ted done?

How much did Laurence know?

'Lovely wedding,' said Betty Sillitoe, who was over-powdered as usual, and she raised her almost empty glass in tribute.

'Thank you,' said Liz.

'No, I mean it. Really lovely. Really really lovely.'

'Well, they do these things well here.'

'Yes, but the point I'm trying to get across is, it's been a lovely wedding.'

'The message is getting through, I do assure you,' said Liz, her voice drier than the champagne, and she hurried on.

'Terrible snobs, those Rodenhursts,' announced Betty Sillitoe to nobody in particular.

'We've made it, haven't we?' said her husband Rodney, the big wheel behind Cock-A-Doodle Chickens.

'You what?' said Ted, who would have been astounded if somebody had pointed out that he was saying 'What?' or 'You what?' to people who had been on their side of the church, and

'Pardon?' or 'I beg your pardon?' to the Rodenhursts and their friends and relations.

'In life,' explained Rodney Sillitoe. 'We've made it in life. Who'd have thought it, a couple of dunces like us at school, and now I'm exporting frozen chicken drumsticks to Botswana and your door knockers in the shape of lions are gracing every front door on a neo-Georgian housing estate in Allwoodley. We've made it. Moderately prosperous. Happily married. Stayed the course. Survived. *And* remained friends. I've never told you this, Ted, but your friendship is one of the most important things in my life.'

'Are you drunk?'

'Ted! Do we have to be drunk before we can express affection?'

'No. Sorry. Sorry, Rodney. No, what you said, it . . . it touched a chord . . . I mean . . . it hit a spot. I . . . sorry.'

'Ted!' Rodney was alarmed. 'Is something wrong?'

'No!' said Ted overemphatically. 'It's an auspicious event. A right good do. A happy day. Nobody's happier than Betty.'

They looked across at Betty, who waved from the other side of a crush of mixed relations and friends, and gave an unmistakeably drunken lurch.

'Oh Lord,' said Rodney. 'I'll see if I can get her off the premises without a scene, bless her.'

'I envy you,' said Ted.

Rita decided that she had summoned up enough reserves of strength to enter the fray. She entered the fray from the garden at exactly the same moment as the happy couple entered it from the hotel.

Ted approached Rita, and the four of them met in the middle of the room.

'Are you all right?' asked Ted.

He was speaking to Rita, but it was Paul who answered.

'She's been sick,' he said.

'Sick?' said Rita.

'Usually only in the mornings, but today in the afternoon,' said Jenny.

'Oh heck,' said Ted.

'Everybody! Please!' shouted Jenny.

57

'What?' said Paul.

'I've got to, Paul,' said Jenny. 'Everybody! Please! I have an announcement!'

Paul and Jenny stood with their backs to the remains of the cake. The guests gathered from the corners of the room, they poured in from the garden, uncles and aunts, friends and colleagues, Simcocks and Rodenhursts, cousins once, twice and three times removed, people who were longing to go home, people who were hoping it would go on for hours because they never knew what to do after a wedding, you felt flat and not entirely sober and there was the whole evening still to go, and you wished it was the first night of *your* honeymoon. Even Percy and Clarrie Spragg, who had been nodding off peacefully in a corner, perked up and hobbled painfully over to join the throng.

The only guests who were not gathered round to hear Jenny's announcement were the Reverend and Mrs Thoroughgood, Rodney and Betty Sillitoe, Elvis Simcock, Simon Rodenhurst, and Neville Badger. The Reverend and Mrs Thoroughgood had gone to their dark, lonely home; Rodney Sillitoe had managed to get Betty out of the room, but was meeting problems in the lobby; Simon and Elvis were arguing in a far corner of the garden; and Neville Badger was walking in the grounds, tears streaming down his face, telling his dead Jane all about the day's events while he waited for the moment when he could decently take his leave.

Jenny looked grimly determined. Paul looked nervous.

'I'm pregnant,' said Jenny.

There were some sharp intakes of breath, but nobody said anything.

'We should have told you when we found out,' she ploughed on doggedly. 'But all the invitations were issued, and we couldn't very well send out a newsletter, and the white dress was ordered and everything. We thought of cancelling it and just doing it quietly in a registry office, but we knew everybody was looking forward to a bit of a do, a white wedding and everything, and you'd probably bought presents – I mean, that's not why we didn't cancel it, but if you've bought the present and then your invitation's cancelled, and you're left with a toaster you don't want, it's a bit annoying, so we decided to go through with it and not tell anybody and then go away or something round about the time so you didn't cotton onto the dates and even if you did cotton on later, well, by then it would be a *fait accompli* anyway.' She began to cry. 'I'm sorry.'

'Jenny!' said Paul. 'Come on, Jenny. Come on, love.'

'I'm sorry,' sobbed Jenny. 'We should have just done it quietly on our own like we wanted, but we wanted you all to have a lovely do like we knew you wanted.'

'Come on,' said Paul. 'Let's go and get changed and be on our way. Come on, love.'

He led her tenderly to the door. Afterwards, Rita felt quite proud of how tender he had been.

'I feel much better now I've told everybody,' wailed Jenny, and off she went with Paul to room 108, where Liz had carefully remade the bed, though Ted would later wonder whether, as they believed nobody had used the bed, the chambermaids would change the sheets before the next occupancy and, if they didn't, whether the next occupants would notice.

There was a massed tactful movement of guests to the four corners of the room, to the walled garden and to the toilets. One or two even set off home without saying goodbye, feeling that it would be the least embarrassing thing to do.

Ted and Rita and Liz and Laurence stood in silence for a moment, and then Clarrie Spragg came forward and asked Ted for the car keys.

'I'm going to sit him in the car,' she said. 'He's had enough.'

Ted started to fish out the car keys. His hands were shaking slightly.

'I 'aven't,' said Percy Spragg. 'I want to stick it out to the bitter end.'

'I'm not sure if I appreciate that phrase,' said Liz.

Clarrie Spragg began to lead Percy out, and everything might have been all right if Betty Sillitoe hadn't lurched in, with Rodney hanging onto her, trying to stop her. Naturally, Percy stopped to watch.

'No, Rodney, it must be said,' said Betty Sillitoe. 'Can't go without telling them. Rude. It was a lovely wedding. Lovely. Obviously it wasn't perfect. The tuna fish vol-au-vents were disgusting, and, all right, there were some of the biggest snobs in this town in this room – no names, no dentists' drills – but it *was* a lovely wedding, give or take a few snobs and vol-au-vents, and that's the main thing.'

Betty Sillitoe staggered out of the room.

'Sorry about that,' said Rodney.

'Never mind,' said Laurence grimly.

'You don't mind much, do you?' said Liz to Rodney.

'Not much, no,' said Rodney. 'I love her for her foibles, you see.'

'I envy you,' said Liz.

Betty blundered in again.

'Come on, Rodney,' she said. 'Can't you see we're interrupting a family row?'

Once more, Betty Sillitoe left the room.

'Goodbye,' said Rodney Sillitoe. 'Thank you. Sorry.' And he too left.

Rita had watched this display by their closest friends with even more horror than Ted, but it was Ted who felt obliged to say, 'I'm sorry.'

'Please!' said Laurence, rubbing it in while appearing to dismiss it. 'You can't be held responsible for the behaviour of your friends.'

'So our Paul couldn't wait, eh?' said the barrel-chested Percy Spragg, who was still only halfway to the door. 'I'm not surprised. She's a right cracker.'

'Or your relatives,' added Laurence, not quite softly enough.

'Go to the car, Dad,' said Rita.

'Wants to get rid of me,' said Percy Spragg. 'Didn't want me to come.'

'Dad!' said Rita, pink spots flaring. 'The things he says!'

'Never has welcomed me in her house.'

'Dad!'

'Pretends it's Ted, but Ted's all right.'

'Dad!' said Ted.

'Come on, Father,' said Clarrie Spragg.

'A bit different from our wedding, eh, Clarrie?' said Percy. 'July the twenty-first, 1938. Long time ago, i'n't it?'

'Jolly well done,' said Laurence.

'I never forget the date 'cos it was exactly two months to the day after our Rita was born,' said Percy.

Rita gasped, and Ted pulled a chair forward. She crumpled into it.

'Percy!' said Clarrie. 'You wicked old man!'

'I wouldn't have said it if she didn't want me out of the way. Come on, Mother.' Percy lowered his voice to a whisper, discreet for the first time now that it was too late. 'I need to go.' Out loud, he added, 'It's the only good thing in this bloody awful business of growing old. You don't have to give a bugger.'

Percy and Clarrie hobbled from the room with agonizing slowness, agonizing to them because of their age and rheumatism and arthritis, agonizing to everyone else for fear that Percy would start up again with further revelations.

Liz flashed Rita a smooth, cool, social, understanding smile, as of one woman to another who is very nearly her equal.

'There's no need to look at me like that, Mrs Rodenhurst,' said Rita.

'I was smiling, Mrs Simcock,' said Liz.

'Well, I don't need your smiles, thank you very much,' said Rita. 'Your family isn't exactly as pure as the driven snow.'

'What exactly do you mean by that?' said Laurence.

'Well, your daughter's pregnant on her wedding day,' said Rita.

'Your son did have something to do with that,' said Liz.

'I hope,' said Ted.

'Ted!' said Rita.

'Mr Simcock!' said Laurence.

Elvis Simcock and Simon Rodenhurst entered from the garden.

'I bet you fifty pounds you never make it as a philosopher,' Simon was saying. 'I mean, who ever heard of a famous philosopher called Elvis?'

Elvis didn't mean to knock Simon out, just to give him a good, hearty biff. But the rising young estate agent, who had also drunk rather more than he should have, fell backwards across the buffet table. He caught his head on the edge of a large plate, which jerked up into the air. Simon Rodenhurst, of Trellis, Trellis, Openshaw and Finch, slid slowly onto the ground, the upturned plate crashed onto his forehead, and a shower of tuna fish vol-au-vents descended on his inert body.

Rita fainted.

The immaculate Neville Badger entered, complete with hat,

and gazed at the scene with eyes that saw nothing.

'I'm off now,' he said. 'Goodbye, and thank you. Sorry if I . . . it was just too soon. I just couldn't cope with the sight of so many people enjoying themselves.'

Second Do

October:
The Dentists' Dinner Dance

Laurence Rodenhurst felt that it was rather vulgar of a three-star hotel to decorate the walls of its bars with signed photographs of celebrities. He appeared to be looking with extreme disfavour on the smiling face of Terry Wogan, who had signed his picture with the message 'Super nosh. Pity about the flab. Love – Tel'. But Laurence's expression might equally have been because he was talking to Larry Benson, of fitted kitchen fame.

The Angel Hotel stood in Westgate, which sloped gently away from the abbey church towards the westerly loop of the Gadd. Seven building societies, four shoe shops and the great concrete frontage of the Whincliff Shopping Centre had replaced its old town houses. Only the Angel's long, peeling facade remained to recall the street's Georgian heyday.

. The Angel's yellowish Georgian facade concealed a crumbling, rambling, heavily altered medieval interior. The Gaiety Bar, whose beamed roof was concealed by plaster except for one small hole, was situated next to the ballroom and was used as a private bar for functions held there. It was just too small to be impressive. The green-and-white striped wallpaper bore the stains of a decade, and there were large damp patches not quite hidden by furniture and radiators. The tables were extremely low, and customers reclined so steeply in the armchairs that their knees were level with the table tops. It was rumoured that the chairs had been designed by the brother of an unscrupulous osteopath. Bar snacks were served in the Gaiety Bar at lunchtimes, although the furniture made it almost impossible to eat them; but perhaps this was the aim, since they were almost inedible. The brown leather upholstery was beginning to burst. Everyone said that the Angel had known better days, though nobody could actually remember them. But it had one great advantage for events such as the

Dentists' Dinner Dance. There was still nowhere else in the town with a function room of the size required, at least not until the Grand Universal opened.

The standing room around the bar was slowly filling up with dentists and their guests. The men wore lounge suits, the women short dresses. Liz Rodenhurst's black dress was restrained and bold, simple and revealing, elegant and sexy. Her back and shoulders and, almost certainly, her breasts were tanned.

Laurence had invited his son Simon, Jenny and Paul, Ted and Rita Simcock, and Neville Badger. None of them had yet arrived.

'In Peru they drink a thing called pisco sour,' Laurence was telling Larry Benson, of fitted kitchen fame. Larry Benson was looking everywhere but at Liz's cleavage.

'Laurence!' said Liz. 'Don't bore Larry to death over Peru. He hasn't paid you for his gold bridge yet.'

She moved off energetically.

'Your wife is stunning,' said Larry Benson, trying to breathe in her lingering aroma without being seen to do so. He ran a small firm called Kitchen Wonderland. His wonderland was situated between two Indian restaurants, at the wrong end of Commercial Street.

'Yes,' said Laurence, whose chosen apéritif that night was gin and tonic. 'It's local brandy mixed with lemon juice and beaten white of egg. Surprisingly enough, it's very good.'

'She must have been quite a sensation in Peru,' said Larry Benson, whose tipple was whisky.

'Yes. Though why I say "surprisingly" I don't know. They wouldn't drink it if it wasn't. Peruvians aren't daft. Oh Lord, here are Paul's parents.'

Ted and Rita Simcock approached bravely. They were already aware that they were the only people in the room in evening dress.

'Oh God, they're in evening dress!' said Laurence. He turned towards them, putting on a smooth, false smile.

'Ted! Rita! Good to see you.'

He introduced them to Larry Benson.

'I'm sorry, Laurence,' said Rita, pink spots showing on her cheeks. 'I feel mortified. Ted said it was evening dress.'

'Never mind,' said Laurence. 'It sometimes is. It's up to the incumbent dentist. In my presidential year, it *was* evening dress.'

It would have been, thought Ted. 'Anyway, you both look terribly distinguished.'

Laurence Rodenhurst was lying. Ted always looked like a head waiter in evening dress, and Rita's long, heavy, dark blue gown hung around her in folds that made her look more curtained than dressed.

'What did his wife see in him?' said Larry Benson, the moment Laurence had gone to buy them drinks. 'She could have had anybody. She's an amazingly lovely woman.'

'Is she? I hadn't really . . . er . . .' For an awful moment Ted thought he was going to blush. He looked round and saw Liz, chatting to Timothy Fincham, president of the area dental association for the year. Helen Fincham was at his side, as always. Ted's eyes practically popped out of his head at the sight of Liz's stunning outfit. 'Yes . . . I . . . er . . . I suppose she . . . er . . . are you a dentist, Barry?'

'Larry. No, I'm in kitchens.'

'So am I, most of the time,' said Rita. 'Perhaps that's why I'm not amazingly lovely.'

There was a pause. Larry Benson, of fitted kitchen fame, sensed that perhaps he had not been entirely tactful. Ted spent longer studying a smiling photograph of Ian Botham than its message, 'A smashing evening. Cheers. Ian', could possibly justify. Rita looked round the room, seeking escape, finding none. Larry Benson seemed on the verge of one or two remarks, only to abandon them. Would it be fanciful to imagine that one of the abandoned remarks had been, 'But you *are* amazingly lovely, Mrs Simcock'?

At last he hit upon a gem that satisfied him. 'Are you a dentist, Fred?' he said.

'Ted. Oh no, no. I run a little foundry, forge type of effort. You've probably heard of us. The Jupiter Foundry.'

'No,' said Larry Benson. After another brief pause he added, 'Well, excuse I. Must go and rescue my lady wife.'

'Rita!' said Ted, when Larry Benson had gone.

'Well! People!'

'I agree, but . . . I mean . . . Rita!'

'I want to go home.'

'Rita!!'

'Is this some memory training like the Americans? Do you keep repeating my name for fear you'll forget it?'

'Rita!'

'Well, you've no interest in me.'

'Rubbish.' He looked round, and met Liz's eyes. She winked. He looked away hastily. 'Absolute rubbish. You're my wife, Rita.'

'Precisely. What on earth gave you the idea he'd said evening dress? I feel awful.'

'Rita! Love! Brazen it out. Show a bit of style.'

'I haven't got any style. I don't like style. I don't trust style.'

Laurence returned with a whisky and American for Ted, and a gin and tonic for Rita. They raised their glasses in acknowledgement of his generosity, and Ted found his head swivelling in Liz's direction. It seemed to have developed a life of its own, his head.

Liz blew him a kiss, a very brief kiss, so discreet that he could hardly believe that he hadn't imagined it, but still a kiss from a dentist's wife in a bar that contained her husband, his wife, several dentists, and guests from all walks of the town's professional life. He turned away rapidly, and found Rita looking straight at him. He went cold all over. How much did she know?

'How's business, Ted?' enquired Laurence with no overwhelming curiosity.

'Oh, absolutely! Absolutely! What? Ah! Oh, it's beginning to move again. I'm pinning great hopes on our new novelty boot scrapers with the faces of famous prime ministers.'

'Good heavens,' said Laurence. 'That sounds . . . that is new.'

'I've got some in the car, if you'd like to see them.'

'Well, I'd . . . but I don't want to put you to any trouble.'

'No trouble. I'd like to see what you think.'

Ted rushed out before anybody could dissuade him.

There was a brief, awkward pause.

'How's Mother?' asked Laurence.

'The doctors seem quite pleased with her,' said Rita.

'Jolly good. I was sorry to hear about it.' There was another pause, mocked by the apparently easy chatter that was welling up all around them. 'How was the South of France?'

'Very nice, considering. We only had rain once, but he came out in this terrible prickly heat.'

'Oh dear! Where?'

'Well . . .' Rita dropped her voice, to make sure that no more dentists would hear her than was absolutely unavoidable. 'In a rather awkward place.'

'I meant . . . in what town?' Laurence's face wore a look of faint amusement at the absurdity of all the world except himself.

'Oh! Avignon. He had to give the bridge a miss.'

There was another pause, in that early evening of pauses.

'The weather in Peru is usually very predictable,' said Laurence. 'It's dry in the dry season and wet in the wet season.'

'Well, I suppose it would be.'

'But, funnily enough, it wasn't when we were there. It had all gone topsy-turvy.'

'It's all these satellites.'

Rita wished she could lose her talent for producing conversation stoppers.

Ted removed his sample case from the boot of his Cavalier 2000 GL, looked round the dark, oily, glassed-in car park of the old coaching inn, and went through the narrow passage that linked it with the outside world. He stood on the pavement of Westgate, gulping in the comparatively fresh air, less polluted these days – partly because of genuine environmental progress, partly because the bulk of the county's pollution was exported on the prevailing winds to the lakes and forests of Sweden, and partly because so many of the factories were shut down.

Dusk had descended on Dolcis, and Lotus, and Saxone, and Freeman, Hardy and Willis, and on the marbled facades of the Halifax, Abbey National, Leeds, Harrogate and Wakefield Building Societies, and on the grimy concrete mass of the Whincliff Shopping Centre, and on the offices of the Argus, which had been painted off-white and were now off-off-white, and on all the other buildings of the sloping, curving, once-lovely street.

Three young welders on a pub crawl were hunched against the rising wind as they struggled from The Blue Posts to The Three Tuns, and a coachload of laughing women descended from a blue village bus and made their way arthritically down West Riding Passage to the bingo in the old Regal in Slaughterhouse Lane.

Simon Rodenhurst, of Trellis, Trellis, Openshaw and Finch, drove his red MGB into the car park of the Angel Hotel, and didn't see Ted.

How Ted wished he was spending this evening somewhere unpretentious, like the dear old Crown and Walnut.

He sighed, and returned to the Gaiety Bar.

Perhaps it was because of the extreme discomfort of the chairs, or perhaps it was because of the natural herd instincts of the English, but the gathering throng of dentists and their guests were standing shoulder to shoulder around the bar, as if penned there by an invisible sheepdog.

'This time last year she would have danced till dawn. She had more energy than anybody.' The immaculate Neville Badger's voice cracked. 'I'm sorry.'

'Neville!' said Liz.

'Embarrassing, isn't it? The man keeps breaking down in public. And him a past captain of the rugby club. Funny how you can never tell the ones with no moral fibre.'

'Neville! Don't be absurd.' Liz kissed him. 'Dear Neville!'

What on earth was Ted showing her husband, with Rita such an aghast spectator?

'Other people's tragedies *are* so desperately boring, aren't they?' said Neville Badger.

'What? Oh, Neville, no! You could never bore me. No, I was just intrigued to know what Ted's showing Laurence.'

Ted was showing Laurence a boot scraper. There were rungs for scraping boots, and beside them, at one end, the upturned face of Clement Attlee, moulded in lead and ridged for the reception of mud.

'Clement Attlee,' said Ted.

'Amazing,' said Laurence.

'Thank you for a great evening – Des,' said a smiling photograph of Des O'Connor. Nobody could remember ever seeing him in the Angel Hotel, but he must have visited it when appearing at the theatre.

'You've got to have them these days, gimmicks,' said Ted. 'I mean . . . who could resist grinding his boots on the face that nationalized the railways?'

He produced a similar object, with the face of Sir Winston

Churchill complete with lead cigar. Laurence frowned his disapproval of this liberty, but Ted said, 'It's got to be bipartisan, has business.'

'Do you . . . er . . . do you have any of the present incumbent?' asked Laurence.

'No,' said Ted. 'I tried, but the mould cracked.'

Jenny entered. She was wearing a patterned south Indian dress which prettily solved the problem of not outraging the conventions while not conforming to them. She was beginning to show distinct signs of pregnancy, if you looked hard enough, and since she was attractive, people often did. Only that week the manager of Beacock and Larkin's, gents' outfitters but a ladies' man, had placed a hand on her stomach 'to see if I can feel it moving', and that hadn't fooled her, and she had taken her custom elsewhere – to Leonard's, of Bridge Street, if the truth be known. The custom in question had consisted of a tie for Paul to wear tonight, his only tie having been chewed by the unruly mongrel of some visiting anarchists. And then, after all that, Paul had refused to wear a tie. All in all, the purchase couldn't be said to have been one of Jenny's most conspicuous successes.

'Dad?' she said, approaching them just as Ted snapped his sample case shut. 'They won't let Paul in without a tie.'

'Oh, the silly boy,' said Rita.

'Do you know how many wars there have been in the world since the Second World War?' said Jenny.

'What?' said Laurence.

'I'll tell you. Fourteen. That's just major international wars. It doesn't include civil wars or border skirmishes. Well, in the context of all that misery, does it honestly matter whether Paul wears a tie?'

'Of course not,' said Laurence. 'So why is he making such a fuss?'

'He isn't. Society is. He isn't saying people can't wear ties. Society is saying they must.'

Dame Peggy Ashcroft looked as if she had heard this sort of thing many times before. None of the regulars could remember seeing her in the Angel Hotel, but she must have been there more than once if her message, 'Excellent as always - Peggy', was anything to go by.

71

'I mean,' said Jenny, 'what difference does his wearing a tie make to his worth as a human being?'

'Not a lot,' said Ted. 'But it makes a hell of a difference to his getting any dinner.'

'You all enjoy laughing at us, don't you?' said Jenny. 'Well, maybe we are naïve, but it's better than dying of terminal smugness.'

'I've got a dental association tie in my car,' said Laurence with suppressed anger. 'If he has no rooted objection to maroon.'

'The nastier the better,' said Jenny. 'He won't care if it's got four crossed molars on a ruptured abscess.'

Laurence stalked out past the inseparable Finchams at a pace his pregnant daughter couldn't match.

Rita wasted no time in asking Ted, 'Why on earth did you show him your boot scrapers?'

'Because.'

'Because what? What do you mean - "Because"?'

'Because there's no room for shrinking violets in the world of the small foundry.'

'Shrinking violets! I don't know. Between you and Paul, I'll have a nervous breakdown. I will. Ask Doctor Gillespie.'

'Be fair to the lad, Rita. He's got principles.'

'Yes, and we all know where he got them from. Before he met her, he lay in bed till twelve and wandered around picking his nose and listening to rubbishy music like any other normal, healthy boy.'

Ted had an uneasy feeling that Dame Peggy Ashcroft had winked at him.

'I'll put me prime ministers in the boot,' he said.

'Don't leave me,' begged Rita, but he was on his way.

As he approached the door, Liz intercepted him and made it look accidental.

'Liz!' he said. 'Don't keep winking and blowing kisses. She'll see.'

'I must see you outside,' said Liz.

'Liz! We were dead lucky at the wedding. I mean . . . aren't they enough for you, our Tuesdays?'

'No, actually they aren't.'

'Oh heck.' Ted raised his eyes imploringly to a photograph of

General Dayan. There was no help from that quarter. The face was stern. The message, 'Good food. Good service. General Dayan', was of no practical value. 'Liz?' he said. 'Are you kinky about this? Does it turn you on, doing it in the middle of dos? It's probably got a medical name. Functionomania. Do-itis.'

'All right. We can do it in here if we're careful.'

'Liz!'

'Talk! I'm talking about talking, Ted. I have to talk to you.'

'Liz! She's watching.'

'It'd be unnatural if we never talked. I mean, we do have a young married couple in common. Just make sure you take it calmly. Pretend to show me those things you were showing Laurence.'

'Oh heck.'

Ted opened his case, and got out a boot scraper with the face of Neville Chamberlain. He could feel the sweat trickling down his back. He had an uneasy feeling that the three eyes of Rita and General Dayan were fixed upon him.

'Make sure I take what calmly?' he said.

'What on earth is that?' Liz was gawping in astonishment at the boot scraper, and Ted realized that he had never seen her gawp in astonishment before, not even at the magnificence of his naked body on their Tuesdays, when she was ostensibly at her aerobics and he was supposedly at work.

'Don't bother about it,' he said. 'I'm only pretending to show you them.'

'It's not the kind of thing you can ignore.'

'Good. If that's a harbinger of the trade's reaction, it bodes well. They're boot scrapers with the faces of famous prime ministers. That's Neville Chamberlain. You're impressed, I can see.'

'Ted, listen, I'm . . .' Jenny and Paul approached with Laurence, who was still simmering. '. . . doomed never to tell you.'

Paul's suit looked a worse fit than ever now that he seemed to be developing the symptoms of a sympathetic pregnancy, and the maroon tie clashed horribly with his green shirt.

Neville Badger wandered slowly round the edges of the bar, pretending to be interested in the photographs, reading the messages as if he expected to find the meaning of life in them, thinking about last year's dance, thinking about Jane. The inseparable Finchams veered away to avoid him, but Rita made a beeline for him.

'Hello,' she began.

He looked at her blankly.

'Sorry?' he said.

You feel rather a fool when asked to repeat a sparkling gem like 'hello'.

'Hello,' she said again.

'Ah. Yes. Rather,' said the immaculate Neville Badger. 'Hello. Absolutely.'

'Would it help to talk about her?'

'What?'

'Your wife. You *were* thinking about her, weren't you?'

'Yes. Yes, I was. How on earth did you . . . ? I was thinking of this same evening last year. She said, "We've been happy, haven't we?" It's true. We were. I mean, we wanted children, we couldn't have any, but . . . that's life, you can't choose. But, we *were* happy. I was wondering, Rita, remembering her saying that, it suddenly struck me. Last year. Did she know? Did she suspect? I'm sorry. I'm boring you.'

'No! Please! I don't mind. I mean, not that you are, but even if you were I wouldn't mind, because I like listening. It saves me from having to think of anything to say. I mean, not that that's the only reason why I enjoy hearing about Jane. I'm very interested.'

Part of Rita was outside herself, listening to herself wittering on, thinking, 'How embarrassing!' Yet she didn't feel embarrassed. And it was a lot better than thinking about her suspicions.

The object of those suspicions was standing with Liz and her pregnant daughter. Laurence and Paul were getting the drinks.

'I'm starving,' Jenny was saying. 'I could eat a horse, except I never could.'

'It's chicken tonight,' said Ted.

'I hope it's free-range,' said Jenny. 'I won't eat it if it isn't.'

'Good for you,' said her mother.

'You think you'll annoy me by not disagreeing with me, don't you?' said Jenny.

'I just have,' said Liz. Ted wanted to bury his head in those smooth, tanned shoulders. He wished she wasn't showing so much to all these people. He wanted it for himself. She was speaking to him. He hadn't been listening.

'What?' he said.

'Rita's rather trapped with poor Neville. A rescue might be diplomatic.'

'Every morning I stretch out my hands to caress her . . . er . . .' Delicacy prevented Neville from continuing, but his hands stroked an exquisite pair of invisible buttocks. 'Every morning it's a shock to find she isn't there. The mornings don't get any better, Rita.'

'They will.'

'Yes, but, you see, I don't think I want them to. That would seem like a betrayal. I'm sorry. I don't mean to burden you with my grief.'

'Oh, please do. I don't mean burden me. It doesn't. I'm glad. I don't mean glad about your grief. I mean, I'm glad to listen to the grief I wish you hadn't got, but since you have got it, I'm happy to listen to it.'

Ted arrived. 'Rita, love, could I have a word?' he said, and to Neville he added, 'Sorry, Neville.'

'No! Please!' said Neville.

Ted led Rita away.

'What is it?' she asked.

'Nothing. I was rescuing you.'

'It's years since I enjoyed a conversation as much as I was enjoying that one with Neville.'

'So how are you feeling?' asked Liz. In the months to come her relationship with her daughter was going to be put under a great strain. She wanted a nice, cosy chat before that happened.

'Fine. It's going to be a girl, incidentally.'

'You've had it tested?'

'I didn't need to. I know.'

'Oh. Are you pleased?'

'I don't mind. I think it's selfish of parents to saddle their children with burdens of expectation.'

'Is that a dig at me or mere disinterested trendy priggishness?'

Oh dear. The nice, cosy chat was going wrong.

'It's a dig at you,' said Jenny. 'Well, you never left me in any doubt that you preferred Simon.'

'Are you serious?'

'Yes. I mean, I'm not resentful. Not now. Not really.'

It was no wonder if her parents did prefer Simon, thought Jenny. He'd always been the perfect son. Never a hint of rebellion. It was entirely typical of him that he should walk past at this very moment, right on cue.

'Oh, hello, Mother,' he said. 'Hello, Jenny. You look nice!'

'There's no need to sound so surprised.'

'Well . . . you're my sister.'

'I mean not that I want gracious compliments, anyway. They're so sexist.'

'Simon?' said Liz. 'Would you say I favoured you as a child, at Jenny's expense?'

'Good Lord, no! You were absolutely fair.'

'You see!' said Jenny triumphantly, when Simon had moved on.

'What?'

'If Simon thinks you were fair, you must have been favouring him outrageously. Which isn't surprising, really.'

'What do you mean by that?'

'Well . . . you've always been a man's woman, haven't you?'

Jenny had never seen the blood rush to her mother's cheeks before.

'You bitch!' said Liz.

'Mum!' said Jenny, as Liz stormed off. 'I didn't mean . . . I only . . . Oh!'

Paul and Laurence returned with Ted's scotch, Rita's gin and tonic, dry white wine for Liz and Jenny, and a pint of bitter for Paul – a pint of bitter as an apéritif at a dinner dance! Were these Simcocks deliberately uncouth or merely ignorant?

'Where's your mother?' said Laurence, and Jenny burst into tears and ran from the room.

'She does that a lot,' said Paul proudly, and he set off to follow her.

'Paul!' said Laurence. 'Sometimes, a woman needs to be alone.'

'Not Jenny,' said Paul. 'Our marriage is a totality of shared experience.'

'Berk,' said Laurence softly to Paul's back, and then Rodney and Betty Sillitoe were bearing down on him. Rodney looked as if he'd slept in his suit for a week. Betty was wearing a mauve dress and a string of real pearls.

'Rodney and Betty Sillitoe,'. said Rodney. 'Ted and Rita's friends. We met at the wedding.'

'I *do* remember,' said Laurence drily. 'What a pleasant surprise! What brings you to these festivities?'

'Timothy Fincham invited us,' said Rodney Sillitoe, and felt obliged to add, 'He isn't our dentist.'

'Rodney's provided the chickens,' said Betty Sillitoe, who was over-powdered as usual.

'Funnily enough,' said Laurence, 'I was listening to Radio Gadd this morning . . . for the news, I can't stand their . . . well, you can't call it music . . . and I heard an advert for your Cock-A-Doodle Chickens.'

'"Which chickens give the best value? Cock-A-Doodle Do."'

'That was it. I suppose it must be a bit of a problem finding decent copy writers for local radio.'

'I wrote that myself,' said Rodney Sillitoe.

'I must go and check the seating arrangements,' said Laurence Rodenhurst.

'Where's my pint?' said Paul, when they returned after Jenny had washed the tears away, and they had kissed passionately in the corridor.

'You're not going to forget to check that the chickens are free-range, are you?' said Jenny.

'Bloody hell!' said Paul. 'Do you want me to die of thirst?'

He went off, with slightly bad grace.

'I didn't mean straightaway,' Jenny called out, but it was too late.

As Paul reached the door, he met Percy Spragg hobbling painfully in.

'Hello, Grandad,' said Paul, surprised. 'What are you doing here?'

'Mr Mercer invited me. He's not my dentist, but he's a friend.'

'How's Grandma? I'm coming to see her tomorrow.'

'The doctors say she's satisfactory. It seems a strange description to me.'

The bow-legged Percy Spragg moved on, seemingly unabashed by the great crush of dentists and their guests. You might have thought he went to dinner dances every night.

He came face to face with Rita.

'Dad!' said Rita. 'What on earth are you doing here?'

'I'm glad you're so pleased to see me,' said Percy. 'Mr Mercer invited me. He drinks at my pub. He drives me to the football.'

'He invited you here? Why?'

'Incredible though this may seem, Rita, he likes me. He thought I might be lonely, with our Clarrie in the General. Unlike some people, he seems to think I know how to behave in public. Des O'Connor! What's he got to look so pleased about?'

'What do you mean – "unlike some people"?'

'Nothing.'

'Well, don't let him down. Don't drink too much.'

'I'll try not to fart too often an' all.'

'It's all right,' said Paul. 'They're free-range.'

'Amazing,' said Jenny. 'I mean, I could just have had the veg, but . . .'

Rodney and Betty Sillitoe bore down on them. The big wheel behind Cock-A-Doodle Chickens gazed with frank admiration at Jenny's legs. He kissed her enthusiastically and said, 'Mmm! Pregnancy suits you!' Jenny recognized the disinterested quality of his admiration and kissed him back, warmly. Betty Sillitoe beamed. Paul spotted his pint. Everybody was happy. Rodney Sillitoe said, 'Well, the moment of truth approaches.' Betty said, 'It's the first time he's been to a do where they're using his chickens. He's like a cat in a hot tinned soup.' Jenny said, 'I didn't realize you did free-range chickens.' Rodney said, 'I don't.' Paul, about to take his first sip, froze.

'Paul!' said Jenny. 'You lied to me.' And she rushed off again.

'Jenny!' said Paul. 'Oh heck!' He put his pint down sadly. 'I haven't even had a drink yet.'

Jenny, halfway to the door, swung round. 'I'm really learning about your priorities tonight,' she said. 'First, drink. Second, me,' and she picked up Paul's pint and poured it over his head.

There was a momentary faltering in the buzz of conversation, and then it burst forth with renewed, excited vigour.

Paul rushed out in pursuit of his weeping wife.

Ted, who was trapped with Larry Benson, of fitted kitchen fame, and his lady wife, who was actually no lady, had watched this scene with some alarm. But at least it gave him an excuse to escape from the Bensons. He stepped forward to intercept the youngsters, but they were gone before he could reach them.

Now he found Liz at his side. 'Don't worry about them,' she said. 'A good row will do them good. We can have that talk on the dance floor later.'

'Are you mad?' said Ted. 'We can't be seen dancing together.'

'We're related by marriage. It'll look very suspicious if we don't dance together.'

They were facing a smiling photo of Frank Carson and a pile of prawns. His message read, 'It's the way I shell 'em'.

'You were quite impressed with my boot scrapers, weren't you?' said Ted.

'Don't get excited if I tell you what I have to say,' said Liz.

'I *thought* you were impressed.'

'I'm pregnant. You're the father.'

'You didn't think I had it in me, did you? You're what??? I'm what???'

'S'ssh! Be calm. Be casual. Rather awful, isn't it? The baby was actually conceived during our children's wedding reception.'

The double doors to the ballroom opened, and there appeared a man who looked almost as much like a head waiter as Ted.

'Ladies and gentlemen, dinner is served,' he announced.

'Oh my God,' said Ted, half to himself, still digesting Liz's news. Rodney Sillitoe, arriving at his elbow as the hungry throng surged forward, said, 'You see! Even my best friend's dreading my chickens.'

The ballroom of the Angel Hotel was just too small to be impressive. It was also slightly too long for its width. The walls were the colour of smokers' fingers. The outside wall, opposite the double doors to the Gaiety Bar, was curtained for most of its length. The curtains had also seen better days. In those better days they had been dark red. Now they were just dark. Ted noticed none of this.

At one end of the room, on a raised platform, the Dale Monsal Quartet had already set up their instruments. On the big drum, in large letters, were the words, 'Dale Monsal Quartet'. Ted noticed none of this.

At the other end of the room, separated from the platform by the dance floor, there were eighteen round tables, where nineteen dentists and their hundred and twenty-three guests were tucking into prawn cocktails. There were only two empty places. Laurence endeavoured to compensate for the absence of Jenny and Paul by being unwontedly free with his claret.

The prawn cocktails were at least reasonably generous. The diners had been consuming rubbery frozen prawns for quite a while before they found that all they had left in their cut-glass bowls was a pile of soggy lettuce in Marie Rose sauce. As far as Ted was concerned, he might have been eating braised toenail clippings in porcupine blood. How like Liz to give him this earth-shattering news seconds before they were to sit at the same table, for a three-course meal, in company with *her* husband and *his* wife.

Rita was too preoccupied to notice how preoccupied Ted was. What *had* happened to Paul and Jenny? And then suddenly she was too preoccupied even to worry about Paul and Jenny. Elvis had entered, also in evening dress, carrying a pile of plates. She almost stopped breathing. The humiliation of it! Her own son, Elvis Simcock, philosophy graduate, the first graduate in the family, working here, tonight, in front of all the Rodenhursts, as a waiter!

Timothy and Helen Fincham's table got their main course first. The Mercers' table had to wait longer, and Percy Spragg entertained them with reminiscences about the golden age of dung. By the time the Rodenhursts got theirs, the chicken was already congealing. And Simon Rodenhurst, of Trellis, Trellis, Openshaw and Finch, had called out excitedly, 'Good Lord! There's Elvis! He's one of the waiters!' and Rita had closed her eyes and felt herself sinking.

Some said the chicken was tasteless. Others were not so complimentary. Fish meal was the main flavour detected. The chicken was burnt on the outside, but almost raw along the bones. No playwright on the first and only night of a West End flop suffered more than Rodney Sillitoe during that meal. Only Timothy Fincham's Bulgarian burgundy kept him going.

With each portion of chicken there was a rock-hard rasher of bacon. The stuffing was from a packet. The service was strained. The frozen beans weren't. The pale green water in which they had been cooked mingled with the anaemic gravy. Thin green streams trickled round the natural dams provided by tinned carrots and greasy roast potatoes. It reminded Simon Rodenhurst of seaside holidays, of building dams to trap the streams emerging from tidal pools, of untroubled youth, before he had realized what a very ordinary, plodding brain he had.

Between the main course and the ersatz meringue, the Dale Monsal Quartet began to play. It comprised piano, drums, saxophone and clarinet. Dale Monsal himself was on sax, a dry, rather sad, withdrawn man, with receding hair. The pianist was black, wiry, all smiles and ivory teeth. The drummer was white, huge and fierce. The clarinetist was middle-aged, with her greying hair done in a severe bun, which contrasted dramatically with the very low cut of her long evening gown. She simpered, smiled and ogled, constantly attempting to impose her personality on the gathering.

After the first, somewhat uninspiring number, Dale Monsal spoke through a microphone held too close to his mouth. 'Good evening, ladies and gentlemen and dentists,' he said in a slow Yorkshire voice, as flat as a fen. 'My name is Dale Monsal and this is my quartet. Our aim tonight is enjoyment. Your enjoyment. We aim to provide music loud enough to make you want to get up and dance, but not so loud that you can't talk if you want to. Thank you. And now, without further ado, take it away, maestros.'

Dale Monsal and his three maestros took it away. Muddy coffee was served. Rita gave Ted an urgent look and, when he ignored it, she kicked him and he said, 'Ow! You kicked me, Rita!' and she glared at him, and performed a brief and surprisingly competent mime, suggesting that she could have had quite a career in street theatre, if fate had willed her life otherwise; and at last the penny dropped, and Ted bought a round of drinks.

At first nobody danced, and it looked as if the event would be a monumental flop. People began to stretch their legs and wander about. Simon Rodenhurst moved off to join some of the younger people, and the immaculate Neville Badger went on a slow though restless wander.

The conversation turned inexorably to Peru.

'It's a fascinating country,' said Laurence, after giving a not notably brief resumé of their holiday, 'but it is very poor. It makes one ashamed of one's greed and over-consumption.'

'Absolutely,' said Ted.

'Same again?' said Laurence.

'Why not?' said Ted.

Laurence moved off, and Ted got a look from Rita.

'Well, if I don't have another whisky, it'll not get transported to the shanty towns of Lima,' he said. 'I mean . . . it won't. It'll just help put some poor sod in Western Scotland out of work.'

Rita sighed. 'I do hope they're all right,' she said fervently.

'Well, a lot of distilleries have closed,' said Ted, 'but . . .'

'I think Rita meant Paul and Jenny,' said Liz.

'Oh, don't worry about them,' said Ted. 'It's just a tiff.'

'They have such high expectations from marriage,' said Liz.

'They'll learn,' said Rita.

There was a pregnant pause.

'Do you think that was what novelists mean by a pregnant pause?' said Liz.

'Liz!!' said Ted, and immediately realized that he'd sounded much too horrified, since nobody else knew that Liz was pregnant. 'I mean it's not exactly tactful, is it?' he went on, struggling to justify his interjection. 'I mean . . . mentioning pregnancy in public. When our son got your daughter pregnant before they were married. I mean . . . is it?'

Neville Badger returned from his wanderings, and asked Liz to dance.

'Come on, Ted,' said Rita.

'Rita! The floor's not crowded enough for me yet.'

'I find talking a strain. I hardly drink. The food's never any good. The only thing I enjoy's the dancing. So come on.' And she yanked Ted to his feet. Her new-found ruthlessness and strength astounded and worried him. How much did she know?

As they made their way between the tables to the dance floor, Ted felt very conspicuous in his evening dress.

Elvis, conspicuous in his evening dress, was passing by with a tray of empties.

'Elvis!' said Ted. 'I mean . . .'

'What?'

'Working here!'

'It's a job. You were scornful enough when I was on the dole.'

'You might have told us,' said Rita.

'You'd have tried to stop me working tonight,' said Elvis, who never told them anything now that he was sharing a flat with friends.

'I would,' said Ted. 'You've embarrassed your mother.'

'But not you?'

'Well . . . I can't say it exactly thrills me. I mean . . . it's not exactly conducive, is it?'

'You should have given me a job in the foundry.'

Elvis moved on, and Simon Rodenhurst called, 'Waiter!' Elvis turned, and found himself facing a table of rather drunk young men who looked slightly too anaemic to be described as 'young bloods'.

'Elvis!' said Simon with mock surprise. 'Good Lord!' To his friends he explained, 'This is my sister's husband's brother.' To Elvis he said, 'I hope this isn't embarrassing you.'

'Not at all,' said the cynical Elvis Simcock. 'Though you might try something a little politer than yelling "Waiter!"'

Simon's companions raised their eyebrows.

'What's rude about that?' asked Simon, and the eyebrows were raised even higher when Elvis replied, 'Well, how would you like it if I popped into your office and yelled "Estate agent!"?'

'That's rather different,' said Simon.

'Yes,' said Elvis. 'You're a member of a profession, and I'm "only a waiter".'

Simon's companions gave little cries of derisive surprise at Elvis's insolence. This was rather fun.

'I think you're rather forgetting your position, aren't you?' said Simon Rodenhurst, of Trellis, Trellis, Openshaw and Finch.

'I was speaking as your sister's husband's brother,' said the philosophy graduate from Keele University. 'Speaking as a waiter . . .' He became insultingly obsequious. '. . . what can I get you, "gentlemen"?'

The Gaiety Bar was almost deserted as Laurence bought his round of drinks from the dark, intense Alec Skiddaw, the thirty-five-year-old barman with the boils.

'This is my strategic defensive position,' explained Betty Sillitoe from a bar stool. 'Here I can keep an eye on Rodney's drinking.'

'Absolutely! Good plan!' said Laurence.

Betty Sillitoe gave a gasp of pain.

'What's wrong?'

'Would you believe, toothache? No need to ask if there's a dentist in the house.'

'We had a heart attack last year at the Doctors' Dinner Dance,' said the dark, intense Alec Skiddaw. 'That was a full dress do.'

'It's ironical,' said Betty, who was over-rouged as usual. 'Rodney chipped a tooth at the wedding. There was an imitation pearl in the cake. He's had no pain, and I've had toothache ever since.'

'I'm sorry about the cake,' said Laurence. 'That makes four. Some distant cousin wrote from Durban to ask if it was a good luck charm. I've complained to the Vale of York Bakery in no uncertain terms.'

'It was the woman what did them keep fit classes on Radio Gadd,' said Alec Skiddaw.

'My dentist can't find anything wrong,' said Betty Sillitoe, with another gasp of pain.

'Who is your dentist?'

'Mr Young.'

'Ah! Sorry, that was unethical. Young Mr Young or old Mr Young?'

'I think it must be old Mr Young. He's as bald as a coot.'

'That's young Mr Young.'

'She's made a complete recovery,' said Alec Skiddaw.

'If you want a change, I can thoroughly recommend Mercer,' said Laurence. 'Odd chap, but a good dentist.'

'She's very attractive. Wasted on radio,' said Alec Skiddaw. 'There were seven doctors fighting to give her the kiss of life.'

'Odd?' said Betty, taking a large sip of gin to ease the pain.

'He's a socialist,' explained Laurence. 'Believes in the National Health Service. Likes football. Supports the United. Must be a masochist.'

'Doctor Spreckley won,' said Alec Skiddaw. 'His wife didn't

half give him what for afterwards. I was amazed she knew such words, but apparently she's a regular theatre-goer.'

'Or,' said Laurence, 'and I wouldn't like to put any pressure on you, I could fit you in as a private patient on Monday morning.'

'I'd like that,' said Betty Sillitoe. 'I'd like to have the job done properly.'

As Laurence took his tray of drinks into the ballroom, he met Percy Spragg hobbling in the opposite direction.

'Hello!'said Laurence. 'How's Mr Sprigg enjoying himself?'

'I've no idea,' said Percy Spragg.

'What?' said Laurence.

'My name's Spragg,' said Percy. 'I'm having a grand time, and this is the first time I've had to go all night.'

The dance floor was beginning to fill up. The Dale Monsal Quartet were playing 'Send In The Clowns'.

Rita danced well, if tautly. Ted was clumsy and self-conscious, resentful of every second spent away from his drink.

Neville Badger was leading Liz towards them. They passed quite close. Ted and Liz exchanged brief looks.

Rita's tongue slid out and moistened her lips as she summoned up her courage.

'Ted?' she said. 'Is there something between you and Liz?'

'What? Between me and Liz? Rita! What on earth gave you that idea?'

'I keep seeing you exchanging looks.'

'Ah.' Ted swung her round just in time to avoid colliding with Rodney Sillitoe, who had miraculously managed to separate the Finchams, and was pushing Helen round the floor. 'Yes. Well . . . the fact is, Rita . . . to be absolutely honest . . . I don't like her. In fact, I can't stand her. So that's what I'm doing, you see. Overcompensating. For the sake of harmony between our two families.'

Ted found himself steering straight for Liz and Neville again, as if they were on the dodgems. Neville steered Liz out of danger. He danced beautifully, immaculately, in an absent-minded, melancholy way.

Ted met Liz's eyes again, and flashed her a warning.

'You are going to dance with her, aren't you?' said Rita.

'What?'

'People'll talk if you don't.'

'What a convoluted mind you've got. All right. I'll dance with her if you insist, but don't you trust me?'

'Trust you? After Ingeborg!'

'Rita! For God's sake! It was exceptional circumstances. I mean . . . love . . . she'd just placed an order for two thousand toasting forks! I mean . . . Rita . . . be fair . . . one isolated lapse, bitterly regretted.'

They swung round beside the Dale Monsal Quartet.

'What about Big Bertha from Nuremberg?'

Ted stared at the musicians, in order to avoid thinking about Big Bertha from Nuremberg. He found himself gazing at the lady clarinetist's slightly blotchy shoulders, which rose to an almost Amazonian bos . . .

'What about Big Bertha from Nuremberg?' repeated this new, remorseless Rita.

'All right,' Ted admitted. 'Two isolated lapses, bitterly regretted.'

He felt his eyes searching out Liz. He yanked them back to the Dale Monsal Quartet. He felt that the lady clarinetist was willing him to meet her eyes. He did so. She dropped her eyes coyly, as if directing him down past her busy blowing mouth to her slightly blotchy shoulders, which rose to an almost Amazonian bos . . .

'What about Doreen from the Frimley Building Society?'

'All right! Three isolated lapses, bitterly regretted!'

'That was carrying "Everyone's friendly at the Frimley" too far.'

'Well exactly, Rita. This is it, love. I was seduced by the power of advertising.'

'You were seduced by Doreen Timperley. And I was impressed by how regularly you were paying in.'

'Rita! Three peccadilloes in twenty-four years of marital bliss. I mean . . . be fair . . . that's one lapse every eight years.'

'It's eight years since Ingeborg.' Rita turned to flash a beaming, insincere smile at Liz. 'I'll be very suspicious if you don't dance with her,' she said.

'I've said . . . I'll dance with her.'

'Don't hold her too close, or I'll know something's up.'

'Bloody hell, Rita!'

'Don't hold her too far away either, as if she's a piece of Dresden china. That'll make me really suspicious.'

'Bloody hell, Rita. Have you brought your tape measure?'

The waltz ended. There was modest applause, as befitted the performance.

The cynical Elvis Simcock approached Simon Rodenhurst, of Trellis, Trellis, Openshaw and Finch, on the tide of that modest applause. He bore a tray of exotic drinks.

'So, Elvis,' said Simon. 'Are you finding your three years as a philosophy graduate helpful in your job?'

'Incredibly.'

'Oh good. That is a relief. You don't feel the taxpayers' money has been poured down the drain, then?'

'Money! Money! Money!' said Elvis. 'I hear the heart of an estate agent beating like a till. No. In my brief spell as a waiter, Simon, I've found the answer to a question that has exercised philosophers down the ages.'

'What question?'

'Is the external world real, or is it just a figment of my imagination? Does this room exist? Does this tray exist? Does your large pernod and blackcurrant exist? Do you exist outside my mind? I know now that you do.'

'How?'

'Because I wouldn't waste time by inventing anybody as futile as you.'

Simon's companions felt that this waiter had gone too far. They glared at him, and waited for Simon to deliver a suitably cutting retort. They weren't sure if Simon rose to the occasion. 'Same to you, with knobs on,' he said.

'Precisely!' said Elvis Simcock. 'Case proved.' He put on his obsequious waiter voice, dripping with respect. 'That'll be nine pounds thirty-six, sir. Call it ten pounds for cash.'

'My ex-brother-in-law from Falkirk, he's an income tax inspector and an amateur ventriloquist. Though when I say amateur, I'm not saying he doesn't accept a bit in the back pocket. Well, they know the dodges, don't they? They're forced to.'

It was very quiet in the Gaiety Bar. Trade was slack, and the

Dale Monsal Sound barely penetrated. The dark, intense Alec Skiddaw was taking the opportunity to regale Betty Sillitoe with tales of his family life.

'Amazing,' said Betty, feeling that some comment was called for. She had just ordered another drink. It would have looked odd if she'd spent so much time in the bar and never ordered anything.

'His first wife came from Lowestoft. I've never known a woman that could do dog impressions like she could when she'd had a few.'

Neville Badger entered from the ballroom, with Liz.

'A dry vermouth and a dry white wine, please. Betty, what will you . . .?' Liz shook her head urgently. 'Ah! Yes!' said Neville. 'That's all, thank you.'

'They took this self-catering holiday in Llandudno,' said Alec Skiddaw, to the considerable surprise of Neville Badger and Liz as he served their drinks. 'Well, you're free to eat what you want when you want, aren't you?'

Paul and Jenny returned, more than somewhat sheepishly.

'Jenny and I have survived our first row,' said Paul.

'Congratulations,' said Neville.

'We've decided that, if the correct lessons are learnt, my lie can cement our relationship,' said Paul.

'Oh good. I'm so glad,' said Liz.

'Well, the man in the next chalet, because that's what it boiled down to, chalets, never mind what it said in the brochure,' said Alec Skiddaw, but Betty Sillitoe wasn't listening, and he abandoned his tale with a sigh and reverted to the more modest pleasure of fingering the boil on the back of his neck.

'Mum?' said Jenny. 'I'm sorry if I was a bit rude earlier.'

'I understand,' said Liz. 'The nerves and emotions sometimes go a bit haywire during pregnancy.'

'So what's your excuse?'

'What?'

'Well, you called me a bitch, and I hardly imagine you're pregnant.'

'Hardly.'

Liz laughed, and Neville and Betty joined in. Even the dark, intense Alec Skiddaw smiled.

'I must apologize for the meal tonight,' said Laurence Rodenhurst to Ted and Rita Simcock at Laurence's otherwise deserted table. Rita was still slightly flushed after her exertions on the dance floor. 'The chicken was a disaster. Oh sorry. I forgot your friend provided it.'

'Oh no! We're enjoying ourselves,' said Ted. 'I mean, let's face it, it isn't everything, food, not by a long chalk.'

They watched the dancers for a moment. The Finchams were together again. How smugly they danced!

'Talking of food not being everything,' said Ted, 'you must be my guests at my angling club Christmas party, Laurence.'

Rita glared at Ted.

'Lovely,' said Laurence without enthusiasm.

'It's in the lounge bar of the Crown and Walnut, closed for the occasion.' Laurence was failing to hide his dismay. Ted couldn't resist turning the screw. 'Of course it won't be a classy do like this,' he went on. 'It's only a little back street boozer, but they're a friendly crowd.'

Rita's glare became almost frantic when Ted called it a 'boozer'.

'It sounds delightful,' said the appalled Laurence.

Jenny and Paul entered, with Neville Badger and Liz.

'Well well,' said Laurence.

'Where have you been? We've been worried sick,' said Rita.

'Sorry,' said Jenny. 'I think I over-reacted.'

She plonked herself thankfully into a chair.

'You didn't,' said Paul. 'Little lies lead to bigger lies, a resultant fatal lack of trust, and the ultimate destruction of the relationship.'

'How true,' said Rita, giving Ted a look.

There was an uneasy pause. Dale Monsal hit a spectacular wrong note right in the middle of it.

'Another pregnant pause,' said Liz. 'The evening seems pregnant with pregnant pauses.'

The music ceased. They all applauded, for want of anything better to do.

'And now, ladies and gentlemen,' said Dale Monsal, as flat as a cap, 'we'll pay a brief visit to the exotic rhythms of Latin America. Yes, it's carnival time in Rio.'

Rodney Sillitoe came over and asked Jenny to dance.

'Will you be all right?' said Paul.

'Yes!' said Jenny. 'Modest exercise is good for you.' Bred into her, and still there despite her politics, was a confident assumption that people of her background didn't have things like miscarriages. (This is not an intimation of impending disaster, dear reader. Jenny will have a fine, healthy baby. There's enough tension in the world without my adding to it.)

Paul raised his eyebrows in exasperation. He'd only been trying to give her an excuse in case she didn't want to dance with the big wheel behind Cock-A-Doodle Chickens, but he couldn't say that.

Rita gave Ted a look, indicating that he was to ask Liz to dance. He gave her a look which said, 'All right! I'm just going to,' and Liz gave him a look, indicating that he was to ask her to dance, so he repeated his look which said, 'All right! I'm just going to,' and while they were all giving each other looks, Laurence asked Liz to dance.

'Rita?' said Neville Badger.

'Oh! Mr Badger! Why not?' fluttered Rita, hating herself for fluttering.

Liz returned.

'Ted?' she said. 'It might be a good idea to prise Betty away from the bar.'

Carnival time began in the ballroom of the Angel Hotel.

In the Gaiety Bar it wasn't carnival time. It was Alec Skiddaw resumption of family reminiscence time.

'Well, the man in the next chalet,' he was saying to Betty Sillitoe, 'he complained of a dog howling at three am, never dreaming it was my ex-brother-in-law's first wife who'd had one too many on a mystery tour of Rhyl night-spots. Well . . .'

'Betty!' said Ted, arriving on the scene. 'You can't sit here all night by yourself,' and he led her back to the ballroom.

'I don't exist, I suppose,' grumbled Alec Skiddaw darkly, intensely to nobody in particular, and his boil throbbed indignantly.

Rodney Sillitoe flung himself into the Latin American rhythm with more verve than finesse. Jenny followed more carefully.

Laurence Rodenhurst danced correctly but stiffly, with a self-satisfied expression as if he thought he was excellent. Liz was going through the motions in a rather perfunctory way, but there was still a hint of distant sexuality, even when she was dancing with her husband.

Neville Badger danced as if he had been dancing with Rita all his life. He smiled warmly. He really was a charming and attractive man. She felt a thrill such as she hadn't experienced for a long while. 'I'm still alive,' she thought, surprised. Once, he squeezed her hand.

Ted resisted Betty Sillitoe's attempts to get him onto the floor. He watched Liz. Turned away rapidly and watched Rita. Watched Jenny and Rodney Sillitoe. Watched Liz. Turned away rapidly and watched the hot, rhythmic Brazilian movements of the clarinetist's breasts. It was carnival time in her outsize bra. Turned away rapidly. Watched Liz. Turned away rapidly and smiled uneasily at Betty Sillitoe and Paul. How much did they know?

The applause was enthusiastic, and several middle-aged people were badly out of breath.

'From Latin America the Dale Monsal Quartet transport you over the Atlantic by magic carpet to the capital of the Austro-Hungarian empire,' said Dale Monsal, as flat as Ted's singing in the bath. 'Take the floor, ladies and gentlemen, for a whiff of old Vienna.'

To Rita's joy, Neville showed no desire to leave the floor. Rodney appeared happy with Jenny's company. Even Laurence was happy to remain. He wanted a private chat, and where was safer?

'Exactly the same thing is happening as at the wedding,' he said, as the Dale Monsal Quartet attacked the Blue Danube, with very few false notes. 'Mrs Chicken is desperately trying to make sure Mr Chicken doesn't drink too much, and she'll be the one who ends up drunk.'

'You find people so amusing, observed from a distance, don't you?' said Liz. 'What a pity you don't like us so much close to.'

'I do, Liz. It's just that the Rodenhursts have never found affection easy to express.'

'Perhaps because you have so little affection to express.'

'I have feelings, Liz. I just keep them bottled up.'

'Like chutney.'

'Exactly. Well, not exactly like chutney, no.' Laurence felt almost certain that the lady clarinetist had just winked at him. He looked away, and met the eyes of the male, black pianist. And the pianist definitely winked at him! And grinned hugely, with what looked like the joy of being alive. Again, Laurence looked away hurriedly. 'I'm British, Liz,' he said. 'My affection doesn't come bursting out in great surges.'

'You can say that again.'

'You don't want to get close to me. You want to get close to the toasting fork tycoon. You're having an affair with him, aren't you? Don't answer that! I don't want to know. Just make sure you're very, very discreet. And, please, don't dance with him tonight.'

'Won't that be guaranteed to set tongues wagging in this town?'

Laurence considered this, and almost missed a step.

'All right,' he said. 'Dance with him once, but don't hold him too close.'

'Yes, sir!'

'But hold him close enough not to arouse suspicions.'

Rodney Sillitoe's hands as he guided Jenny sedately round the floor were firm, tactful, not a bit naughty. The expression in his eyes was appreciative of her attractions, but not lustful. He seemed to be glad that she was attractive, for Paul's and the world's sake. She really didn't understand it.

'I just don't see how a nice man like you can enjoy dancing while you're keeping thousands of living creatures in conditions that would make a Siberian prison camp seem like a Young Conservatives' disco,' she said. 'I'm sorry. I shouldn't have said that. Not when you've asked me to dance. But I don't.'

The music stopped. There was gentle applause.

'Oh, Jane!' said Neville Badger.

'I'm Rita,' said Rita.

'Yes. Yes. Of course you are,' said Neville Badger.

Laurence and Liz and Jenny joined Ted and Paul and Betty Sillitoe at the table. Neville Badger led Rita off for a drink, in case she was upset at being mistaken for Jane. The Dale Monsal Quartet launched themselves into a quickstep.

'Come on, Paul,' said Jenny.

'Leave him alone, Jenny, if he doesn't want to,' advised Laurence.

'No,' said Jenny. 'Marriage is a totality of shared experience.'

'So that's where I went wrong!' said Laurence, and he left the table abruptly.

'Why are my parents so touchy today?' said Jenny, watching her departing father, wondering. Then she pulled Paul onto the dance floor.

'Don't overdo it,' he said.

'I'm all right!' she insisted.

'I can only do disco dancing,' he said.

Ted and Liz and Betty Sillitoe watched Paul and Jenny bopping vaguely in a far corner of the floor, hardly moving, holding each other tight, swaying gently.

'He's slipped off to the bar. I'm sure of it. Excuse me,' said Betty, and she slipped off to the bar to see if Rodney had slipped off to the bar, and there were Ted and Liz, secret lovers, alone together in the middle of the crowded, noisy, smoky ballroom.

'. . . night-life. Well, he thought it was a bona fido labrador. He never dreamt it was my ex-brother-in-law's first wife, who'd been on the sauce in Colwyn Bay. Well, you wouldn't, would you?' The dark, intense Alec Skiddaw appeared to have found an unexpectedly good listener in Rodney Sillitoe, the big wheel behind Cock-A-Doodle Chickens. He was getting nearer to telling the whole of his tale without interruption than he had ever been. 'Then up pipes the tax inspector, doing his amateur ventriloquy, saying to the dog, his then wife, now his ex-wife, "Gelt up, you stupid gitch." Well . . .'

'There you are!' said Betty Sillitoe. 'Come on, love. You had an awful lot of wine with the meal. Better give it a rest or you'll regret it.' And she led Rodney back into the ballroom to rejoin Timothy and Helen Fincham, their almost-inseparable hosts.

'I'm just a figment of the imagination, I suppose,' muttered Alec Skiddaw darkly, intensely.

'How can you be so sure it's mine?' said Ted urgently.

'Look casual, Ted. People may be watching.'

'Hell's bells.' Ted smiled excessively casually at a passing lady dentist, who almost stopped because she thought she must be supposed to know him. 'I mean . . . Liz . . . how can you be so sure?'

'There's nobody else.'

'What about Laurence?'

'Laurence and I don't sleep together any more.'

'I assumed you . . . you know . . . took precautions.'

'No point if there's nothing to take them against. You could have, though.'

'Liz!' Ted suddenly remembered to smile cheerfully. 'I don't go to wedding receptions armed with rubber goods.' A casual wave to Larry Benson's lady wife, who was actually no lady. 'Anyroad, I'd have thought . . . I mean . . . that the chances were pretty remote at your age.'

'Oh thank you!'

'Oh Lord. Oh heck. Sorry.' Liz's face was like thunder. 'Look casual. Look happy.'

Liz smiled sweetly. 'What a tactless, uncouth man you are,' she quipped.

'No . . . I meant . . . you don't look your age,' he riposted smilingly. 'So sometimes I forget how . . . how you aren't quite as amazingly young as you seem.'

'Don't try to recover,' said Liz. 'I like you because you aren't smooth. I like you for what you are. Your own man. Proud. Rough.'

'Good Lord. Liz? I suppose you've thought of . . .' A nod to the Mercers, smile as if not a care in the world. '. . . er . . . having a . . . I mean . . . not having the . . . er . . . you know.'

'Yes. I have. I've decided to have the baby. But I absolutely adore York.'

'What?' Ted saw Neville Badger and Rita approaching, and understood. 'Ah! Yes. Right. York. The Minster. The Shambles. Hello, love.'

'It was rather, wasn't it?' said Neville, sinking wearily into a chair with the air of a man who has sunk into many, many chairs in his lifetime. 'Poor Rodney.'

'Sorry?'

'I thought you said the dinner was a shambles.'

'No. York.'

'York a shambles? I can't agree. Delightful city.'

'No. There's a street in York called The Shambles.'

'I know.'

'I know. I mean, I know that you know. I mean, I assume that you know. Most people do.'

Neville Badger looked bewildered, Ted embarrassed, Rita suspicious, Liz amused.

With one accord Rita and Liz gave Ted a look, indicating that he should dance with Liz. 'Right,' he said, and they both gave him another look, indicating that he shouldn't have acknowledged their first look. 'Sorry,' he said, and they both raised their eyes in irritation with him for acknowledging the second look. He was sweating. He was no good at this sort of thing. 'Liz?' he said. 'Are you prepared to brave the perils of my clumsy feet?'

'Well, if you insist,' said Liz.

They moved onto the dance floor, and the music stopped.

Liz laughed.

Ted didn't.

'Another dance, Neville?' said Rita. Her boldness surprised her.

'No. Please. Thank you.'

'It might help to take you out of yourself.'

'I don't want to be taken out of myself. Who'd I be then?'

Rita's pink spots returned, but Neville Badger didn't see them. He was already halfway to the bar.

'It's worse than being on the telly,' said Ted.

He was trying to remember the name of the slow foxtrot. They were dancing self-consciously, taking care not to be too near each other, or too far away. Both were aware of Rita, seated alone now, and of Laurence, standing with young Mr Young and old Mr Young and giving them not an inkling of his low opinion of their professional ability. Both knew that Rita and Laurence were watching with eyes like tape measures. Ted remembered the title of the music. It was 'Embraceable You'. Some chance of embracing.

'Don't be grumpy,' said Liz.

'I am grumpy,' he said. 'Making me make love during the

wedding reception. Choosing just before dinner to tell me you're pregnant. Constantly referring to pregnant pauses. Blowing me kisses in a crowded bar. You flirt with danger as much as with me. It turns you on.'

'You turn me on. I'm having your baby.'

'Oh heck. What are we going to do?'

The Dale Monsal Quartet seemed to be in a trance. Dale Monsal was swaying almost imperceptibly. The black pianist was smiling dreamily to himself. The drummer was glaring. The clarinetist ogled, smiled, simpered, fluttered, and her great breasts bobbed slowly in time with the quietly seductive rhythm, to which more than thirty couples gently moved and slowly sweated.

'It's impossible to dance to this music,' complained Paul, who was disco dancing a couple of feet away from his hot, tired, pregnant, almost immobile and apparently rather worried wife. 'What's wrong?'

'Nothing.'

Paul moved closer, and took hold of her. They moved round, very slowly, in each other's arms.

'Jenny, there is.'

'No.'

'I can tell. Come on! No secrets. A totality of shared experience.'

'I think my mother and your father are having an affair.'

Paul stood still, thunderstruck, and the managing director of White Rose Carpets Ltd collided with him. Paul was oblivious of this. He was watching Ted and Liz.

'You shouldn't have told me,' he said.

'Don't you want me to have your baby?' said Liz softly.

'Of course. It's a great thrill. But.'

'Ah. "But" again. But what?'

'Well . . . I mean . . . at your . . .?'

'. . . age?'

'Oh heck. But . . . I mean . . . isn't there? Some risk?'

'I suppose so.' Like her daughter, Liz felt that the risks were negligible for Rodenhursts, née Ellsworth-Smythes. 'I know some people probably think I'm selfish.' She paused, giving Ted time to deny this, but he didn't. 'But I've had two children. Watched them grow up. I couldn't have an abortion after that. The third child is already real for me. It's a person.' She lowered her voice still more. 'I want your baby.'

'Well . . . good. Good. But . . . I mean . . . Laurence! . . . I mean . . .'

'Well, obviously I shan't be able to go on living with Laurence.'

'No. Quite. Well . . . good. Good.'

'Look bright and jolly.'

'Oh. Yes. Right. Sorry. Oh heck.'

Ted was finding it harder than Liz to seem bright and casual. He found it difficult to believe that the other dancing couples were interested only in each other, and not in them. He wondered if Rita or Laurence could lip-read. The clarinetist was smiling straight at him. He looked away, as if there was a danger of having her baby too. Oh God.

'I think we should live together,' said Liz.

'Absolutely. It's the only way.' Too close. Dangerous. Push her away just a little, without offending her. Oh God. 'I mean . . . is there absolutely no possibility that it's his?'

'Don't you want to live with me?'

'Absolutely. It's like a dream. I was just . . . exploring possibilities. 'Course I do. Like the clappers. But.' He saw her expression. 'I mean not but.'

'Your enthusiasm sounds pretty temperate to me.'

'No. No, love!' Too far apart now, pull her closer, lovely feel of her flesh. Push her away! 'It's just . . . Rita, Laurence, the family, everything.' Smile. Ha ha! Oh God! 'Yes, of course I do. Madly. But . . . oh heck. That's all. How?'

'How? How what?'

'How do we go about it?'

'Oh. Well . . . we just go away together. Quickly. Suddenly. A clean break.'

'Yes. Yes. Absolutely.' Almost trod on her feet. Swing round. Bump gently into manager of National Westminster Bank. 'When?'

'Tonight.'

'Tonight?? You are function-fixated.'

'It's not easy for me either. I've never left Laurence before, you know. I'm worried my courage'll run out if I don't. *Now*, Ted! When the dance finishes. Before the realities of our daily life engulf us for ever.'

The music finished. There was applause.

'Thank you very much, ladies and gentlemen,' said Dale Monsal, as flat as a London pint. 'We're going to take a very short breather now. We'll see you again in a very few minutes.'

Possibly, thought Ted. Or possibly not.

Finding Rita still alone, Laurence felt obliged to dance with her on the resumption of the musical activities. It was a particularly nondescript tune, which neither of them knew. In fact, it was an extraordinarily nondescript tune. In fact, it was so extraordinarily nondescript as to be, in the final analysis, not nondescript at all.

He held her as lightly as he could, with the tips of his fingers. They were both embarrassed by even this degree of physical contact, and they were glad when the memorably forgettable dance ended.

Rita went to the ladies' powder room. On her way back she lingered briefly in the bar. Betty Sillitoe bought her a drink and, to keep her company, bought one for herself as well.

Rita became aware that it was quite a while since she had seen Ted.

Laurence wandered among the tables, stopping to exchange a word here and there with colleagues. Some felt that they should advertise, to correct the popular misapprehension that dentistry under the National Health Service was becoming extortionate. Laurence was not in favour. He wanted people to believe it was extortionate, so that he could continue to charge high prices. He edged swiftly past the Mercers' table, for fear that Mr Mercer would invite him to the football, or Percy Spragg would wax lyrical over horse shit. He took Neville Badger to the bar and bought him a drink. The dark, intense Alec Skiddaw thought they looked depressed, so he started to tell them about his ex-brother-in-law from Falkirk, but the inseparable Finchams were waiting for service and looking impatient, and they never heard the end of the tale.

Laurence became aware that it was quite a while since he had seen Liz.

Eventually Rita and Laurence both returned to Laurence's empty table. The Dale Monsal Quartet were in skittish vein, and some fifty of the dentists and their guests were making chicken gestures as they performed a comic dance. Rodney Sillitoe was imitating his product with enthusiasm. Simon Rodenhurst was cavorting overenthusiastically with the rather embarrassed fiancée of a dental mechanic. The pianist beamed. The clarinetist sparkled and fluttered her eyelashes. Dale Monsal managed a tiny, light-hearted twitch of the lips.

If the town was on the verge of a new, uninhibited bacchanalian era, where impersonating dancing chickens was considered *de rigueur* in respectable professional circles, it seemed that Rita and Laurence were to be excluded. They were linked in disapproval, and yet as far away from each other as ever.

After the chicken dance was over, the Dale Monsal Quartet flirted coyly with the world of pop. Their choice was too radical for the old and too conservative for the young. The Angel Hotel's repertoire of strobe effects had never looked less adequate.

Rita was beginning to realize that it was quite a while since she had seen Liz, and Laurence was beginning to realize that it was quite a while since he had seen Ted. Both of them were beginning to realize that the other might well be beginning to realize what they were beginning to realize.

The Dale Monsal Quartet erupted into 'Rock Around The Clock'. The lady clarinetist looked very audacious. Middle-aged people relived their youth with dangerous abandon.

The Dale Monsal Quartet subsided into another waltz. Now Laurence felt the need to talk, because otherwise he would have to ask Rita to dance.

'How were the beaches in the South of France?' he asked.

'Too full of overweight topless German women for my taste.'

'Oh dear.'

'Bottomless too in many cases.'

'Oh dear!'

There was a pause, while Laurence reflected on these horrors.

'I mean, I know Filey has its critics,' said Rita, 'but it's not full of

99

overweight nude German women.'

'They'd catch their death.'

'It's an ill wind.'

'Absolutely.'

The immaculate Neville Badger approached unsteadily.

'I must go home,' he said. 'It's past my bedtime. Thank you, Laurence, for a . . . er . . . an . . .' He lapsed into silence, unable to find an adjective which would describe his evening truthfully but not hurtfully.

'You're in no condition to drive,' said Laurence.

'Paul'll drive him,' offered Rita. 'He won't mind.'

'Oh, that's very kind,' said Neville. 'Where's Liz? Must say goodbye to Liz.'

Rita's eyes met Laurence's briefly.

'Come on, Neville,' she said hurriedly, and led him off.

Neville stopped by the double doors. He seemed embarrassed.

'I owe you an apology, Rita,' he said, in a voice only slightly thickened by alcohol. 'I was a trifle abrupt earlier.'

'You're under a strain,' said Rita. 'I understand.'

'That's no excuse. Jane believed in good manners. She'd have been deeply shocked. That sort of thing lets her down, it lets me down, it lets Badger, Badger, Fox and Badger down.'

'Never mind,' said Rita, touching his arm quite naturally as she could never have touched Laurence's. 'The point is, already you're coping better. You're going to be all right. Time is a great healer.'

'Oh shut up,' said Neville Badger.

Paul and Jenny would have looked uncomfortable on the edges of the impossible chairs in the sparsely populated Gaiety Bar, even if a signed photograph of Michael Heseltine hadn't been staring at them.

'Do you promise never to lie to me again?' said Jenny, as Neville Badger strode angrily through the bar, unseen by them.

'If I say "yes" and later on I do lie to you,' began Paul, as Rita passed through more slowly with a look of stunned shock on her face, 'the "yes" will have been a lie as well. If I say "no" and later I lie to you again, at least I won't have lied about lying to you. If I say "no" and I never lie to you again, which I hope to do – not to lie, I mean – I won't have told a lie today saying "no" because I'll only have said that I can't promise not to tell a lie, I won't actually have said that I will tell a lie. So the answer's got to be "no".'

'I love you!' said Jenny.

Paul kissed her, and they went up to the bar. They had an uneasy feeling that Michael Heseltine's eyes were following them. Before Paul could order their drinks, Rita and Neville came back in.

'Are you sober?' Rita asked him.

'Of course I am,' said Paul. 'I haven't been here long enough to get drunk.'

'Oh good. You won't mind driving Neville home, then, will you?'

'Thank you, Paul. That's very kind of you,' said Neville, who had his overcoat on.

'Thank you, Paul,' said Rita. 'It's good of you to volunteer.'

Neville Badger turned to Rita and said, 'Goodnight, Rita. What can I say? I . . .' and he kissed her, and he said, 'I'm sorry' again, and then he said, 'Where's Liz?' and Paul exchanged a look with Jenny and Jenny said, 'I'll say goodnight to her for you,' and Neville said, 'Am I being a nuisance?' and Jenny said, 'Of course not, Uncle Neville. Paul's happy to do it,' and Paul grunted, and Rita stood watching Neville's back as he went out with Paul, and remembering his insults and his kiss, and wondering, and then she thought of Ted and Liz, and her eyes met Jenny's, and they both looked away, and didn't quite meet the eyes of Michael Heseltine, and Rita sighed and set off for the ballroom and came face to face with her father.

'How's tha doing, our Rita?' said the barrel-chested Percy Spragg. 'Tha hasn't had much time for thy old father, whatever tha's been up to.'

'Dad!' said Rita. 'I do wish you wouldn't say "our Rita".'

'I know tha does, our Rita. Well, don't mither thysen. I've been on my best behaviour. My table are right interested in my tales of the olden days. They had no idea of the traffic problems posed by horse manure in big cities.'

'Dad!' said Rita. 'I can't take you anywhere.'

'Aye, I've noticed.'

'Well, are you surprised? I mean . . . why do you always have to be so crude?'

Percy Spragg gave the malicious, irresponsible, infuriatingly crafty, heart-achingly smug grin of a man on the verge of second childhood. 'Because you don't take me anywhere,' he said.

Rita went back into the ballroom. Laurence was sitting on his own, and she felt that she had no alternative but to rejoin him.

'I'm watching your friend Rodney,' said Laurence.

Rodney Sillitoe was dancing on his own, much too flamboyantly. Rita wished Laurence hadn't described him as 'your friend'.

'So this time it's Rodney who's got drunk,' he said. 'I'll say this for your friends, Rita. They've a high entertainment value.'

Rita began to steel herself for the question that would have to be asked.

Elvis Simcock, off duty now, entered the Gaiety Bar for a drink.

The first thing he noticed was a signed photograph of Professor A. J. Ayer. The great philosopher's message to the world was, 'I ate well, therefore I was. Freddie.'

The second thing he noticed was Simon Rodenhurst.

'Another shipping order for your drunken friends?' he asked cheerfully.

'I could get you sacked, if I reported your behaviour tonight,' said Simon.

'Oh, please do! I loathe the job, and if I'm sacked I can go straight back on the dole.'

'There's not much point, then, is there?' said Simon. 'Besides, I enjoy having you waiting on me, and we've got the Estate Agents' Dinner Dance next month.'

'Oh my God! They haven't got one of those as well!'

Alec Skiddaw refused to serve Elvis. He wasn't supposed to serve staff, he explained intensely. Rules were rules, and it was more than his life was worth to break them, he added darkly.

'Give him one on me,' said Simon.

'Oh well, that's different, sir,' said Alec Skiddaw. 'Sorry about that, sir,' he repeated to Elvis, 'but rules are rules.'

'They are,' said the cynical Elvis. 'That is indisputably true. Boring and tautologous, but true. Rules aren't fishnet stockings. They are rules.'

Alec Skiddaw stared at him in amazement. Simon Rodenhurst scurried off with his tray of drinks. Betty Sillitoe felt the need to explain her presence on the bar stool.

'I only try to stop him drinking because it makes him so miserable,' she said. 'He's so happy when he's sober and he's so miserable when he's drunk. It worries me. Which is his real self?'

'I only studied philosophy for three years, Auntie Betty,' said Elvis Simcock. 'I'm afraid I can't answer questions like that.'

Rita closed her eyes and ran naked into the cold sea of her fears.

'Laurence?' she said. 'Do you think there's anything between Ted and Liz?'

There! It was done! It was out in the open! For about three seconds, it was a relief.

'You mean . . . are they having an affair?'

'Well, I wouldn't have put it quite so . . . but, yes, I suppose I do.'

'Yes.'

'What?'

'Yes, I do think they're having an affair.'

'Oh my God! Oh no! Laurence, they can't be.'

Rodney Sillitoe was cavorting more flamboyantly than ever.

'But you've just asked me,' said Laurence. 'You must have thought they were.'

'Yes, but I hoped you'd tell me I was imagining things. I hoped you'd say I was sick in my mind and tell me to pull myself together.'

'Sorry.'

'Oh my God.'

'Keep calm, Rita. People may be watching.'

'Calm! Our youngest children have only been married for two months, my husband is having an affair with your wife, and you tell me to keep calm!'

'Absolutely. Because it won't last, you know. Liz is far too much of a snob.' Laurence saw Jenny approaching. 'Close ranks,' he said urgently. 'Make small talk.' He turned to Jenny, as if noticing her for the first time, and said, 'Oh hello, Jenny! Rita was just telling me that they found the scenery in Provence very spectacular, but not as green as England.'

Jenny sat down, scraping her chair along the floor.

'Yes,' said Rita. 'It was . . . very spectacular, but . . . not as green as England.'

Jenny looked from one to the other, somewhat astonished.

'The scenery in Peru is very spectacular,' said Laurence. 'Especially the Andes. They're so . . .' He searched for the *mot juste*.

'. . . high?' prompted Rita.

'Exactly! Very high indeed!'

'Come on, Laurence,' said Rita. 'Let's dance.'

'Oh!'

Rita practically dragged Laurence onto the floor. Her behaviour shocked Laurence, astounded Jenny, and was quite a surprise to Rita herself. But, appalling as dancing with Laurence was, it was better than enduring conversations like that. And there was something that he had to explain.

'What do you mean . . . "Liz is far too much of a snob"?' she asked.

'Nothing.'

'Then why say it?'

'You're forcing me to spell it out. Ted is not quite her social equal.'

'He's got his own business.' They swung round slowly underneath the Dale Monsal Quartet. Rita had to raise her voice. 'He employs twenty-two men. He exports to sixty-three countries.'

'He's done extremely well for himself,' said Laurence, 'but socially, Rita, socially selling door knockers to Arabs hardly compares with being a dentist's wife. I mean, do you want this affair to last?'

'Of course not, but I don't want it not to last because he isn't good enough for her.'

'The indestructibility of English snobbery!'

'The snobbery's on your side, Laurence.'

'Without wishing to be snobbish, Rita, I would suggest that you are far more snobbish than me. People who are . . . "upwardly mobile" . . . always are.'

Rita didn't mind these particular pink spots. They were the children of anger, not shame. How typical of those who had never needed to be 'upwardly mobile' to mock so ruthlessly, to put the whole concept, which was so desperately important to many people who had a natural wish not to remain at the bottom of any heap if they could avoid it, into patronizing verbal inverted commas.

The music ended. There was applause, momentarily giving Rita the unpleasant feeling that the dancers were applauding Laurence's remark.

She glared at him. His face was smooth, impassive, cool. She understood why people killed.

'And now, by popular request,' said Dale Monsal, as flat as a wet Sunday in unlicensed Aberystwyth, 'we pay a return visit to the rhythmic paradise that is Latin America. Take it away, señors and señoritas.' (He pronounced them 'seniors and senior eaters', turning graceful, dark-skinned dancers into a Darby and Joan hot-pot supper.)

The seniors and senior eaters took it away, and Rodney Sillitoe grabbed hold of Rita while she was still staring at Laurence.

'Oh,' she gasped.

Rodney was a bull-fighter. Rita was his red rag. The whole of the Dentists' Dinner Dance was his bull.

Rita squirmed. The more she squirmed, the more she imitated the swirling of a red rag, and the more hugely pleased Rodney was.

It was a very different Rodney Sillitoe who entered the Gaiety Bar three minutes later, when the Latin American music had ended. All the liveliness had gone out of him. The big wheel behind Cock-A-Doodle Chickens was maudlin and morose.

Betty Sillitoe was talking with Jenny.

'There she is!' said Rodney. 'The girl who once told me I was the Hermann Goering of the British food industry.'

'Rodney!' said Betty.

'No, but I sort of did,' said Jenny. 'Oh Lord!'

'No! Please!' said Rodney. 'You did right. A drink for my friend, Eric.'

'Alec,' said the dark, intense Alec Skiddaw.

'Well, just an orange juice,' said Jenny.

'And a whisky for me, and a . . .'

'. . . tonic for me,' said Betty.

'Tonic??'

'I'm looking after you.'

Above the bar there was a photograph of a smiling Joan Sutherland, with the message 'Magnifico! Joan Sutherland'.

'Typical of an opera singer,' said Rodney. 'Always use Italian.

Their own language isn't good enough for them. Bloody snobs. But you did right, Jenny.'

'What?'

'I am Hermann Goering. As I stand here, warm and well fed, but thirsty . . . hurry up with that whisky . . . but, apart from that, in the pink, out there, under the stars, except that it's raining, but you know what I mean, are rows of low huts. Stalag Hen Thirty Two. The battery chicken archipelago. A monument to man's inhumanity to chicken. Eric, you're a total idiot, what do you say?'

'Eighty pee, sir,' said Alec Skiddaw coldly.

'About my chickens. And where's my whisky? Don't you think my chickens lead a dog's life?'

'I'm not here to have opinions, sir. I'm just a minion. I'm here to serve.'

'Well, serve me my whisky, then!'

'I'm sorry, sir,' said Alec Skiddaw. 'I have discretionary powers not to serve those who in my judgement have had enough.'

Rodney Sillitoe gasped.

'That incident with the Rotarians would never have happened if I'd been on that night,' said Alec Skiddaw. 'That chandelier cost three hundred and forty six pounds.'

'You mean . . . we go on living with them as if nothing's happened?' After escaping from Rodney, Rita had returned to Laurence's table. Angry with him she might be, but their fortunes . . . or misfortunes . . . were inextricably linked.

'It's easy enough, if they're discreet,' he said.

'But I mean . . . what sort of marriage is that?'

'The best available under the circumstances.'

'I can't live with him . . . knowing!'

'Rita! I implore you not to rock the boat.'

'Maybe they've already rocked the boat. They've been gone a long time.'

'You mean . . . they're . . . "at it" now?' Laurence could hardly bring himself to say 'at it'. 'Where?' A dreadful thought struck him. 'In your car?' An even more dreadful thought struck him. 'In *my* car? Liz wouldn't.'

'I mean, maybe they've walked out on us.'

'They wouldn't. Not tonight. Ted's my guest!'

'I agree it would be very rude.'

'Rude? Unforgivable. Those tickets cost me fourteen pounds fifty.'

'Laurence!'

'I know. Extortionate for that rubbish, when you think the wine was extra.'

'I meant . . . how can you talk about money at a time like this?'

'Because now you are imagining things. Liz wouldn't leave me. Certainly not for . . . and not tonight. The Dentists' Dinner Dance is the highlight of my social calendar. She knows that. She wouldn't. She just wouldn't. Would she?'

'Come on, Jenny,' said Rodney Sillitoe. 'We have a job to do.'

'A job?'

'You were right. We're going to let my chickens go free. Woof! Open the doors. All fly away to a better life.'

'Stop him, Jenny,' said Betty. 'He might even do it.'

'Come on, Jenny,' said Rodney, clambering off his stool with difficulty. 'Help me make amends for a wicked life.'

'I can't,' said Jenny. 'I'm waiting for Paul.'

'Jenny!' Rodney put his face close to hers and breathed alcohol fumes over her, as if he thought that might help to persuade her. 'Jenny! Did Che Guevara say "Sorry, chaps. The revolution's cancelled. We've got visitors." Did he? He did not!!' These last words were roared with such ferocity that Larry Benson's lady wife spilt her sweet martini and made a very unladylike comment.

'It isn't the way to do it,' said Jenny.

'Oh. What is the way to do it?'

'Close down the factory.'

Rodney Sillitoe considered this option seriously, head on one side, like a song thrush.

'All right,' he said at last. 'I will. On Monday. Well, not close down. I'll make umbrellas.' He peered into Jenny's face anxiously. 'You aren't one of those umbrella liberation people, are you?' he asked.

The moment Rita entered the car park she knew that their car was gone. She picked her way carefully among the patches of oil, and stood in the empty space between the Volkswagen Golf and the Rover 3000, as if still refusing to believe the evidence of her eyes. She looked around, as if searching for clues to where they had gone. She felt as if all the blood had been drained out of her body. She couldn't possibly survive. She wouldn't possibly have enough strength to remain standing.

She walked slowly back towards the ballroom, surprised to find that life was still going on, surprised to find that her legs still obeyed her.

She would continue to keep up appearances. It was the strongest motivation for survival that she could find.

Rodney Sillitoe seemed to have forgotten the umbrella idea. He was again trying to persuade Jenny to let his chickens out.

'I can't take advantage of you in that condition,' said Jenny.

'Never mind my condition! What about my chickens? Do they ever get a chance to go to dinner dances and eat frozen people? You're all talk and no do. You armchair rebels make me sick!'

Jenny burst into tears and rushed out.

'Rodney!' said Betty.

'I know. I've made her cry,' said Rodney. 'Hermann Goering? More like Adolf Hitler.'

Once again Laurence was alone at his table, on this the highlight of his year. He was the eye of a social cyclone, motionless in the middle of the room, while the Dale Monsal Sound washed all around him, and the buzz of the Dentists' Dinner Dance rose steadily towards its crescendo. Among the dimly lit tables he was hardly noticed and outwardly he looked serene, as if waiting for a gin and tonic rather than bad news. When Timothy Fincham, hurrying back to Helen, called out breathlessly, 'Where's your lovely wife got to?' he replied with a smile, 'Just taking a breather.' This meaningless response satisfied the self-centred oaf! When Larry Benson, of fitted kitchen fame, said, 'Chicken was foul, wasn't it?' he said, 'Chicken. Fowl. Very good!' and laughed as if the mindless berk were Oscar Wilde.

As Rita approached, she gave him a smile which he couldn't interpret.

'Our car's gone,' she said brightly, as she slid into her seat.

'Oh my God!' He clutched at a straw. 'Maybe they've . . . gone for a drink?'

Laurence couched this in question form to involve Rita in the effort of trying to find it a not totally unconvincing suggestion. She made no effort to oblige.

'I hardly think so.'

'Gone for a quick . . . erm . . . in some deserted spot?'

Laurence couldn't hide his distaste as he thought of his wife having a quick . . . erm . . . with Ted in the back of a Cavalier 2000 GL on the waste ground beside the canal. But even this disgusting prospect was a palliative to the even more unwelcome possibility which Rita now repeated with apparent calm.

'I think they've left us,' she said.

'Oh my God! What are we going to do?'

'Smile.'

'What?'

'Keep up appearances. You said so yourself. At least until we're sure.'

'Yes. Yes.' Laurence smiled. It was as surprising as an owl's grin. 'This is dreadful.'

'Yes.'

Rita laughed, a merry little trill that was almost successful.

'What's funny?'

'Nothing. I'm keeping up appearances.'

'Oh. Right. Well done.' Laurence chuckled horribly, and switched the chuckle off much too suddenly. It sounded like an aberration in the plumbing. 'Not being rude, Rita, but I'd have expected you to go completely to pieces.'

'Thanks,' said Rita. She almost added, 'I'm so glad you weren't being rude.' She was almost light-headed. Was this hysteria? Hang on, Rita. You never lacked courage. 'Well, yes, so would I. It's odd. I've spent most of my life dreading the worst. Now that it's happened . . . well . . . it's odd, but it doesn't seem quite as . . . I mean, it does, it's awful, but . . . well, I suppose there's nothing more to fear, and that's almost a relief. I mean, the world's still here. We're still alive.'

'At least she didn't take my car,' said Laurence, as if it were a private thought which he'd said out loud by mistake.

'I really believe you find that a consolation.'

'No. No! But it means she may still have some feeling for me. Why, Rita? We were happy. Well, perhaps that's a slight exaggeration. We . . . existed pretty satisfactorily, on the whole. Rita, she must come back. I can't face it. The empty house. Telling the family. Facing my friends. The patients. The girls at the surgery. The cleaning lady. All that sympathy. All that pity. All that emptiness. Oh my God.'

'Keep calm,' said Rita. She looked round, and gave a short bark of a laugh, like a walrus that has heard a dirty joke.

'Calm!' said Laurence. 'You tell me to keep calm when my wife . . . it's my fault. I've failed her.'

Rita overcame her natural revulsion, and put a consoling hand on Laurence's arm.

Jenny, approaching, saw this, looked alarmed, and veered away. They didn't notice her, but they couldn't miss Percy Spragg. If Aunt Gladys from Oswestry was a tea-clipper, Rita's father was an old Thames barge. The wind was failing. Would he make it?

'Oh my God, here comes your father. That's all I need,' said Laurence.

Rita withdrew her hand. Laurence realized that he hadn't been tactful.

'Oh Lord. Sorry,' he said.

'Make small talk,' said Rita, and she laughed. 'The funny thing was it wasn't even our shopping.'

Laurence gave a painfully forced laugh, like an elderly cat sicking up chair stuffing.

'Very good,' he said. 'Hello! How are you doing?' He didn't feel brave enough to venture on Percy's surname.

'I'm having a good time,' said Percy Spragg. 'I've had my table in tucks with my impression of Staff-Sergeant Crabtree.'

'Oh no,' groaned Rita. 'You didn't do Staff-Sergeant Crabtree.'

'I've never seen Mr Mercer laugh so much,' said Percy. 'It's a pity you weren't there, Mr Robinghurst.'

'Rodenhurst. My loss was Mercer's gain.'

There was an awkward pause.

'Is everything all right?' said Percy Spragg.

'Absolutely.' Laurence laughed. 'It's a wonderful evening.'

'Absolutely wonderful,' said Rita, and she laughed also.

The hokey cokey was in full swing. The wonderful evening was nearing its end.

'Come on,' said Percy. 'Let's dance.'

'Me?' said Rita.

'Well, I'm not dancing with 'im. I'm not a bum-boy.'

'Dad!'

'Come on. Dance with your old dad.'

'All right!'

Percy and Rita walked slowly towards the dance floor. Rita held his arm, with no little embarrassment. Surely he looked grotesque? Was it possible, so stiffly and painfully did he hobble, that he would be able to dance at all?

Just as they reached the floor, the hokey cokey ended. The massed, sweating dentists and friends subsided into mirth at their own antics. The pianist gleamed. Sweat glistened on the shoulders of the clarinetist, and her eyes shone.

Dale Monsal looked tired. 'Thank you very much, ladies and gentlemen,' he said, as flat as a soufflé in the Angel Restaurant and Grill. 'Well, I'm afraid the licensing authorities have beaten us once again.' There were groans and protests from the same people who had been so reluctant to dance earlier. Percy Spragg looked very disappointed. 'We like to end on a gentle, romantic, traditional note. Take your partners, please, for the last waltz.'

Percy brightened up. They stepped onto the floor. It was crowded. They couldn't have moved otherwise than slowly and sedately, even if Percy had been capable of it.

'Dad! Why did you have to be so crude?' said Rita.

''Cos he hates it.'

There was a wistful, intense quality to the Dale Monsal Sound now, as if the four musicians feared that they would cease to exist when the dance ended.

'Why do you have to hurt me?' said Rita.

'Because you've hurt me,' said her father.

'Dad!'

'Oh, I understand. I clash with your contemporary furniture.'

'Dad!'

'Oh, I daresay you'll have me more now my Clarrie's dying.'

'Dad! She isn't dying.'

'She's dying. I know that. Like I know summat's wrong between thee and Ted. I'm not such a fool as you think.'

They were having to shout to make themselves heard above the music and the dancers. What a time to choose to have a proper talk together at last, thought Rita.

'What's up, our Rita?'

She lowered her voice as much as she dared. 'I think he's run off with Liz.'

'What? Oh, Rita!' He had very good hearing, when it was vital. 'Oh, Rita! The bloody fool! I'd give one of these dentists summat to do. I'd kick his bloody teeth in!'

'Dad!'

'Well, that's no way to treat my little girl.'

'Dad!' Rita was amazed.

'Come on, Rita. Defy the world. You had such spirit when you were little. Where's it all gone, Rita? What's happened?'

'Life, Dad. Life's happened.'

'Come on, Rita. You can do it. Show a bit of style.'

'It's funny. He said that.'

'Well, show him. Show her. Show them. Defy the world.'

'Right!' There was astonishment in Rita's voice, astonishment at herself as much as at her father. 'Right! Come on, our Dad!'

Despite the lack of space, despite Percy Spragg's creaking old limbs, they began to show real style. Percy's eyes sparkled. The years seemed to drop away from him.

The last waltz was drawing to its conclusion. The Dale Monsal Quartet were putting their all into it.

Rita grinned at her father. His response began as a grin, but then his face became convulsed with pain.

'Oh, Rita!' he gasped. 'Oh, Rita!'

He collapsed onto her.

The dance ended. There was warm applause. Rita lowered her father slowly to the floor, and silence fell rapidly.

'Dad!' she cried, and she didn't care that everyone was listening. Appearances didn't matter. They never had!! That was what was so awful. She knew now that they never had. 'Dad! You can't be dead! I haven't told you that I love you.'

Third Do

December:
The Angling Club
Christmas Party

'I'm sorry we couldn't finish the decorations,' said Lester Griddle, landlord of the Crown and Walnut, lugubriously. 'We've had the bloody VATman here all day, excuse my French.'

Liz Rodenhurst smiled faintly as Ted took her coat. She was wearing an elegant yellow-and-white dress which was too expensive and too revealing. You still wouldn't have thought she was pregnant, if you didn't know.

Lester Griddle stared at her cleavage, blinked, and said, 'I mean, would you believe it? Friday before Christmas, a function in the evening, bloody VATman poking around in my drawers all day.'

Outside, along the dimly lit Knapperley Road on the southern edge of town, where municipal dumps and used car lots formed a muddy no-man's-land between the housing estates and the gently rolling farmland, it was black, wet and raw. In the lounge bar of the Crown and Walnut it was warm, smoky and pink.

Half the bar was festooned with decorations. There were plastic chains in crude primary colours. There were cardboard angels that swung gently in the smoky breeze every time the door opened to admit an angler and his wife and a swirl of arctic night. There was a profusion of holly clinging to light fittings, to pictures, to the mantelpiece, to the glass cases of stuffed fish, to Lester Griddle's collection of exotic matchboxes, to any flat surface, like climbers bivouacking all over an overbooked Mount Everest.

'I mean, what do the silly buggers want, excuse my French?' continued Lester Griddle, that smouldering volcano of complaint. 'Receipts for every packet of pork scratchings?'

The other half of the bar was entirely innocent of decorations. Ted Simcock thought it typical of Lester and Mavis Griddle, when time was pressing, to decorate half the room completely rather than half decorate the whole of the room.

'Never mind, Lester,' said Ted. 'Half the room looks lovely.' He didn't say which half.

There wasn't a single object in the bar with which Liz felt she could happily spend an evening. Oh God, what bad taste the British had.

If Ted had thought about taste, he would have said that the whole point of the lounge bar of the Crown and Walnut was its bad taste. You couldn't relax in up-market country pubs where you were frightened to pass remarks less stylish than the antiques. Here, among these tables with tops of beaten copper and elaborately carved legs with eagles' feet, among the over-large brown chairs which dwarfed the tables, among the curved lampshades which sent a dim, sinful red glow over the pink curtains and walls, the gold-and-brown carpet, the nicotine ceiling and Lester Griddle's exotic matchboxes, here a man could be free from feelings of inferiority, from the need to compete with his fellows. Here you could drink good beer or bad beer – there were both – bad wine or worse wine – there were both – and eat snacks that filled you up without bankrupting you. And that was all the people around the Highcliffe Estate and the Knapperley Road wanted or could afford. Long live bad taste, Ted might have said. If he'd ever thought about such things. Which he hadn't.

They came from different worlds. It was part of the attraction. They were living in limbo, in a world of their own, alone together, self-centred lovers, cocooned in their own sensuality. Ted had never been admitted to Liz's world. It was the first time he had taken her to his. Already he realized that it was going to be more difficult than he had thought.

He looked round his world. About twenty people had arrived so far. They included his son Elvis, the Sillitoes, and a group of men of various ages who looked as if they would be happier in their normal haunt, the public bar.

'Come and meet the Pilbeams,' he said.

'I don't want to meet the Pilbeams,' said Liz.

'How can you say that?' said Ted. 'You've never met them.'

'Exactly. I feel as though I know enough people. I don't want to meet any new ones.'

The Pilbeams were standing between the artificial log fire and the Christmas tree, on which three of the fairy lights were failing to twinkle. George Pilbeam was that rare fish, an angler who doesn't drink. Liz felt that she and they were the three fairy lights that were failing to twinkle. But that didn't mean that she wanted to meet them.

'Oh, come on, Liz. I'm chairman. It's my social duty, is mingling.'

'I don't know any of these people.'

'Exactly. So, if you meet them you will know them, and then it'll be no problem to meet them. So come and meet them. Liz! It's no problem to you anyroad. I mean . . . you've got social poise. Oh heck! I used to think, "why can't Rita be more like Liz?" Now I'm with you and you're getting like Rita. It's very unfair sometimes, life.'

'Could it possibly be that the fault is yours?'

'Mine? Don't be ridiculous.'

'Is that what you want me for, my "social poise"?'

'Of course it isn't!' He looked round. Nobody was within earshot, but he still lowered his voice to a whisper. 'I want you for your body.' He saw Liz's look. He added hurriedly, 'Plus your mind and personality, obviously. That goes without saying.'

'Did Rita mingle at these dos?'

'That was different. That was marriage. You and I are in love. Aren't we? Well, then! So . . . we make sacrifices for each other. So . . . come and meet the Pilbeams.'

'Still working as a waiter, are you?' said Rodney Sillitoe, the big wheel behind Cock-A-Doodle Chickens. He was wearing a new Harris tweed jacket which wouldn't have looked crumpled on anybody else.

'Oh no,' said the cynical Elvis Simcock, whose black tee shirt bore the legend, 'I think, therefore I am. I think'. 'It turned out I was a holiday relief. At the end of October, when the regular waiters had finished their holidays, they sacked me. It's a non-union hotel. Therefore, no comebacks.'

All the customers were clustered into the decorated half of the bar, perhaps hoping that the good cheer of Christmas would rub off onto them. Elvis was trying to edge the Sillitoes towards the undecorated half.

'It must be tough for you,' said Rodney. 'You haven't got any marketable skills, have you?'

'I've got a philosophy degree. I've spent three years studying the world's greatest thinkers.'

'This is what I say. You haven't got any marketable skills.'

'No. My business is merely logical analysis. Since the nation is collapsing because nobody seems capable of thinking properly about its problems, you'd think it'd be worth employing somebody trained in how to think properly. But no.'

'Well, don't get bitter, Elvis.'

Betty Sillitoe's eyes moved from one to the other, as if she were umpiring their conversation. Her black-and-gold dress went perfectly with her platinum hair and dark roots.

'Wouldn't *you* be bitter if your dad left your mother and shacked up with your younger brother's stuck-up wife's even more stuck-up mother?'

'Elvis!' Rodney joined willingly in the move into the unmapped half of the room, the uncharted seas where Liz would be unable to overhear them. 'Jenny isn't stuck up.'

'No? Well, her mother is. Couldn't you have stopped him?'

'I tried. He wouldn't listen.'

'I nearly didn't come. There's a lot hasn't.' Leslie Horton, water bailiff and organist, who hated to be called Les, was just arriving with his wife Patricia, who hated to be called Pat, but there were still only about twenty-five people present, and Mavis had catered for fifty.

'I think that's mainly internal,' said Rodney. 'There's been some bad feeling since the fracas at Wisbech.'

'Yes, well, it's always been very cliquey, has the angling club,' said Elvis. 'You're very quiet tonight, Betty? Are you all right?'

'I'm fine,' mumbled Betty Sillitoe, hardly opening her lips.

'She's upset about her dental work,' said Rodney. 'She's had a bridge done and she hates it.'

'I didn't want to come,' mumbled Betty, 'but I've had to, to see he doesn't have too much to drink while I'm not here.'

'Betty!' said Rodney. 'As if I would!'

Ted and Liz joined them, Ted having abandoned his effort to get Liz to meet new people.

'Hello,' said Liz. 'And how's Elvis?'

'Thirsty,' said Elvis, downing the remains of his pint and going off to the bar.

'Don't worry, love,' said Ted. 'He'll come round in time.'

'Dry white wine, Liz? Usual, dear? Give me a hand, would you, Ted?' said Rodney. He led Ted away without waiting for replies to any of these questions, but before they reached the bar, he stopped. 'Betty saw Rita outside the Knaresborough Building Society,' he said.

'Oh yes?'

'She looked awful.'

'Well, what can I say?'

'How about . . . "I'm sorry"?'

'Rodney! You know I am!'

'She's not long lost her father, Ted.'

'I know. I know. Not that they ever got on, but still . . . I know.'

'She's had her mother in the General for months, not getting any better, it seems.'

'I know. I go to see her.'

'I promised Betty I'd ask you. Take her back, Ted.'

'I can't.'

Ted picked up a Paraguayan matchbox, looked at it unseeing, and put it down again.

'None of this is doing anybody any good,' said Rodney.

'I know. I know. But . . . I mean . . . I can't. I love Liz. I'm having her baby.'

'What?'

'I mean . . . she's having mine. It's a new life for me. Bliss. Joy unimagined. Oh heck, Rodney.'

Liz was finding Betty Sillitoe hard work.

'Do you fish?' she asked.

'No,' said Betty through closed lips.

There was a pause.

'Does Rodney fish?'

'Yes,' mumbled Betty, who was over-jewelled as usual.

Another pause.

'I realize you probably resent me,' began Liz.

'It's not that,' mumbled Betty. 'I mean, yes, I suppose I do. Well, wouldn't you, in my shoes? But, as I say, it's not that. It's my teeth. In the unlikely event of your running into your husband, tell him I'm going to sue.'

'You mean Laurence has made a . . .' Liz laughed, then hurriedly stopped laughing. 'I'm sorry. To you it can't be . . .' Betty turned away. '. . . remotely funny. Oh Lord.' Liz developed a sudden, unlikely interest in a large pike in a glass case. A plaque indicated that it had been caught by B. Kitchen in Broadfurze Lake, wherever that was, in 1979. When she had maintained her interest in this attraction to the absolute limits of credibility, she sighed, and went to meet the abstemious Pilbeams.

'You're not the entertainment, are you?' said Pete Ferris, who had volunteered to man the door and make sure no awkward customers defied the notice which said, 'Private Party. Sorry'. Pete Ferris was always happy to do these unrewarding jobs. He never tired of telling people about the good deeds he did for the club, unbidden, without anybody even knowing that he'd done them. He regularly listed these unknown deeds, in case nobody believed him.

'No. Sorry,' said Paul, who was wearing a Greenpeace tee shirt and a battered black leather jacket with a CND badge. He didn't know why he had apologized. There was no reason why he should have been the entertainment.

'I can see that now,' said Pete Ferris, the self-appointed doorman.

'What?'

'Well . . . she's pregnant.'

Pete Ferris hadn't needed the observational powers of a Sherlock Holmes to make this deduction. Jenny was getting pretty big, though she still looked attractive in her hand-woven Kashmiri smock.

'Can't entertainers be pregnant?' she said. 'Is that one more thing pregnant women can't do?'

'No, but you aren't the entertainment, are you?' said Pete Ferris.

'It's the same with newsreaders,' said Jenny. 'Do they think we wouldn't listen if they were seven months pregnant? Do they think we'd all be going "Oooh! Isn't she big? I wonder if it's twins. I wonder if it'll grow up to be a newsreader. Ooops! Missed that! Who's invaded who, Dad?"?'

Pete Ferris paused briefly, as if considering the points Jenny had made.

'Only the entertainment's cutting it a bit fine,' he said.

Ted approached, beaming.

'Hello! You've come!' he said.

'We've decided there's nothing to be gained by pretending what's happened hasn't happened,' said Paul.

'But we wouldn't want you to think that because we've come this means we approve of the situation,' said Jenny.

The smile went swiftly from Ted's face. 'Is that the end of the joint communiqué?' he enquired.

'Incidentally, I should have told you, I've gone vegetarian,' said Jenny. 'I wonder if they could do me a salad or something?'

Liz approached. Beaming was outside her range, but she was smiling.

'You've come!'

'Yes,' said Ted, 'but we'd be wrong to think it means they approve of the situation.'

Another smile froze on another face.

'I see,' said Liz. She turned to Ted, pointedly excluding the young marrieds. 'Well,' she said. 'I've met the Pilbeams. What was the fracas at Wisbech?'

'Nothing,' said Ted unconvincingly. 'Just a ripple on the waters.'

Paul and Jenny hovered uneasily. They didn't want to be so friendly as to offer Ted and Liz drinks, or so rude as to refuse to do so. And neither Ted nor Liz offered them drinks.

'George Pilbeam told me all about the problems he's having with his spigotted ferruleless rod, whatever that is,' said Liz. 'I suggested he see a doctor. It didn't go down too well.'

'Do you think they could do me one?' said Jenny.

'A spigotted ferruleless rod?' said Liz.

'A salad.'

'Why? You've not turned vegetarian?' Jenny's silence proclaimed her guilt. She resented feeling guilty. Liz resented her daughter's vegetarianism. Paul resented Liz's resentment. Ted resented all their resentment. The air crackled with resentment.

'Still trendy, then?' said Liz. 'I thought marriage to Paul might knock that out of you.'

'It's not a trend,' said Paul indignantly. 'It's a conviction. I don't share it, but I respect it.'

'I'm not going to not do the things I believe are right just because other people are doing them,' said Jenny.

'I'll go and see if Mavis can rustle up a salad,' said Ted grimly. 'It shouldn't be totally beyond her.'

Paul asked Jenny what she'd like to drink, but didn't ask Liz.

Kevin Loudwater intercepted Ted before he reached Mavis. He was a tall, sensually handsome man of forty, with permed, crinkly hair and tight, complacent buttocks. He was a pork butcher. He kept his life outside the pub very much to himself, and was variously rumoured to be a great womanizer and a homosexual. There was no hard evidence either way.

'Can I have a word outside, Ted?' he asked.

'Outside? It's freezing, Kev.'

'I know, but . . . I don't want people to hear what I have to say.'

'What is all this?'

'Blackmail,' said Kevin Loudwater.

'You what?'

'I've got some dirt on you, Ted, and I'm afraid I'm going to have to blackmail you.'

'Say what you have to say, Kev. Shout it through a megaphone. I've got no secrets.'

'Oh, come on,' pleaded Kevin Loudwater. 'Play fair. How can I blackmail you if everybody overhears? I won't have any hold over you any more.'

'You haven't got any hold over me now. I mean . . . there is no dirt on me. There isn't.'

'It's about the fracas at Wisbech.'

'Let's go outside.'

'Cast your mind back to Wisbech,' said Kevin Loudwater, the permed pork butcher. 'A rotten day. Grey clouds over the flat, black Fens. A howling easterly wind blowing straight from Russia.'

It felt as though there was a howling easterly wind blowing straight from Russia to the car park of the Crown and Walnut.

'You're getting carried away, Kev,' said Ted through chattering teeth.

The Crown and Walnut was an old canal pub, with fishing rights over five hundred yards of the Rundle and Gadd Navigation. At the back of the pub, beyond the car park, there were six rustic tables with rustic benches on a thin strip of coarse grass beside the canal. In summer this was gay with drinkers and their squealing children, and the bank was dotted with old crisp packets and discarded tissues. Now it was deserted except for the blackmailer and his victim, hunched against the gale. Behind them, a dim light almost lit up the neatly parked cars. In front of them, the canal and the housing estate beyond were invisible in the inky night.

'Aye, but it's not irrelevant,' said Kevin Loudwater. 'It all contributed to the frayed tempers. It made the fracas inevitable.'

'There'll be another fracas if I die of exposure here,' said Ted.

'Right. So the argument occurs. The pretext is the habits of tench. The real cause is the habits of a redheaded waitress called Janet Hicks.'

Ted was transported back, far away to the distant flat lands south of that mythical line from Birmingham to the Wash, which used to be so popular with weather forecasters. He was on the long, straight bank of the Ouse, on that grey Fenland day of endless horizons, so dreary in bad weather, so miraculously beautiful in the vastness of sunny days.

'Trevor Barnwell makes repeated boasts regarding himself, the redhead and Derek Wiggins,' continued the inexorable pork butcher. 'Derek Wiggins responds with counter allegations, casting doubts on Trevor Barnwell's ability as angler and lover. Trevor Barnwell pushes Derek Wiggins in. Derek Wiggins can't swim. Trevor Barnwell refuses to rescue Derek Wiggins. Alan Wallis pushes Trevor Barnwell in.'

Listening to Kevin Loudwater's account, Ted had a ridiculous hope that this time the outcome would be different. It reminded him of his boyhood, when he was still an avid supporter of the United. Sometimes he'd bought an evening paper on the way home, in the hope that he'd read that they hadn't lost 3–1 after all.

'Trevor Barnwell can swim, but it takes three men to rescue Derek Wiggins. You are not among them. Your Elvis is, but you aren't.'

'I was prepared,' said Ted. 'I mean . . . I was. If necessary. Which it wasn't.'

'I don't dispute that, Ted,' said the sensual pork butcher. 'But you didn't, did you? What did you do? While all eyes were on the water . . . except mine . . . you removed two roach and a bream from Trevor Barnwell's keep-net and put them in yours, thus winning the Arthur Tong Cup under false pretences.'

Ted didn't reply immediately. When he did, the wind tore his words away and scattered them to the night.

They turned, and walked slowly back along the bank, with the wind behind them.

'Kev!' said Ted. 'It's ridiculous, is that. Ludicrous. I mean . . . why should I do a thing like that? I mean . . . tell me . . . just tell me. A respectable citizen, owner of his own foundry, a recently elected Rotarian. I mean . . . Kev! . . . be sensible! . . . Why should I do a thing like that?'

'Because it was about to be won by your son. You resent him for having a university degree. You feel inferior. You couldn't bear to see him beat you. Suddenly, on an impulse, you saw your opportunity.'

'Kev! It's ludicrous, is that. Ridiculous. I encouraged our Elvis to join the angling club. And why should I envy him, anyroad? I'm the premier maker of toasting forks and door knockers in Yorkshire. He's an unemployed waiter. I mean . . . Kev! . . . really! You're a pork butcher, not a psychiatrist.'

'I saw you take them fish.'

Ted stopped walking, and watched a car's headlights swing wildly across the sky as it mounted the humped canal bridge.

'What do you want?' he asked at last.

'Nine hundred and ninety-nine pounds seventy-three pee.'

'You what?'

'That's the estimate for my roof. I'm not greedy. I won't even ask for the extra twenty-seven pee.'

The car turned carefully into the crowded car park.

'I need the money,' said Kevin Loudwater. 'It's no picnic, being a pork butcher in this town. A high Jewish influx, the price of meat, the depression, the common market, the greed of the farmers, the collapse of the traditional pattern of family eating, the health food fad, vegetarianism. We're a persecuted minority, surrounded by enemies. It's our name. Take history. The Butcher of Magdeburg. The Butcher of Lyon. Never the Greengrocer of Magdeburg. Never the Ironmonger of Lyon. We are, Ted. We're a persecuted minority.'

'What if I don't pay?' said Ted.

'I denounce you at the next committee meeting. Your sons despise you. Your mistress finds out what a hero she's hitched her wagon to.'

'Oh heck.'

The car's headlights were extinguished. Inside the car, Henry the Eighth released his seat belt, gave a deep sigh, and wondered whether it might not be better to drive off home.

Ted made an unobtrusive return to the lounge bar, where thirty-five people were now present. The abstemious Pilbeams and Hortons had formed a tiny, respectable party within the more raucous, larger party.

Ted approached Liz, trying to look casual.

'Where have you been?' she asked.

'Just chatting to Kevin Loudwater. He's a bit upset.'

'I wish you wouldn't leave me on my own!'

It was like an echo of Rita!

'Liz! Talk to people! Mingle!'

'What was he upset about?'

She was suspicious. She could see that he was shaken. He should have prepared his story. He cast around for inspiration.

'Having fish and chips,' he said. 'He wanted meat. Well, he would, wouldn't he? I mean . . . he's a butcher. It's a devil sometimes, the responsibility of office. I said to him, "Kev! You're letting your business interests cloud your judgement. It was democratically decided on. Majority verdict." No use. Stubborn.'

He never found out whether she believed him. Their thoughts were diverted by the arrival of Henry the Eighth. All conversation in the rosy lounge bar faltered momentarily, as anglers and their wives and friends and the lads from the public bar and their lugubrious hosts Mavis and Lester Griddle gawped at him.

'Are you the entertainment?' asked Pete Ferris, the self-appointed doorman, hopefully.

'What? Oh! No! No no!' said Henry the Eighth. 'No, I'm Neville Badger, of Badger, Badger, Fox and Badger. I'm an old friend of . . . of Mr Simcock's . . . er . . . his . . .' Neville could find no suitable word for Liz's present status in Ted's life. '. . . of Liz.'

'Only they said they'd be here by half eight, and it's nearly nine fifteen,' said Pete Ferris.

Ted approached the magnificently padded figure. 'Neville!' he said.

'You were kind enough to say that if I could drop in I'd be very welcome,' said the immaculate Neville Badger.

'Oh yes. Yes. Good.' In Ted's expression there was the unstated addition, 'But not dressed as Henry the Eighth.'

'I'm sorry about the garb,' said Neville, answering the unstated addition. 'I was invited to a fancy-dress party, and I couldn't find it.'

Ted laughed, then quickly recovered himself.

'Sorry,' he said. 'I'm sorry.'

Liz approached. She'd hung back, thinking it was some maniac fisherman of Ted's acquaintance. Only now had she recognized Neville. 'Neville!' she said. 'It's you!'

'He was invited to a fancy-dress party, and he couldn't find it,' said Ted.

Liz laughed, then quickly recovered herself.

'Sorry,' she said. 'I'm sorry. I really think that's the saddest thing I've ever heard.'

She kissed Neville. A tiny bit of false beard adhered to her face.

'I'm Henry the Eighth,' said Neville.

'Well, obviously.'

'She loved fancy dress. I felt she'd have wanted me to go. We did every year. But they've moved, and I couldn't find them, and I didn't like to knock on people's doors dressed like this.'

The red wall lights and the fairy lights on the tree flickered as the gale hurled the overhead cables against the swishing tops of the frantic poplars by the Mead Farm. Mavis Griddle gave Lester Griddle a look which said, 'Get the candles ready.' But the lights recovered.

'Nobody ever knew what I was supposed to be,' said Neville. 'Nobody. Ever. Now at last I succeed, and I can't find the blasted party. I combed the streets for Napoleons and Nell Gwyns. I followed somebody dressed like Hitler. It turned out to be some wretched youth going to a disco. Well, I couldn't go on all night. And I knew that if I went home to change, I'd lose impetus. I wouldn't find the courage to come. And I'd be a bit of a sore thumb in a round hole here anyway in these surroundings . . . oh, not that they aren't nice. Awfully jolly little place. All those match-boxes. Fascinating . . . So in a way being Henry the Eighth might make it easier. I felt. And I certainly haven't the courage to stay at home, on my own. I dread this Christmas.'

'You're welcome to spend it in our cosy little penthouse with us,' said Liz. 'Isn't he, Ted?'

Ted tried to hide his dismay at this suggestion, also at their diminutive attic flat being described as a cosy penthouse. It wouldn't have been difficult to guess that Liz was the mother of an estate agent. 'Yes! Yes, of course!' he said.

'Well, thank you,' said Neville. 'Thank you! We'll see.'

'Telephone call for you, Ted,' said Lester Griddle lugubriously as they approached the bar. 'Summat about an accident,' he added rather more cheerfully.

'Oh no,' said Ted. 'If that's the entertainment, we're sunk. Incidentally, Lester, can Mavis rustle up a salad or something? We have a vegetarian in our midst.'

Ted hurried off. Liz bought a drink for Neville Badger, and Lester Griddle said, 'A vegetarian, in the angling club! It's a contradiction in terms.'

Neville and Liz went to sit at one of the beaten copper tables, near the curtained bay window. Behind them was a garishly improbable painting of the canal and bridge. No water was ever so blue, no sky so purple, no clouds so manicured.

'How are you feeling?' said the immaculate Henry the Eighth. 'Fine.'

'Morning sickness?' He spoke about it as something very distant, which he had read about but never encountered.

'Not really.' Liz spoke of it as a phenomenon experienced only by lesser mortals.

'I ran into Laurence outside the Rotherham Building Society on Tuesday.'

'Oh?'

'Aren't you going to ask me how he is?' continued Neville, when he realized that 'Oh?' was all Liz was going to say.

'No.' Liz had the feeling that Neville looked shocked, under all his Henry the Eighth paraphernalia. 'I shock you.'

'Yes.'

'Neville, I can assure you I wouldn't have left Laurence if I had a shred of feeling left for him.'

'I know, but . . .'

'. . . I ought to worry about what I've done to him. Although it was at least as much what he's done to me. All right, if my scorn for the social niceties appalls you . . . how does he seem?'

'He seems to be bearing up reasonably well.'

'Oh good,' said Liz in a flippant tone. And she mocked the stuffiness in Neville's voice. 'He's "bearing up reasonably well", is he?' And then she was contrite, less about Laurence than about the pain she was inflicting on this decent, honourable man, whose personal life had been so sheltered that after thirty years he still shook his head in dismay at the dark side of life which his work so often revealed. 'No, I am glad,' she said. 'Of course I am.'

When Ted came back from his phone call, Paul buttonholed him before he could return to Liz.

'Dad?'

'Bloody Crutchley. What does he expect me to do? Drive to Hemel Hempstead at this time of night? I mean . . . does he?'

'I saw Mum on Tuesday.'

'Oh good. A lorry's shed its load near Hemel Hempstead. Fire dogs and toasting forks all over the M1. Punctures *ad infinitum*. "I thought you ought to be informed, Mr Simcock." Delighted to have the chance to ruin my evening. Bloody southern runt! What?'

'I saw Mum on Tuesday.'

'How is she?'

'I think the new pills are doing her some good.'

'Oh good. Good. I'm glad. You're a good lad. I mean that. Look after her.'

'Dad!'

'It's over, Paul. I mean . . . I'm sorry . . . but . . . it is.' Oh God! Elvis was talking to Kevin Loudwater. Oh God! What had he done to his sons? 'It's over, Paul. You don't think I'd have hurt her like this if it wasn't, do you?'

'No, but . . .'

'You're a good lad. I'm sorry if I've ever given you the impression I thought anything else. A very good lad.'

He *was*, too. In some ways. Ted decided that, in view of Paul's feelings for Rita, he would forbear to make any sarcastic remarks about the Greenpeace tee shirt.

'I'm not thinking of me, Dad. It's her.'

'I know. I know. You're a good lad. But . . . you see . . . it's over. Where the hell is the entertainment? I'm going to phone Dave Willcocks and blast him from Christmas to next Thursday. I mean – he bloody well booked them.'

'Dad!'

'I know! I know! But I'm still chairman, Paul. One's personal feelings clash with the burdens of office. That's what it's like, public life. Oh heck!'

Laurence had come! He was standing in the doorway, wearing an impeccable lounge suit and assuring Pete Ferris, with a faint air of astonishment, that he wasn't the entertainment.

'Laurence!' said Ted.

'Don't sound so surprised,' said Laurence. 'You were good enough to invite me at the Dentists' Dinner Dance. Don't you remember? "Only a little back street boozer, but they're a friendly crowd," was your description. How accurate it was!'

Ted flashed Liz a dismayed look, and she glared at Laurence.

Laurence smiled, well pleased with the effect of his unexpected arrival.

Say what you liked about Mavis Griddle, and people often did, but nobody ever said she couldn't make batter. The fish and chips were good, though they would have tasted better washed down by several cups of tea. It was an informal supper, and people formed their own groups at the beaten copper tables. Ted sat with Liz and Laurence and Henry the Eighth, but had little appetite. He found it hard to laugh when Arnold Haygarth, his predecessor as chairman, called out, 'That fish on your plate's bigger than any you ever caught, Ted.' Neville Badger and Liz gave each other shocked glances as they received their first taste of the white wine. Liz and Laurence gave each other no glances. Laurence wore a fixed smile. He looked as stuffed as the salmon in the glass case above his head. Ted had chosen his seat before he realized that he was condemning himself to stare at a photograph of a smiling Kevin Loudwater, standing beside the record shark he had caught at Aberystwyth on the Welsh trip.

The dessert took the form of Mavis' trifle, for which she was famed, unjustly in Liz's opinion.

After the meal, it was time for the prize-giving. Ted stood in the raised area by the bay window. On the table in front of him there were two small silver cups, one large silver cup and a silver shield.

Most of the guests were seated at the tables and on bar stools, but four of the men lolled against the bar.

Ted felt nervous. He wished he hadn't brought Liz. He found that he was seeing the evening through her eyes. He was ashamed of these people, his friends and colleagues. He was ashamed of feeling ashamed. If only they were having a nice quiet evening, just the two of them, making amorous plans in a secluded corner of the Gaiety Bar of the Angel Hotel, out of sight of Michael Heseltine.

He wished his two sons, the fruits of his loins, the pride of his life, both unemployed, weren't sitting there with Jenny. He wished Kevin Loudwater, the complacent pork butcher, wasn't there, his smug backside perched on a bar stool.

'Ladies and gentlemen,' he said. 'I now have great pleasure in climaxing my year as chairman . . .' There were suggestive cries. Ted glared. Laurence smiled thinly. '. . . by giving away the trophies for what has been another excellent year . . . apart from the . . . er . . .' He found his eyes being drawn to Kevin Loudwater. '. . . the fracas at Wisbech. The sea fishing shield goes to Bert Kitchen.'

There was generous applause. Bert was popular.

'Unfortunately, Bert can't be here tonight, as he's in Tenerife.'

'Lucky Bert,' said Arnold Haygarth, and even this innocent comment, coming from his predecessor, struck Ted as an implied criticism of his handling of the event. He took the shield and put it at the other end of the table. If only Bert hadn't sent his postcard. If only he didn't know how upset Bert would be if his carefully written festive card wasn't read out in full at the party. If only he hadn't had the absurd idea that Liz could share the whole of his life.

'But he *has* sent a postcard. "Dear all. Weather fair to good, local talent fair to brunette, just my luck, I'm with the wife and there's a knocking shop right opposite the hotel."' Ted looked uneasily at his lover, seated between her husband and Henry the Eighth. '"I'll be thinking of you all on the big night. Sup some Fothergills' Best for me." Good old Bert! Next . . .' He picked up one of the smaller cups. '. . . we come to the prize for the biggest trout, which this year goes to Derek Wiggins.'

There was generous applause. Derek Wiggins, who drove a lorry for Jewson's, was well liked.

'Unfortunately Derek can't be here tonight, as he's in bed with his leg.'

'Not to mention a certain redheaded waitress,' called out Elvis.

'Thank *you*!' said Ted. 'That will do! I mean! . . . really!' He couldn't believe it. His own son, a philosophy graduate! And it didn't really seem in character. Cynical, yes, but not usually crude. And in front of Liz, too.

Well of course! The boys were taking it hard. You couldn't really blame them. Oh God. Ted became aware that it was too long since he had spoken. People were looking at him strangely. He was drenched in sweat. He put the cup down beside the shield. He caught sight of Liz, looking as if there were nowhere she'd like to be less, and of Laurence, faintly supercilious, and Neville Badger, distant and sad behind his costume. 'Next, the spring competition, held this year at the Newark gravel pits. This was won by Trevor Barnwell.'

Ted applauded. Nobody else did.

'Come on! It's petty, is this. It's a sign of small minds, pettiness. Now come on! Let bygones be bygones, you miserable lot.'

Ted applauded. There was some response from his audience.

'That's better. Not much, but better. Unfortunately, Trevor can't be here tonight, as he has parted company with us following the . . . er . . . the fracas at Wisbech. However, your committee felt . . .'

'Not unanimously,' said Pete Ferris, the self-appointed doorman.

'True, Pete, but by a majority verdict, on my casting vote.'

'Since when could you cast?' said Elvis, just loud enough to be heard by the whole bar, just soft enough for it to be possible that he hadn't intended it to be heard.

'Look, will you belt up?' snapped Ted.

'Just a little joke, Dad.'

Ted glared at Elvis, then slowly regained control of himself. 'Right. Good,' he said. He adopted the bland, grammatically tortured tones in which men reveal the sentiments of committees. 'Your committee felt that the award to Trevor should stand, as awarded, in the hope that, in the fullness of time, good sense may prevail.'

Ted put the second small cup with the other trophies. There now only remained the large cup to be awarded. He braced himself.

'Finally, I come to the Arthur Tong Cup,' he said. 'This cup was kindly donated by the late Arthur Tong . . . before he was late, of course . . . for the winner of the autumn competition, which was held this year . . . at Wisbech.'

His perverse noddle was at its tricks again, swinging his eyes round, against his will, to meet the eyes of the person he least wanted to see.

Kevin Loudwater, the permed pork butcher, returned his gaze blandly.

'I'm glad to say,' said Ted, not looking in the least glad, 'that at last we do have a winner present tonight, and it's . . . er . . . it's me, Ted Simcock.'

He applauded, realized that he shouldn't be, and stopped. There was modest applause, more than for Trevor Barnwell, less than for Bert Kitchen and Derek Wiggins. Kevin Loudwater applauded enthusiastically. So did Elvis. Liz looked uneasily at Laurence as she clapped gently. Laurence gave two soft, perfunctory claps.

'Your new man cuts quite a dash in public,' he said, and Liz looked as if she would like to throttle him. 'Door knocker tycoon, prize-winning angler, accomplished public speaker. A man of many parts. You must be very proud of him.'

Paul and Jenny approached the table where Liz was sitting with Laurence and Neville Badger. They looked determined and united. Clearly they had a purpose that was more than social.

'Hello!' said Jenny. 'That's a very good Henry the Eighth, Uncle Neville.'

'Thank you, Jenny,' said Neville. 'You see! Everyone knows who I am this time.'

'We . . . er . . . we wondered if we could have a word,' said Jenny.

'Of course,' said Laurence.

'I went as Sir Francis Drake. Boadicea. I even went as the Eddystone lighthouse,' said Neville. 'Nobody ever knew who I was.'

'Er . . . we wanted a word with . . . er . . . my . . . er . . . about something personal,' said Jenny.

'Ah!' said Neville Badger. 'Sorry. I was a bit slow there. It's the syphilis, I expect. It rots the brain.'

They stared at him in horror.

'I was being Henry the Eighth,' he explained. 'Sorry.' And he made his regal way towards the gents.

'Poor Neville,' said Liz. 'He's trying to be jolly.'

'Look, as we've got you two together,' said Jenny. 'Paul and I felt . . . I mean . . . we made our marital vows much more recently than you, obviously . . . so we feel that . . . er . . .'

'Yes,' said Paul. 'We do. We feel that in this cynical, materialistic age people give up far too quickly. I mean, if a marriage has really broken down, fair enough, but we also feel . . . er . . .'

'. . . that people oughtn't to give up before they've . . . er . . .' said Jenny.

'. . . explored every avenue,' said Paul.

'Believe me,' said Liz, 'we've explored both sides of every avenue in both directions several times.'

'Could we please change the subject?' said Laurence.

There was a lengthy silence, while they hunted around for subjects to which they could safely change.

'The fish and chips looked nice,' said Jenny.

'Do you know I think it's the first time I've ever actually had fish and chips,' said Laurence.

'Your snobbery is so boring, Laurence,' said Liz.

'My snobbery! Who was it who when I offered the Simcocks Bucks Fizz said you weren't certain if we had any orange juice?'

'The point being that it was assumed that we had champagne,' explained Jenny to Paul.

The lights flickered again.

'I understood it, Jenny,' said Paul. 'I may be as common as muck, but I happen to know what Bucks Fizz is.'

'Paul!' said Jenny. 'I wasn't . . . I wouldn't . . . I hate snobbery as much as you do. It's of no importance to me that you're from a lower class than I am.'

'Oh Christ! Thank you!' said Paul, and he stormed off, past the crowd at the bar, past the abstemious George Pilbeam surreptitiously looking at his watch, out towards the car park.

'Well, you are,' Jenny shouted, as she followed him more slowly, in view of her condition. 'That's a fact. That's not snobbery. Not being snobbish means not caring about class differences, not pretending they don't exist.'

As Jenny pursued Paul they passed Betty Sillitoe, who was taking a drink to Rodney. She was trying to buy all their drinks that night, so that she could control his consumption. She gazed at Paul and Jenny without surprise, and continued on her way. As she passed Laurence and Liz, she looked away.

'Betty!' said Laurence.

Betty, who was over-rouged as usual, cut him dead, and he reproached himself for having given her the opportunity.

'She says she's going to sue,' said Liz.

'That'll be fun for you,' said Laurence.

Ted reached them at last. On his long voyage across the room, clutching his trophy, he'd been forced to discuss the fracas at Wisbech, his long-overdue triumph, how big a refund would be given in view of the absence of the entertainment, and Trevor Barnwell's treachery – nobody had ever really liked him. He had just heard for the fifth time that night about the Irishman who was buried at sea and the eighteen men who tried to dig the grave. He had laughed each time. All jokes made by members were fresh and funny when you were club chairman.

He flopped into a seat.

'Well done, Ted,' said Laurence. 'You must feel very . . .'

'Yes, I do,' said Ted.

'Seeing you there, smiling shyly, acknowledging the storms of applause, it suddenly occurred to me . . . you still haven't come for your final scaling and cleaning.'

'I won't be coming any more, Laurence.'

'That's rather an extreme course, isn't it? Surely we're sophisticated enough to separate our professional from our private lives?'

'Maybe your reputation is crumbling, Laurence,' said Liz. 'Maybe the saga of Betty's bridge will destroy you. Maybe they'll film it. "The Dentist's Downfall" or "A Bridge Too Far".'

'Liz!' said Ted.

'Or maybe Ted doesn't trust you not to go berserk when you've got him there helpless with his mouth open. He knows what a passionate nature you have.'

Liz swept across the bar to rescue Neville Badger, who was being told by the abstemious Pilbeams and Hortons that angling was the only true antidote to the agonies of widowerhood.

'Ouch!' said Laurence.

'Absolutely,' said Ted. 'I don't want to hurt you any more than I . . .'

He couldn't finish the sentence. Laurence did it for him.

'. . . have already?'

'Exactly. Sorry.'

Ted came face to face with Elvis in the passage outside the bars. It was a bleak, draughty corner, unfurnished except for a fire extinguisher, with six doors, one to each bar, one to each toilet, one marked 'Private', and one leading to the arctic car park. Ted was on his way out to put his undeserved prize in the boot of the car, far from the ironic eyes of Kevin Loudwater, and Elvis was on his way back from performing one of those natural functions which are necessary even for philosophers. They looked at each other uneasily, father and son.

'Elvis!' said Ted. 'Look . . . I mean . . . I know you don't like . . . you know . . . what's happened . . . Liz and me. I understand. I mean . . . I do . . . really . . . I do. I wouldn't if I was in your shoes. But.'

'But what?'

'It's happened. It's a fact. Try and accept it.'

'Dad!'

'Oh, incidentally. You're going to have a little brother. That'll be fun, won't it?'

Elvis stared at Ted in horror. 'Oh my God . . . you mean . . . ? oh my God.'

'Elvis? Everything that's happened. I . . . I mean . . .'

Elvis held out his hand. 'Congratulations, Dad,' he said.

'Thanks,' said Ted, trying not to sound too surprised. 'Of course, it could be a sister.'

'Not that! On winning the Arthur Tong Cup. You beat me fair and square.'

Elvis went into the lounge bar.

Did he know?

Ted hurried out to his car, and put his trophy in the boot.

He heard crying, over by the rustic tables. It was Paul and Jenny. He went over to them. They were shivering and shuddering in each other's arms.

'We're all right now,' said Paul. 'We've just had our first real row. It's done us good. We've got things into perspective.'

Suddenly, Rodney Sillitoe made up his mind. He approached Elvis Simcock.

'What a fiasco,' said Elvis. 'I told them Barbra Streisand wouldn't turn up.'

'How would you like to work in the frozen chicken industry, Elvis?' said Rodney.

'What? Well . . . I mean . . . it's never exactly been my burning ambition.'

'I've been thinking. You're right. If we can't employ fellows like you, the blokes with the brains . . . we're expanding next year, I hope. Think about it.'

'Well. I mean . . . what as?'

'On the management side. I wouldn't expect a philosophy graduate to be knee-deep in chicken shit. Think about it. No hurry. If you . . . er . . . you know . . . give my Miss Wainscot a tinkle.'

'Well, thank you, Rodney. I . . . er . . . I will think about it. And if I . . . er . . . you know . . . I will give your Miss Wainscot a tinkle.'

'Good. Good. Now I must make sure the old girl doesn't drink too much, bless her.'

•

136

'I'm finding it difficult to make myself understood,' mumbled Betty Sillitoe through lips that barely moved.

'Sorry?' said the immaculate Neville Badger.

'I said, I'm finding it difficult to make myself understood.'

'Nonsense. You're as plain as a pikestaff. Your speech, I mean, of course, not your . . .'

'It's undermining my self-confidence and ruining my social life,' said Betty. 'What do you think our chances are?'

'Sorry?'

'I said, It's undermining my . . .'

'No, no, no. I *heard*. I didn't understand. Chances?'

'Sorry. I find it difficult discussing business when I have to mumble and you're Henry the Eighth.'

'Business? I didn't know we were discussing business.'

'Well, of course! I'm suing Laurence for defamation of appearance and character change. I want you to represent me.'

'Ah! I don't know, Betty. Laurence is an old friend.'

'I see. Old pals stick together. Friendship is more important than justice. Fine. Just as long as we know where we stand.' Betty was finding it difficult to get up a real head of anger while mumbling. Her indignation subsided. 'Excuse me,' she said. 'I must go and make sure the old fool doesn't drink too much, bless him.'

'Tell Liz about the time you went to Paris to see the rugby, and ended up inside,' said Ted.

They were parked on bar stools, talking to their lugubrious host, Lester Griddle. Ted had promised her that Lester was a barrel of laughs when you got to know him, and she'd said, 'Oh Lord. Is he? How awful!'

'We did,' said the barrel of laughs. 'We went to Paris to see the rugby, and ended up inside.'

'Those were the days,' said Ted.

'Aye, and you know why? 'Cos there was no V A bloody T, excuse my French,' said Lester Griddle lugubriously.

'There was Lester and Archie Wainwright and these three French polishers from Sunderland,' said Ted. 'Between them they polished off thirteen bottles of French champagne.'

'Inland Revenue, fair enough, give and take, swings and

roundabouts, we understand each other,' quipped Lester Griddle. 'VATman, no chance. He's got you by the short and curlies.'

'Are you going to come and serve or do I have to do it all myself, Lester Griddle?' said Mavis Griddle. Had she always been as sour as a bad pint, or had Lester Griddle slowly curdled her?

Lester Griddle raised long-suffering eyebrows and moved off.

'He's a character,' said Ted. 'Oh God!'

Kevin Loudwater was standing beside them.

'He deserved that trophy,' said the sensual pork butcher to Liz. 'He worked hard at Wisbech.'

'Kev!'

'I know. I saw him. I know what determination he showed.'

'Kev!'

'Well, aren't you going to introduce us?' asked Kevin.

'Oh . . . yes . . . of course. Liz Rodenhurst, Kevin Loudwater. Kevin has the pork butcher's in Newbaldgate, between the unisex hairdresser's and the organic food shop.'

'Hello, Kevin.'

'Hello, Liz. By heck, you're a cracker.'

'Well . . . thank you very much. So, you were upset that they chose fish and chips!'

'You what?' said Kevin, puzzled.

'Being a pork butcher, Kev,' said Ted hastily. 'That's what we were talking about outside, remember?'

'Oh! Right. Right. It does rile me, Liz. It does. Well, I've no time for fish, me. Never have had. I'll catch 'em, but I won't eat 'em, no thank you! You must come and visit me one day, Liz,' he said, as he strode off with his pint. 'It'll be right snug when the roof's repaired.'

'I want to go home,' whispered Liz.

'Liz! You don't mean . . . back to . . .?'

'No! How can you say that? I want to go and make love.'

'Oh! Right! Well . . . right! So do I. But.'

'Oh dear. Another thundering great "but". Well, come on. But what?'

Ted stared at her as if it was obvious.

'I'm chairman.'

'Is your passion cooling? Is your ardour on the wane?'

''Course it isn't. But.' He continued hurriedly, before she could wax sarcastic about his 'but'. 'I mean . . . Liz! This do is the final responsibility of my term of office.'

'I see. Well, I'm flattered that you're so keen.'

'I am keen! Madly! Deliriously! But! Oh God, Liz! Does a judge say, "Right. I'm feeling randy. Court adjourned"? Does the Archbishop of Canterbury break off after the first hymn and say, "That's all for now, folks. I'm going home for a bit of hanky-panky. Same time next Sunday."? Well . . . it's the same difference with angling club chairman.'

The jackpot paid out noisily on the new fruit machine in the public bar.

'Would you say you were a popular man?' said Liz.

'Well . . . yes . . . I mean . . . rather than no. Yes. Reasonably popular. Well liked. Widely respected. Why?'

'I thought your reception was distinctly lukewarm. I felt angry.'

'Well . . . a lot of them knew Rita. They liked her, though she never believed it.'

'You talk about her as if she's dead.'

'She is for me.'

'Will I be dead for you, one day?'

'Course you won't! Love! How can you even say that? Really! I mean . . . you mean more to me than anything in the world. You are my world.' He kissed her. 'Now go and talk to the Pilbeams while I sort out the entertainment.'

Rodney and Betty Sillitoe bore down on Jenny and Paul at their corner table like two sailing dinghies beating into a safe harbour. Was there a slight wobble in their wakes, or was this just imagination?

'May we join you?' Rodney asked. 'Only Betty's embarrassed to show her teeth, and with you you'll understand and she needn't talk.'

'Of course,' said Jenny.

Rodney and Betty sat down. The big wheel behind Cock-A-Doodle Chickens raised his glass to the youngsters. He looked embarrassed, uncertain, almost as if he were quite a small wheel.

'Betty tells me I may have been a little rude to you at the Dentists' Dinner Dance, Jenny,' he said.

'Well . . . a bit, perhaps, but I didn't mind,' said Jenny. 'I was fascinated to find out how guilty you feel about the way you treat your chickens.'

Betty was searching in her handbag, and Paul showed his moral support for Jenny over the chicken question by clasping her hand.

'Did I say that?' said Rodney. 'I think I may have had a little too much.'

'Have you thought seriously about umbrellas?' Jenny asked.

Rodney stared at her. Beside him there was a ledge crammed with Scandinavian matchboxes, including, did he but know it, one specially produced for a bar in Trondheim, and featuring a photograph of that cosy refuge from the arctic night. Above the ledge there was an aerial photograph of *this* cosy refuge. More than half the photograph consisted of car park.

'Umbrellas?' he said at last.

'You said you'd switch production to umbrellas.'

'Oh Lord. I *was* drunk!'

'It's not a bad idea, though, is it?'

'You can't do things like that, Jenny. I sell to butchers. Supermarkets. Hotel chains. I can't suddenly say, "Sorry. No chickens this week. How would you like some umbrellas?"'

'No, but in time you'd find new outlets,' said Paul, removing his hand, as if speaking and clasping Jenny's hand were alternative expressions of support, and to give both at the same time would be excessive.

'I'd love to make umbrellas,' said Rodney. 'But they're dodgy in this climate. Get a wet summer, and you can't satisfy demand. Get a fine summer and you're knackered.'

Betty had produced a notepad from her bag and was writing a note. There was a painting of a sheaf of wheat on each sheet of paper.

'It doesn't have to be umbrellas,' said Jenny, and Paul squeezed her hand. 'It could be . . . oh . . .'

'. . . socks,' said Paul, letting go of her hand.

'I don't know about socks,' said Rodney. 'I don't know about umbrellas. I know about chickens. It's a boom industry in which British technology leads the world. Our product is cheap, standardized and almost totally tasteless. Other countries can't manage that.'

'I should have helped you set your chickens free,' said Jenny, 'but I couldn't.'

'You chickened out!' said Rodney.

'There's nothing funny in discovering what a coward you are,' said Jenny, and she burst into tears and hurried out to the toilets.

'I always seem to end up making your wife cry,' said Rodney.

'Oh, don't worry,' said Paul. 'She cries a lot,' he added proudly.

'Doesn't it worry you?'

'The kind of world we live in, it'll worry me when she doesn't cry.'

'Shouldn't you go to her?'

'No. There are moments when a woman needs to be alone.'

Betty handed Rodney the note she had been writing, and he read it aloud before she had a chance to warn him not to.

'"It must be tough on the dole, whatever some people say,"' he read. '"Buy them large drinks without looking as if you're patronizing them. And get me one while you're at it. You've had enough." Betty!'

The abstemious Pilbeams were saying good night to Leslie and Patricia Horton, who hated to be called Les and Pat. Ted could wait no longer, if his evening was to be saved from collapsing around his ears.

He leapt onto the little platform by the curtained bay window.

'Ladies and gentlemen!' he cried. 'Ladies and gentlemen!'

The noise, never terrific, soon died down. A gust rattled the windows, and Lester Griddle almost smiled. He'd made sure that all the windows rattled. There was nothing better than rattling windows for emphasizing the cosiness of the pink-and-red womb over which he presided.

'Thank you!' said Ted. 'Thank you! Unfortunately, through no fault of ours, we have been badly let down by our entertainment. Never mind. I mean . . . so what, eh?'

Jenny returned, and tiptoed to her seat. When she saw Ted addressing the assembly, she wished she could leave again.

'So come on. Let's prove to our visitors that we have unexpected talents in our midst,' said Ted. 'We'll make our own entertainment.' The Pilbeams were edging their way towards the door. 'George? Sybil? Not going, are you? Come come. The fun's just beginning.'

The Pilbeams gave each other looks, and everyone turned to look at them, and they went very red and returned to their seats in much confusion and mortification.

'I'm very glad to be able to tell you,' said Ted, 'that Norman Penfold will do some amazing things on his instrument.'

The bachelors and those who hadn't brought their wives jeered, whistled and made cat calls and suggestive cries. So did some of the wives. The Pilbeams and the Hortons smiled bravely. Liz, sitting between Laurence and Henry the Eighth, tried to look loftily detached. Laurence smiled his supercilious smile. Neville Badger looked puzzled, a king unused to the amusements of his subjects.

'Now come on,' said Ted. 'That's not the spirit. I mean . . . is it? Is it the spirit? It isn't, is it? Right. So . . . let's hear it for Norman Penfold and his squeeze-box.'

A tiny, wizened, elderly man stepped onto the platform with his accordion. The audience applauded and cheered.

'Thank you,' said Ted. 'That's better. And to set the ball rolling, I'm going to start things off myself.'

There was a mixture of cheers and jeers. Liz looked mortified. Ted avoided looking at her. He wished he didn't have to do this but, if he didn't, history would record that his year's tenure of office had ended in fiasco.

'After me, you'll all sound good,' he said. 'Ladies and gentlemen, a witty little ditty from the days of the music hall, en-tittled "The Tuner's Oppor-'tuner'-ty".' Surely even Liz would find mild vulgarity acceptable if it was historical?

Norman Penfold played with more enthusiasm than skill. Ted sang as one would expect of a man whose more usual audience consisted of toothbrushes, sponges and face-flannels.

> Miss Crotchety Quaver was sweet seventeen,
> And a player of exceptional skill.
> She would play all the day, all ev'ning as well,
> Making all the neighbourhood ill.
> And to keep her piano in tune she would have
> A good tuner constantly there.
> And he'd pull up the instrument three times a week
> Just to keep it in proper repair.

Even before he flung himself upon the first chorus, Ted's hopes that Liz would find it amusing were fading fast. In private she might be extremely sexy, but in public . . . he caught a glimpse of her embarrassed face, and of Laurence looking amused at her discomfiture.

He launched into the chorus, and he was very nearly in tune with Norman Penfold. Every now and then the wizened old musician sensed that he was falling behind his own rhythms, and produced a sequence of very fast notes, like an overexcited and slightly asthmatic blackbird, until he was satisfied that he'd caught up with himself.

And first he'd tune it gently, then he'd tune it strong,

sang Ted.

Then he'd touch a short note, then he'd run along.
Then he'd go with vengeance enough to break the key.
At last he tuned whene'er he got the oppor–'tuner'–ty.

Paul and Jenny were also embarrassed. They raised their glasses to Rodney Sillitoe, thanking him for their unpatronizing large drinks, and settled to listen to the second verse with fixed smiles.

He came there so often I thought I'd complain
That in March, April, May and in June
That tuner had been there once ev'ry day,
To keep her piano in tune.
I said, 'He's too often here, hanging about,
And he's costing you no end of pelf,
If your instrument wants such a lot of repairs,
I'll attend to the business myself.'

Towards the end of the verse, Liz walked out. Ted wavered, longed to follow her, couldn't follow her, didn't follow her. Instead, he launched rather viciously into the second chorus, somewhat behind the accordion. Norman Penfold played excitedly, breathlessly, jerkily and, just occasionally, squeakily. Ted signalled to the audience to join in, and here and there somebody did remember the odd word, and some of the words they remembered were very odd indeed.

By the end of the chorus, Ted had just caught up with Norman Penfold. He began the third verse.

> But vainly I spoke to Miss Crotchety Q.–
> She said, 'Fred, I'll do just as I please.'
> And the very next time I called I saw
> That tuner still fingering the keys.
> I said 'Get out.' They said 'Get out yourself.'
> And they meant it – for out of the place
> I went with a foot (his or hers) in my back,
> And the door, it was slammed in my face.

Again, Ted signalled to the audience to join in the chorus. This time Norman Penfold was careful to wait for Ted, and Ted leapt in as fast as he could, so it was Norman Penfold who was behind throughout and only caught up at the end of the last line.

And at that moment of rare synchronization between singer and musician, Rita walked in. She was wearing a bottle-green outfit that was deeply unflattering.

Ted looked thunderstruck, and Norman Penfold's accordion gave out a surprised, excited squeak.

'Rita!' muttered Ted under his breath.

There was a pause, then Ted signalled to Norman, and they began again.

> I got over my folly, I courted again
> A bewitching but sensible maid.

Rita gave Ted a challenging look, then searched the bar for Liz.

> But I went in for tuning, and in less than a month
> I was quite an adept at my trade.

Rita gazed in amazement at Henry the Eighth, alias Neville Badger.

> Now we're married, and all my doubts and fears
> Are for evermore laid on the shelf.

'But are they?' thought Rita, as she met the astonished eyes of Paul and Jenny. 'Where's Liz?'

> For if ever her instrument gets out of tune,
> I am able to tune it myself.

Rita caught Elvis's more detachedly surprised expression. Her elder son joined in the last chorus defiantly, making up the words that he couldn't remember.

And first I'd tune it gently, then I'd tune it strong,

roared Ted.

Then I'd touch a short note, then I'd run along.
Then I'd go with vengeance enough to break the key.

Ted signalled to them all to make one last effort, and they thundered out, with a fair degree of gusto:

At last he tuned whene'er he got an oppor–'tuner'–ty.

There was a fair round of applause. Ted acknowledged the applause briefly, then rushed out, straight past Rita.

'It was just a song, Liz. Just a bit of fun.'
'I hated seeing you making such an exhibition of yourself.'
They were sitting in Ted's Cavalier 2000 GL. He had had GB plates and Townsend Thoresen stickers put on even though the car had never been abroad, but it wasn't really cheating because he had been abroad, in Rodney's car.

The engine was running. Ted wasn't sure whether he'd started it to work the heater or because they were going home. He hoped they weren't going home. He had to speak to Rita. He had to see his year of office through to the bitter end. It was impossible to go home.

Nevertheless, he felt that if he didn't handle the conversation very carefully, they would be going home.

'I went to a wedding on Clydeside once,' he said, though this wasn't at all what he'd planned to say. 'Everybody did a turn. Everybody. Nobody minded. And because nobody minded, everybody was good. I mean . . . really . . . everybody. You lot, you're so . . . not cold, because you aren't, well *you* aren't . . . so knotted up . . . private . . . snobbish.'

'You were making a fool of yourself.'
'No, because I didn't mind making a fool of myself. Don't you realize? You can only make a fool of yourself if you mind.'

A car pulled into the car park, briefly floodlighting them.

'It doesn't matter with these people,' said Ted. They were in darkness again. He put his hand on Liz's knee, and she didn't remove it. 'These people are my people.'

'Nonsense. You're managing director of your own factory.'

'I haven't forgotten my roots.'

'Asparagus has roots, but one keeps them well hidden.'

'Liz! Love! Asparagus is asparagus. People are people. I mean . . . we use asparagus and chuck it out when it's exhausted. We don't treat people like that.'

'Don't we?'

'Exactly! But we shouldn't.'

The car shuddered as a particularly violent gust swept over the car park. A white fish and chip bag soared over the roof of the Crown and Walnut like a joyful barn owl.

Ted was in a quandary. After a few minutes you feel self-conscious about resting your hand on somebody's knee. He couldn't slide it up Liz's leg. You didn't do things like that to Rodenhursts in pub car parks. He felt that he had no alternative but to remove it, and rely entirely on the persuasive qualities of his voice.

'So . . .' he said. 'Come back in. Show them you like them. Show them you care about them.'

'I don't like them. I don't care about them.'

'Liz! Oh heck! Love! These people are the salt of the earth.'

'Were they the salt of the earth at Wisbech?'

'Liz! It wasn't typical, wasn't Wisbech. I mean . . . they're Yorkshiremen. When they're outside the county boundary, well, it's a bit like being abroad. It's a bit like being on a cross-channel ferry. I mean . . . they're liable to go a bit berserk.'

'They didn't just go a bit berserk. It sounds as though some of them went thoroughly nasty.'

'All right. All right. I'm not saying they're any better than anybody else. I'm just saying they're no worse. Look . . . I mean . . . I'm chairman. I must go back. Come with me. Please.'

'What's the point?'

It was time to play his joker. Ted knew that it would decide the issue one way or the other, but he didn't know enough about women to be absolutely sure of the outcome.

'Rita's turned up,' he said.

'Well, why didn't you say so?' said Liz.

The tiny, wizened Norman Penfold was playing 'Send In The Clowns' and losing to it narrowly. Ellen Ferris, self-appointed contralto and burly wife of Pete Ferris, the self-appointed doorman, was belting out the words and only just failing to reach the top notes.

Laurence felt that if Ted and Liz were talking together, he ought to talk to Rita, out of respect for symmetry if nothing else. So he bought her a drink. They installed themselves in an alcove, beneath a shelf devoted to matchboxes of the subcontinent, including a rare family-size box with a joke on the back in Gujerati.

Laurence saw Betty Sillitoe go to the bar, and said, 'I wonder whether Betty or Rodney will win the race to get drunk tonight.' Rita didn't reply, and he wondered if she was offended. 'I'm sorry,' he said. 'I don't mean to be rude to your friends.'

'They're Ted's friends really,' said Rita, and instantly regretted this small betrayal. 'Though I like them,' she added. 'I think they've taken our side.'

'I should hope so,' said Laurence. 'We're the wronged parties.' He gave Rita a sharp but not hostile look. 'With respect, Rita,' he said, 'I'm astounded you've found the courage to come.'

'So am I,' said Rita. 'You don't know what you can do till you try, do you? I think, to be honest, it was anger that gave me the strength.'

'You're fed up with giving them a clear field?'

'Exactly.'

'And this is a chance to create maximum embarrassment for minimum outlay.'

'That makes it sound awful.'

'My dear woman, you have every right.'

Ted and Liz entered. Ted murmured something to Liz, but neither Laurence nor Rita could lip read. (He actually said, on hearing the closing moments of Ellen Ferris's song, 'It could be worse. It could be "My Way".')

'Talk as if we're being intimate,' said Laurence.

'Pardon?' said Rita.

'For effect. To worry them. Say something intimate.'

There was silence from Rita.

'I've gone blank,' she said.

'Well . . . pay me compliments. Say you find me . . . very attractive . . . or something. Just for effect.'

Again, there was silence.

'I'm sorry,' she said. 'I can't.'

'I see.' Laurence sounded slightly piqued. 'Look, just . . . choose my best features. Compliment me on them.'

Again, there was silence from Rita.

'Sorry,' she said.

'For goodness sake,' said Laurence. 'Just say . . . oh, I don't know . . . er . . . "You have nice eyes. Do you know you have an elegant, shapely, rather distinguished nose?" Whatever!'

Again, Laurence waited expectantly.

'I'm sorry. It's no good,' said Rita.

'I see!'

'I'm sorry.'

'It doesn't matter! It was just . . . to say something. For God's sake, Rita, it doesn't matter if it's utter nonsense. Just look as if it's intimate.'

Laurence tried not to look fierce as he waited.

'I'm not very good at nonsense,' said Rita at last.

'Well, anything!' Laurence was becoming irritated now.

Why didn't *he* start, thought Rita, if he was so keen? Why did he have to put all the burden onto her?

'Tell limericks,' he commanded.

'Limericks??'

'Why not?'

And suddenly Laurence did start. Rita was astounded, as he leant forward and talked very intimately indeed, even, in so far as he was capable of it, sexually.

> A certain young gourmet of Crediton,
> Took some pâté de fois gras and spread it on
> A chocolate biscuit,
> Then murmured 'I'll risk it.'
> His tomb bears the date that he said it on.

'This is ridiculous,' said Rita.

'Try,' urged Laurence.

'What are they talking about?' said Ted, as they settled down at the table so recently vacated by Laurence and by Neville Badger, who had joined Betty Sillitoe at the bar.

'You aren't interested, are you?' said Liz. 'You aren't worried?'

'No! I'm not remotely interested. I'm not remotely worried. I'm just mildly intrigued, that's all. I mean . . . they look quite intimate.'

Rita tried hard to sound and look sexy and intimate as she whispered to Laurence:

> There was a young lady from Spain
> Who was dreadfully sick on a train.
> Not now and again,
> But now . . . and again . . .
> And again . . . and again . . . and again.'

'They're not going to start up as well, are they?' said Paul, watching the alcove with ill-concealed interest.

They were alone again, Rodney Sillitoe having gone to the bar to keep an eye on Betty's drinking.

'Well, I suppose it would solve the problem,' said Jenny.

'I know, but I don't think I could cope with it. It might scar me permanently.'

Again, Laurence spoke in his idea of an intimate, sexy voice.

> There once was a pious young priest,
> Who lived almost wholly on yeast.
> 'For,' he said, 'It is plain
> We must all rise again
> And I want to get started, at least.'

Rita thought hard. She leant forward and gazed dreamily into Laurence's eyes.

> There was a young lady from Spain,

she murmured.

'Again!' said Laurence.

Who was dreadfully sick on a train.
Not now and again,
But now . . . and again,
And again . . . and again . . . and again.

'It's the only one I know.'
They laughed.

'They're laughing!'
'Ted!'
'Oh, I don't *care*. I'm just astounded.'
'It's all for show. It must be, if Laurence is involved.'

Young Rod Wagstaffe, who had recently sacrificed his beloved
hippie appearance in order to get accepted on a TOPS course in
plumbing (a victory for common sense but a defeat, Rod still felt,
for the richness of human life), had popped back to his home in
Admiral Benbow Crescent on the Highcliffe Estate, and fetched
his guitar. He had been conferring with Norman Penfold, and the
result of their deliberations now began to assault the ears of the
assembly.
    'Er . . . if you . . . er . . . feel like coming over any time over
Christmas, don't hesitate,' said Laurence. 'I'll be there.'
    'Well . . . I may . . . yes . . . thank you . . . I may,' said Rita.
    'It's going to be a funny old Christmas.'
    'Yes. Yes, it is.' .

'Have you asked them for Christmas Day yet?' said Jenny, trying
not to keep looking across the smoky room to Rita and Laurence in
their alcove.
    'I'm beginning to wonder if we should. Your mum and my dad,
fair enough. Well, I don't mean "fair enough", I mean "absolutely
dreadful and shocking and all too typical of parents today, but . . .
I can understand". But my mum and your dad! The mind boggles!
If they went for a lie-down full of turkey and I heard them
tiptoeing to each other's rooms, I think I'd have a nervous
breakdown. My tender and idealistic young mind wouldn't be able
to comprehend the unimaginable.'
    'They wouldn't be full of turkey,' Jenny pointed out. She was

finding the bar stifling. It must have been a man who had described pregnancy as an 'interesting condition'. Just now it seemed a distinctly boring condition. She felt too hot all the time. She felt enormously heavy. Chairs were incredibly uncomfortable. She grew tired easily. She couldn't drink, and had almost stopped breathing several times in her efforts not to inhale cigarette smoke and stunt her baby's growth. 'They'd be full of soya bean loaf.' They had decided that it would be ridiculous to have a turkey for one. Paul would be eating it till February.

'Well, this is it, Jenny. What'd we give them? It's not just the turkey. It's the trimmings. Mum says the trimmings *make* a Christmas dinner. She'd be lost without her chipolatas. Well, you can't have vegetarian chipolatas, can you? You can't have bread sauce and cranberry sauce and two kinds of stuffing with soya bean loaf.'

'Will you miss your Christmas dinner?'

'Of course not. You're what matters to me, not turkey.'

They kissed, a spontaneous and delightful kiss, bringing Christmas joy to the undecorated half of the room. Lester Griddle, watching lugubriously, twitched. Mavis Griddle, as sour as a bad pint, lugubriously watching Lester Griddle watching lugubriously, narrowed her bloodshot licensed victualler's eyes. Lester Griddle returned rapidly to the pulling of pints. The whole room burst into generous applause. Paul and Jenny broke off shyly, as if they thought the applause was for them. Then they realized that it was an ovation for courage at the end of the guitar and squeeze-box recital.

'It'd be worth your having turkey if they come,' said Jenny.

'I'd rather have soya bean loaf and just us, but maybe we ought to ask them.'

Ted jumped up onto the platform.

'Right,' he said. 'Now. Who else is going to entertain us?'

'I will,' said Rita.

She stepped forward, leaving Laurence looking astounded.

Ted also looked astounded, and more than a little put out.

'Rita!' he said.

Rita stared at him defiantly. Her heart was thumping.

'Ladies and gentlemen,' said Ted. 'My . . . er . . .' He couldn't say 'my wife'. 'My . . . er . . .' He couldn't say 'My ex-wife'.

151

'. . . my word, this is a stout effort, so let's hear it for Rita Simcock.'

Ted moved to the side as the applause rang out, and stood there, as if ready to interrupt if Rita's material turned out to be unsuitably blue. He was feeling a mixture of anger – what right had she got to do this to him? – and protectiveness – you couldn't wipe out twenty-four years of marriage just like that. Ted felt that he must be there to rescue her, should the need arise. And surely it must? His Rita, trying her hand at being a pub entertainer? It wasn't possible. He glanced uneasily at Liz, who was watching him with a faintly sardonic expression.

'We live in troubled times,' said Rita, to the astonishment of everybody except Lester Griddle, who nodded his fervent agreement. Rita gave Ted a long, cool look. 'Sometimes I wonder if mankind has gone stark, staring mad.'

Ted looked extremely uneasy.

There was a pained, throbbing tension in Rita's voice, but she ploughed on.

'Womankind has on the whole done rather better.' She fixed her gaze on Liz. 'But there's no room for complacency in this area either. People have abandoned moral standards in order to gratify their greed for pleasure.'

It was Liz's turn to look uneasy. Laurence, alone in his alcove beneath the oriental matches, wore his fixed, stuffed, supercilious smile. The cynical Elvis Simcock, standing at the bar with a group of fairly drunk young anglers, seemed to be relishing the drama.

'It's the pills,' whispered Paul. 'It must be.'

'So,' said Rita, 'I would like you to remember that it is a Christmas party. If Norman would accompany me, I would therefore like to sing "Hark, the Herald Angels Sing".' She turned to Norman Penfold. 'Do you know it?' she asked.

The little old man gave an almost imperceptible nod of his wizened head, as if to say that he thought he knew it, but wasn't guaranteeing anything.

'Good.' Rita fixed a fierce eye on Elvis and the young anglers. 'You may all join in the chorus. And I don't want any funny words.'

Elvis felt strangely abashed. He glared at the young anglers, indicating that he didn't want any funny words either.

Rita cleared her throat. Norman Penfold's lips moved as he

rapidly recalled the tune. Jenny closed her eyes, unable to witness a fellow female making a fool of herself. Paul felt sick.

They were totally unprepared for the attractive, clear, strong, tuneful voice which flung out the words defiantly.

> Hark, the herald angels sing
> Glory to the newborn king.
> Peace on earth, and mercy mild,
> God and sinners reconciled.

Jenny opened her eyes in astonishment. Paul smiled. Elvis gawped. Mavis Griddle, who had a singing voice like a butch corncrake, twitched sourly. It would be an exaggeration to say that Norman Penfold was accompanying Rita, but he was following her quite closely, and there was a smile on his wrinkled old face.

Rita signalled to the gathering to join in the chorus. Many of them did.

During the second verse Laurence began to look uneasy, as he found his supercilious smile becoming inappropriate and couldn't discover any more suitable expression. Ted was looking quite moved. Liz was looking somewhat caustic at the sight of Ted looking quite moved. Laurence found his new expression. He was able to look faintly amused at the sight of Liz looking somewhat caustic at the sight of Ted looking quite moved.

The second chorus was a distinct improvement on the first, and Rita even ventured a little smile of encouragement at Norman Penfold.

Alternative naughty words froze on the lips of cynical young anglers. Lester Griddle, their lugubrious host, sang as he hadn't sung since the introduction of VAT. Norman Penfold became so inspired that for several bars he was in time and in tune with Rita. Rodney and Betty Sillitoe watched in delighted amazement, almost carried away. But Rodney wasn't so carried away that he couldn't find the time to raise his glass to his lips. And Betty wasn't so carried away that she didn't notice this and take the drink away from him. She poured the contents into her own glass. It was the least she could do for the man she loved.

By the final chorus the noise was quite thunderous, as anglers and wives and guests belted out, in almost perfect unison:

Hark! The herald angels sing
Glory to the newborn king!

For a few seconds it might have been Bethlehem. There was a
burst of applause. Then it was the lounge bar of the Crown and
Walnut again. The applause died down. Norman Penfold became
a little old man again. Lester Griddle returned to the mundane
business of taking orders, grimacing with irritation at the need to
keep the money for crisps separate from the money for drinks.

Rita rushed out of the bar. Ted followed her, passing Liz's table
without even giving her a look.

Laurence's supercilious smile was well and truly back in place.

'Well, well, well!' he said. 'Can the king of the coal scuttles be
scuttling back to wifey, do you think?'

'Rita! Rita!'

She was just disappearing round the side of the pub. He hurried
after her. He felt as if he were spending half this cold, windy
evening out here.

He caught up with her just before she reached the Knapperley
Road. Here, on the very edge of the town, as a result of a recent
economy measure, only half the street lamps were lit.

'Rita! Where are you going?' he asked.

'Home.'

'Rita!'

'Shouldn't you be with her?'

'Yes, but . . . I wanted to say I'm very sorry for what's
happened.'

They had turned left along the Knapperley Road, towards the
canal bridge. Rita was walking more slowly, and Ted stopped, in
the hope that she would stop too, in order to continue their
conversation.

The ruse was a success!

'What's brought this on?' she said.

'You sang well. I was amazed.'

'Thank you!'

'Rita! Not that you sang well! That you sang. In public. I mean
. . . it's not like you.'

'Ah, but who am I? I saw Mrs . . . whose husband used to work at that special school before he collapsed . . . in Tesco's yesterday. Harrington. I heard her whispering to her friend, "You know who that used to be. That used to be Rita Simcock."'

Rita set off again. Ted hurried after her.

'Rita!'

'Lately, it's seemed as if you think everything would be made right by constantly repeating my name. It's not enough!'

'Rita!'

The last bus from Bradeley Bottom was approaching, with only three people on board. Rita held out her hand. Ted pulled her hand down, but the driver was already stopping.

'Sorry,' said Ted to the conductor. 'Mistake.'

The conductor scratched his turban in mystification, and the bus growled angrily on its way, groaning as it mounted the steep, hump-backed bridge over the Rundle and Gadd Navigation.

'I want to talk, now you've come!' said Ted.

'Why?'

'I care what happens to you.'

'In case I do something dreadful and it's in the papers, and brings disgrace on you and your precious foundry.'

'No! Rita! That's very unfair. I mean . . . love . . . I care about you. I do. That's why I've come outside, in the cold, without my coat, to say, I'm sorry.'

'Well, you've said it now. Twice.'

They were on the canal bridge now. An oval blue plate announced that it was bridge number 163, although they couldn't see this. It was the last bridge on the canal's tortuous, heavily silted, unromantic, forty-three mile journey north-east from Thurmarsh, where it began its course. Two hundred yards to the east, invisible on this cloudy starless night, was Gadd Stop Lock, where the navigation fell all of two inches into the navigable lower reaches of the only marginally more romantic Gadd, haven of herons, gulls and old prams.

A sports car roared up much too fast. Ted held Rita tightly in to the side of the bridge, in case she should do anything stupid. The car roared on. 'Maniac!' yelled Ted uselessly.

He could have continued to hold onto Rita. He could have run his hands over her not uncurvaceous body. He could have smothered her with hot, frenzied kisses. He didn't. He let her go,

155

sighed, and said, 'At least come back and get your coat, or you'll die of pneumonia.'

'That *would* be embarrassing,' said Rita. 'Foundry owner's wife dies of exposure on scantily clad mystery walk while he boozes with "other woman" in angling club Christmas orgy.'

'Rita!' said Ted. 'Come on! Love!'

He began to walk back towards the welcome pool of light around the whitewashed pub. To his relief, Rita followed.

'I didn't want all this to happen, you know,' he said.

'You're just putty in her hands.'

'No! I mean . . . what I mean is . . . obviously I want to be with her, or I wouldn't be . . . but I don't positively want not to be with you. I mean . . . I just have to be not with you because I'm with her . . . that's all, love.'

'You're splitting hairs as well as families now.'

'I'm sorry.'

'Three times!'

The first spears of rain were coming in almost horizontally on the gale.

'Look, you were great in there,' said Ted. 'Fantastic. I was proud of you.'

Rita stopped dead. 'Proud?' she said angrily. 'Proud? What have you got to be proud of? Do you think I'm your creation or something?'

'Rita! Look! All I'm saying is . . . you did well. Don't spoil it by running away. Look. I've got to go in now.' After a brief pause, he added, 'I have! I really have. I mean . . . I'm chairman,' as if Rita had said, 'Why have you got to go back in?' although she had said nothing. 'I mean . . . all I'm saying is . . . come back in, now that you've come in the first place, or it'll look like a victory for her.'

'They *have* been gone a long time,' said Laurence.

'What?' said Liz, trying not to look in the direction of the door.

'You're wondering if, under the influence of song, they are being reunited with each other and their God.'

'I'm not. Ted wouldn't. He couldn't. It's inconceivable.'

'Methinks the lady doth protest too much.'

The door opened, and Liz couldn't help looking. It was only Neville Badger returning from the gents, where he had experienced slight difficulties with his costume. Laurence smiled.

Ted and Rita entered. Liz tried to hide her relief. Laurence tried to hide his disappointment.

Paul and Jenny approached Ted and Rita.

'You were marvellous,' said Jenny, kissing Rita warmly.

'Not bad, Mum,' said Paul, kissing her shyly.

'I saw you trying to hide your head in your hands, before you realized you didn't need to,' said Rita.

'Er . . . excuse me,' said Ted.

'Please! Don't let me keep you from her!' said Rita, whose teeth were chattering.

'Rita!' said Ted.

'Dad!' said Paul.

'I'm sorry,' said Ted.

'Stop saying that,' said Rita.

'I'm sorry. Oh heck,' said Ted. He went over to join Liz and Laurence at their beaten copper table. 'I'm sorry,' he began. 'But I had to speak to her. I can't be completely callous. Well, can I?'

'I'll leave you two alone,' said Laurence.

'Don't feel you have to go, Laurence,' said Ted.

'Oh, I don't. I want to go, believe me,' said Laurence.

'I love you!' said Ted, when Laurence had gone. 'I do. Utterly.' He saw that the Hortons were leaving. 'Les! Pat! Not going, are you? There's an extension.'

'It's past our bedtime,' said Leslie Horton, organist and water bailiff, who hated missing his bedtime almost as much as he hated being called Les.

'You care more about them than about me,' said Liz.

'No, love,' said Ted. 'I don't. Of course I don't. But! . . . I mean . . . it's down to my responsibility, the conduct of the function. I said I'd be chairman for a year, not till such time as I wanted to go home and have it off with my lover. I mean . . . be fair . . . I'm committed morally.'

Pete Ferris, the self-appointed doorman, approached.

'Ted?' he said. 'Can I have a word?'

'No, Pete,' said Ted. 'I'm afraid you can't. I'm otherwise engaged.'

'It's about what Kev said in the car park.'

'Oh heck. Sorry, Liz.'

Ted left behind a Liz Rodenhurst who was not only angry, but puzzled.

'Bloody hell, Pete. It's raining,' said Ted.

'Did Kev blackmail you in this car park, Ted?' asked Pete Ferris.

'Why on earth should you think that?' said Ted.

'I don't know,' said Pete Ferris, and proceeded to tell him why. 'The way you looked at Kev. The way Kev looked at you. Rumours. Things people have said. Summat Trevor Barnwell said. Things I've heard about Kev when he was in Heckmondwyke. We can't afford to have rotten apples in the angling club, Ted. Can we?'

'Oh, all right. Yes, he did blackmail me.'

'Why?'

'What?'

'Why did he blackmail you?'

'That's my business.'

'Is it?' said Pete Ferris, self-appointed keeper of the angling club's conscience. 'If we get Kev expelled for blackmailing you, people may just ask what hold he had over you.'

'Is this blackmail, Pete?'

'Ted! 'Course it isn't. I've given my whole life to this club. It is my life. Naturally, therefore, I don't want rotten apples contaminating the whole barrel.'

Ted sighed wearily. People who gave their whole lives to things were always a menace.

'When you say rotten apples, who are you referring to?' he asked. 'Kev or me?'

'You tell me, Ted. It goes without saying that whatever can be done discreetly will be done discreetly. But we must scotch the rumours. Because if I've learnt anything about angling clubs in my lifetime of service to this club, it's this. Mud sticks. Mud bloody sticks, Ted.'

'Oh to hell with it,' said Ted. 'To bloody hell with it.'

And he stomped off to his car. Already, puddles were forming on the raddled, pock-marked face of the car park.

In the cosy, dry, smoky, roseate warmth, Rita approached Neville Badger, who was making a slightly unsteady return after yet another visit to the toilets. It was beginning to look as though Henry the Eighth had prostate problems as well as syphilis. Rita tried to make it look as if the encounter were casual.

'Being a king suits you,' she said.

'Oh. Thank you very much,' said the immaculate Henry the Eighth.

'You'd look good as George the Sixth.'

'Oh. Thank you very much.'

'If you'd like to come over at all at Christmas, Neville . . .'

'Oh. Thank you very much. I'd have loved to, but . . . thank you, no.'

'You can't make the world into a shrine for her, Neville.'

'Why don't you mind your own business?' said the senior partner in Badger, Badger, Fox and Badger.

Rita turned away, flabbergasted. The pink spots on the cheeks made a reappearance, and she was shocked to find that she was face to face with Liz.

'Oh!' she gasped.

'I must say, Rita,' said Liz. 'It wasn't exactly tactful to come tonight.'

'That's why I came,' said Rita.

'How nasty!'

'I wouldn't exactly describe it as nice to steal my husband and have his baby.'

'I wouldn't exactly describe taking things that turn up on one's doorstep as stealing,' said Liz.

'I feel that events have forced us to become enemies,' said Rita. 'What a pity we couldn't have got to know each other under happier circumstances. Then we could have been enemies of our own free will.' And off she rode on the tide of her exit line.

Liz Rodenhurst, née Ellsworth-Smythe, had not often looked flabbergasted during the first forty-eight years of her life. She did now.

Laurence approached, eager not to miss such a rare moment entirely. It occurred to Liz with a swift return of her normal spirit that he had never looked more like a rat *joining* a sinking ship. But before either of them could speak, attention was stolen by Ted, returning with the Arthur Tong Cup. He strode onto the platform, just as Norman Penfold finished a solo to modest applause from the somewhat diminished gathering. The abstemious Pilbeams had managed to make their exit at last.

'Ladies and gentlemen,' said Ted. He held his hand up for silence. It fell swiftly. Everyone gathered round, sensing that something was afoot. Rita found herself back at Liz's side. 'Thank you. I have to announce a change in the result of the winner of the Arthur Tong Cup. This is no longer me. I am also resigning as of now my chairmanship. I have besmirched this high office. During the . . . er . . . the fracas at Wisbech, I . . . I took two roach and a bream from Trevor Barnwell's keep-net. The new winner is my son Elvis. A well-deserved winner, too, in every sense. Let's hear it for Elvis Simcock.'

There was a bewildered round of applause, led by Ted.

'Well, come on, Elvis,' said Ted.

Elvis came forward reluctantly.

'Well done, son,' said Ted, not meeting Elvis's eyes.

'Dad!' said Elvis.

Ted handed Elvis his silver trophy.

'Play something, Norman, for God's sake,' he said.

Laurence, Liz and Rita stared at each other. There was a moment, in the stunned silence, when any of them could have said something, but none of them did. Then there was a buzz of conversation throughout the bar. Never mind the absence of the entertainment. Rarely, if ever, had there been such a dramatic event in the history of the angling club. Chairman resigns after admitting shameful petty crime, hands trophy to son in presence of wife, mistress, mistress' husband and Henry the Eighth. Several people volunteered to telephone the Pilbeams and the Hortons the next day to tell them how much they had missed by leaving early. And then the wizened old maestro of the squeeze-box also burst into noise, as he accompanied himself on one of his many railroad numbers.

Elvis had to pass Laurence, Liz and his mother. He spoke quickly, irrelevantly, to forestall any possible comment about his trophy.

'I wish there were more British railroad songs,' he said. 'Last train to Tulse Hill. The Chatham New Cross Choo Choo. There ought to be a British equivalent of Boxcar Willie.'

'We have him here,' said Liz. 'Guardsvan Norm.'

The cynical Elvis Simcock moved on, having given them back their tongues.

'Come on,' said Laurence. 'I'm taking you home.'

'No, Laurence. I shall stand by him,' announced Liz.

'Not you, dear,' said Laurence, trying not to sound too smug. 'I was talking to Rita.'

Ted and the Sillitoes converged upon them.

'Well!' said Ted. 'That's that.'

'Good night, everybody,' said Betty Sillitoe, struggling into her coat. 'Happy Christmas. Happy New Year. Happy . . . what is it these people do?'

'Angling,' said Rodney, helping her out of the tangle she was getting into with her coat.

'That's it,' said Betty. 'Bloody boring occupation it's always seemed to me.'

'Come on, my love,' said Rodney. 'Shut-eye time.'

'Sitting for hours watching a worm wriggling on a hook. Ridiculous. I've had more fun watching pimples grow.' She called out to the remainder of the assembly. 'Lovely party, everybody, apart from the singing and that berk going on about VAT all the time.'

Mavis Griddle gave Lester a fierce glare.

'And if that was trifle,' announced Betty, as she lurched away, 'then I'm the Queen of Sheba.'

Lester Griddle gave Mavis a fierce glare.

'She's forgotten all about her teeth,' whispered Rodney.

'Oh Lord!' said Betty, and she swung back towards them. 'Oh my God!' she said, mumbling again through lips that barely opened. 'They've all seen.'

'It doesn't notice,' said Rodney, as he led her tenderly away. 'Not really. I mean, it's thoroughly incompetent dental work, but it doesn't notice.'

Betty Sillitoe glared at him, and hurried out with a burst of dangerous speed. Rodney Sillitoe scurried after her protectively.

'Come on, Rita,' said Laurence coldly, stung by Rodney's description of his dental work.

'Don't go, everyone,' pleaded Ted. 'There's an extension!'

'Oh, do shut up about your blasted extension,' said Liz.

'You're beautiful when you're angry,' said Neville Badger,

arriving on the scene.

'Neville!' said Liz. 'That is so corny.'

'Ah, but I'm Henry the Eighth. It was original in my day!'

Neville laughed strangely, just as Paul and Jenny joined the group, and Jenny said, 'You won't mind giving Neville a lift, will you, Paul?'

'No!' said Paul. 'It can't be more than twelve miles out of our way.'

'No. Please. I'm all right,' said Neville. 'I'm not likely to be stopped.'

'In that costume?' said Liz.

'Oh Lord,' said Neville Badger.

'What's all this talk about going?' said Ted.

'Let them go, Ted,' said Liz. 'I want to talk to you.'

'I know,' said Ted.

The Sillitoes had not yet managed to extricate themselves from the bleak passage outside the bars and toilets.

'You fool!' Betty had said, as soon as they were out of the bar.

'You what?' her astounded husband had responded.

'I was making out my bridge is even worse than it is, so as to sue Laurence. Ruined social life. Can't face opening my mouth in public. Severe psychological disturbances. And you say "it doesn't notice"!'

'I didn't know what you were doing. Why didn't you tell me?'

'Because you're no actor.'

'We don't need their money.'

'It's not the money. Why should that family get away with anything? I hate them for what they've done to our friends. I hate them!'

Her legs had given way. She'd fallen in a crumpled heap by the fire extinguisher. Rodney was just helping her up when Neville Badger and Rita and Laurence and Paul and Jenny came out. Paul and Rita helped Rodney get Betty to her feet, then Laurence took over from Rita and helped steer Betty to the car. Jenny tried to help, but Paul wouldn't let her because of her condition. Neville Badger took the opportunity to have a quick word with Rita.

'I . . . er . . . I'm sorry I was rude again,' he said.

'It's natural,' said Rita. 'You resent other women because they aren't Jane.'

'Do I? Oh Lord,' said Neville.

'Good night, Neville,' said Rita, and she kissed him as warmly as she could through his rain-damp false whiskers.

As Rodney Sillitoe drove off, Betty shouted, 'I hate them, Rita.'

Rita stared at the departing Volvo Estate in surprise. Laurence led her over to his car, opened her door first, ushered her inside. No kissing would take place when he dropped her at Presley, the pleasant detached three-bedroom house on the York Road, where she now lived all alone.

Neville Badger and Jenny squeezed with difficulty into Paul's elderly car. Citroën Dianes weren't designed for pregnant women and Tudor monarchs.

It was half past eleven. Half an hour to go till the end of the extension. Very few guests remained. Lester Griddle was clearing empties lugubriously. Mavis Griddle was feeding them sourly into the glass-washing machine. Norman Penfold was asleep, his wrinkled old face resting wearily on his trusty squeeze-box.

Ted and Liz sat at a table beside the artificial log fire.

'It's been a fiasco,' said Ted. 'It has. I mean . . . it has. A total fiasco.'

'Not total,' said Liz. 'You made a brave speech. Not everyone could admit something like that with so much dignity. I was proud of you.'

'Oh heck,' said Ted, partly because Liz was proud of him, partly because Elvis was approaching.

'Right. I'm off,' said Elvis, clutching his trophy. ''Night, Dad.'

He went towards the door. Ted hurried after him.

'Elvis!' he said. 'There's twenty-nine minutes of the extension unexpired.'

'I'm going down the Plough,' said Elvis. 'You can drink late there without an extension.'

'Elvis! Have a drink with us.'

'I told some of the lads I'd go,' said Elvis. 'They're getting one in for me. They're the sort that only enjoy late drinking if it's illegal. They were CB fanatics till it was legalized. Make vandalism compulsory and you'd wipe it out overnight. 'Night, Dad.'

'Elvis!' Ted looked over his shoulder at Liz, hoping she didn't realize that he was imploring Elvis to stay. 'Never mind them. You're my son.'

'I can't cope with all this, Dad,' said Elvis. 'Tonight. Everything. I don't know if I admire you or despise you. I don't know if I love you or hate you.'

'And this is what your three years of philosophy have taught you!'

'Yes! I've learnt how impossible it is to know anything. 'Night, Dad.'

'Say good night to Liz! Please!' implored Ted, dropping his voice to a whisper.

''Night, Liz,' called out the cynical Elvis, without turning round. He raised his right arm, waggled it casually, in a parody of a farewell, and hurried off towards the Plough. All evening he had felt that something was missing. Only now had he realized what it was. It was Simon Rodenhurst, of Trellis, Trellis, Openshaw and Finch. He just hadn't found anybody he enjoyed insulting so much.

Ted returned slowly to his lover.

'Sorry about that,' he said. 'Families! Who'd have them? Oh God!'

Kevin Loudwater was coming over to speak to them.

'I suppose you think you've won, don't you?' said the blackmailing pork butcher with the crinkly perm. 'I've lost anyroad. I'm to be expelled from the club if I don't resign. Bloody Pete Ferris playing God again. And how am I going to get my roof repaired now?' He moved off. Ted breathed a sigh of relief. Too soon! Kevin Loudwater returned! 'You invited the vegetarian, didn't you?' he said. 'It's the thin end of the wedge. You'll be flooding the town with them. Pork butcher? I'm living in the past. So bollocks to you both.'

Kevin Loudwater's tight buttocks didn't look so complacent as he swung out of the bar. Just angry.

'What did he mean about being expelled?' said Liz. 'What did he mean about his roof?'

Ted didn't reply.

'What's been going on, Ted?'

Ted sighed.

'Oh hell!' he said. 'Oh, bloody hell, Liz. I wasn't being brave. You've no cause to be proud of me. I mean . . . you see . . . oh Lord . . . I only admitted what I'd done because Kev saw it. He blackmailed me in the car park.'

Lester Griddle dropped a glass. Ted jumped. Mavis Griddle scowled.

'Why did you do it?' said Liz.

'God knows!' Ted bent forwards, towards the artificial log fire. He felt colder, older. 'Well! . . . I suppose . . . Kev thinks it's because I resent Elvis because he's got a third-class degree in a useless subject at a new university and I've got nothing. Maybe I do, but I don't think so. It's been my hobby for nearly forty years, and I've never won anything. Other people are good at their hobbies. Suddenly I saw my chance. I mean . . . simple as that. End of story. What a hero.'

Liz kissed him on the lips. Her tongue made its way into his mouth. Lester Griddle almost dropped another glass. Ted was astounded. Astounded that she still cared for him. Astounded that she could kiss him like that, in front of people. Then he realized that nobody was there except the Griddles, and people like Liz didn't think of people like the Griddles as people. Landlords, waiters, shop assistants, they were part of life's furniture. Ted felt guilty about thinking such things while Liz's tongue was inside his mouth. The truth was, he couldn't respond. He was too tired. He had only one need. Drink.

At last the kiss ended.

'Let's go home,' said Liz.

'There's twenty-six minutes of the extension unexpired.'

'The failure of the evening is no longer your responsibility. You've resigned.'

'I know, but I need a drink. Just one, love. After that ordeal. Because it was.' He called out, 'Same again, please, Lester,' and then they noticed that Norman Penfold was still there. He looked even smaller than usual when he was asleep.

'Let's dance,' said Liz.

He had won over the question of going home. He would have to concede in the matter of the dance. He shook Norman Penfold, who woke up with a start and immediately began playing an Irish jig.

Ted and Liz danced dreamily, romantically, wearily, slowly, in a manner utterly unsuited to the accompaniment of an Irish jig. The wind rattled and the lights flickered and Lester Griddle plonked their drinks on the bar lugubriously and the rain beat against the windows like late drinkers requesting entry diffidently. Norman Penfold jigged. The cardboard angels swung gently in the breeze that Ted and Liz created as they smooched across the old, stained, gold-and-brown carpet, from the decorated half of the bar to the undecorated half and back again.

'Thank you for standing by me,' said Ted. 'A lot of people are going to have to eat their words.'

'What on earth do you mean?' said Liz.

'Oh heck. They say you're . . . oh heck.'

'They say I'm what?'

'They say you're . . . well . . . shallow and self-centred and . . . you know . . . out for what you can get and . . . I mean . . . Liz . . . I know you aren't. Oh heck.'

Ted kissed her, and began to feel amorous at last.

'You don't like it when I take the initiative, do you, Mr Macho-Man?' said Liz. 'You like to remain in control.'

'Rubbish. Rubbish, Liz. It's rubbish, is that. I mean . . . it is.'

'Methinks the man doth protest too much.'

'Liz!'

'When we get home I'm going to take the initiative, and if you don't like it you can lump it,' said Liz. 'I'm going to start by taking all your clothes off, very very slowly.'

'Me too,' said Ted. 'Yours, I mean. Oh Liz!'

'Look at him,' said Lester Griddle. 'I don't know how he bloody does it, excuse my French.'

'Does what?' said Mavis Griddle, as sour as a bad pint, impatient to close down now that only three customers remained.

'Dancing!' said Lester Griddle lugubriously. 'As if he hasn't got a care in the world. And he's been paying VAT for years.'

Fourth Do

April:
The Charity
Horse-Racing Evening

The long picture windows of the golf club restaurant and bar faced
west across the gently rolling hills on which the golf course had
been built. The sun was dipping below the distant Pennines, and
the last golfers were walking up the eighteenth fairway.

Behind the clubhouse lay the untidy sheds and converted
hangars of the Wartley Industrial Estate. The windows of the
kitchens and lavatories faced that way.

Graham Wintergreen, the manager, a bluff, egg-shaped man
with a small bald head and a pot-belly, surveyed his kingdom
uneasily. His bloodshot eyes roamed briskly over the panelled
walls, engraved with the names of the winners of the various 'in-
house' competitions since the year dot, over the beige carpet, the
varnished tables and adequately elegant chairs, over the well-
stocked bar run by the dapper, ageless Eric Siddall, barman
supreme. Everything was spotless. In the centre of the room there
was a huge, false, stone chimney breast. The golfing prints and
cartoons which adorned the chimney breast and the panelled
walls were free of dust and hanging straight.

His gaze travelled up the short flight of stairs to the restaurant
area. Tonight there was to be a fork supper, and the tables had not
been laid. The place mats, with more golfing scenes, were stacked
in a cupboard. So were the menus, on which starters were
described as 'drives', main courses as 'iron shots', desserts as
'putts'.

Everything was in order, but Graham Wintergreen's uneasiness
remained. When he had agreed to hold a horse-racing evening to

raise money for the Theatre Royal, he hadn't been worried. It had seemed a good idea to mark the thirtieth anniversary of that great day when the town had at last been put on the world's theatrical and cultural maps, when the Mayor and Mayoress and all the councillors had attended, and Agatha Christie herself had sent a very nice letter regretting that she couldn't see the production of her play, due to 'unavoidable archeological commitments'. He had even invited an actor as guest of honour tonight. Harvey Wedgewood was one of the few surviving members of that opening cast. He was apparently well thought of 'in the business'. Graham Wintergreen, whose interests were golf, drink, food and women, in that order, had imagined a cheery, extrovert type, good company apart from his theatrical 'tales'. Then the blow had fallen. He had been asked to provide 'some vegetarian meals'.

Vegetarians, in the golf club! It would be the thin end of the wedge! The tip of the iceberg! Now he expected Harvey Wedgewood to be a revolutionary socialist homosexual intellectual. In place of his normal clientele, who swapped golfing boasts, risqué stories and, just occasionally, wives, there would be weirdos, poofters, intellectuals, Marxists. Possibly even people of an ethnic nature.

How he wished that the club professional, Harry Hopworth, was here to give him moral support. But Hopper, as he was known to his many friends, was far away, lying twenty-seventh in the Tunisian Open, and looking set for his best result on foreign soil for five years.

Imagine the relief of the uncharacteristically edgy clubhouse manager when the first to arrive was Ted Simcock! No Marxist revolutionary here!

Nevertheless, Graham Wintergreen's relief was mixed with embarrassment. He had no idea what to say to Ted. Yet he couldn't just ignore what had happened.

'Hello, Ted,' he said.

'Hello, Graham,' said Ted.

So far so good! Graham Wintergreen thought of following up this opening gambit with 'How are you?' But Ted might tell him! To talk about the weather seemed cowardly. Golf? That might seem callous, under the circumstances.

'I was sorry about . . . er . . .' he said gruffly.

'Thanks,' said Ted equally gruffly, moving off towards the bar.

A wave of relief swept over Graham Wintergreen. He had handled the situation in masterly fashion. He had expressed his sympathy, without touching on hurtful or unpleasant matters, and had elicited the information that Ted didn't want to talk about them either.

Graham Wintergreen battened onto the next arrivals gratefully. He knew where he was with Rodney Sillitoe, the big wheel behind Cock-A-Doodle Chickens, and his wife Betty, who was over-adorned as usual.

'Large Scottish wine,' said Eric Siddall, barman supreme. He was a small man with an elegant, polka-dotted bow tie. 'Certainly, sir. Just the job. Tickety-boo. No problem. Here we go.' He hesitated, as if about to make a personal remark. Then the dangerous moment passed, and he poured Ted's large whisky. He was one of the few men who have ever told their careers officer that they wanted to be a barman. After a searching apprenticeship on lesser-known cruise liners he had been in charge of the golf club bar for seventeen years. In that time he had never served a bad drink, given the wrong change, been at a loss for an exotic cocktail, or made a personal remark. He seemed untouched by age, but over the years an increasing collection of catch-phrases had adhered to him. They poured out, as if beyond his control. Perhaps he didn't even realize that he was saying them. 'Same again of water, sir? Very good. That's the ticket. There you go, sir. A fiver? No problem.'

'No, I'll get that,' said Rodney Sillitoe, hurrying over in his crumpled Harris Tweed jacket.

'I'm not broke yet,' said Ted.

'Ted! You're my guest. That's all I meant.' Rodney ordered his and Betty's drinks with some dismay. He'd felt that he must invite Ted, under the circumstances, but he'd had a sneaking hope that Ted wouldn't be able to face up to coming. 'You're early,' he said.

'I wasn't sure if I could face walking into a crowded room,' said Ted.

'Nobody'll gloat,' said Rodney. 'We aren't like that. You'll have the sympathy of every man and woman in this room.'

'It's worse than gloating, is sympathy,' said Ted. 'It's a bugger, is sympathy.'

'Gin and tonic, ice and a slice, one Scottish wine, just the job, tickety-boo, there you go. A fiver? *No* problem,' said the dapper, ageless Eric Siddall.

'Thanks.' Rodney hesitated. There was a little matter which he wanted to raise with the barman before Betty returned from her titivations. Did it matter if Ted witnessed it? He didn't really think it did. 'Can you do me a favour, Alec?' he asked.

'Eric, sir.'

'Eric! Sorry! Can you do me a favour, Eric?'

'If I can, sir. What can be done will be done. Have no fear.'

'Thanks. If my wife . . . er . . . if you think she's having a bit too much at any stage . . . let's face it, she has been known to, bless her . . . could you try and catch my eye, and signal to me?'

'Signal to you, Mr Sillitoe?'

'Yes. Say . . . er . . . oh . . . raise your right arm high above your head with a glass in it.'

Rodney indicated the gesture by raising his right arm with a glass in it.

'Certainly, sir,' said Eric Siddall. 'Can do. *No* problem. No snags anticipated.'

Damn! Laurence was approaching, and he'd seen Rodney raising his right arm, and he was looking faintly surprised.

'Touch of rheumatism,' Rodney Sillitoe explained, raising his arm again and flexing it. He offered Laurence a drink. Laurence asked if Eric had such a thing as a really dry white wine. Eric's reply suggested that he did indeed, he anticipated no problem, indeed he seemed confident that it would be just the job, thoroughly tickety, and probably boo as well.

Ted Simcock and Laurence Rodenhurst greeted each other cautiously. Their eyes met, weren't quite sure what they saw, and slid away from the contact.

'Is Betty not here?' said Laurence, who was wearing a very smart suit.

'Oh yes,' said Rodney. 'We must all help to save our theatre, mustn't we? It'll be a tragic loss to the town if it goes under.'

'Tragic,' agreed Laurence. 'It's a nice little theatre, isn't it?'

'Well, we've never actually been,' admitted Rodney. Like many people in the town, the Sillitoes went to London at least once a year, stayed at the Strand Palace, Went on a Shopping Spree, Had a Slap-up Dinner, Took in a Show, and spent a small fortune. Like many people in the town, they were loth to spend eight pounds for two seats in their own theatre, especially when you had to add in the cost of the programme and the drinks in the interval.

'Oh, you should. You must,' said Laurence. 'It's very attractive. You'd never know it was built on the site of an abattoir.'

'How's Liz?' said Ted suddenly, as if he couldn't bear to avoid the subject any longer.

'I haven't the faintest idea,' said Laurence. 'I haven't seen her.'

'Oh!' Ted seemed surprised.

'No. I haven't heard a word,' said Laurence.

'Oh!'

'Ah!' said Rodney Sillitoe, welcoming with relief the arrival of Betty, who was over-titivated as usual. She was wearing a white trouser suit, with her best pearls, her second-best pearls, two rings, a silver brooch and a gold necklace.

'Hello, Ted, love,' she said, giving him a warm kiss which said everything. It's so much easier to sympathize with somebody if they're of the opposite sex.

'Hello, Betty,' said Laurence. 'You look . . . er . , .'

'Thank you,' said Betty, choosing to assume that if Laurence had felt able to finish his sentence he would have said something complimentary, although it wasn't clear why, if he had been going to say something complimentary, he hadn't been able to finish his sentence. 'It's the teeth,' she said, flashing him a bright smile. 'I've decided not to sue you after all. I'd have had to keep them as you left them for months, and mumble at everybody. I've had the bridge redone on the National Health. Half the cost and twice as good.'

'Betty!' said Rodney. Women, even wonderfully sociable women like Betty, didn't always seem to understand the value of social decorum, of club rules, of applied hypocrisy.

'How's Rita?' asked Betty, ignoring Rodney's rebuke.

'I haven't the faintest idea,' said Ted. 'I haven't seen her.'

'Oh!' Betty seemed surprised.

Ted didn't feel like telling them that he'd written Rita three letters and torn them up, that he'd phoned her and rung off when he'd heard her voice, that he'd gone to Tescos twenty-three times and bought one item each time, braving the strange looks of the check-out girls and the suspicious eyes of the store detective, in the hope that he would bump into her.

'You'll see her tonight,' said Betty.

'What?' His heart was thumping.

'Neville's bringing her.'

'Neville!!!'

'He's giving her a lift. It's on his way.'

Ted wished he hadn't said 'Neville!!!' with three exclamation marks. He knew, really, that there couldn't possibly be anything between Rita and Neville Badger or indeed anybody but especially somebody like Neville Badger which could justify one exclamation mark, let alone three!!

The bluff Graham Wintergreen approached.

'Hello, all,' he said breezily. 'Good to see you. Awful lot of non-golfers turning up. The actor's arrived. He's freshening up upstairs. Tote opens in ten minutes. I'll get the actor to make a little speech.' He moved off, then returned. 'Nearly forgot,' he said. 'Congratulations, Laurence.' He flicked his head at Laurence, indicating that he would like a word in private.

Laurence followed him.

'I don't know if this is good news or bad news,' said Graham Wintergreen. 'I met Liz in town. She's coming tonight.'

'Ah!' Laurence's tone was carefully neutral. 'Well, she's always been a great aficionado of the boards.'

He rejoined the others, determined not to show that he was feeling weak at the knees.

'I don't know why Graham had to be so mysterious,' he said. 'That was just to say that Liz is coming.' He looked into Ted's eyes, searching for pain.

'Oh good!' said Ted. 'I hope that makes you very happy.'

Ted strode off towards the windows. Laurence's lips twitched in slight triumph.

'"Congratulations"?' said Rodney Sillitoe.

'Didn't you know?' said Laurence. 'I'm a grandfather. Jenny's had a little boy.'

'Oooh!' said Betty Sillitoe. 'Lovely! Bless her!'

'He weighed eight pounds ten ounces. They're calling him Thomas.'

'She was so sure it was going to be a girl,' said Rodney.

'Well, there you are,' said Laurence. 'That's life. Can I get you a drink, to celebrate?'

'Oh well,' said Rodney. 'Under the circumstances. Thank you.'

'"Under the circumstances"!' said Betty, when Laurence had gone. 'You make it sound as if there were circumstances under which you'd have refused.'

'There are.'

'Such as?'

'If it was *Laurence* who'd gone bankrupt.'

'He should have. Or been defrocked. Or struck off, or whatever dentists are.'

'Drilled out, I expect,' said Rodney.

'People never fail to amaze me,' said Betty. 'I just wouldn't have thought Laurence was the sort of man to remember a baby's weight.'

'Eight pounds ten is probably the price of a fillet steak at the Clissold Lodge,' said Rodney. 'Well, it could be a very interesting evening.'

'It could be a marvellous evening.'

'Marvellous?'

'Reconciliation. Between Ted and Rita. Between Laurence and Liz.'

'I wouldn't have thought you cared about Laurence and Liz.'

'Oh, I do. They deserve each other. Here's Rita now.'

The room was filling up. Several tables were already occupied. A few women were wearing trouser suits, but most wore dresses that ranged from the sober to the sexy. The men wore suits or sports jackets, with one or two blazers and sweaters. There wasn't much evidence of Marxism, but there were two men in jeans and tee shirts and, as they made their slow journey to the bar, Neville Badger and Rita passed the man in the orange wig, who had been to all the shows for the last twenty years, from Ibsen to 'The Wombles'.

The immaculate Neville Badger looked over-immaculate for the occasion. Rita looked as if she was curtained, but at least these russet-and-gold curtains suited her.

'Hello,' said Neville to the Sillitoes. 'How are things in the world of intensive chicken farming?'

'Not bad,' said Rodney.

'Unless you're an intensive chicken,' said Betty.

'Betty!'

'Good. Good,' said Neville Badger. 'What are you two . . . er . . .' Rita was shaking her head with a movement large enough to be clear to Neville but small enough to remain undetected by the Sillitoes. Neville rather spoilt the effect by saying 'Ah!' very pointedly. 'What are you two . . . er . . . planning to put your money on in the first race?'

'I haven't studied the form yet,' said Betty.

'I don't intend to study the form,' said Rodney. 'Winning isn't the object of the exercise. The object of the exercise is to give for our theatre.'

'Absolutely,' said Neville. 'Well done. Well done indeed.'

Neville went off to the bar, but Betty caught Rita's eye, and Rita stayed.

'Ted's here,' said Betty.

'I know,' said Rita. 'I've seen him.'

'I think he wants to talk to you,' said Betty.

'I think that's an excellent idea,' said Rita. 'I'll look forward to hearing what he has to say,' and she joined Neville, just in time to hear the dapper, ageless Eric Siddall say to Laurence, 'There you go, sir. One whisky and Canadian, *not* American, one fruit of the grape, white, medium-dry, chilled. Just the job. Tickety-boo. One pound eighty, sir. The exact change? You're a gentleman, sir.'

It was still not Neville's turn to be served, but he waited patiently. Very few people mind waiting for drinks, they only mind other people being served out of turn before them, perhaps because most people have a secret fear that they are so insignificant as to be to all intents and purposes invisible. Eric Siddall, barman supreme, had never, in seventeen years, served anybody out of turn, so there was no problem.

'That sounds promising,' said Betty.

'What?' said Rodney.

'She's looking forward to talking to Ted.'

'She said she was looking forward to hearing what he had to say. That's not quite the same thing.'

Laurence arrived with their drinks. They raised their glasses and said, 'To Thomas.'

Laurence sipped his drink like a mouse nibbling cheese.

'I've seen more repulsive babies,' he said. 'He isn't totally bald and wrinkled.'

'Exactly!' said Betty.

'What?' said Laurence.

'You've never struck me as a great lover of babies. I was amazed you remembered his weight.'

'Well, funnily enough, eight pounds ten happens to be the price of a rump steak at the Clissold Lodge.'

'God! Their prices have got worse,' said Rodney Sillitoe. 'I thought it was fillet.'

'What?' said Laurence.

'Thanks, Neville,' said Rita, as they left the bar to make room for others. 'To you. To the future.'

'To you, Rita,' said Neville Badger. 'Thank you for coming with me.'

They raised their glasses and drank. Their eyes met. Neville was the first to look away. He found himself looking at the list of winners of the ladies' individual championship. There she was. 1966 Mrs J. Badger. 1971 Mrs J. Badger. 1973 Mrs J. Badger. 1978 Mrs J. Badger.

'Excuse me a moment, Rita, dear,' he said, adding the 'dear' to take the sting out of his impoliteness.

Rita watched him walk over to the window. Her legs felt rubbery. She felt such a fool. But was it so foolish? He had looked away, as if to look into her eyes was more than he could bear. He had called her 'dear'.

The scarlets and mauves and purples were slowly darkening. When he was a small boy, Neville Badger had thought that the sun went to Lancashire when it dropped behind the Pennines, and that when it was night in Yorkshire, it was day in Lancashire.

Over to the right, along the edge of the golf course, ran a row of pleasant villas, rambling brick houses from the years between the wars, with one or two outbreaks of Mock Tudor. Over there, just visible in the fading light, was the seventeenth green, where

Charlotte Ratchett, of the furniture Ratchetts, had three-putted in 1978, giving Jane the last of her four titles.

He waited for the pain, that sharpness of loss which surged through him as if he had just taken a huge bite out of a lemon. It didn't come. There came instead a vague melancholy, a distant sadness, an emptiness.

Briefly, as it darkened, the sunset looked like a great bruise. That was all Neville could feel in his heart. A great bruise.

He knew the colour of her eyes, it was on her passport, but he could no longer see those eyes. Her mouth had been wide and generous. He remembered the words which described it. He could no longer see the mouth. Jane was the sunset, fading, soon it would be night.

Huge green curtains slid slowly, electronically, across the picture windows. With an insensitivity that verged on genius, the bluff Graham Wintergreen had decided that it was night.

Paul and Jenny arrived, with little Thomas in a carrycot. Jenny was wearing an attractive Taiwanese dress which emphasized her return to normal size and clung revealingly to her milk-large breasts. Paul was wearing jeans, an anti-apartheid tee-shirt, and a defiant air. To his fury, he felt embarrassed about the tee-shirt.

Rita praised Jenny's dress, made no remark about the tee-shirt, gazed fondly, hungrily at the baby and said, 'Bless him! He looks just like you, Paul!'

'Mum!' said Paul.

'Like you did at his age, I mean.'

'What?' said Jenny. 'Do you mean he'll grow up to look like Paul?'

'Jenny!' said Paul.

'Are you disappointed it's a boy?' said Rita.

'No,' said Jenny. 'I'm glad. I felt guilty about being so sure it was a girl. I'd hate to burden it with sexist favouritism before it was even born.'

People came from all sides to see the new arrival. Neville Badger was the first. He beamed carefully, said 'Ah! Little Thomas' and bent immaculately over the cot. He was still there when Liz arrived. Her entrance was a little too defiant to be described as self-possessed. She knew that she was the object of many looks, some disapproving, some rather less friendly. Infuriatingly, to those who disapproved of her conduct, she still looked sexy and attractive, managed in fact to make it seem that looking almost eight months pregnant in a shapeless grey smock was *the thing* to be that spring.

'Hello,' she said, rather too cheerily.

Neville Badger gasped. As he looked at the sleeping baby, he had experienced a feeling that he was Jane. The pain of his loss of her became the pain of her sorrow at being childless. The emotions that he had sought swept over him. He hurried away, in the presence again of his loss, in the joy again of his sorrow.

Liz turned to watch him.

'Oh Lord!' said Jenny.

'What?' said Paul.

'Uncle Neville wanted children so much.'

Liz forced her eyes off Neville. 'Hello, Rita!' she said, as if seeing her for the first time.

Rita went through a bad moment when she thought the pink spots were going to appear, but she fought them off.

'My word!' said Liz, peering at the sleeping baby. 'He's getting to look just like you, Jenny.' To the baby she whispered, 'That's right, Thomas. You sleep on. Very sensible. Nothing so very extraordinary about a pregnant granny.'

She says granny to emphasize that she doesn't look like one, thought Rita.

The next admirer was Leslie Horton, water bailiff, organist and theatre-goer, who hated to be called Les.

'What's her name?' he asked.

'Thomas,' said Jenny.

'Ah. It's a boy. I can see that now,' he said. 'Hello, little Tom.'

'Thomas,' said Jenny firmly.

And then there came the cynical Elvis Simcock, in dark blue cords and Peruvian sweater. He was smoking a large cigar.

'God!' he said. 'I suppose I'm an uncle now.'

'Keep that thing away from him,' said Jenny.

'Sorry.' Jenny's fierce protectiveness wrung a rare apology from him. He held his cigar ostentatiously out of harm's way, at the end of his outstretched arm, as he looked down at his sleeping nephew. 'Hello, Thomas,' he said. 'I'm your Uncle Elvis. Oh God, that doesn't sound right.' He turned away from the baby, looked his younger brother in the eye and said, 'He's boring.'

'Shut up, Elvis,' said Paul. 'It's your pseudo-macho cynicism that's boring. I'm suspicious of people who don't like children and animals.'

'I'm suspicious of people who're overcareful to show how much they do like children and animals,' said Elvis. He kissed Jenny, blushing slightly. 'Is your brother going to be here?' he asked.

'I think so. Why?'

'I enjoy insulting him. He takes it so seriously.'

Elvis moved on. He hadn't acknowledged Liz's existence. Rita wouldn't have believed that she could ever be so proud of rudeness in one of her sons.

People became aware of a large bear-like man who had just entered the room. He had a lined, lived-in face with deeply pitted cheeks. He wore a bow tie and a burgundy velvet jacket. This was Harvey Wedgewood, the actor. They took furtive looks at him, while pretending to be too sophisticated to be interested in this rare appearance of the almost famous in their midst.

Paul and Jenny set off to take young Thomas upstairs, where Angela Wintergreen would watch over him, giving her a great excuse not to come downstairs.

Ted hurried over to them, now that they were no longer with Rita.

'Well well well! How's my little grandson?' he said.

'He's doing well,' said Jenny.

'He looks grand,' said Ted. 'Just grand. I mean . . . he really does.'

Looking at his grandson, he felt a deep longing to be back with his family again. And, as if reading his thoughts, Jenny said, 'Have you seen Rita?'

'Yes, I . . . er . . .'

'How did it go?'

'Oh, I haven't spoken to her. I mean . . . what can I say?'

'You'll have to talk to her, Dad,' said Paul.

'Oh, I know. I know. But . . . I mean . . . I was hoping she'd speak to me.'

'I really think under the circumstances it's up to you to speak to her,' said Jenny.

'Oh, I know. I know. But . . . I mean . . . I'm frightened she'll snub me.'

Paul promised to have a word with his mother, and Ted moved on. He found himself face to face with a large man of about sixty, who looked vaguely familiar.

'I know you, don't I?' he said.

'Very possibly,' said Harvey Wedgewood, trying not to look too pleased.

The penny dropped.

'You used to run the off licence in Frog Lane, didn't you?'

'I'm Harvey Wedgewood, the actor.'

'Oh Lord. I'm sorry.'

'Please!' Harvey Wedgewood raised his hand in a gesture eloquent of self-deprecation. 'It's so boring being constantly recognized!'

Ted moved on, in such confusion that he was almost upon Rita and Liz before he realized it. He called 'hello!' to somebody he'd never met, and bolted round the side of the chimney breast, where he spent what seemed like several minutes studying a cartoon of Adolf Hitler struggling unavailingly in deep sand while a sultry woman watched contemptuously. The caption was, 'I'm never going to get out of this bunker, Eva.' Ted had never felt less like laughing in his life.

'It'll be embarrassing for you if yours grows up looking like Ted, won't it?' said Rita, as they watched Ted bolt behind the chimney breast. Their conversation so far had been cool and cautious.

'Please, Rita. I did love him, you know,' said Liz.

'For several months. Your persistence does you credit.'

'I'd have thought you'd be pleased I've left him.'

'It makes me livid. You broke up my marriage, and for what? The moment he's bankrupt, you're off like a shot.'

'That's unfair.'

'Is it? You shied away from the social disgrace like a terrified horse.'

'That's an exaggeration. I stayed with him for three and a half weeks after it happened.'

'Do you want a medal?'

People tried to look as if they weren't watching Rita and Liz. But the suave Doctor Spreckley, in the middle of a hilarious story about a ruptured spleen, which had never yet failed, realized that he had completely lost the attention of Zoë Brookes, the pale, thin but immensely tough ballet teacher, whose choreography had won plaudits for the Operatic over more years than she would ever admit to remembering.

'It was an awful time,' said Liz. 'We had no money. We couldn't go out.'

'Millions have to live their whole lives like that,' said Rita.

'Yes, and I've realized how much I admire them,' said Liz.

'It's a start, I suppose.'

'You didn't make it easy, Rita. He can be a difficult man.'

'Really?? Thank you for the information! I hadn't noticed that! But then I've only been married to him for twenty-five years. I had a lovely silver wedding anniversary on my own, incidentally.'

'I want to say one thing, Rita,' said Liz. 'Please don't blame Ted. This whole affair was entirely my fault.'

'Ladies and gentlemen!' called out the bluff Graham Wintergreen. 'Ladies and gentlemen! Please!'

Silence fell rapidly. Graham Wintergreen stood on top of the steps that led up from the bar area to the restaurant area. People on the far side of the chimney breast moved round so as to be able to see him. Rita and Liz remained motionless. Behind Graham stood Harvey Wedgewood. Ted thought that if a photograph of Harvey Wedgewood's face was blown up to enormous size, it would be difficult to distinguish it from the car park of the Crown and Walnut. Yet the women were drooling over him. He certainly was immaculately groomed. Ted felt that he ought to carry credits for make-up and wardrobe.

'Good evening, ladies and gentlemen,' said Graham Wintergreen, in a voice in which the last obstinate traces of a childhood in Rugeley still persisted. 'Welcome to the golf club and our racing evening, on behalf of our splendid Theatre Royal, the so-called "Gem of Slaughterhouse Lane". For those who haven't been to a racing evening before, it works like this.' Jenny and Paul returned, free of care and ready for fun. 'We show you films of six races. You have the opportunity to bet on the tote – that's me. Fifty per cent of all bets goes to the winners, the rest to our charity. We also auction off the ownership of all the horses in the race. Again, half the money goes to the owner of the winning horse, the rest to the theatre. There will be a fork supper after the third race, and Brenda's goulash is never forgotten by those who have experienced it.'

Harvey Wedgewood gave a good-natured grimace in recognition of Graham's recommendation of the goulash. There was a gratifying amount of largely female laughter, suggesting that the women were looking at his velvet, grey-haired elegance, rather than at old pot-bellied baldy Wintergreen ha ha! Be careful not to look complacent, Harvey, modest acknowledgement of the laughter, almost hear the purr of matronly sexuality, good God, what's this, old Baldy looks as if he's about to break bad news or wind or both.

'There is also . . .' said Graham Wintergreen, as if announcing the death of someone whom nobody had liked. 'There is also a vegetarian casserole, as I understand there are some vegetarians here tonight.'

Paul squeezed Jenny's hand.

'Now we are very honoured to have with us a very popular actor,' said Graham Wintergreen. 'He starred in the very first production at the Royal, and he certainly seemed more like a literary lion than a lamb being led to the slaughter.' There was almost no laughter at this beautifully turned epigram, which combined praise of Harvey Wedgewood with a subtle reference to the history of the theatre's site. Graham Wintergreen felt a spasm of hatred for Harvey Wedgewood, who got laughs just by raising his carefully manicured eyebrows. He had thought he liked the man, in gratitude for his being a boozy womanizer with a fondness for fivers in the back pocket, and not a homosexual vegetarian revolutionary Marxist intellectual. Now he wasn't so sure. But he was careful to keep all this out of his voice. 'I refer of course to Harvey Wedgewood. Harvey has come all the way from Princes Risborough to support our cause. So let's have a big welcome for Harvey Wedgewood.'

There was a storm of applause. Some of the women applauded so generously that their husbands looked at them, so they stopped applauding rather more quickly than Harvey Wedgewood expected.

'Good evening,' he said, in a Christmas cake of a voice – rich, fruity, and soaked in brandy. 'I must say my mouth waters at the thought of Brenda's goulash.' There was laughter, although Graham Wintergreen could see nothing amusing in the remark. 'I am not the point of this Eisteddfod of culture.' He looked briefly round the hundred and fifty people crowded all around him, and all the women except Liz and Rita thought the gesture was for them alone. 'The fact that I've made seventy-seven films and been nominated for an Oscar three times is of no account tonight. What matters is *you* . . . and *your* theatre, which I had the honour of opening. I thought I was rather a good Hercule Poirot, incidentally. But enough of that. Go to it. Enjoy yourselves. I hope to meet each one of you in the course of the evening, especially all you lovely ladies. If you wish to purchase an autographed copy of *With A Hey Nonny No*, my slim little memoirs, please don't feel shy. I shan't be cross. Copies will be available at the table to the left of the exit. Thank you.'

There was applause, eighty per cent of which was from women. Graham Wintergreen applauded rather too fervently for fear that people would realize that he was jealous.

The moment the applause had died down, Rita and Liz came to life again.

'"Entirely your fault"?' said Rita, as if the speeches hadn't happened. 'How dare you insult me by suggesting I'd spend twenty-five years with a man so pathetic that he can't be held responsible for his actions? But I suppose you could never admit to anything as common as being seduced.'

'Let's not argue in public, Rita,' said Liz. 'We're supposed to be supporting the drama, not making it.'

'All rather bad form, would you say?'

'Well yes, I would.'

'What *will* people think?'

'Well, yes.'

'I've worried about that all my life. Now I hardly seem to give a damn.'

Liz stared after the retreating Rita.

The moment Liz and Rita were separated, Paul and Jenny steamed in.

Paul tackled Rita.

·'Mum?' he said. 'Aren't you and Dad going to talk to each other at all?'

'I think that's rather up to him, isn't it?' said Rita. 'I'm not going to humiliate myself by making the first move.'

'Oh. No. No. I wouldn't expect you to. But I think he's a little worried that if he approaches you, you'll snub him.'

'Of course I won't.'

'Can I tell him that officially?'

'Yes. I don't guarantee that the conversation will be entirely pleasant, but yes – it's official – I won't snub him.'

Paul had an uneasy feeling that his mother was making fun of him. Could such a thing be?

Jenny tackled Liz. Her task was much more quickly done.

'Will you talk to Dad?' she said.

'Of course I will,' said Liz.

Jenny led her over to Laurence, who was standing in the queue for the tote with a faint air of embarrassment.

'Mum,' said Jenny self-consciously. 'There's someone I'd like you to meet. Dad. Dad, this is Mum.'

Jenny moved off, well satisfied with the role that she had played.

'Hello, Laurence,' said Liz.

'What a memory you have for names!' said Laurence.

Betting for the first race was in full swing, and Paul didn't get a chance to talk to his father.

Ted plumped for number three, because it was his lucky number. Rodney Sillitoe plumped for number five, because it was his unlucky number. The screen was set up on the side of the false chimney breast, facing the restaurant area. The projector was on one of the tables.

Harvey Wedgewood stood by the bar and tried to look loftily detached. The dapper, ageless Eric Siddall was drying glasses with studious intensity, ignoring all life beyond the bridge of his ship. Rita sat with Neville Badger. Liz was with Paul and Jenny. When they left their seats to watch the race, Liz stayed where she was, until she saw that Laurence, who had joined suave Doctor

Spreckley and his nervous wife, was also staying where he was, so that as the crowd cheered and yelled with excitement, she and Laurence would be alone in amused detachment behind the chimney breast, and might even have to speak to each other. So she joined the throng, and pretended to be excited by these animals thundering half a mile over some tinder-dry American racecourse with hard-bitten dried-up little men on their backs wearing ludicrously complicated and clashing colours on their quartered caps and shirts.

As the race proceeded, Betty Sillitoe and Ted got quite excited. They both had a chance of winning. Rita jumped up and down, and Neville Badger gave her an astonished look. Harvey Wedgewood, the actor, had become Harvey Wedgewood, the punter. He was staring fixedly at the screen, and his knuckles were white. It was an exciting finish. The cheering rose to a crescendo. Rodney's horse won, and he looked sheepish.

'Well done, love,' said Betty.

'Excuse me,' said Ted, and he set off abruptly across the room.

Rodney gave Betty a meaningful stare. It was quicker than explaining, and he was anxious to pursue Ted. Unfortunately the meaning of his meaningful stare escaped her, and he had to stay to explain.

'I'm trying not to win,' he said. 'I don't want to rub it in with Ted. So don't say "Well done".'

Ted was already halfway across the room. Rodney caught up with him as he struggled through the queue of successful punters, who were already waiting at the tote, even though they were all disclaiming that they had any interest in winning.

'Ted! Don't go!' said Rodney.

'I must, Rodney.'

'Ted! People aren't gloating. They're thinking, "there but for the grace of God." I know I am.'

'I'm only going to the gents,' said Ted.

'Ah. That's a relief.'

'It will be, if you'll let me go.'

'I'd like a word with you, in private.'

'What?'

'I'll be in the locker room.'

'Oh. Right,' said Ted, puzzled.

'One fruit of the grape, on the dry side, you're a person of taste, madam, an excellent choice, can do, no delays anticipated, here we go.'

'And one for yourself, Alec.'

'Eric. Oh thank you very much, madam. Much appreciated. I'll have twenty penn'orth with you. Why not? Just the ticket. They can't touch you for it.'

'Eric? If you . . . er . . . if you think Rodney's had a bit too much . . . let's face it, it has been known, bless him . . . will you give me a signal?'

For once Eric Siddall, barman supreme, was almost lost for words.

'It's . . . er . . . it's a bit awkward, Mrs Sillitoe,' he said eventually.

'Nonsense. Just . . . oh . . . raise your right arm with a glass in it.'

'Oh dear. No can do, I'm afraid. It'll have to be the left arm.'

'Why?'

'Er . . . I've put me shoulder out.'

'Hello, Elvis,' said Simon Rodenhurst of Trellis, Trellis, Openshaw and Finch, as the cynical Elvis Simcock strolled casually to the back of the pay-out queue, as if collecting his winnings was seventy-fifth on his list of priorities and he was only actually collecting them at all for administrative convenience. 'How's our great philosopher enjoying life among the frozen poultry?'

'If you weren't my brother's wife's brother I'd make my highly desirable manual extremity extremely convenient for your spacious breathing and blowing organ.'

'Sorry?'

'I'd punch you on the nose. I was using estate agent-ese.'

They shuffled slowly forward beside the chimney breast, past a print of an Edwardian golfer bending to pick up his ball on a shingle beach and getting a view right up the blowing voluminous skirts of two buxom matrons. The caption read, 'Out of bounds!'

Simon Rodenhurst looked pained. 'This is a false image of our profession, Elvis,' he said.

'Oh yes? We've got to move from our flat. I went to look at that place in Power Station one yesterday. You said, "Plenty of scope for improvement." You meant, "It's falling down." You said, "Totally secluded garden." You meant, "The cooling towers block off the sun completely." Lies, Simon.'

'Not lies, Elvis. Sensible rearrangement of the truth.'

'I'm not thrilled that the only job I can get is with Rodney's battery chickens,' said Elvis Simcock, 'but I work hard and accept that there are people all over the world far worse off than me, and if you continue to make fun of me, you supercilious, snobbish, dark-suited, light-minded, overprivileged, undereducated, over-paid underling, I'll make a sensible rearrangement of your face.'

Paul gave them a cheery wave as he passed by on his way back from checking on Thomas, who was asleep. 'Building the family friendship? Great,' he said. He moved on, barely noticing the sickly looks they gave him. He was wearing a much sicklier look, which was surprising, in view of the fact that an attractive, long-haired, full-breasted young lady with a creamy complexion was approaching him with a broad smile.

'Paul!' said Carol Fordingbridge.

'Oh heck!' said Paul, turning the colour of putty. 'We can't talk here, Carol. Meet me in the men's locker room in a couple of minutes.'

Faint echoes of a thousand battles between sweat and deodorant eddied feebly around the cold, dank locker room. Beneath the rows of pegs there were long benches, and at the far end, through a wide arch, was the shower room. Rodney Sillitoe wondered if open champions entered places like this immediately after they had been cheered in the crowded amphitheatre of the eighteenth green.

'What's all this about?' said Ted.

'I'd like to give you my winnings. If you're a bit short. So you've something to bet on. I didn't want folk to see.'

He held out thirty pounds. Ted's face went red. 'I don't want charity,' he said. 'I'm a Yorkshireman.'

'It isn't charity, Ted. It's lifelong friendship. Look, it's no use pretending you haven't gone bankrupt.'

'I haven't,' said Ted. 'I've gone into voluntary liquidation. It isn't bankruptcy, isn't voluntary liquidation. I mean . . . it isn't. I'm moving sideways into design.'

'Design? What of?'

'Fire irons. Toasting forks. Door knockers. The things I know.'

'All right, but . . .'

'I should have gone into voluntary liquidation long ago, instead of waiting till I was forced to,' said Ted, sinking onto a bench.

'You've got cash problems as of now, though, haven't you?' said Rodney, sitting beside him. 'In that you're skint. And I know you'd help me if I ever went ba . . . into voluntary liquidation.'

'Of course. But you haven't, have you?'

'Do you resent my success, such as it is?' said Rodney. 'It's a poor sort of friendship if you do.'

'No! 'Course I don't! What do you mean, "such as it is"?'

Rodney's hand moved towards Ted's shoulder, then seemed to think better of the physical contact, hovered there for a moment, and drew away. Ted didn't appear to have noticed. It was very quiet in the locker room. If a drip had fallen from one of the showers, they would have jumped.

'I'm on the horns of the same knife edge as you were, Ted. And I can't move sideways into design. "Hello, Mr Ponsonby. I've come up with a rather novel three-legged chicken that I think might be a winner." It's not on.'

'You're taking on staff. You took on our Elvis.'

'And you weren't too pleased either.'

'Well . . . I mean . . . it rubbed it in a bit that I couldn't. I mean . . . didn't it? My boys have asked me for jobs several times. I couldn't take them on, knowing how things were. It wouldn't have been fair to keep them from other jobs, would it?'

'Well, there you are. So you should be glad Elvis has got a job. Which I didn't give him to rub anything in. I gave it out of family friendship.'

'Are you saying *you'll* soon be going . . . into voluntary liquidation?'

Ted picked up a sock, covered in dust, then dropped it hurriedly when he realized what it was.

'I'm not saying I will,' said Rodney. 'I'm saying I could.'

'Bit irresponsible to take our Elvis on then, wasn't it?'

'I have to take staff on to create the confidence to avert the crisis that might cause me to have to sack them if I hadn't taken them on.'

'How could you sack them if you hadn't taken them on?'

'Look, let's not argue,' said Rodney. 'I mean, I'm being friendly.'

'I can't take your money if things are that bad.'

'a) it isn't my money. It's only my winnings. b) You said you'd help me if I ever got into trouble. So, I'm just paying you back for your kindness. Tit for tat. Only I'm doing it in advance. Sort of . . .'

'. . . tat for tit.'

'Exactly.'

'Well . . . all right,' said Ted grudgingly. He realized how ungracious he sounded, and added, 'Thanks,' much more warmly.

Just as Rodney was handing Ted the money, Carol Fordingbridge entered. She had nice legs and a good figure, but it was her magnificent long hair that men noticed first. Ted and Rodney sprang apart instinctively, and Ted stuffed the money untidily into his back pocket. Grown men don't like to be witnessed either offering or receiving charity. But by the time they were standing several feet away from each other, they both realized that this must look infinitely worse. Ted must look like a council official, accepting a bribe for overlooking planning regulations, or a petty crook accepting his share of the sale of a stolen video recorder, or a homosexual prostitute receiving his payment for giving Rodney a happy half hour in the shower room. So they hurried back towards each other, and smiled horrible, falsely innocent smiles, which made them look guilty of all these things, and more besides.

Carol Fordingbridge stared at these two middle-aged men as they lurched back and forth across the locker room.

'Sorry,' she said. 'Am I interrupting something?'

'No. Nothing. Absolutely nothing,' said Rodney Sillitoe. 'We were just . . . er . . .'

'. . . leaving,' said Ted. 'We were just leaving.'

'That's right,' said Rodney. 'We were just leaving.'

'I'm just . . . you know . . . waiting for somebody,' said Carol Fordingbridge. 'Speak of the devil,' she added, as Paul entered.

'Paul!' said Ted.

'Ah, there you are, Dad,' said Paul. 'I've been looking for you everywhere. I've spoken to Mum, and she's authorized me to guarantee that she won't snub you.'

This was a rare piece of quick thinking on Paul's part. It deserved a better fate than to make his meeting with Carol seem even more clandestine than it was.

'Thanks,' said Liz, as Neville Badger handed her her drink at the crowded bar. 'So you at least are still prepared to talk to me.'

'My dear Liz!' said Neville.

'I'm not wildly popular just now. The same people who were furious with me for going to live with Ted are even more furious with me for leaving him.'

Neville shook his head slowly several times in sorrowful amazement at the pettiness of humankind.

'My dear Liz!' he repeated. 'It's always a joy to talk to you. And now, if you'll excuse me, I must take Rita her drink.'

'You seem to be being very attentive to her.' Liz tried to sound casual.

'I've had her on my conscience.'

'What?'

'It's awfully embarrassing. She keeps trying to cheer me up. Tells me I'll get over it. Time is a great healer. All that rot. She doesn't seem to realize that I don't want to get over it. I want to hang onto my grief, Liz. It's all of Jane I have left. I've been inexcusably rude to Rita several times. Jane was very upset.'

'Neville!'

'Oh, I'm not going mad,' he said hurriedly. 'I know she's dead. But she comes to me in dreams, and she seems so real. Last week she ticked me off for being so rude to Rita. Jane lays great store . . . laid great store . . . by manners. I'm being very charming to Rita, for Jane's sake.'

'Rita does have a point,' said Liz.

'What?'

'You must try to live in the present.'

'Why don't you shut up?' said Neville. 'What do you know about what it's like?'

As he stormed towards the restaurant area with Rita's drink, Neville met Harvey Wedgewood, the actor, wandering expansively towards the bar.

'Hello, I'm Harvey Wedgewood, the actor,' said Harvey Wedgewood, the actor.

'Really? I'm Neville Badger, the lawyer,' said Neville, and he continued on his way, leaving Harvey Wedgewood stranded.

All Neville's anger left him immediately, and he hurried back to Liz. 'My dear Liz. I'm so sorry,' he said. 'I don't know what I'm saying these days.' He gazed into her eyes, remembering suddenly how vulnerable she must feel tonight, hoping he hadn't hurt her. He squeezed her hand and kissed her. 'Dear Liz,' he said. 'We must have dinner one day. I'll phone you.'

Liz watched him as he made his way towards Rita, giving Harvey Wedgewood a wide berth. She saw him smile. She saw Rita's answering smile. She wouldn't have believed, if somebody had told her at Jenny's wedding, that, less than eight months later, she'd look across a crowded golf club, heavily pregnant, and feel jealous of Rita.

Harvey Wedgewood couldn't have looked more staggered after his encounter with Neville if he'd been the Duke of Edinburgh opening a traditional knitwear centre, and a tourist had approached him and said, 'Don't I know you?' and he'd said, 'I'm the Duke of Edinburgh' and the tourist had said, 'Oh yeah? And I'm the Archbishop of sodding Canterbury.' But no man who has toured Egypt in a British Council production of *Titus Andronicus* is at a loss for long, and by the time he'd bought his drink his public persona was back in place. He even felt able to smile at that idiot who thought he ran an off licence. After all, the incident would be worth a self-deprecating chuckle in his local in Princes Risborough.

Ted was looking round rather anxiously. He wanted to avoid Liz, but catch Rita on her own. He found himself staring at the man whom he now knew to be Harvey Wedgewood, the actor. He'd better apologize.

'I'm sorry about that,' he said, 'but you're so familiar to us in our lounge that I couldn't believe I hadn't met you.'

'Please! The incident is closed,' said Harvey Wedgewood, mollified by Ted's explanation. 'Now, tell me about yourself. I want to meet everybody. You are?'

'Ted Simcock.'

'And what do you do for a crust, Ted Simcock?'

Ted found that he was on the verge of concealing the truth. That wouldn't do. His only hope was to face it head-on.

'I had a small foundry,' he said. 'I've just gone into voluntary liquidation.'

'I *played* a bankrupt once,' said Harvey Wedgewood. 'The critics said I was too cheerful. They always do. They said my Lear looked about as tragic as a man who's just discovered that the spare wheel's flat. But I believe in looking on the bright side. What's wrong with that? They've paid good money. They don't want to go home feeling depressed.'

Liz was almost upon them before she saw Ted. She attempted to veer away, but Harvey Wedgewood shot out a firm but friendly arm with an agility that would have been surprising to anybody who didn't know that in his palmier days he had played in goal for Equity, and drew the captured Liz slowly towards Ted.

'Ted!' he said. 'I'd like you to meet a lady I've been lucky enough to be introduced to tonight. Liz Rodenhurst. Ted Simcock.'

'How do you do?' said Ted, grasping Liz's hand in a painful grip.

'Ow!' said Liz. 'You're hurting.'

'Oh good,' said Ted. 'Now you know what it feels like to be squeezed through a mangle.'

'I have the impression that you two know each other,' said Harvey Wedgewood.

'Inside out,' said Ted.

Far away, on the peripheries of the world, the social hubbub could be heard as if through water. Here, between Ted and Liz and the watching Harvey Wedgewood there was a silence that was like the ice age must have sounded, if there had ever been a brief lull in the screaming of the wind.

'Er . . . excuse me,' improvised Harvey Wedgewood. 'Uncle Harvey must go and place his bet on the next race.'

He scampered away, as if he'd seen three critics approaching.

Eyes were straining on the edges of their sockets as people studiously avoided looking as if they were watching Ted and Liz. They stood just far enough away to be socially respectable, but near enough to hear if things should really hot up. Ted and Liz were left facing each other like stags in a clearing. Liz was amazed at how coarse Ted's features were. Ted noticed that she was beginning to develop a double chin. Neither of them could believe that not many weeks ago they had found each other deeply attractive.

'What's it like back in the upper middle classes?' asked Ted.

'You didn't exactly make it easy for me to stay,' said Liz.

'You didn't exactly make it easy for me to make it easy for you to stay. How's Laurence looking forward to bringing up my baby?'

'I haven't seen him. I must say, Ted, I admire your courage in coming.'

'Not as much as I admire yours. They're saying far worse things about you than they are about me.'

Anger had given Ted an eloquence to which he rarely aspired. For a few seconds, as he strode away, he felt like a successful matador. But instead of a cheering crowd of Spaniards exalted by their vicarious courage there was a gathering of middle-class Anglo-Saxons pretending that they hadn't even noticed him. Already, by the time he found himself face to face with his daughter-in-law, his triumph had been eroded, and when she said, 'Have you seen Paul?' the most eloquent and elegant reply that he could manage was, 'Oh! Er . . . yes. Yes. He's . . . er . . . he's gone for a walk. He's got a headache.'

Paul and the long-haired Carol Fordingbridge sat with their feet dangling in one of three particularly vicious bunkers which guarded the tight, awkward green of the short thirteenth. It was a mild, soft, still spring night, but Paul could take no pleasure from its velvet charms.

'So what do you want to talk about?' said Carol Fordingbridge.

'Well . . . you know . . . what happened. As we'd met, I thought . . . well . . . it'd be nicer to talk than just . . . not talk. Pretend it hasn't happened. I didn't want to arouse suspicions so . . .'

'. . . you suggested meeting in the men's locker room.'

'I didn't know my dad would be there.'

'And now outside.'

'No one'll notice we're missing. It needn't take long. I just . . . didn't want it to . . . er . . . end messily. You know. And . . . er . . . my wife doesn't know anything about it, Carol. And I'm a happily married man and I don't want to destroy that.'

'Perhaps you should have thought of that before you . . .'

'I know. I know.'

The moon came out from behind a bank of quiet cloud. Paul felt very visible. Supposing the whole gathering decided to admire the night.

'But . . . she needn't know. Need she?'

'I don't even know your wife.'

'She's here tonight. I just thought . . . if you could avoid her . . . it might be best.'

'I've no burning desire to meet her.'

It wasn't an unqualified assurance, but Paul sensed that it was all he'd get.

'I didn't mean to do what I did,' he said. How could he say that he'd been drunk without seeming rude and unsympathetic to feminine sensitivities? His reserves of tact were stretched to the full. 'I . . . I was . . . I'd been celebrating the birth of my first child. I was . . . in a state of . . . exaltation.'

'You were drunk.'

'Carol! I'd had a few. Who wouldn't? You overwhelmed me. In my . . . emotional state . . .'

'You were as emotional as a newt.'

'You knew I was married. You knew I'd just become a father. You shouldn't have done it if you disapprove.'

'I was pretty emotional myself.'

'Exactly. You said yourself you'd been in the pub for hours. Oh, Carol. I'm not like that really. I'm a young idealist brimming over with concern and respect for all forms of life. My ambition is to eliminate poverty from the Third World, not have a drunken sex orgy the night after I've become a father. I long to go back to that night, and do something different. Anything. March through central Leeds protesting about unemployment. Break into Molesworth Camp and sit on a cruise missile. Be a kidney donor while still alive. Anything, rather than meet you.'

'Thanks very much.'

He heard the cheering as the guests watched the second race. It made him feel safer.

'No! Carol! What I mean is . . . lovely though that was. Particularly because that was lovely. I mean I must admit that afterwards . . . what I could remember . . . I wondered if it was

195

only because I was . . . so emotional . . . that I'd thought you were so lovely. It isn't. You are. You're amazingly lovely.'

The moon went in again, hiding her amazing loveliness. He longed to take her creamy body out here, now, in the dewy grass. Well, not take her body, he was a sensitive enlightened feminist. He·longed to give her pleasure, to let·her take *him*, here among the rabbits, beneath the floating owls. He closed his eyes and fought against it. 'Down, down!' he told his penis, as if it were an overexcited dog. He forced himself to think about asexual things – golf, Graham Wintergreen, the Tory Party Conference. He sighed with relief. The moment of danger was over.

'We'd better go in,' he said.

Half the world was starved of water, but they could hear the soft hiss of the sprinklers, making sure that the green wouldn't be too fast the next day. In view of this, and his youth, and the dark, and his emotional turmoil, golfing readers may perhaps excuse Paul for not tidying up the bunker where their heels had scuffed a pit in the sand.

As they walked back, Paul put round Carol Fordingbridge an arm that was intended to be comradely, affectionate, respectful, grateful, apologetic, non-sexist and unpatronizingly protective. To his horror his hand squirmed its way down her back and felt the outline of her superb buttocks as they swung rhythmically through the night. She removed the hand and gave it a smack. Three startled rabbits scuttled off into the rough.

The second race was over. Ted had lost five of his thirty pounds. The cynical Elvis had explained to his employer·that he was making a simple error of logic. If he wanted to lose, it was no use backing his unlucky number. Since it was unlucky, he would win. He must back his lucky number, and thus achieve the desired effect – defeat. Luckily, Jenny had been too busy to worry about Paul's absence. Laurence had asked her to indicate to Liz that he regretted his earlier sarcasm, and wished to discuss the situation in a civilized way. Jenny had conveyed this message to Liz, who had indicated that if her father wished to have a civilized discussion, he should approach her and have it. He had been rude and it was up to him to make an apology, which she would accept in handsome fashion. Jenny had conveyed this message to Laurence, who had sighed. Ted had bought one more large whisky, to give him the courage to approach Rita. Harvey Wedgewood, as he walked away from Graham Wintergreen's one-man tote, pocketing his betting slip for the third race, needed no such courage. After all, he was Harvey Wedgewood, the actor.

'Hello, dear lady,' he boomed fruitily. 'You are . . .?'

'Rita.'

'Rita! What a lovely name!'

'Thank you.' Rita felt a glow suffusing her cheeks, a faint flush, quite unlike those pink spots. 'You're Harvey Wedgewood, the actor, aren't you?'

'Alas! My anonymity is shattered!' said Harvey Wedgewood with a gesture of regret, which he hoped would seem like self-effacing modesty, though it was actually an attempt to hide a spasm of irritation. It was all very well his using the suffix 'the actor', but when the punters used it it reminded him that he had never become quite as famous as he had expected. This Rita woman would have said to Sir Alec Guinness 'You're Sir Alec Guinness, aren't you?' not 'You're Sir Alec Guinness, the actor, aren't you?' as if it was necessary to distinguish him from all the other Sir Alec Guinnesses that were clogging up the civilized world. He switched off the irritation and turned a charming smile onto Rita. 'But don't let's talk about me,' he said. 'Actors are boring. Our job is to observe, to listen. Tell me about yourself.'

'I'm just a very ordinary woman.'

'Rita!' Harvey Wedgewood's outrage at this description was so loud that the headmaster of the Abbey School almost dropped the half-pint of bitter which was all he ever allowed himself in public in case one of his boys saw him setting a bad example. 'Nobody's ordinary!' There was deep concern on his richly cratered face. 'Don't sell yourself short. My agent used to say to me, "Harvey, never sell yourself short. You're a genius. Never forget it."'

'I saw you in *The Dance of Death* at Dewsbury,' said Rita, who had never been told she was a genius by anybody.

'I thought I was quite good in that,' said Harvey Wedgewood. 'I thought I brought out an optimistic side that is usually sadly overlooked in Strindberg. But don't let's talk about me. What's your favourite food, Rita? Your favourite colour? Your deepest hope? Your greatest fear? I'm fascinated by people's dreams. What did you dream about last night? Spill the beans to Uncle Harvey.'

'Well . . . last night, actually . . .' Rita didn't want to talk about her dreams. '. . . it's so silly, but . . .' You just couldn't disappoint this great bear of a man. '. . . last night I dreamt I was a rabbit.'

'A rabbit! Good Lord! Sounds like one for Clement Freud rather than Sigmund.'

Rita shook her head. She knew that the repeated images of her own insignificance in her dreams were definitely for Sigmund.

Ted found himself approaching Rita on his way from the bar with the large whisky which was to give him the courage to approach her. He was in a quandary. He didn't want to talk to her when she was with the actor, but he didn't want to snub her by veering away. While he was debating his course of action, Harvey Wedgewood grabbed him in a bear-like hug so affectionate that most men would have reserved it for old friends who had just returned to freedom after seventeen years in a Siberian labour camp.

'Rita,' said Harvey Wedgewood. 'I'd like to introduce you to a *very* old friend of mine, Ted Simcock. Ted has recently liquidated his foundry, Rita. Ted, meet Rita, who dreams she's a rabbit. I didn't catch your other name, Rita.'

'Simcock.'

'What?'

'Exactly.'

'You mean . . .?'

'Precisely,' said Ted.

'But I thought Ted and . . .' Harvey Wedgewood stopped, wishing he hadn't started.

'Absolutely,' said Rita.

'Ah!' improvised Harvey Wedgewood.

'Rita?' said Ted. 'It's time we had a talk.'

'My friends!' said Harvey Wedgewood, putting one hugely affectionate arm round each of them. 'Take a leaf out of old Harvey's book. Look on the bright side. Be reconciled. Forgive and forget. Life's too short. 'Nuff said? Exit Harvey Wedgewood left, tactfully.'

Harvey Wedgewood exited left, thankfully. A young lady was approaching him, tall and gauche. He was about to speak, but she blushed and bolted. She was the daughter of Colonel Partridge, who was on the theatre management committee. Colonel Partridge was no intellectual, but he knew what he liked. He liked mystery plays (Agatha Christie and Francis Durbridge, not York and Oberammergau); port; stilton; hunting; shooting his namesakes; being kind to the poor and driving them to polling stations to vote Conservative; and his dear, over-loved, over-protected daughter Davina. How horrified he would have been if he had seen the swift exploratory sniff which Harvey Wedgewood gave her before she rushed from his aura. He smelt expensive perfume, horses, dogs, tomato soup and fear. Then the more general aroma of the room assailed him. Sweat, aftershave, cigarette smoke, alcohol, furniture polish and heat, the whole confection bound together with a hint of distant goulash. Hello! Who was this stick approaching?

'Excuse me,' said Laurence. 'You're Mr Wedgewood the actor, aren't you?'

'Please! No formality. Call me Harvey. And you are . . .?'

'Laurence. I saw your Othello in Leeds.'

'Yes, yes, never mind that. What do you do, Laurence?'

'Me? I'm just a dentist.'

'Priceless! Absolutely right!' exclaimed Harvey Wedgewood so loud that several people turned their heads.

'What?' said Laurence faintly.

'You being a dentist. Well done, the great casting director in the sky. A slightly up-market dentist, but ... . very good. I suppose, Laurence, as you went through all the business of sitting through it, it'd be selfish of me not to ask you what you thought of my Othello.'

'Well . . . I thought the critics were *unnecessarily* cruel.'

'I never read the critics. If the *Daily Telegraph* want to say that I showed all the passion of a man who has just discovered that Desdemona has been buying rather expensive curtain material, let them. What do they know? Can they act, Laurence? You're quite right. They can't. Don't they realize that I want to send the audience home feeling there's still some hope in life? But let's talk about you. Your hopes. Your fears. Your dreams. I love other people's dreams. Tell me, Laurence, what did you dream about last night?'

'Well . . . actually . . .' Laurence didn't want to go into great detail about his dream, in which he had been judging an Eisteddfod in which every contestant had been Liz. But he felt obliged to say something. 'It's stupid, but I dreamt I was Welsh.'

'A nightmare, eh? Probably you'd had cheese. Unfair. Just because they booed my Peer Gynt in Port Talbot. Laurence, why did you say "*just* a dentist"?'

'Well . . .'

'Laurence! Don't say that! I merely pretend to be non-existent people. Or, which is worse, real people saying things they never said. Pathetic! But you . . . well . . . without people like you many of us would no longer have any . . .' Harvey Wedgewood stopped as he saw Liz approaching.

'. . . teeth.' Laurence finished the sentence, wished he hadn't, and also saw Liz.

And then Liz saw them, but it was too late. Harvey Wedgewood had her in his vast yet gentle embrace.

'Laurence!' he said. 'I'd like you to meet an *extremely* good friend of mine, the very ravishing and deliciously naughty Liz Rodenhurst. Liz, you of the wonderfully wandering eyes, meet Laurence, the dreaming dentist. I didn't catch your other name.'

'Rodenhurst,' said Laurence drily.

'Oh my God!' said Harvey Wedgewood.

'Precisely,' said Liz.

'Liz . . .?' began Laurence, and hesitated diffidently.

'". . . don't you think it's about time we had a serious chat about things?"' prompted Harvey Wedgewood.

Laurence and Liz were briefly united in giving Harvey Wedgewood distinctly unfriendly looks.

'Sorry,' said Harvey Wedgewood. 'But one picks up the conversational style of the place. Exit Harvey Wedgewood, left, in much confusion.'

Harvey Wedgewood exited left, in much confusion. He took an enormous swig of his drink, and sank exhausted onto a bar stool. He had come on a long and painful journey to this watering hole.

So had Paul.

'Shan't keep you, gentlemen,' said Eric Siddall, barman supreme, as he slid past as if on rails to serve the drama teacher at the Abbey School. 'No problem. Don't go away. All under control. We're on our way.'

Paul gave Harvey Wedgewood an uneasy smile.

'Don't look so frightened, young man,' said the exhausted Thespian in a kindly tone. 'I'm human.'

'No. That thing you did on the telly. I loved that when I was a kid,' said Paul.

'*The Forsyte Saga?*'

'Chocky Bar, the between-meals meal that doesn't spoil your meals.'

'Yes! I daresay that is what I'm best remembered for after forty-three years,' sighed Harvey Wedgewood. 'And you are . . .?'

'Paul Simcock.'

'Another Simcock! Well, congratulations, Paul Simcock. You have a very lovely young lady.'

'Well, thank you very much. I think so, anyway.'

'I felt the need of air, and saw you.'

'What?'

'Slipping off to the golf course for a swift quickie.'

'Will you shut up?' hissed Paul.

'Harvey Wedgewood, this isn't your day,' mused Harvey Wedgewood.

But at two widely separated tables, two married couples who had been widely separated were in conversation again, thanks to the efforts of that egotistical old actor.

Seated round the side of the false chimney breast by the huge curtains, three tables away from the Sillitoes, sat Laurence and Liz.

'So . . . er . . . where are you living?' began Laurence.

'I've rented a very cheap and thoroughly nasty flat,' said Liz.

'My heart bleeds for you,' said Laurence, and he closed his eyes and wished he hadn't said it.

There was silence between them.

'How this icy silence takes me back,' said Liz, and she closed her eyes and wished she hadn't said it.

'There's so little to say to one's wife,' said Laurence. '"Where were you born?" "Are you an outdoor person?" "Do you prefer books or TV?" "Would you describe yourself as a political person?" One knows the answers.'

'My views may have changed,' said Liz. 'I've been in a different world.'

'I imagine that was part of the attraction,' said Laurence. 'Unfortunately, the attraction between people from different worlds rarely survives unless they remain in those different worlds.' Again, he closed his eyes and wished he hadn't spoken.

There was more silence.

'More silence,' said Liz.

'It's called the companionship of marriage,' said Laurence.

Ted and Rita were tucked away in a corner table in the restaurant area, beside the wine racks.

'I've got a job,' said Rita, not without a hint of pride. Getting a job had been a minor moral victory. Bringing herself to apply in the first place had been a major moral victory.

'Splendid!' said Ted. 'Wonderful. What a turnabout! The whole family's working except me.'

'Oh, Ted!' said Rita. Don't allow yourself to be flattened by him, she told herself.

'Well!' said Ted. 'I mean . . .'

'I was dreadfully sorry to hear about the foundry,' said Rita.

'Were you?'

'Ted! Of course I was. I felt physically sick.'

'I didn't feel too grand meself.'

'No.'

'So . . . what are you doing?'

'The old exciting stuff. Secretarial. With a finance company.'

'Well, it would be. I mean . . . nobody's creating wealth round here any more. They're just moving it around.'

There was silence between them.

'I was very sorry about your mother,' said Ted.

'It was better than lingering,' said Rita.

'I . . . er . . . I'm sorry it happened while I was away,' said Ted awkwardly.

'You make it sound as if you'd gone for a weekend break in Morecambe,' said Rita.

'Ladies and gentlemen,' announced the bluff Graham Winter-green, breaking in on these conversations. 'All bets are now placed for the third race. It's auction time again. Who will start me off for horse number one?'

'Twenty pounds,' said Rodney Sillitoe.

'Thank you, sir. Any advance on twenty pounds?'

There was silence. The first horse in the first race had gone for twenty pounds, and since then nobody had liked to offer less or wanted to offer more. The auctions had been dull, but brief.

'Sold to Mr Rodney Sillitoe, managing director of Cock-A-Doodle Chickens,' said Graham Wintergreen. 'Would you like to name your horse?'

'Yes, I would,' said Rodney. 'Could I call it Beautiful Betty?'

A sentimental breeze of 'Aaah's pervaded the golf club restaurant and bar.

'What a lovely man!' said Betty Sillitoe, kissing him.

There were eight horses in the race. Others were bought by Colonel Partridge; the drama teacher at the Abbey School; the headmaster of the Abbey School, who could hardly refuse after the drama teacher had been so generous; the suave Doctor Spreckley; and Melissa Holdsworthy, the handsome, statuesque, grey-haired sculptperson whose controversial piece representing the agonized emergence of life from the primordial slime adorned or disfigured the foyer of the theatre, according to one's tastes, and who was assumed by most men to be lesbian because she was tall and had never met a member of their sex whom she liked enough to marry. Doctor Spreckley knew better. He had removed her appendix once and her putty-smeared jeans seventeen times. She was a very independent woman and sent him messages when she was ready for him. He interpreted her purchase of the adjacent horse in a race for three-year-old American geldings as being one of those messages.

'Go on. Don't be mean for once,' said Liz, just loud enough for people at neighbouring tables to hear, as the last horse came up.

'Oh God, how undignified!' said Laurence. He called out shyly, 'Twenty pounds.'

'Thank you, sir. Any advance on twenty pounds?' said Graham Wintergreen, as a pure formality.

'Twenty pounds fifty,' called out Rita from the restaurant area, and heads craned to see her.

'Rita!' said Ted.

'Push them up,' said Rita.

Heads swivelled back towards Laurence.

'Go on,' hissed Liz. 'Don't let them beat you.'

'Twenty-one pounds,' called Laurence self-consciously.

'Twenty-one fifty,' called Rita immediately.

'Rita!' said Ted. 'I can't afford it.'

'I can,' said Rita.

Rodney and Betty Sillitoe were swivelling back and forth like two footballers on the same rod in a football game in an amusement arcade.

'Laurence!' hissed Liz.

'She's making us a laughing stock,' said Laurence. The words 'twenty-two pounds' emerged thickly, as if pulled out of his throat against his will.

Rita's reply of 'Twenty-two fifty' was absolutely instantaneous.

'Rita!' Ted was getting desperate. The last thing he wanted on his very first public appearance as a bankrupt was to have a hundred and fifty people staring excitedly in his direction. The sweat was surging down his back.

'She'll make him go on, which will mortify him,' said Rita. 'Or he'll stop, which will mortify her.'

And indeed, as the excitement buzzed round the room – nobody needed to be tactful about their curiosity now – Liz whispered to Laurence, 'Don't let them get it. Just for once, win.'

'Sir?' said Graham Wintergreen, whose great moment this was. There was nothing the actor could do to steal attention from him. 'With you, sir?'

Laurence shook his head, an almost imperceptible gesture which he hoped nobody would notice.

Graham Wintergreen noticed. 'Thank you, sir,' he said. This wasn't going to end quickly, if he could help it. 'Twenty-three pounds. With you, madam.'

'Twenty-three fifty.'

'Thank you, madam. Sir?'

Laurence tried to remain totally immobile. All eyes were upon him. He wanted to sneeze.

He sneezed.

'Twenty-four pounds! Thank you, sir!' Graham Wintergreen's eyes twinkled maliciously, and there was a loud laugh. Eat your heart out, Harvey Wedgewood.

Rita waited till the laughter had died down, before saying, 'Twenty-four fifty' quite softly.

'Sir?' said Graham Wintergreen to Laurence, who was looking fiercely embarrassed. 'Nice round twenty-five?'

Liz's eyes implored Laurence to continue, but he remained totally immobile. He was desperately fighting off the urge to blink and to twitch. He was terrified that another sneeze was on its way. He even had a fear that he might fart.

'Twenty-five, sir? No? For the last time! Going. Going. No, sir? Are you sure, sir? Sold to Rita Simcock for twenty-four pounds fifty!'

'Oh God,' said Ted, as angry at the victory of the Simcocks as Liz was at the defeat of the Rodenhursts.

'Do you have a name you'd like to give it, madam?' asked Graham Wintergreen.

'Give me a name for it, Ted,' said Rita.

'Tremendous Ted,' said Ted.

'You must be joking,' said Rita.

'A gesture of reconciliation,' said Ted.

'That's a nice thought,' said Rita.

Ted smiled.

'I'd like to call it Karl Marx,' Rita called out.

There was a stir, then a burst of talk erupted all round the room.

'Rita!' said Ted.

'Stir them up a bit,' said Rita.

And Betty Sillitoe, exhausted from all the swivelling, limp after all the excitement, and above all pleased that Rita had won, leant on her husband's shoulder and said, 'Wonderful!'

'Karl Marx?' said Rodney. 'It's a ridiculous name.'

'No! They're competing against each other as couples. They're together again. Everything's going to be all right.'

The crowds gathered round the screen, the lights were dimmed, the projector whirred, the American geldings carried their grotesquely garbed jockeys along the unbelievably green, white-fenced, neat-as-a-toy racecourse in some corner of America which none of them would ever know. It was as if an over-coloured photograph in the *National Geographical Magazine* had burst into movement. Many people cheered with genuine excitement, others with frenzied excitement, to make sure the evening went with a swing. Laurence and Liz tried to look as if they were Mr and Mrs Einstein and this was the Eurovision Song Contest, but in fact they were dreading a victory for the horse that they had so nearly bought. Simon Rodenhurst, of Trellis, Trellis, Openshaw and Finch, got so excited that the cynical Elvis Simcock worried that he might have a hernia. Elvis adopted a cooler pose, reflecting on the absurdity of cheering an event that had happened months ago, of urging a result different from the inevitable one. Ted and Harvey Wedgewood felt their hearts beat faster as they longed for victory, and Rodney Sillitoe felt his heart beat faster as he longed for defeat. Then, as the winning horse flashed past that distant post, giving the same result for the two hundred and seventy-ninth successive time, there was a great cheer from a few, and a huge sigh from many.

Beautiful Betty beat Karl Marx by a short head. Rodney should have realized that he was bound to win if he switched to his lucky number.

And then it was time for the fork supper. Two huge trolleys were wheeled in from the kitchen. On the trolleys there stood a vast pot of goulash, and a smaller pot of vegetarian casserole. To accompany them there was rice, buttered potatoes and mixed salad. There was a wide selection of sauces, dressings and condiments on a table nearby. On every plate there was a picture of Tony Jacklin holding the Ryder Cup. It seemed sacrilege to cover him with goulash.

Some people hurried to be first in the queue for food. Others, longing to hurry, ambled. Others waited with dignity for the rush to die down. Upstairs, as if the idea of a meal had been transmitted to him in his sleep, Thomas awoke and began to bawl. Jenny fed him gladly. She felt that it was indefensible to scramble for food while there was so much starvation in the world.

'Rita?' said Ted, in a tone which rendered immediate goulash impossible. He had decided to ignore her extraordinary behaviour. 'Rita? What I wanted to say was . . . I mean . . . love . . . I won't. I'll never stray again. I promise.'

'You seem to assume I'm having you back,' said Rita.

'But, Rita . . .'

'You wouldn't expect me to have you back, after what you've done to me, without making you beg for forgiveness, would you?'

'Well . . . I suppose not . . . I . . .' Ted looked round, desperately, hoping nobody in the restaurant area was looking at them. 'Oh heck,' he said. 'It just isn't me, isn't begging.' He lowered his voice almost to a whisper. 'I'm very sorry, Rita,' he croaked. 'I've been a fool.' Betty and Rodney Sillitoe, craning their necks to watch, foregoing goulash in their excitement for their friends, were pleased to see this evidence of intimacy. 'When I saw her for what she was . . .'

'Would you ever have seen her for what she was if you hadn't gone bankrupt?'

'Voluntary liquidation!'

'If you were still in business, you'd still be with her.'

'No! Rita! Honestly! I'd long since realized what a fool I'd been. I had, love! I mean . . . I had! Honestly! Love! I had!' He paused. 'Right,' he resumed. 'Well . . . I've begged. So . . . will you take me back, my love?'

'No.'

'Thanks. What?'

Rita stood up.

'Where are you going?' he asked.

'I'm hungry.'

'Sit down!'

Rita sat down.

'Rita! What's got into you?' he said.

'Life.'

'You what?'

'In the last few months I've lost both my parents and my husband. I've had to learn to stand on my own feet.'

There was a slight kerfuffle as Mrs Spreckley nervously tried to persuade her suave husband to leave the vegetarian casserole for the vegetarians. He refused, saying that he didn't like goulash. The real reason was that he wanted to stand behind the tall, handsome Melissa Holdsworthy in the vegetarian queue and murmur 'Tuesday' suavely, sexily into her ear. Ted and Rita, oblivious to anything except each other, would never know of this.

'You don't have to have lost me, my love,' said Ted.

'I've lost you whether you come back or not,' said Rita. 'I've changed. I've gained confidence.'

'What? You mean . . . on your own . . . without me?'

'Yes. Sorry.'

'I just don't understand it.'

'It's simple. When you step out of the shadows you feel the sunshine.'

'Rita! I know it seems as if I've failed. I know it looks as if I'm a flop. But . . .'

It didn't sound like one of Ted's old, confident, infuriatingly final 'buts'. It practically begged her to say 'But what?' Rita had no intention of being deliberately cruel to Ted. It was impossible to feel much hostility for him now. 'But what?' she said.

'But I haven't. Failed. I haven't. I'm moving laterally into design, that's all.'

'I'm not not having you back because you're a failure.'

'Rita! Are you saying you'd rather be on your own without me?'

Rita tried hard to admit no element of coyness or smugness into her voice as she said, 'Those aren't the only alternatives.' She wasn't entirely successful.

Ted's mouth dropped open. 'Oh, come on, Rita,' he said. 'I mean . . . Rita! Who'd . . .? He stopped.

'. . . look at me? Is that what you were going to say?'

'No! Of course not! Love! Really! But.'

This was more like a 'but' of the old school. It hung there, infuriatingly, in the silence. She couldn't let him get away with it.

'But what?'

'Well! . . . I mean . . . you aren't young any more.'

And she'd been on the verge of sympathizing with him!

'I mean . . . Rita! . . . you aren't! Are you? So . . . I mean . . . not being rude . . . but! . . . who'd have you that's worth having?'

'Neville. And now I'm going to get some of Brenda's goulash.'

'You know the younger of the Kirkstall girls?' said Laurence. 'The one we sometimes think isn't quite right. Her mother rang me on Saturday afternoon. Saturday afternoon! She'd had an abscess for eight days, and nobody'd done a thing. Eight days, and then they ring me on Saturday afternoon.'

There was a pause, during which Liz slowly realized that the story was over.

'Much as I admire your gift for story-telling, Laurence,' she said, 'can I go and get my fork supper?'

'No! Please! I was just making small talk to . . . er . . . well, it's my halting, clumsy way of saying what for some reason I find very difficult to say. I'm . . . er . . . I'm prepared to forgive and forget.'

'I believe you could forgive too!' said Liz, patting his hand. 'I don't deserve it. But *forget*? How could you? There's the baby.'

'It'll bring us together again. It'll breathe new life into our marriage.'

'But it isn't yours.'

'We're talking about a human being. The idea of possessing it seems terribly wrong to me.'

'All right, but not only is it not yours, but you know whose it is.'

'That's a bit more serious, I admit, but . . .'

'You hate Ted. You drove all the way to the municipal dump to throw away his companion set.'

'Because it was falling to bits, not because it was his!'

'You'd never even been to the dump before. You pretend decay doesn't exist except in teeth, where it's profitable.'

'I went because the tongs were bent, the brush-head came off, the poker kept unscrewing, and the shovel buckled if you put a piece of coal larger than a plover's egg on it. Every time I looked at it, it reminded me that I'd wasted thirty-six pounds ninety-nine pee. If that's a sample of his product, I'm not surprised he went into voluntary liquidation!'

'Bankrupt! And you hate him. Supposing our child's a boy and looks like him. Supposing it's a *girl* and looks like him!'

'It'll be a challenge. I need a challenge, Liz. In the current jargon, I need to be stretched as a human being.'

'Laurence!'

There was a slight kerfuffle as Colonel Partridge discovered that he had taken the vegetarian casserole by mistake. The gauche Davina blushed scarlet and said she would have it. One day she would pluck up her courage and tell him that she disapproved of hunting. Liz and Laurence, oblivious to anything except each other, would never know of this.

'Please!' pleaded Laurence. 'I'm serious! I don't think I can stand living in that empty great house alone.'

'Oh, Laurence! It's not really any wonder I went off, is it?' said

Liz. 'That cry came from the heart, and there wasn't a mention of me in it. Move from that empty great house to à little service flat. Join clubs. Go to lounge bars. Expand your practice. Play golf. Play bridge. Be happy. Without me.'

'Liz!'

'You're a natural bachelor. Accept it at last. It's better for both of us.'

'You mean . . . this is final?'

'I'm afraid so. There's somebody else.'

'Already?'

Liz gave him a sharp look, searching for sarcasm. His face showed no emotion whatsoever.

'There's no reason why you should believe me,' said Liz. 'But this is serious. It's the real thing.'

'Who is this somebody else, who's serious and the real thing?'

'Neville. And now I'm going to get some of that fork supper.'

Rodney Sillitoe bought the drinks, while Betty fetched the goulash. Rodney reminded the dapper, ageless Eric Siddall that he had agreed to signal, should Betty overindulge, and Eric assured him, 'No problem, sir. Leave it with me. All under control. It shall be done, sir. If it's needed, sir. Which we hope it won't be, sir. A tenner, sir? Can do. No panic.'

The goulash came up to expectations, although the vegetable casserole lacked conviction. The fourth race proved as exciting as the first three. Paul was among the winners, and went to the bar to buy drinks for himself and Jenny. He found his brother and Simon Rodenhurst there, and bought them drinks too.

'Congratulations, Paul,' said Simon Rodenhurst.

'What on?' said Paul.

'Everything,' said Simon. 'Winning. Marvellous. The baby. Terrific. And I hear you've landed a job.'

'Yes. He's a municipal highways operative,' said Elvis.

'Ah! Really!' said Simon. 'Jolly good. Well done. Er . . . what exactly is a municipal highways operative?'

'It's estate agent-ese for road sweeper,' said Elvis.

'Still prepared to be seen talking to me, Simon?' said Paul.

Simon ignored this. 'Why does everyone think we're purveyors of untruths?' he said.

'That's estate agent-ese for liars,' said Elvis.

'I know you all think I'm an upper middle-class twit,' said Simon.

'No,' said Elvis. 'We don't, Simon. Honestly. We think you're a middle-class twit.'

'Well, I'd just like to say one thing,' said Simon, with a burst of anger. 'I love my little sister.'

'Well . . . good,' said Paul.

'But, you see, your cosy flat . . .'

'Our tiny flat.'

'Your compact, easily maintained flat is one of the many places to which I've never been invited.'

'Paul!' said Elvis, stiff with mock outrage. 'I thought you always did your bit for the world's underprivileged.'

'Oh, shut up, Elvis,' said Paul. 'I'm sorry, Simon. We will invite you . . . soon . . . I promise.'

He felt dreadful. He wondered what Jenny would have thought of him if she'd seen him taking part in baiting Simon. He wondered what Simon would have thought if Simon knew what he had done on the night Jenny became a mother.

He hurried off to give Jenny her drink. He longed to be with her. He loved her more deeply than he had ever realized.

His father intercepted him. 'Paul?' he said. 'Who was that girl in the locker room?'

'Nobody, Dad. I mean . . . it's nothing important. What were you and Mum talking about just now?'

'Never mind that. What were you and that girl talking about?'

'It's nothing serious, Dad.' He was blushing. Oh God!

'I hope not,' said his father. 'I mean . . . really . . . Paul!'

'Yes . . . well . . . you're hardly in a position to give me moral advice, are you?'

'I'm not giving moral advice. I'm giving practical advice. They're bad news, women. They're fickle.'

'And we're as solid as rocks, are we?'

'Paul! We're different. Men are different. They are!'

'When women play around, they're fickle bitches and nymphomaniacs. When men play around, they're men of the world. That really is rock bottom old-fashioned clapped-out male chauvinist hypocrisy, Dad.'

'Whose side are you on?'

'Women's. Jenny's.'

'You've got a bloody funny way of showing it.'

Ted was shouting. People were looking round.

'Don't you think I don't know that, Dad?' said Paul. 'I just hope she never finds out.'

'I thought there were going to be no secrets in your marriage.' Ted couldn't help looking smug as he made his thrust.

'I was very young,' said Paul. 'I've found out since that it's possible to be too idealistic.'

'Well, anyway, you haven't done anything serious,' said Ted. 'I'm glad to hear it. You won't be too worried that that girl's talking to Jenny then.'

'What??' Paul followed Ted's eyes, and his blood ran cold as he saw Jenny talking to Carol Fordingbridge, over by the entrance to the kitchens, by the piled remains of the fork supper. 'Oh my God!'

Carol hadn't actually promised not to tell. He rushed off, then realized that he ought to look calm, and did the last few feet extremely casually. He handed Jenny her drink and made no comment to Carol.

'Paul! This is Carol Fordingbridge,' said Jenny. 'She used to be receptionist at the surgery. Carol, this is my husband Paul.'

Paul realized that Carol was as surprised at discovering that Jenny was his wife as he was at discovering that Carol had been Laurence's receptionist. All was not yet lost.

'Hello, Paul,' said Carol.

'Hello, Carol.'

They shook hands demurely.

'You look as lovely as ever, Carol,' said Jenny.

'Absolutely,' said Paul. 'I mean, not that I know how lovely she looked before. But I mean, put it this way, if she's gone off significantly she must have been absolutely unbelievably fantastic before, so, yes, I would say on balance that I'd assume that she must be as lovely as ever, as you so rightly say.'

Jenny and Carol both showed a certain amount of surprise at this speech.

'Well . . . thanks,' said Carol. 'Hey, I hear you've got a little boy.'

'How did you hear that?' said Jenny.

'Oh . . . you know how news gets around in this town. If you burp in the Highcliff Road flats, you've got a duodenal ulcer on the Wartley Industrial Estate by morning.'

Paul felt that he was going to faint. He murmured an apology to some people at a nearby table as he sat down beside them. He heard the two women's voices as if from a long way off.

'What are you doing these days, Carol?'

'I'm the distribution manager's secretary at Cock-A-Doodle Chickens.'

'Are you all right, Paul?'

Paul! That was his name! That must have been for him. He would have to reply.

'Marvellous,' he said with a sickly smile. 'Terrific.'

Then he passed out.

Ted's opportunity came when Rodney Sillitoe went off to place the bets, including one for Ted.

Betty Sillitoe had stationed herself at the bar, just in case Rodney decided to drink all the profits from the fourth race after he had placed their bets for the fifth race.

Ted just hoped she was still sober.

'Not a bad evening,' she said. She sounded sober enough. 'Not bad food.'

'I've never rated goulash, me,' he said. 'In my book it's just foreign stew.' He lowered his voice so dramatically that several people turned to listen. 'I need your advice, Betty.' He mouthed the final words. 'About Rita. A woman's advice.'

He led Betty away from the bar. Rita was sitting with Jenny and Paul, who was recovering from his fainting fit. Ted took Betty right to the far corner of the restaurant area, where they could talk inconspicuously. Several people watched them and wondered why they had suddenly gone to talk together in the far corner of the restaurant area.

'I . . . er . . . I was talking to Rita earlier,' began Ted.

'I saw you.'

'Yes . . . well . . . she says there's another man.'

'What?'

'I know. I know. But . . . that's what she says. She says . . . she says it's Neville.'

'What???'

'I know. I know. But . . . I mean . . . she did come with him. Didn't she? And I mean . . . I thought . . . being a woman . . . well, couldn't you? Find out? If you could. I mean . . . if there's anything in it. I mean . . . not that there can be. I mean . . . it's impossible. It's ludicrous. It's ridiculous. But.'

Ted stood by the restaurant stairs and watched. He saw Rita leave Paul and Jenny and walk across the room, without any apparent purpose. And there . . . oh God . . . was the immaculate Neville Badger moving towards her, an elegant figure, always so gentlemanly, but bent on seduction. Good old Betty! She managed to get to Rita before Neville. She put a friendly arm round Rita and led her away from the danger area. Now there *was* a friend. Not many left. Friends. Less than ever now.

'It's a very enjoyable evening, isn't it?' said Betty Sillitoe, as she steered Rita over to their table by the curtained windows.

'Yes. Very enjoyable.'

'It wasn't a bad meal, was it, considering?'

'I enjoyed it. Ted hates goulash.'

'Rita!'

'Well!'

'You had a nice long chat with him, didn't you?'

'Well, long, anyway.'

Betty gave Rita an assessing look, raised her glass to her lips, realized it was empty, looked round, saw Rodney going over to the bar, sighed, gave Rita another assessing look, and spoke.

'You get on well with Neville, do you?' she asked.

'Ted's told you what I said, hasn't he?'

'No!' Betty met Rita's disconcertingly amused stare, and quailed, and amended her reply slightly, to 'Yes', and wondered, because Rita was not a person before whom one usually quailed. 'Is there . . . er . . . I mean . . .?'

'I don't know, Betty. I really don't know.'

'What?'

'I think it surprised me almost as much as Ted when I said it. But I've been thinking. He has been behaving oddly. Neville. Very

214

rude sometimes. Really abrupt. Then sometimes, like tonight, incredibly charming. Really attentive. When he came round to pick me up he brought flowers. Ted has never ever brought flowers. I mean . . . is it that impossible? Am I that awful?'

'Rita! Of course not!'

'And I just wondered . . . I don't know . . . maybe he was being so rude because he was fighting against the fact that he was beginning to find me . . . I can't say it. It sounds too silly.'

' . . . attractive.'

'Yes. I mean it looks like it tonight. And I thought maybe the rudeness was out of a sort of loyalty to his wife's memory. Then I thought maybe I'd been reading too many stories in the doctor's waiting room. But if you've noticed it too . . . I don't know.'

Neville walked past, and gave them a charming smile, completely unaware that they were discussing him. They smiled back. Rita blushed a little, but no pink spots appeared.

'What would you do if he did?' said Betty.

'Did what?' said Rita.

'Did anything.'

'He's a very attractive man.'

'Rita!'

Silence fell between these old friends.

'Would you like a drink?' said Betty, as a device for creating movement.

'Just a tonic, please.'

'Stay there. I'll get them.'

To Betty's relief, Rita did stay there. Betty took her empty glass towards the bar, turning to give Ted a meaningful look. Ted waited for a few seconds, and then, seemingly casually, joined her at the far end of the bar from Rodney.

'Well?' he said.

'It's possible,' she said. 'It's just possible.'

'Oh heck,' he said. He wanted to move off, but Betty insisted that he stay and have a drink, in case Rita was watching.

When Betty had returned to Rita, Ted set off in pursuit of Neville Badger. Neville was talking to Colonel Partridge. He introduced Ted.

'Oh yes,' said Colonel Partridge. 'You're the chap whose firm's failed, aren't you? Bad luck. Thing like that, tragic. Makes a chap feel so useless.'

'I wonder if I could have a word in private, Neville,' said Ted.

If Neville Badger felt any displeasure at this interruption, one faintly raised eyebrow was all he showed of it.

'You're a kind-hearted man, aren't you?' said Ted, when they had detached themselves from Colonel Partridge.

Neville looked surprised.

'Well . . . I . . . er . . .' he said.

'Exactly! I mean . . . you are. You're known for it.'

'Well . . . thank you. I try to be.'

'Your late wife was a kind-hearted woman, wasn't she?'

'Very much so.'

'I think you're the sort of man who'd . . . out of respect for your wife's memory, if nothing else. I mean . . . aren't you?'

'What?'

'The sort of man who'd never want to hurt anybody deliberately.'

'Well . . . yes . . . I hope I am, Ted.'

'Right! So! You may think . . . well, nobody seems too bothered, nobody will get hurt. You'd be wrong, Neville. Very wrong. Need I say more?'

Neville Badger peered gravely at Ted, straining to understand. 'Yes, I think you do need,' he said.

'You mean . . . you haven't caught my drift?'

'Frankly, Ted, I haven't the faintest idea what you're talking about.'

'Oh. Oh!' Ted thought for a moment. 'In that case, maybe we'd better say no more about it,' he said at last.

'About what?' said Neville.

'Good man,' said Ted. 'You won't mention any of this to anybody, will you?'

'I couldn't, if I wanted to,' said Neville.

Ted felt vaguely reassured by this conversation, but didn't know if the feeling was justified. Neville Badger felt vaguely alarmed, but didn't know if the feeling was justified.

The fifth race proved as exciting as the first four.

Simon Rodenhurst approached Rodney Sillitoe and Ted, as they queued for their winnings. 'Congratulations,' he said.

'I didn't want to win,' growled the big wheel behind Cock-A-Doodle Chickens. 'I wanted to give.' Rodney handed his ticket to Graham Wintergreen, who gave him his winnings.

'You do give, Mr Sillitoe,' said Simon. 'You'll be giving new jobs to the community when we find those new premises for you.'

Ted, in the act of handing his ticket to Graham Wintergreen, froze. 'New premises? Are you moving?' he said.

'Expanding,' said Simon Rodenhurst, of Trellis, Trellis, Openshaw and Finch, proudly. 'I'm handling it personally.'

Ted hardly noticed that Graham Wintergreen had given him his winnings. He couldn't have claimed it as a great triumph – he'd only won because he'd chosen to back the same horse as Rodney – but he'd still felt pleased at the prospect of collecting some money. Now even that pleasure had been spoilt. He pocketed the money automatically, as they walked away from the tote desk.

'Sorry. Was it a secret?' asked Simon, looking from one to the other.

'It *was*, yes.'

'Only from me, Simon,' said Ted. 'Clearly I wasn't supposed to know.'

'Ted!' said Rodney.

'Well, according to your story you were on a knife-edge, not expanding,' said Ted.

'I am,' said Rodney, trying hard not to sound like an even bigger wheel behind an even bigger Cock-A-Doodle Chickens. 'I'm forced to expand in order not to collapse. I'm on a treadmill of failure. You don't want me to collapse, do you?'

''Course I don't,' said Ted. 'But . . . I mean . . . I'd appreciate being told the truth. I mean . . . I'd appreciate not being patronized because you think I can't face the truth because you think I'm a failure.' He stomped off.

'Sorry,' said Simon Rodenhurst.

'Take my advice, Simon,' said Rodney. 'Don't have friends. They're more trouble than they're worth.'

Rodney Sillitoe moved off to the bar. It was only right, if he kept on winning, that he should buy a few drinks for the less fortunate. Betty tried to stop him buying a large one for himself, but he explained that it would look mean if he didn't.

Ted queued and placed his bet for the sixth race, glad to have something to do. All around him there was chatter and warmth and self-assurance. There was smug enjoyment of success. Only *he* was bankrupt. Only *he* had failed. Only *he* had lost his lover. Only *he* was in danger of losing his wife. As he moved away from the tote he found himself approaching Neville Badger, and decided to veer away. Before he could do so, Neville veered away from him. The insufferable cheek of the man.

Graham Wintergreen announced the auctioning of the horses for the last race, and Ted knew that he couldn't face the humiliation of sitting there again, unable to afford to bid. But he didn't want people to say that he hadn't had the courage to stick it out to the end.

The gents! That was the answer. He locked himself in a cabinet, away from that petty and ignorant throng. What did they know? His boot scrapers with the faces of famous prime ministers had been ahead of their time. His toasting forks were too elegant for a utilitarian age. He was a man out of his time.

He heard the distant cheering for the sixth race. How hollow it all was. How false that undiscriminating rabble were. Anger coursed through him, and he pulled the chain savagely. He had forgotten that he was sitting there fully dressed. The water splashed up and soaked the seat of his trousers.

Betty Sillitoe had won at last, and queued for her winnings, hoping that, as Rodney had lost, it would be safe to leave him on his own for a few minutes.

Rodney bought drinks for everyone at the bar, to celebrate the fact that at last he had lost.

Ted slid back into the bustling bar and stood with his back to the radiator.

Rita couldn't decide whether to approach Neville Badger, so she walked slowly towards him, giving him the chance to approach her. But Harvey Wedgewood approached her first.

'Are we going to meet again, Rita?' he demanded.

'I very much doubt it.'

'Now listen. I've landed a very small part in a new production of

Hamlet. They seem to think I can bring a bit of much-needed light relief to the gloomy ramparts of Elsinore. I want you to promise to come and see it and come backstage afterwards.'

'You'd be horrified if I did. If you remembered me.'

'I'm not that drunk! Now promise!'

'All right. I promise!'

'Good. Good. Good Rita.' He spoke to her as if she were a puppy. 'A little kiss for Uncle Harvey.' He kissed her expansively, fruitily, boozily, not at all as if she were a puppy. He broke off as he saw Laurence passing by, on his way to have a talk with Neville Badger, for which he had been screwing himself up for half an hour. 'It's Dan, Dan, the dental man,' he cried, catching Laurence in his huge goalkeeper's clasp.

Laurence wriggled free from the human contact like a desperate eel.

'My good friend Laurence,' exclaimed Harvey Wedgewood. 'Do you know my good friend Rita? Of course you do. Now listen to Uncle Harvey. You two have been badly bruised. Why don't you lick each other's wounds?' He saw the distaste on Laurence's face and added, hurriedly, 'As it were.' He lurched away from them, had a thought, and was among them once more. 'Laurence dreams he's Welsh,' he announced. 'Rita dreams she's a rabbit. Together you can dream you're Welsh rabbits.' He laughed, and was gone.

'What an awful man,' said Laurence.

'I rather like him,' said Rita. After a pause she added, 'Don't worry. I prefer you.'

'What?' gasped Laurence.

'Your place or mine?'

'What?'

'For our affair. Harvey has a point, don't you think? We undeniably have the wounds. So . . . why don't we lick them?'

Laurence was making heroic efforts not to look too horrified.

'Thank you,' said Rita.

'What for?'

'For making those heroic efforts not to look too horrified. I'm teasing, Laurence.'

'Teasing? *Teasing?* You?'

'I know! What *can* have got into me?'

Rita bobbed away from him, feeling wonderfully irresponsible, drunk with the delicious power of not caring what people thought of her. She would speak to Neville Badger before the bubble burst, as burst it must, that being the fate of bubbles.

Laurence watched her in astonishment, and scurried off, also to speak to Neville, who seemed a safe haven after the typhoons of Rita's appalling playfulness. Laurence reached him before Rita. Neville felt apprehensive. Something in Laurence's manner reminded him of Ted. He feared another conversation which he wouldn't understand.

'Neville?' said Laurence. 'May I have a word?'

Neville Badger's heart sank. It sounded ominous. 'Well . . . yes . . . of course,' he said.

Laurence interpreted Neville's apprehension as evidence of guilt. 'As one of my oldest friends,' he said, and Neville flinched slightly, 'would you think very hard before embarking on a course of action that would hurt and humiliate me?'

It was a nightmare! 'Well, of course,' he said, 'but I'm afraid I . . . er . . .'

'I think you know what I'm talking about!'

'No! I don't!' The sincerity, even desperation, in Neville's denial was unmistakeable.

Laurence stared at him. 'You don't know what I'm talking about?' he said.

'I don't know what you're talking about. What are you talking about, Laurence?'

Laurence thought furiously. Maybe he was on the wrong tack altogether. Liz could be very mischievous. 'I'm not sure,' he said. 'If you don't know what I'm talking about, I'm not sure that I know what I'm talking about.'

Laurence moved off hurriedly, and Rita was able to approach at last, wondering why the immaculate Neville Badger, that urbane and dignified man, was gawping in total mystification and disbelief, as if he were the Messiah and had just made his Second Coming in the middle of an English Christmas.

Neville recovered slowly, and waited for her opening gambit with stoic resignation. Used in these last months to being avoided, he was suddenly being approached from all sides.

'I'm all right for a lift home, am I, Neville?' Rita asked.

Neville slowly realized, with a feeling of immense relief, that somebody had said something which he understood. Perhaps the nightmare was over. 'Oh, absolutely!' he said. He put an arm round Rita and hugged her warmly, in impulsive gratitude for her comprehensibility. 'Dear Rita! You're a breath of sanity in a mad world!' He realized that he had his arm round her, and withdrew it as speedily as good manners permitted.

What *has* happened? thought Rita. Had she suddenly become a raging beauty? True, 'You're a breath of sanity in a mad world' was hardly what every woman wanted to hear from the man in her life, but Neville's hug had proclaimed a different message. Rita tried not to show how fast her heart was beating.

What *has* happened? thought Neville. Here's another one approaching. Suddenly I'm not poor embarrassing old Neville any more. I'm the sparkling epicentre of a town's social whirlpool!

'You couldn't by any chance give me a lift home,' said the new arrival.

'Absolutely,' said Neville with a hint of disappointment, for it seemed that his popularity was as much for his car as his personality. Rita noticed the hint of disappointment, and her heart leapt. 'The more the merrier,' said Neville, and Rita saw with pleasure the displeasure that Liz couldn't quite hide when she realized that she was going to have to share her lift with Rita. 'Come on, girls!' said Neville, and he put one arm round Rita and the other arm round Liz, and Rita and Liz gave each other false smiles and wondered which of them Neville would drop off first, or, more important, which he would drop off last and, as he yawned and lurched at the same time, whether he would drop off before he dropped either of them off, and Laurence and Ted tried to hide their dismay as they watched the trio depart, and Rita's last sight of Ted that night was of him lolling nonchalantly against a radiator, with steam . . . yes, steam! . . . rising from his backside! And Betty Sillitoe, flushed with her winnings, felt the pleasure drain away as she witnessed the total failure of her plans for reconciliation all round, and Neville Badger, utterly oblivious of the effect their exit was having on so many people, breezed out, his weariness forgotten in the pleasure of having a woman on each arm, and the moment he was out of the door, he remembered Jane and felt . . . yes yes! . . . a sharp pang of the old loss, so that it wouldn't matter at all which of them he dropped off last.

And at the bar Rodney Sillitoe found himself between Harvey Wedgewood and Jenny, who was handing back their empty glasses because she counted barmen among the world's underprivileged, which would have hurt the dapper, ageless Eric Siddall deeply if he'd known.

'Help me, Jenny,' said Rodney.

'What?' said Jenny cautiously, alarm bells ringing.

'I keep my chickens in conditions that would make the average Siberian labour camp look like a Masonic dinner by comparison with.'

'Oh, Rodney!'

'My chickens never go to Masonic dinners. My chickens never get the chance to roll one trouser leg up and become chief constables. You'll help me let them out this time, won't you?'

'I'm sorry,' said Jenny. 'I just don't think it's the right way to go about it.'

'I'm disappointed in you, Jenny.' Rodney turned to Harvey Wedgewood, the actor, who wasn't as pretty, but might prove more receptive. 'How do you feel about doing something really amazing tonight?'

'Absolutely,' boomed Harvey Wedgewood, the actor. 'But with whom?'

'With me.'

Harvey Wedgewood fixed a withering glare on Rodney.

'Sir!' he thundered. 'You have allowed a popular prejudice against the theatre to cloud your judgement!'

'No! Not that!' said Rodney, but Harvey Wedgewood had stalked off with a greater sense of being wronged than he had ever shown as Lear. Rodney turned to Eric Siddall, his last chance. 'Alec?' he said. 'Will you help me?'

'If I can, sir,' said Eric Siddall. 'What can be done will be done. Have no fear.' He made no further attempt to correct Rodney's belief that he was called Alec. In the end, the customer is always right. 'What can I do for you, sir? Speak and I shall listen.'

'All my chickens have come home to roost and it's time to let them roost where they like.'

'What? Sir.'

'We're going to let my chickens out of the factory. Set them free.'

Eric Siddall slid off along his invisible rails, grabbed an empty glass, and hesitated. The perfect barman was about to make his first mistake. He flung his right arm up in the air.

'Oh no,' said Rodney. 'Is she?'

Betty hurried over. To Rodney she said, 'Oh, Rodney!' To Eric she said, 'Thanks, Alec, but I thought you said you couldn't raise your right arm.'

'Oh dear!' said Eric Siddall, barman supreme.

'Oh, Betty,' said Rodney. 'Are you drunk again?'

'Not me!' said Betty. 'You!'

Betty and Rodney stared at each other, then turned to stare at Eric Siddall.

'Alec!' they said.

'Oh dear,' said the dapper, ageless Eric Siddall, suddenly naked of catch-phrases.

Now there was much putting on of coats. The room rang with good nights loud and good nights soft, good nights sincere and good nights false. There was a sudden rush for copies of *With A Hey Nonny No*. Harvey Wedgewood signed them both with pleasure.

'Your taxi's arrived, Mr Wedgewood,' said Graham Winter-green to Harvey Wedgewood's surprise, since he hadn't ordered one.

Melissa Holdsworthy, the tall, handsome sculptperson, strode out majestically with a last, meaningful glance at the suave Doctor Spreckley. Betty Sillitoe managed to get Rodney Sillitoe to the car. At last the actor was gone. Graham Wintergreen breathed a sigh of relief.

'No reconciliation, then?' said Ted, as Laurence put his coat on prior to leaving alone.

'No. Nor you?'

'No. Well . . . we're better off without them, Laurence. We are!'

'Please don't try to pretend you've done me a favour,' said Laurence.

'Laurence! Don't be like that,' said Ted. 'I mean . . . we're in the same boat, you and I. I mean . . . we are!'

Then Laurence was gone, and Paul and Jenny were approaching

with the carrycot and Elvis Simcock and Simon Rodenhurst converged on them too, and Elvis turned and gazed straight into the gauche Davina Partridge's hot, uncomfortable eyes, and she blushed and bolted for the last time that night, and the cynical Elvis said, 'I wonder how much her parents paid for the education that screwed her up. Probably sent her to a finishing school in Switzerland which finished her completely,' and Simon Rodenhurst knew that Elvis was really talking about him, and couldn't think of anything witty to say, and scowled, and scurried off with an impulse to ask Davina Partridge out to dinner, but as usual with women he was too late, the whole covey had gone. And Elvis hurried off to insult Simon one last time, and Paul and Jenny were left alone with Ted.

'You certainly find out who your friends are at a time like this,' said Ted, whose backside was now completely dry.

'We're your friends, Dad,' said Paul.

'Definitely,' said Jenny.

'I thought you were angry with me for what I did,' said Ted.

'We are,' said Paul. 'But I don't think we expect people to be perfect any more.'

Ted and Paul hugged each other, and Ted and Jenny kissed each other, and Ted set off for his lonely home, and Paul and Jenny kissed each other.

'Except you,' said Jenny.

'You what?' said Paul.

'I think you're perfect,' said Jenny.

She turned to wave cheerfully to the long-haired Carol Fordingbridge, who was in a group that were just leaving. Carol managed to catch Paul's eye, behind Jenny's back, and her look said, 'Don't worry. I'll never tell,' and then she was gone.

'I have a perfect husband,' said Jenny. 'I have a perfect marriage.'

'Oh heck,' thought Paul.

Fifth Do

May:
The Crowning of
Miss Frozen Chicken (UK)

The mournful swish of the windscreen wipers was making Rodney Sillitoe feel nervous. If only he hadn't decided to act as compère as well as host.

It was established policy to give all the regions a turn at hosting the most prestigious event in the intensive poultry farming calendar. It was established tradition that the managing director of the largest firm in the chosen region should act as host. Last year, when the chicken caravan had rolled into Dumfries, Norman Preston, the ebullient head of Border Frozen Products Ltd, had also acted as compère, and by common consent he had handled a difficult evening with skill and humour. 'Anything Norman Preston can do, I can do better,' had been the sentiments of Rodney Sillitoe, the big wheel behind Cock-A-Doodle Chickens. Now he wasn't so sure. He wished he'd chosen one of the disc jockeys from Radio Gadd.

He had been thrilled to learn that the Grand Universal Hotel would be opening at last a fortnight before the crowning. Instead of the drab ballroom of the clapped-out Angel, his great moment would come in the gleaming new Royalty Suite of the Grand Universal. Now he wasn't so sure about that either. It would be too new, too impersonal, too efficient. He longed for the cosy, raddled charm of the Angel. He even felt nostalgic about Alec Skiddaw's boils. What was good enough for Terry Wogan, Ian Botham, Des O'Connor, Dame Peggy Ashcroft, General Dayan, Frank Carson, Michael Heseltine, Professor A. J. Ayer and Joan Sutherland, should have been good enough for him.

Rodney sighed deeply as he pulled off the Flannerly Roundabout into the cul-de-sac. Onto the top of the signpost, which for many years had read 'C.E.G.B. Only', the Automobile Association had tacked a rather pathetic small yellow sign which stated, but only for those with excellent eyesight, 'Hotel And'.

'It'll be all right,' said Betty Sillitoe, who was overdressed as usual.

'Welcome to Yorkshire's first Grand Universal Hotel,' said a dripping billboard.

'I wonder if I was wise to invite Ted,' said Rodney Sillitoe.

Twenty minutes later the cold, relentless spring rain was still falling on the bare flowerbeds and immature saplings of the muddy, semi-landscaped gardens of the Grand Universal Hotel. In front of the hotel, facing the ring road, the flags of all the nations were flapping petulantly in the breeze, indignant at landing up in this bleak corner of the globe. Beside the hotel, a large car park, studded with yet more immature trees which in less than twenty years might become adequate windbreaks, stretched down to the concrete banks of the muddied, rain-swollen Gadd.

Ted Simcock looked up defiantly at the glass-and-concrete structure of the hotel. He was delighted to see that it was already disfigured by one narrow, rusty, dribbling stain. He hoped it was a harbinger of structural problems to come.

The glass doors hissed open like alarmed snakes at his approach, and hissed shut behind him with the disapproval of puritanical women. He walked smack into a wall of plastic sexuality. There was a faint smell of air freshener. Piped music tinkled all about him, and in the centre of the vast foyer a fountain tinkled. He found it hard to lift his feet across the luxurious carpet. He felt clumsy, cloddish, wet. He was sure everyone knew that he was bankrupt. He glared about him with a defiance which he thought concealed, but which in fact revealed, his lack of confidence. His prized raincoat, the most expensive that Beacock and Larkin's stocked, felt like a flasher's mac. How fervently he wished that he didn't have to ask the way to the Royalty Suite.

To his right, a huge noticeboard told him, uselessly, what time it was at that moment in every Grand Universal Hotel in the world.

Behind the reception desk, a much smaller noticeboard announced the day's events. 'Royalty Suite: Miss Frozen Chicken (UK). Hawaiian Room: Consolidated Linen. Balinese Room: Mr E. G. Davies (Private Party). Your duty manager: Mr F. Lombardo.'

The music tinkled to a stop, and a sing-song female voice, its human equivalent, announced, 'We have a message for Sir Hamish McTaggart. Will Sir Hamish McTaggart please contact the reception desk situated in the ground floor foyer immediately? Thank you.'

Ted felt tempted to pretend that he was Sir Hamish McTaggart, a rich eccentric in his flasher's mac. It was lucky he didn't. There was no Sir Hamish McTaggart. There was no Consolidated Linen or Mr E. G. Davies (Private Party). Early bookings were poor, and the manager, Mr Gilbert Pilgrim, was as frightened of looking a failure as Ted.

The Royalty Suite was on the first floor. Ted only took the lift because he couldn't find any stairs. There wasn't the slightest noise when the doors closed, no sickening lurch of his nervous stomach as they set off, not a groan, not a hiss, not a shudder, to indicate that they were moving. Ted was reluctantly impressed.

The doors slid open silently, and he stepped back into the foyer.

'Sorry, sir. Bugger's been on the blink all week,' said an elderly porter, who appeared to be wearing the uniform of a colonel in the New Zealand Army.

He was quite surprised when Ted gave him fifty pee.

The patriotically decorated bar of the Royalty Suite was airy, well lit and gleaming. The carpet was red. The wide, square armchairs were blue. The walls were white. Everything was set at right angles. The chrome ashtrays revolved when pressed, and could mash large cigars into tiny pieces.

The moment Rodney Sillitoe saw Ted, he approached him. The room had an enormous capacity for devouring crowds and didn't yet appear at all full, but he knew that it would take courage for Ted to enter it.

'Ted!' he said. Ted would have known who he was even if he hadn't been his best friend, because Rodney wore a name tag. All the representatives of the intensive poultry industry wore name tags. 'I'm glad you came!'

Ted took some pieces of paper from his pocket, and handed one to Rodney.

'*Thank you for inviting me*,' read Rodney. 'What's up, Ted? Have you lost your voice?'

Ted handed another piece of paper to Rodney, with grim satisfaction.

'*No. I'm not talking to you*,' read Rodney. 'Ted! There's no need to take it like that.'

But Ted was already on his way to the bar, by a circuitous route which took him right past Simon Rodenhurst, of Trellis, Trellis, Openshaw and Finch, so that good manners obliged Simon to turn away from a group of name-tagged chicken executives to greet him.

'Ted! Good to see you!' lied Simon.

Ted handed Simon one of his pieces of paper.

'*Or to you*,' read Simon. 'What?'

But Ted hadn't waited for a reply.

The males wore drab, sombre suits. The females wore colourful, glamorous evening dresses. It was the bird world in reverse. Simon joined drab Rodney and his gleaming gold-and-red mate Betty.

'Ted wouldn't talk to me,' he said.

'He isn't talking to me,' said Rodney. 'He's accepted my invitation, and he isn't talking to me.'

'I'll talk to him,' said Betty.

'Will he talk to you?' said Simon Rodenhurst.

'If he doesn't, I'll give him a talking to such as he's never had,' said Betty Sillitoe.

'Thank you for inviting me,' said Laurence Rodenhurst.

'Don't thank me,' said the immaculate Neville Badger. 'Thank Cock-A-Doodle Chickens. Rodney's invited me and my guests at his expense. It's my reward for fifteen years of legal service. I think he genuinely believes he's doing me a favour.'

'And you thought that if you have to endure it, why shouldn't I?'

'Exactly. No!'

'Neville?' Laurence led Neville over to the wide windows, which afforded an excellent view over the rain-drenched ring road. All the main function rooms looked east, away from the town, over the ring road to the twee, red-brick houses of an almost completed executive housing estate. Right opposite the hotel and the flags of all the nations, across the busy, perilous ring road, there was a smaller row of sodden, flapping flags marking the Show House, which would soon afford its lucky executive purchaser a magnificent view of the Grand Universal Hotel. 'I'm probably being a bit rude, as your guest,' said Laurence, 'but will you give me a straight answer to a straight question?'

'It depends what the question is,' said Neville Badger frankly.

'The question is . . .' Laurence pressed down on an ashtray. Its top spun fiercely, as it mashed the air. '. . . are you involved in an intimate relationship with Liz?'

'This is what you were hinting at the horse-racing evening, isn't it? I didn't understand at the time.'

'Don't prevaricate. You aren't in court now. Are you having an affair with my wife?'

'Certainly not! When I realized that must be what you'd been driving at, I couldn't understand why. Why on earth should you think that?'

'On the slenderest evidence. Liz told me she loved you.'

'What???'

A taxi detached itself from the stream of traffic, and slid into the cul-de-sac. It carried Rita Simcock. She hated spending money on taxis, but if she'd come by bus she'd have got splashed with mud between the ring road and the hotel, and she didn't want Neville to see her all splashed with mud.

Neville, unaware of this, was staring at Laurence with something near to horror. Laurence didn't take his eyes off the ring road.

'She said it was serious and the real thing,' he said.

'She did? Good Lord. Good Lord! She said . . . she loved me? I assure you this is complete news to me, Laurence.'

'Is it? You took her to dinner at the Clissold Lodge last Thursday fortnight.'

'My God! Have you been employing a private detective?'

'The wine waiter told me. He's a patient of mine. He's an awful gossip.'

'He's an awful wine waiter. I've seen Liz twice since that

evening at the golf club. It was pleasant. Intimate in the manner of old friends. But totally platonic. Well, there may have been the vaguest tingle of sexuality. You know Liz.'

'Who doesn't?'

'Me, in that sense, I do assure you,' said Neville Badger, with all the hurt dignity at his command.

Betty Sillitoe waited until Ted had got his drink from the dark, intense Alec Skiddaw, who had seen not only the signed photographs but also the writing on the wall, and had left the Angel the moment the Grand Universal opened.

'Hello, Ted,' she said, approaching him warily. 'I gather you aren't talking to Rodney.'

Ted didn't reply.

'Aren't you talking to me?' she asked.

'I'm talking to you, Betty,' said Ted wearily. 'I've no quarrel with you.'

They sat, side by side, on the square blue chairs with gleaming chrome arms.

'Ted!' said Betty. 'Life's too short. Rodney's your best friend.'

'Was.'

'Ted!'

'Was, Betty! I mean . . . Betty . . . it was my life, the foundry.'

'It was a tumble-down mess of rusting sheds.'

'It was mine, Betty. I mean . . . it made things. Good things. The best toasting forks this side of Scandinavia. I mean . . . it did. So when it fails, what does my "best friend" do? He rushes in and buys it. I mean . . . stupid birds crapping on the very spot where quality door knockers had been lovingly fashioned by skilled craftsmen. I mean!'

'You got a quick sale at an excellent price. Rodney was helping you in your fight to return to solvency.'

'It wasn't an excellent price. It was the market price.'

'For a site in that condition in that area sold at that speed under those circumstances, the market price was an excellent price.'

'He was helping himself. A quick sale when he needed it. Be honest, Betty. He was.'

'I won't deny it was convenient. But . . . business is business.'

'Exactly. This is it. It doesn't count for much, when business is concerned, doesn't lifelong friendship. So . . . I won't speak to him.'

Tinkle tinkle of piped music. God, its complacency was irritating when you were angry. And Betty was angry. It was another reversal of bird life, the glamorous female being fiercely protective of her drab mate. She pulled angrily at her chair to swing it round, to face Ted, to use her anger. But the bloody things were fixed to the floor. Everything conspired to keep people at a distance from each other. Tinkle tinkle. Only piped emotions please. 'This is his big night,' she said, fighting her anger down. 'Please . . . for me . . . don't spoil his big night.'

'I'm sorry,' said Ted.

'Why have you come?' said Betty.

'To spoil his big night,' said Ted.

Laurence Rodenhurst and Neville Badger were also finding that the only way to sit was side by side. If you sat facing each other, you were so far apart that you had to shout. It reminded Laurence of an airport lounge. No wonder he felt a tension which grew with every tinkle of music, so carefully chosen to dispel tension by Grand Universal's consultant industrial psychologists.

'Do you promise me there's nothing behind these dinners with Liz?' he asked tensely.

'Nothing. I've taken Rita out more than Liz.'

'Maybe, but only because you keep having to make up to her for being rude to her.'

'I suppose so, though actually I find her quite good company. I admire her spirit in refusing to have Ted back.'

'Do you admire Liz's spirit in refusing to come back to me?'

'That's different. I wish she would come back to you.'

'Will you . . .?' Laurence closed his eyes. He found appealing for help difficult. 'Will you use your influence to make one last appeal to her? As my oldest friend.'

'Well, if you put it that way, I . . . yes . . . I'll talk to her tonight.'

'Tonight?'

'She's my other guest.' Laurence looked appalled. 'I thought I'd try a bit of peacemaking. Get you together in public, where you're forced to be polite.'

233

'That principle doesn't seem to have worked too brilliantly recently,' said Laurence.

Paul Simcock looked round the corridor furtively, for evidence of closed circuit television. Then he realized that, if anybody was watching him on some distant screen, the last thing he should be looking was furtive, so he tried to look extremely casual, but that didn't work very well, and it was all wasted effort anyway, because there was no closed circuit television.

'Do we have to?' he said again.

'There's nothing illegal in opening a door,' said Jenny.

'You can't say it's just opening a door, when we know perfectly well that fifteen fanatical feminists are going to pour in through it and disrupt the crowning.'

The corridor had a green carpet. There were tubs of plastic flowers, complete with plastic greenfly. On one side there were several small windows and, on the other side, doors numbered 108–126. The very absence of atmosphere seemed redolent of furtive sexuality.

'Why can't they take their chance coming in the front door?' said Paul, stopping to look out of a window onto a small gravel courtyard studded with weeds, and overlooked by the windows of other corridors.

'It's too risky,' said Jenny. 'There's bound to be a security system.'

'Exactly,' said Paul. 'So this is risky.'

'I'll do it on my own if you're scared.'

'Of course I'm not scared. It's just that . . . . he's my Uncle Rodney.'

'He isn't a real uncle. He's just a friend.'

Paul was wearing his elderly teenage suit, Jenny a multi-coloured long dress hand-knitted in the Punjab.

'"Just a friend"? Is anything more important than friendship?' said Paul.

'Yes. Right and wrong. Justice. Sexual equality. Human dignity.'

'I know, but our Elvis works for him.'

'More shame on him. With a philosophy degree he ought to know it's wrong to keep chickens in conditions of abject misery.'

'With a philosophy degree he knows how superior people are to chickens.'

'Not morally. Chickens don't keep people cooped up in conditions of abject misery.'

'They would if they were superior to people.'

'We don't know that. Maybe they'd be wonderful employers.'

'Anyway, they aren't protesting about cruelty to chickens.'

'Er . . . I think there may be some animal rights people as well.'

'Oh, Jenny! I mean you yourself have refused twice to let Uncle Rodney's chickens out.'

'Because I've realized it's the wrong way to do it! You can't suddenly say to a chicken, "Push off. You're free-range now." It's like letting prisoners out with no after-care.'

A slim, almost thin girl came down the corridor in a swimsuit. She wore a sash which proclaimed 'Miss West Midland Oven-Ready Poultry'. She passed them rather hesitantly, and they suddenly became deeply interested in gravel.

Paul tried not to turn to look at the girl's back view, but it didn't prove possible. Her legs and arms were too thin, and she had goose pimples, but her bott . . .!

'Miss West Midland Oven-Ready Poultry!' said Jenny, as soon as the girl had disappeared round the corner. 'It's humiliating.'

'Oh. Yes. Right.'

'Treated as if she's a lump of meat, like the chickens.'

'Exactly.'

'Battery people.'

'Appalling.'

'Well come on, then.'

'Right.'

Paul and Jenny continued towards the other end of the corridor. As soon as they had disappeared round their corner, the girl peered round her corner, saw that the coast was clear, and hurried back along the corridor.

She knocked on the door of room 114. The door opened almost immediately, and she stepped into the room.

Rita's increasing confidence in entering crowded rooms was suffering a setback. On the credit side, she was entirely free of mud, but this had to be balanced against the fact that she was wearing one of her bottle-green outfits which she now knew to be hideous. Yet she couldn't bear to get rid of all those old clothes. Waste and extravagance were wrong. Oh God, there was Ted. Avoid him without having to snub him. Make a beeline for Betty.

'Thanks for the invitation, Betty.'

'Well, we just hope that if you meet Ted often enough, it'll lead to a reconciliation.'

'Is it you who've invited Ted tonight?'

'Yes.'

'Oh, Betty!'

'Rita! You and Ted breaking up. Ted refusing to talk to Rodney. It's as if a whole era is ending.'

'Maybe it is, Betty,' said Rita. 'Eras do.'

At the back of the hotel, at the end of a labyrinth of characterless corridors, a door marked 'Emergency Exit' led to a flight of stone steps. At the bottom there was another door, which opened only from the inside. Jenny pushed this door open, and Paul hurried out into the rain.

He hurtled across a muddy, uneven, lunar landscape which would one day be a landscaped garden. He splashed through puddles as he searched for something with which to prop the door open. He felt as if eleven security guards were training rifles on him.

He picked up a large stone. An indignant toad jumped off and terrified him. He splashed back to safety, wondering how he would react if he should ever find himself under gunfire. Would he have the courage to move at all? Would he have the courage not to?

They wedged the stone against the door, holding it open. Again, Paul felt that he was being watched. He turned to look. He caught a brief glimpse of faded blue jeans at the top of the steps, and a shapely backside. He was almost certain that it was a girl's.

'Rita?'

They sat side by side in the thinly populated rows of chairs. They would have had a good view of the departures board, if it *had* been an airport lounge. Rita hoped Betty wasn't going to appeal to her to appeal to Ted to talk to Rodney. She would never appeal to him about anything again.

'Not being inquisitive, Rita . . . '

Rita braced herself for the inquisition.

'. . . but did there turn out to be anything in that business with Neville?'

Rita's heart began to pump at the mention of his name. This was ridiculous. 'I think so, yes,' she said cautiously.

'What do you mean, you "think so"?'

'Well. . .' Rita waited till a man with a name tag had passed by. She didn't want J. Hedley Watkins overhearing her private business. '. . . he keeps taking me out to dinner. He's very charming. Very generous. He seems to like me, but it never gets any further than a friendly good-night kiss. I think I'm the first woman he's taken out since his wife died, and he's having to learn the whole process of going out with somebody else step by step. I . . .' She glanced round the room. Neville was miles away. She'd have to go and say hello to him soon. 'I think I'm falling in love with him.'

'Rita!'

'Don't sound so shocked. I'm not a nun. My God, I must have led a dim sort of life. You all seem to think I'm about as emotional as a pumice stone. Be honest with me, Betty. Does a relationship between me and Neville strike you as totally impossible?'

'I wouldn't say that. I've seen the most unlikely and unsuitable liaisons.'

'Thank you very much.'

'Oh, Rita!' Betty Sillitoe reached out and touched Rita's arm. 'All this change! What'll happen to our friendship?'

'It'll survive, if it means anything.' Rita turned to look Betty straight in the eyes, and Betty flinched, as if Rita were a pea-shooter. 'If it doesn't, why should it survive? You two don't need me. You have so much affection for each other.'

'That's true.' Betty sighed. 'Oh God. I feel sick with nerves for him. I just hope he doesn't get drunk.'

'He oughtn't to,' said Rita. 'According to my calculations, it's your turn.'

Betty gawped. 'What on earth do you mean?' she said.

'Nothing.'

'Are you suggesting Rodney and I take it in turns to get drunk?'

'Well . . . it does tend to happen like that.'

'I see!' Betty stood up abruptly. 'Well . . . we do learn about the value of our friendships.'

'Betty! It's one of the many things we love and adore about you.'

But Betty Sillitoe had swept off towards the bar. Rita watched her stop abruptly as she realized that she might look as if she were about to fulfil Rita's prediction. She turned, gave Rita a defiant glare, and swept out towards the toilets, for want of anywhere better to go.

'Comment on it and I'll belt you one,' said the cynical Elvis Simcock.

'Comment on what?' said Simon Rodenhurst, of Trellis, Trellis, Openshaw and Finch.

'My name tag. *Elvis* Simcock. My shame revealed for all the world to see.'

'Why are you wearing it?'

'Because I'm a masochist.'

'What?'

'Because I have to, you twit. Philosophy graduate learns hard lesson about nature of freedom.'

'I presume you know that I don't like being called a twit,' said Simon Rodenhurst.

'Of course. That's why I call you a twit, you twit.'

'Do you know why I don't like being called a twit?'

'Because it offends your inflated ego.'

'Utterly wrong! It's because I know I'm a twit, you twit.'

'What?'

'Do you think I chose to be a twit?'

Elvis was appalled. 'Simon! Please!' he said. 'This is terrible. We'll end up as friends if you go on like this.'

Jenny and Paul entered nonchalantly. They approached Simon and Elvis nonchalantly. 'Hello,' they said nonchalantly.

'What have you two been up to?' said Elvis.

'Nothing. Nothing at all. Have we, Jenny?' said Paul nonchalantly.

'No. Nothing,' said Jenny nonchalantly. 'Why?'

'You look too nonchalant to be true,' said Elvis.

'I think some swift naughties have been going on,' said Simon.

'Oh belt up, you twit,' said Paul.

On their way to the bar, Paul and Jenny met Rodney Sillitoe. He greeted them with a warmth that made them feel dreadfully guilty. Jenny blushed as he kissed her.

'No need to blush,' he said. 'You're forgiven for not helping me let my chickens out. I'm glad you didn't.' And Jenny blushed all the more. Rodney pushed on towards the bar. Jenny called after him, 'You didn't forget the two vegetarian meals, did you?' and Ted, approaching to greet them now that Rodney had gone, stopped dead in his tracks.

'Two?' he said. 'You've not turned vegetarian as well, Paul?'

'Yes.'

'I credited you with a mind of your own, but your mother was right.' Ted closed his eyes, as if wishing to erase his mention of Paul's mother.

'I do have a mind of my own,' said Paul. 'It so happens that when I use my mind of my own I find that my mind of my own finds that most of what Jenny thinks with her mind of her own is right.'

'Paul doesn't have any false machismo hang-ups which force him to argue just to assert his independence,' explained Jenny.

'Oh good, I am glad,' said Ted, and he stomped off sourly.

'Did I ever tell you about my ex-brother-in-law from Falkirk, who was an income tax inspector and an amateur ventriloquist, and his first wife did these amazing dog impressions,' said the dark, intense Alec Skiddaw, as he served Rodney his large drink.

'You certainly did, Eric,' said Rodney. 'A fascinating tale.'

'Alec! Well, the most amazing thing has happened.'

'Has it really? How amazing! Excuse me. I have to pop out for a moment.'

'It won't take a minute,' said Alec Skiddaw intensely as he gave Rodney his change. 'He was in this motel with his second wife, who came from Nailsworth . . .'

'Look, I'm sorry,' said Rodney. 'I really do have to go. You see, in past years the girls have paraded after dinner in their swimsuits, then there's been entertainment while they've changed into their sophisticated evening wear, and there's still been the five finalists to interview after that, and the judging hasn't ended till nearly midnight, and people have lost interest.'

In the face of this conversational onslaught, Alec Skiddaw

darkly fingered what he suspected to be the beginnings of the first boil he'd had since he'd joined Grand Universal. He'd begun to think that the boost to his morale had transported him into a happier, boil-free existence.

'Plus which,' continued the big wheel behind Cock-A-Doodle Chickens remorselessly, 'last year's comedian managed to offend the Irish, the Welsh, the Jews, the Mayor of Dumfries and our guest colleagues from the tandoori chicken industry, who walked out. So this year we've dispensed with the entertainment, which will be a big improvement, and they're parading in their swimsuits before dinner and changing into their sophisticated evening wear during dinner. I've got to go and make sure they've grasped all that. They aren't all Einsteins.'

'I could have told you the whole story twice by now,' said Alec Skiddaw.

Rodney Sillitoe moved off, taking his drink with him. He intended to keep himself nicely topped up until his duties were over.

Jenny had waited reasonably patiently through all this, and wasn't too upset when Alec Skiddaw served the bluff Graham Wintergreen, of the golf club, next. But when he began to tell Graham Wintergreen the tale of his ex-brother-in-law, she snapped.

'Excuse me,' she called out. 'Are we going to have to wait all night while you read "A Book At Bedtime"?'

'I do apologize for being a human being, madam,' said Alec Skiddaw.

'I'm going to complain to the manager about your attitude,' said Jenny.

'Jenny!' said Paul, trying to keep up with her as she made her way to the door. 'You aren't one of those trendy upper-middle-class socialists who treat real working people like dirt.'

'Oh!' said Jenny.

'We laugh at people like that, Jenny! That trendy couple who went to that play about the evils of apartheid and were rude to the coloured girl in the box office. That left-wing playwright who had that play about the horrors of elitism on at the technical college, and it was so obscure that nobody could understand it except other left-wing playwrights.'

Jenny gasped, and ran from the room.

Paul hurried after her, and came face to face with Rodney Sillitoe.

'Ah! Paul! The very man,' said Rodney.

'I can't stop,' said Paul. 'I've got to talk to Jenny.'

'You've got to talk to Carol Fordingbridge and all. She says it's urgent.'

Rita watched Neville Badger stand up and walk away from Laurence. Her heart missed a beat. Her legs refused to move. By the time she had got herself to her feet, she had already realized that Neville was on his way to greet Liz, who had just entered, nine months pregnant and still alluring.

She sat down again, and watched.

'Hello, Liz, you look . . .!' said Neville. Liz hoped that if he had finished the sentence he'd have said 'beautiful' and not 'enormous'. Thank goodness the human eye couldn't detect the thumping of hearts. 'Come and meet my other guest.'

'Other guest?' She tried valiantly to hide her disappointment.

'Laurence.'

Liz tried valiantly to hide her horror. The object of her hidden horror and disappointment approached across the vastness of the angular room, concealing . . . what?

'Hello, Liz,' he quipped.

'Hello, Laurence,' was her sparkling rejoinder.

The trio were an islet of silence, in a rippling river of talk.

'Oh dear,' said the immaculate Neville Badger. 'I feel rather like the Secretary General of the United Nations.'

The long-haired Carol Fordingbridge stood in front of the mirror in room 205 in her bright golden swimsuit, and tried to see what the judges would see. They would certainly see her magnificent long hair, but was length of hair an important factor? Her breasts didn't seem quite large enough, her waist quite slim enough, her hips quite rounded enough. Her calves were fractionally muscular. She told herself that she felt happy with her body, that men liked it, that she was incredibly lucky, that the contest was all nonsense anyway, that it really didn't matter whether she won or not.

It was no use. It was the most important day of her life. Winning could change her life.

She tried several poses, hoping to make her breasts look larger.

Her sophisticated evening wear was lying on the mauve coverlet of the bed, with clean undies beside it.

She jumped when the knock on the door came, even though she was expecting it.

'Come in,' she said. Too late, she thought of hiding the undies.

Paul came in. He too was nervous. 'What is this?' he said. 'Good God!' he added, as he saw her swimsuit.

'I've aimed to be stunning but tasteful. Do you like it?'

'Oh. Yes.' He looked round the impersonal, fawn-and-mauve bedroom. Anywhere rather than at her stomach. He examined the etching which hung above the bed. It showed the North Bridge in olden days. The Gadd was lined with half-timbered hostelries leaning tipsily towards each other, where now there stood the massive DIY Centre. Oh God, let her not be pregnant. He ventured a quick, nervous look at her stomach. It looked reassuringly flat. 'Yes,' he repeated. Perhaps she'd sent for him so that he could take her, there and then. She looked tense and tension sometimes made people very sexy. If she did want him to take her, would he be a) thrilled b) appalled c) both d) indifferent? 'Very much. Lovely.' He couldn't. Not with Jenny outside. Not with Uncle Rodney knowing where he was. 'Very much. As you say, stunning but tasteful.' He felt relieved at discovering that he knew that he wouldn't take her, and then he felt disappointed at discovering that he felt relieved. He felt a wave of desire. He felt that he would take her. The fear switched his desire off. 'I like it a lot. I . . . er . . . what do you want, Carol?'

'Sit down.'

Carol Fordingbridge sat in the armchair. Paul removed a sash which was lying on the upright chair by the writing desk. It read 'Miss Cock-A-Doodle Chickens.'

'Good God,' he said, and sat down.

'When you had your one-night stand with me, you never dreamt you were having the future winner of the in-house beauty contest and second favourite for Miss Frozen Chicken (UK), did you?' she said.

'Oh God,' he said.

'I'm 9–2 at Ladbrokes and 6–1 at William Hill's.'

'Carol? Why have you dragged me here?'

'I saw you and Jenny opening that door. Why?'

His first reaction was of relief. She wasn't pregnant. She didn't want him to take her there and then. But the relief didn't last long. He was in trouble.

'We like fresh air,' he said, flinching at the lameness of his reply.

'Paul! I know Jenny. What are you two up to?'

'I can't tell you.'

He held his hands clasped together, for fear one of them would find its way onto one of Carol's magnificent knees.

'Do you want me to tell Jenny about us?' she demanded. '"Hello, Jenny. Your heroic, caring, feminist husband had it off with me the night after his son was born."'

'You wouldn't.'

'Wouldn't I? This is my big night.'

There was silence. Paul knew that he would have to be the one to break it. He let it go on a little longer, to preserve his dignity. He was surprised to find that he could be as calculating as that.

'We're letting in a group of protestors against exploitation of women . . . and chickens. They're going to disrupt the judging.'

'Get it called off or I'll tell Jenny.'

'You don't need to tell her. Why don't you just tell the authorities what's going to happen? You needn't tell them how you found out or about us being involved.'

'I can't. I've a good chance of winning.'

'Well, that would improve it. You'd be a heroine.'

'Exactly. So if they gave me the title then, it'd look as if that was why they were giving it, so they wouldn't give it. So you get it called off or I'll tell Jenny.'

'But Carol! We have to do it. Exploiting female flesh is wrong, and fatally inhibits the establishment of female equality through all aspects of human endeavour. Can't you see that? There'll never be an equal number of women MPs and women judges while women agree to be assessed on beauty rather than brains.'

'It isn't just beauty. There's personality and deportment. That's the next best thing to brains.'

'Personality and deportment! It's an insult.'

He loved Jenny so much. He was full of indignation on her behalf. He hated his own sexuality, which had made him behave so out of character. There were two Pauls – sensitive man and selfish animal. He looked at Carol Fordingbridge's flesh, so near to him, and was pleased to find that it no longer held any appeal for him: it was utterly theoretical in its attractions.

'This beauty contest can open avenues for me that I never dreamt of,' Carol was saying. 'Miss Frozen Chicken (UK) 1981 went on to be Miss Kidderminster, Miss West Mercia and Miss European Processed Meat Products (Category Two). It's my chance to escape from the "Take a letter, Miss Fordingbridge" syndrome, which is female exploitation.'

'I can see that from your point of view,' he said, 'but from the point of view of women as a whole . . .'

'From the point of view of women as a whole, why don't you protest about my sister?' She leapt up, towered over him, paced the little bedroom like a tigress. She was magnificent. He adored her. He had to fight the tiger in him. 'She works on the supermarket check-out. Hour after hour taking dog food and baked beans and Hungarian courgettes and frozen bubble-and-squeak out of wire baskets and having to ring for Miss Priddle because there's no price on them, and Miss Priddle acting as if it's *her* fault. Hour after hour with hardly a word of human contact, till her head buzzes and aches and her brain dries up and she comes home pale and knackered, just because she doesn't happen to be as attractive as me. That's exploitation of women. This is fun.'

There were times when Paul wished he'd never developed a moral conscience at all. Moral issues were so complicated.

'I agree maybe we should go down there as well,' he said, feeling like a candidate who is failing to convince on the doorstep at the end of a very long day, 'but that doesn't make this right.'

There was a knock on the door. 'Two minutes, Miss Fordingbridge.'

'Right.'

'How can I call it off, anyway?' he said, with a last flicker of doomed defiance. 'What'll I tell Jenny?'

'That's your problem.'

'Oh heck.'

When Jenny returned to the Royalty Suite, her first thought was to apologize to Alec Skiddaw. The piped music still tinkled, and there was a harsh, grating, unlovely sound as a group of middle-aged men laughed at a dirty joke told by Mr Gilbert Pilgrim, the manager, who had been invited as a guest at this, the first major function in his hotel. Despite his efforts to be one of the lads, Mr Gilbert Pilgrim remained a man whom one could never think of as mere Gilbert Pilgrim, without the 'Mr'. He was short and dark-haired, with a bulbous nose.

Alec Skiddaw was talking to the classless Nigel Thick, who was recording the evening for posterity. Nigel Thick was saying 'terrific' and 'amazing' at suspiciously regular intervals.

Jenny waited patiently. At last Alec Skiddaw saw her and broke off. 'Yes, madam?' he said, so coldly that she almost didn't apologize after all.

'I want to apologize for my behaviour just now,' she said. 'It was inexcusable.'

'Thank you very much indeed, madam,' said the dark, intense Alec Skiddaw, looking somewhat embarrassed.

Jenny moved on, her good deed done. She approached Rodney Sillitoe, who had just finished his rounds of the contestants.

'Where's Paul?' she asked.

'He was taken short,' whispered Rodney. Inspired lies had never been his forte.

Neville Badger had left Laurence and Liz on their own, in the increasingly faint hope that this would force them to talk to each other. Indecision swept over Rita. Should she approach him? Would he approach her? He didn't approach her. She must approach him. He seemed quite happy to be approached. She hoped he couldn't see how flustered she was.

'Hello, Rita,' he said – quite warmly, she thought.

'Hello, Neville. Have you been avoiding me?' Rita wished she hadn't said that, but Neville didn't seem to mind.

'Good Lord, no!' he said. 'No! I've been rather occupied. Attempting reconciliations.' He shook his head slowly, in disappointed mystification at the behaviour of the human race.

'Thank you for last Tuesday,' said Rita. 'It was a lovely evening.'

'It was, wasn't it? I thought it was a good place.'

They'd been to the new Italian place in Tannergate. Neville had said that, next time, Rita must try the seafood salad. But when would the next time be? There was a brief pause, during which he might have asked her to dinner again, but didn't. Perhaps he was shy. He seemed shy. She must be positive. She didn't feel positive.

'I . . . er . . .' she began. Come on, Rita. It's really very simple. And he can always say 'no' if he doesn't want to. 'I . . . er . . . I wondered if you'd care to brave the perils of my cooking . . .' Oh why had she phrased it so coyly? '. . . and come to dinner some time.'

'That would be lovely, Rita! I'd like that!'

Before they had a chance to discuss dates, the music stopped and a disembodied male voice announced, 'Are about to begin. Would you kindly make your way to the flexible multi-purpose function room? Thank you. Ladies and gentlemen, the main events of the evening.'

There was laughter and cheering at this recorded cock-up. A vein throbbed dangerously near the left temple of Mr Gilbert Pilgrim, the manager. Rodney Sillitoe felt a pit opening up in his stomach. They should have stuck to the Angel. What further teething troubles would there be? Betty clutched at him, perhaps to give support, perhaps to receive it, perhaps a bit of both.

Two panels in the wall that separated the bar from the flexible multi-purpose function room slid open without snags. Neville Badger escorted Laurence and Liz. Laurence wore a slightly twisted smile that seemed to have been set in concrete. Liz was approached by Simon, who took the arm of his pregnant mother. He smiled bravely, trying to ignore her swollen belly, pretending that this embarrassingly obvious evidence of her recent regrettable peccadillo didn't worry him in the slightest. Rodney assured Jenny that Paul would find them, and she drifted in with the rest of the gathering. Rodney frowned as he heard Elvis telling a mystified EEC Rolled Turkey Breasts Standards Coordinator that flexible multi-purpose function room sounded like some form of advanced superloo.

Slowly they edged through into the main room, like sand through an egg timer. The room was brilliantly lit, and filled with tables. At one end there was a stage, with a prettily curved

stairway at each end. Rodney made his way onto the stage, while
the guests hunted for their places. Some of the tables were laid for
four, others for six. The elegant cutlery was the admired product of
Danish craftsmen, while the artisans of the five towns need have
felt no less proud of the china. The lime-green napkins had been
most elegantly arranged. Each place setting had a red, white and
blue name card, stuck in the turbot mousse or, in the case of the
cards that read 'Mr P. Simcock' and 'Mrs J. Simcock', the carrot
mousse. The mousses looked like tiny sandcastles, topped by
Union Jacks.

Simon Rodenhurst, although invited by Rodney in return for
services rendered in the purchase of the Jupiter Foundry, was
sitting with his parents and Neville, to make up a four. Paul and
Jenny, should they both be present, would make up a six with the
Sillitoes and Ted and Rita.

Immediately below the stage, there was a table with six pencils
and six notepads in addition to the table settings. This was the
judges' table. The judges were, in descending order of age, Mr
Edgar Hamilton (69), president of the Food Additives Consultancy Council; Alderman George Cornwallis (64), monumental mason and mayor; Mr Jimmy Parsons (58), manager of the
United, formerly a star with Tottenham Hotspur, Middles-
brough, Fulham, Hereford, Halifax, Crewe, Barnet, Kettering,
Northwich Victoria and Burton Albion, known as 'Lino' because
he was so often on the floor; Miss Ginny Fenwick (55), fashion
editor of the *Argus*, who was also Marjorie Boon, cookery editor of
the *Argus*, Gloria Honeycake, agony aunt of the *Argus*, Auntie
Daphne, compiler of Kiddies' Korner for the *Argus*, and Mr
Binoculars, tipster for the *Argus*; Craig Welting (50), managing
director of Radio Gadd, formerly Dutch correspondent of the
Australian Broadcasting Corporation, and author of one play, a
brilliantly inventive farce about a Dutch correspondent of the
Australian Broadcasting Corporation, which had never been
performed because its title *No Litter, Please, We're Dutch*
reminded everybody of another, only marginally less inventive
farce; and the baby of the bunch, Miss Amaryllis Thrupp (22),
real name Lesley Brown (30), whose recent Juliet had led even
hardened aficionados of the Theatre Royal Repertory Company to
declare that they had never seen anything of quite that standard in

247

their lives.

The lights dimmed. Rodney Sillitoe stood in a spotlight at the microphone. Betty Sillitoe, who was overanxious as usual, clutched at Rita in panic. Nigel Thick was poised, classlessly, for action. Laurence looked as if rigor mortis had set in. The long process of finding this year's Miss Frozen Chicken (UK) was about to begin.

Silence fell. For a dreadful moment Betty thought that Rodney was suffering some kind of nervous paralysis. Then he spoke, and his voice, though tense and nervous, was strong and clear.

'Good evening,' he said. 'I'm delighted to inform you that we aren't having chicken tonight.'

There was laughter and applause. Betty had never felt prouder of Rodney than at that moment. Eat your heart out, Terry Wogan.

'So now, without further ado,' thundered Rodney, 'let's meet, in a veritable cornucopia of beauty and charm, the twenty young lovelies who have been selected by the regions of our great boom industry. Don't forget. The judges . . .' He inclined his head slightly, in the direction of those worthies. '. . . are looking not only for beauty and physical attributes, but also for style, elegance, charm, personality, intelligence, honesty and moral fibre.'

Unseen by each other in the dim light, Laurence and Elvis each raised an eyebrow, briefly uniting their divided families in a gesture of cynicism.

'Ladies and gentlemen, meet beauty number one, Hannah Macpherson, of Border Frozen Produce Ltd,' said Rodney.

There was a fanfare. Hannah Macpherson entered stage left, in her swimsuit. A spotlight picked her out as she walked slowly across the stage, turning round as she did so, so that the judges and the diners could admire every curve and bulge of her breasts, waist, hips, thighs, style, elegance, charm, personality, intelligence, honesty and moral fibre.

There was loud applause. The judges made notes, shielding their notepads from each other.

'Hannah hails from Motherwell,' said Rodney. 'She's nineteen, she's a chicken trusser, she has chestnut hair, hazel eyes, she's five foot seven and her vital statistics are 35–25–34.'

Hannah Macpherson made her exit stage left, and Paul hurried into the multi-purpose function room. He looked round for Jenny, but couldn't see her in the dim light.

'Our second charmer is Denise Saltmarsh, of Choice Chicky Chunks Ltd.'

There was another fanfare. Paul and Jenny both recognized Denise Saltmarsh. She was the rather thin girl they had seen in the corridor.

Edgar Hamilton, Alderman George Cornwallis, Jimmy 'Lino' Parsons and Craig Welting also recognized Denise Saltmarsh, and made doodles which would have been an open book to even a moderately competent psychiatrist and, if they hadn't hidden them hurriedly, to Ginny Fenwick who, as Doctor Ernst Hochbender, made occasional contributions to the *Argus* on medical matters.

Denise Saltmarsh walked and revolved self-consciously, a little awkwardly, but with a hint of infuriating self-confidence.

The audience applauded. Rodney held his hand up for silence. Jenny saw Paul and waved.

'Denise, the reigning Miss West Midland Oven-Ready Poultry, is a native of Halesowen,' said Rodney. 'She's a promotional assistant, she has blonde hair, grey-green eyes, she's five foot six, and her statistics are 33–22–33.'

At last Paul saw Jenny waving. He hurried over to her.

'Our third Aphrodite is Beverley Roberts of Happy Valley Poultry.'

Beverley Roberts's magnificent, long, black legs glistened as she walked. Her movements were both graceful and awkward. She looked like a fast bowler with breasts, and moved like an immature gazelle. When the audience saw that she was black they made it clear that this was of no account to them by giving her twice as much applause as the others. Beverley Roberts grinned spontaneously, and won everybody's hearts. Truly, there wasn't a person in all that gathering who wouldn't have forgiven her anything, except perhaps buying the house next door.

'Where have you been?' whispered Jenny.

'Can I have a word?' whispered Paul.

'What?' whispered Jenny.

'Beverley resides in Basildon,' thundered Rodney.

'In private,' whispered Paul. 'A word.'

'She's twenty years of age,' thundered Rodney. 'She has black hair, dark brown eyes, she's five foot ten, her statistics are 37–26–36, and she works as a chicken stripper.'

'What about?' whispered Jenny, before the applause resumed.

'If you come, I'll tell you.'

Beverley Roberts made her exit to loud applause. Paul practically yanked Jenny to her feet.

'Our next Venus is Bernadette O'Riordan, of the Ulster Poultry Marketing Board.'

The applause for the representative of that unhappy country was as great as the applause for Beverley Roberts. It was heartwarming to know that a young woman could survive the troubles and enjoy a moment of glory such as this.

'Bernadette's place of domicile is Antrim. She's twenty-one years of age, an assistant feed processor, with red hair, blue eyes, she's five foot five, and her statistics are 36–26–36.'

The applause rang out again. Then Paul shut the door behind them, and they were in the almost total silence of the bar. You had to hand it to the Grand Universal Hotel. Its soundproofing was magnificent.

'What's going on, Paul?'

The curtains were not yet drawn, but neither of them availed themselves of the view over the sodden ring road.

'Nothing.'

The dark, intense Alec Skiddaw and his two assistants were clearing up the debris from a hard hour's drinking.

'What have you dragged me in here for, then?'

'It's nothing, really. Nothing important.'

Alec Skiddaw approached. He was feeling gloomy. It *was* a boil.

'Can I get you anything?' he said.

'No, thanks,' said Paul. 'We're just . . . er . . . you know . . . thanks.'

'I must apologize again for being so rude earlier,' said Jenny, to let Paul know that she had apologized.

'Oh, that's all right,' said Alec Skiddaw. 'I shouldn't have been telling stories when I was busy. Only I was that full of it, I had to. You see, my ex-brother-in-law from Falkirk . . .'

'Look!' snapped Paul. 'We are trying to have a vital conversation on which the future of our marriage may depend, so just sod off and leave us alone, will you?'

'I do apologize for breathing,' said Alec Skiddaw, with a depth of hurt dignity which would have been beyond the range of Harvey Wedgewood.'

'A vital conversation on which the future of our marriage may depend?' said Jenny, as soon as Alec Skiddaw was out of earshot. 'I thought you said it wasn't important.'

'It isn't,' said Paul. 'I just said it to get rid of him.'

'My God, you're a hypocrite! You're furious with me when I'm rude, and then you're even ruder. Well, I apologized. So should you.'

'Oh heck. Listen, Jenny . . .'

'I'll listen when you've apologized. You said it wasn't important, so it can wait.'

'Bloody hell!'

Paul made the long trek to the bar. He felt very small. Alec Skiddaw was washing glasses, and pretended not to see him. Paul coughed. Alec Skiddaw looked up.

'Sir?' he said, implying, with a subtlety again beyond Harvey Wedgewood's capabilities, that he really meant, 'What is it now, you spoilt and arrogant young hypocritical pipsqueak?' Had fate willed otherwise, he might have enjoyed a glittering career on the boards, given average luck and relative freedom from boils.

'Look,' said Paul. 'Sorry. Nothing would please me more normally than to hear about your ex-brother-in-law from Selkirk . . .'

'Falkirk!'

'Falkirk! Selkirk! What does it bloody . . .?' Paul recovered his self-control desperately. 'I'm sorry! I came over to apologize and now I've . . . look, normally I'd love to hear about your friends and relations from Falkirk, Selkirk, Thurso, Alloa, Brechin, Forfar, anywhere, but Jenny and I are having, though she doesn't know it yet, the most serious crisis that has ever blighted our comparatively privileged young lives, so I honestly can't listen now.'

'I'd be finished by now if you'd let me go on.'

'I know. I'm sorry. Look, we're a bit on edge tonight, but I'd like to assure you that we regard you as our complete social equal.'

'Thank you very much indeed, sir,' said Alec Skiddaw drily.

Paul had felt small as he walked away from Jenny towards Alec Skiddaw. He felt even smaller as he walked away from Alec Skiddaw towards Jenny.

'What's going on?' she said. It took his brain a fraction of a second to instruct his vocal powers to say 'Nothing'. During that fraction of a second, Jenny spoke. 'And if you say "nothing", I'll hit you.'

'Carol saw us opening that door. She wants us to call off the protest.'

'Well . . . she would.'

'I know, but it's her big night. Her chance to escape from a life of drudgery.'

'At what a cost to her sex!'

'I know. I know. But Carol thinks . . . and she's got a point . . . Carol thinks we'd be better off protesting down the supermarket about the way her sister on the check-out is treated like a machine and Miss Griddle blames her for there being no price on things, which isn't her fault.'

Jenny gave Paul a look. He didn't like the look of it. It said, 'What's behind all this?' But what she said was, 'Why are you taking her side like this?'

'It isn't just beauty. It's character and deportment. They're looking for an honest girl of high moral calibre.'

'Is sleeping with your uncle and having an abortion when you're sixteen honest and of high moral calibre?'

Paul's mouth dropped open. 'What?' he said. 'Did Carol do that?'

'It was ages ago. It's irrelevant.'

'The judges might not think so.'

'They're hardly likely to find out.'

'True.' He doubled up, and clutched his stomach. 'Oh God!!'

'What is it?'

'I don't know,' he said, gasping. 'I think it must be something I ate.'

'You haven't eaten anything.'

'That's it! It's something I didn't eat.'

He rushed out. Jenny stared at his departing back with puzzlement. And anger. And fear.

Carol Fordingbridge was in her undies. She was eating a packet of plain crisps.

'I've . . . er . . . I've had a word with Jenny,' said Paul, perching nervously on the upright chair.

'Oh yes?'

'Yes.'

'And?'

'Carol? Did you . . . er . . . did you . . . er . . .?' He couldn't look at her. Poor girl. To have this raked up! But he had to. 'Did you . . . er . . . have relations with . . . with a relation . . . and an . . . er . . . when you were sixteen?'

'You sod!'

'I could tell the judges that, couldn't I? If you can tell Jenny about us.'

'Jenny told you that, didn't she?'

'Yes, but . . .' He was sweating. The room seemed to have got extremely small and hot. Yet Carol looked so cool and soft and absurd, sitting there in her bra and panties, nibbling plain crisps.

'But what, Paul?'

'She didn't know that I was going to . . .'

'. . . blackmail me?'

'Well . . . yes.'

The long-haired Carol looked him straight in the face. Her lovely, soft face looked troubled and disappointed rather than angry. She was forcing him, in her quiet, seemingly unassertive way, to return her gaze. He longed to turn away.

'He was a pig,' she said, with a slight shudder. 'He got me drunk. Drink and sex don't seem to mix very well with me.' Paul closed his eyes. 'When Mr Rodenhurst found out, he sacked me, even though it had happened three years before. I couldn't go for unfair dismissal, could I, with all the publicity?' She turned away, tired of it all. 'Oh go on. Tell the judges. Ruin my chances. I probably wouldn't have won anyway.' She swept the packet of crisps off the dressing table.

'Oh heck,' said Paul. 'I can't. I can't blackmail you, Carol.' He picked up the packet of crisps. 'I'll tell Jenny.'

'There's no need,' she said. 'I can't tell Jenny either.'

He kissed her gently, on the cheek. She smelt of plain crisps.

'I'm going to,' he said. 'I've got to. I can't live with it.'

'Paul!' It seemed important to her. 'Don't tell her!'

He squeezed her hand gently. 'I hope you win,' he said. 'I adore you.'

'Paul!'

'Oh no. Just as a friend. It'll be a disgrace if you don't win.'

'I know. I'm a bloody genius.'

He hurried out, before she saw his tears.

When he returned to the bar, he tried to look sick. He sat in the chair beside Jenny and squeezed her hand. He tried to move his chair closer, and set it at a more intimate angle.

'Oh God, this place!' he said. 'Jenny?'

Jenny turned a frightened face towards him. She hadn't liked the sound of that 'Jenny?'.

'Jenny? There's something I've got to tell you. When you were in hospital . . . having Thomas . . . the night he was born . . . it was a very . . . well, not disturbing . . . emotional experience. I mean I'd never been a father before. I was knocked all of a . . . not that there's any . . . I got drunk. Very drunk. Because I was happy. Because we . . . oh God. Carol and I . . .'

'Oh no!! Oh God!!!' It was the cry of a rabbit cruelly caught in a trap. It was a dark, helpless, three-in-the-morning scream. Its anguish horrified him.

'It only happened once.'

'Oh good! What a relief!' Her sarcasm was glacial. It came from two hundred thousand years before mankind began to evolve.

If only mankind hadn't evolved.

'Listen! Jenny! Please!' He'd do anything to make up to her for that moment. Hack off his legs at the knees. Hack off the offending organ. Fat lot of good that would do for his marriage. Oh God! 'When I went out there the first time tonight, it was to see Carol. She said she'd tell you about us if we didn't call off the protest, but when you told me about her and her uncle I went back and told her I'd tell the judges about her if she told you about us. Then I realized I couldn't tell the judges, and she said she couldn't tell you about us. So I needn't have told you. I'm telling you because I want to.'

'Is that supposed to make a difference?'

'It does to me.'

254

'Sod you!' She set off towards the exit. He followed her desperately.

'Jenny! It means I'm terribly sorry! It means I love you!'

She turned and faced him. He shrank back from her hostility.

'So!' she said. 'It's over. Our pathetic marriage. Your laughable commitment. Your brief career as a father.'

'No, I . . .' He tried to touch her.

'Take your dirty hands off me,' she screamed.

Alec Skiddaw entered, with olives borrowed from Norbert in the Polynesian Bar.

'You pathetic little rat!' shouted Jenny, as she swept past him.

The dark, intense Alec Skiddaw looked stunned, then hurt, then furious. Paul broke off his chase to turn back and explain to him. He felt they owed him that much. 'Not you!' he said. 'Me. She was shouting at me.'

He had only stopped for a moment, but when he emerged into the wide corridor in front of the lifts, she had gone.

The last of the scantily clad girls had passed across the stage, and the diners had turned to their turbot mousse at last.

'Mmm!' said Rodney Sillitoe, the even bigger wheel behind an even bigger Cock-A-Doodle Chickens. 'Very subtle. Very delicate.'

Ted Simcock glared at his former friend and, just for a moment, wished that he could stop not speaking to him. He wanted to say, 'In other words, totally bloody tasteless.'

They were served by a waitress in her late fifties, with a heart of gold, a face like a chipped gargoyle, and huge veined legs like pillars of Stilton. Her name, though they would never know it, was Annie Smailes. 'I couldn't be in it tonight, 'cos I'm working,' she told them cheerfully.

Rodney and Betty Sillitoe laughed. Rita tried to laugh. Ted tried not to laugh.

Annie Smailes removed Paul and Jenny's uneaten carrot mousses with mock horror.

'He'll be livid, him,' she said.

Paul had pressed for the lifts, but no lift had come. He had found the bare, stone service stairs, and had hurtled down them to the

255

ground floor. There had been no sign of her in the foyer. A bald, albino man had emerged from the lift. Paul had rushed into the lift and returned agonizingly slowly to the first floor. He had asked a plump woman to check if there was anybody in the ladies. There hadn't been. He had gone down the service stairs again, and run to the crèche.

Thomas was gone. Jenny had taken their boy.

Now Paul rushed out into the rain. There was no sign of her. He went over to their battered old ecology-coloured Citroën Diane. It was still there, but that wasn't surprising, as Jenny didn't drive.

He felt deeply angry with Carol Fordingbridge. This was all her fault. If she hadn't led him on . . .! He wondered if she had closed the emergency exit as she had threatened. He felt a deep disgust with the whole evening, and hurried round to the back of the hotel.

The door was closed, and he couldn't open it from outside. Paul couldn't remember when he had ever hated a door as much. He banged on it furiously, and almost broke his hand.

Annie Smailes waddled back, a gloriously unsuitable figure in this temple of the impersonal. She served the Sillitoes and Ted and Rita with their entrecôte steak *marchand du vin*. When she found no takers for the two portions of soya bean loaf *marchand du vin* she said, 'I daren't think what he'll say now. I don't. I daren't think. He'll go bloody spare, him.'

Rodney basked in glory. Betty basked in Rodney's glory. Ted imprisoned himself in self-pity. Across the room, Liz felt the first faint indications that her time was near.

Only Rita was really worried about the absence of Paul and Jenny. She told herself that it was foolish. They were adult. They knew their own minds. But she couldn't help it. She had carried Paul in her womb. She would carry him there till she died.

Paul made his way through the labyrinth of corridors, and reached the emergency exit from the inside. He pushed it open, looking for something to wedge against it to keep it open while he went outside to find something to wedge against it to keep it open. There was nothing. Except his shoes. Oh God, was it worth it? Yes!

He wedged his left shoe in the door, and hopped out into the rain. He hopped across the muddy waste. There was still just enough light to see, and he soon found the very same stone that he had used before, where Carol Fordingbridge had dropped it. He picked it up, overbalanced, put his left foot in a puddle and dropped the stone, which splashed him from head to foot. He picked it up angrily and stormed back. He replaced the shoe with the stone, put the shoe on over his sodden, muddy sock, and squelched off through the rain to the car.

Jenny had the car keys! He'd given them to her to keep in her bag, in case he lost them, which he once had.

He shouted abuse at the weeping skies.

Dinner came to an end. The locals agreed that it had been better than the Angel. The visitors made mental notes never to go to the Angel. The locals felt it was much on a par with the Clissold Lodge. The visitors made mental notes never to go to the Clissold Lodge.

The girls paraded in their sophisticated evening wear. Carol was the nineteenth to appear. There was deafening applause. Her sophisticated evening wear consisted of a silver gown glittering with sequins. It clung to the curves of her body.

'Carol's hobbies are travelling, cooking, roller skating, and collecting antique jewellery,' announced Rodney Sillitoe. 'Her ambition is to drive a formula one power boat.'

Betty felt that Rodney was getting tired, yet she wished that there were a hundred girls, so proud was she of him.

There was more applause as the long-haired Carol Fordingbridge made a pretty, unaffected exit.

'Last, but not least, of our tremendous twenty, all the way from Bridport, in Dorset, Jocasta Winkle, of the Ambrosia Poultry Corporation.'

There was another fanfare. Jocasta Winkle entered to cheerful applause and a few whistles. She was a short girl with a huge personality, and an even larger bust. Her sophisticated evening wear had been designed to make her look like a peacock, with holes instead of eyes. It hadn't worked. She looked as if she were wearing a blue-and-green parachute which the mice had enjoyed. She knew she wouldn't win, and gave a cheerful, totally uninhibited wave. There was another roar.

'Jocasta's hobbies are sketching, meeting people, dancing, keeping fit, watching rugby, and designing all her own clothes,' said Rodney. 'Her ambition is to open her own fashion house.'

There was a last burst of applause as Jocasta Winkle made her cheerful exit.

A buzz of conversation burst out in the flexible, multi-purpose function room. Rodney stilled it with his hand.

'And now, ladies and gentlemen,' he said, 'the judges will begin the hard work of reducing the terrific twenty to the fabulous five. In the meantime, the staff will take your orders for coffee and liqueurs.'

He got a good round of applause as he stepped down, and when he got back to their table, Betty kissed him and said, 'You were wonderful.' Rita said, 'Yes, Rodney. Well done.' Ted passed Rodney a note. He read it, and passed the after-dinner mints. Betty raised her eyebrows to heaven, and Rita passed Ted a note under the table.

Ted read the note aloud. '*Please talk to Rodney. All this passing notes is so childish.*' To Rita he said, 'What are you doing if you aren't passing notes?'

'That's completely different,' said Rita. 'I passed you a note because I didn't want them to know, not because I'm not speaking to you. Rodney's enough on edge with his compèring without your contribution.'

'I am not on edge,' said Rodney. 'I have the natural pent-up excitement of the performer. That's not being on edge.'

'I didn't intend "on edge" to be rude, Rodney,' said Rita. 'I just meant the success of the whole evening depends on you. You can do without overgrown schoolboys passing you notes.'

'Rita!' said Ted. 'I have a real grievance. I've been stabbed in the back by my best friend. That's standing on your adult dignity, not behaving like an overgrown schoolboy.'

'Oh God, Betty,' said Rita. 'Why do men have to take umbrage so easily?' She turned to Ted. 'Ted! Whatever the rights and wrongs of the affair, make it up with Rodney.'

'What do you mean, "Whatever the rights and wrongs of the affair"?' said Betty.

Rita screamed. The conversation in their vicinity faltered, then carried on as if nothing had happened, so that Rodney and Betty wondered if they'd imagined it, until Ted spoke.

'Rita!' he said. 'What are you doing?'

'Screaming,' said Rita calmly. 'We all used to be such good friends, and now we can't open our mouths without rubbing somebody up the wrong way. And I find that very unpleasant. So I screamed. All right?'

'No, Rita, it is not all right,' said Ted. 'I mean . . . Rita! . . . people do not scream at public functions.'

'All the more reason for doing so, then,' said Rita.

And she screamed again.

'Am I imagining things, or did Rita just scream?' asked Neville Badger.

'I think she did,' said Laurence. 'I wonder if she's going off her head.'

'I think she's discovering how to express her feelings,' said Liz. 'That can be quite intoxicating, Laurence.'

'Is the insinuation in that particular verbal hand grenade that I can't express my feelings?' said Laurence.

'Good Lord, no!' said Liz. 'I'm sure you'd be able to express them, if you ever had any.'

'Children! Please!' said the immaculate Secretary General of the United Nations.

Simon Rodenhurst turned to Neville Badger earnestly. 'Don't be discouraged,' he said. 'They wouldn't bother to be rude if they didn't care.' He leant forward, to include Laurence and Liz. 'That's psychology,' he added, with a hint of pride.

'Is it? Ah!' said Neville. 'I've always assumed that people are nice to each other because they like each other, and nasty because they don't. But I'm probably very naïve and simple.' There was a brief silence. 'I'd rather hoped somebody might deny that.'

A young Italian waiter took their orders. Southern Comfort for Simon, malt whisky for Laurence, vintage port for Neville, nothing for the expectant Liz. The young waiter's name, though they would never know it, was Sandro Bernini. He was feeling sad about the death of the olive trees on his parents' farm and excited about the arrival of his girlfriend from Poggibonsi. Being young, he was feeling more excited about his girlfriend than he was feeling sad about the olive trees. Being a waiter, he concealed all these feelings.

'Was that Elvis's psychological theory?' asked Liz.

'Well . . . yes, actually,' said Simon.

'You're becoming rather friendly with him, aren't you?'

'No! We argue all the time.'

'According to his theory, that makes you bosom pals.'

'Would you object?'

'I wouldn't say it would be a friendship that would advance your career.'

'Are you in a strong position to criticize liaisons with the Simcock family, "dear"?' asked Laurence.

'I'm sure Paul will be a good husband to Jenny,' said Neville.

'She could have done a lot worse,' said Simon.

'Oh yes,' said Liz. 'Virtually every other road sweeper in England would have been worse.'

'You really are a terrible snob, mother,' said Simon.

'I think I'm rather a good snob,' said Liz.

'Olympic class,' said Laurence.

Liz turned her face on her husband like a hose. 'You're not so bad yourself,' she said, 'which is just as well, as it's your only talent.'

Laurence held her look, and gave a faint smile. 'I am a snob,' he said. 'And I regret it. If I wasn't, you wouldn't have married me.'

There was an icy silence. The Secretary General of the United Nations looked extremely discouraged.

'Cheer up, Uncle Neville,' said Simon Rodenhurst, of Trellis, Trellis, Openshaw and Finch. 'This is very encouraging.'

Rodney Sillitoe returned to the microphone. The lights dimmed, and Sandro Bernini arrived with the liqueurs. There was a loud fanfare.

'Ladies and gentlemen,' said Rodney. 'The judges have selected their short list of five. I shall now introduce the girls individually, and put a few questions to them. Finalist number one is . . .' He paused, relishing the power. '. . . Denise Saltmarsh, of Choice Chicky Chunks Limited.'

Jimmy 'Lino' Parsons nudged Alderman George Cornwallis,

monumental mason, monumental bore, and mayor. Alderman George Cornwallis woke up abruptly, and fingered his mayoral chains as if to check that he really was mayor. He looked at Denise Saltmarsh as she entered in her swimsuit to modest applause and yet another fanfare, and remembered what he had done. It had been understandable. Attractive young girls didn't offer themselves to Alderman George Cornwallis every day, or even every decade, but still . . . Ginny Fenwick was staring straight at him, as if reading his thoughts.

The applause died down. Denise Saltmarsh smiled radiantly.

'Hello, Denise,' said Rodney Sillitoe. 'How are you feeling now?'

'I don't know really,' said Denise Saltmarsh in her mournful Halesowen accent. 'I feel quite . . . you know . . .'

'Confident?'

All four male judges were tense, willing Denise Saltmarsh to be brilliant.

'Well . . . yes . . . sort of,' she said.

'Jolly good,' said Rodney, and paused, momentarily at a loss. Interviewing was proving harder than compèring. 'Tell us more about this interesting hobby of yours,' he said. 'These ancient Ming vases.' There was a pause. Denise Saltmarsh didn't speak, so Rodney had to continue. 'How did you get interested in them?'

Denise Saltmarsh thought. She smiled radiantly. The male judges willed her on. She smiled radiantly. 'I don't know, really,' she said. 'I just like them.'

There was a sticky pause. Rodney was sweating. Denise Saltmarsh was smiling radiantly. 'You were telling me your great-uncle had a house full of Chinese curios, and they fascinated you,' said Rodney, with only a hint of irritation.

'Yes, that's right, he did,' said Denise Saltmarsh. Rodney waited, and she realized that more was expected of her. 'And they did,' she added. 'Fascinate me, I mean.'

'Jolly good,' said Rodney, and he became aware that he was saying 'jolly good' too often, and it was something he never said. 'Tell me more about this unusual ambition of yours. Why do you want to be a freelance hair stylist?'

'I don't know really,' said Denise Saltmarsh. 'I just do.'

'Jolly good,' said Rodney. 'Thank you, Denise Saltmarsh.'

There was modest applause, as Denise Saltmarsh left, smiling radiantly.

'And now,' said Rodney, 'our second finalist . . .' Again, the pause. '. . . our very own Carol Fordingbridge.'

There was loud applause as the long-haired Carol Fordingbridge entered in her stunning but tasteful swimsuit.

'So, how are you feeling now, Carol?' asked Rodney.

The four male judges willed her to say something really dumb.

'Well, I'm a bit tense,' she said. 'But not too bad. I'm pleased to have got into the last five, and if I can go further, it'll be a bonus.'

'Too good to be true?' wrote Craig Welting, managing director of Radio Gadd, shielding his note from Ginny Fenwick.

'Jolly good,' said Rodney. 'Tell us about this unusual ambition of yours. Why do you want to drive a formula one power boat?'

'Well, I love the sea,' said Carol, 'and I love boats, and I enjoy speed, and I don't see why the men should have it all their own way.' She smiled, to take the sting out of her words, but Edgar Hamilton, president of the Food Additives Consultancy Council, clutching at straws and shielding his note from Ginny Fenwick, wrote 'Feminist?'

Ginny Fenwick wrote, 'These judges are a load of wankers,' in shorthand, and shielded it from nobody.

'Jolly good,' said Rodney. 'Tell us more about this unusual hobby of yours. What got you interested in collecting antique jewellery?'

The doors burst open, and ten women and five men, mostly young, mostly wearing jeans, poured into the room. They were led by the tall sculptperson, Melissa Holdsworthy, prematurely grey, fiercely handsome. She carried a banner which read, 'We're people too.'

Other banners stated, 'Ban beauty contests', 'Stop treating women as objects', 'End this humiliation', 'Ban intensive farming', '"No" to battery chickens', '"No" to battery people', 'Don't judge us by our bodies' and 'Preserve British manhood – pickle a man tonight'. One girl had a tee shirt with 'Chicken farmers are pigs' on the front, and 'Pig farmers are chicken' on the back. They all shouted at the tops of their voices.

Alderman George Cornwallis thought it was a terrorist attack, and hid under the table. Miss Amaryllis Thrupp fled. It was important, out of professional loyalty to the Theatre Royal Repertory Company, that her beauty remain unscarred. Jimmy 'Lino' Parsons hurled himself at the nearest protestor, slipped, twisted his ankle, fell, spraining his knee, and ended up, as always, on the floor. Craig Welting, the Australian entrepreneur of the air-waves, enjoyed the happiest moment of his life to date. He punched an attractive leftist activist viciously in the mouth. Ginny Fenwick sat calmly at the judges' table, writing furiously in shorthand.

Rodney Sillitoe rushed out to inform the reception desk and summon help. Several fights broke out. Simon Rodenhurst yelled 'Scrag them. Scrag them,' from the safety of his seat. Ted did battle with one of the male protestors. Graham Wintergreen, completely forgetting to look bluff, snarled and scowled and loudly regretted that he couldn't take part. 'Bloody high bloody blood pressure,' he grumbled furiously. 'Can't do anything with bloody high bloody blood pressure.' 'Calm down, dear,' said his wife Angela. 'Remember your blood pressure.'

Craig Welting grabbed a male protestor's banner, and tried to hurl it onto the stage. Unfortunately, as he wound himself up to throw, the male protestor twisted him round, and he flung the banner right into the middle of the judges' table, where it knocked his own large glass of vintage port all over Ginny Fenwick's despatches. She looked up, stood up, hurled the banner back at him, sat down, and calmly continued to write. She looked as if she thought it was the Intercontinental Hotel, Beirut, and the vintage port was blood. The banner sailed far over Craig Welting's head and poleaxed the hotel's duty first-aid officer as he rushed into the room.

Rita watched with a distaste which Ted completely misunderstood.

Mr Gilbert Pilgrim, the manager, could remain on the sidelines no longer. He strode towards the smallest of the female protestors and attempted to capture her, thus incurring the full and mighty wrath of the tall, handsome Melissa Holdsworthy. She strode up to him, grabbed him by the hair, and attempted to yank him fiercely backwards off the poor, overwhelmed girl. All that happened was that his wig came off. Melissa Holdsworthy, expecting to grapple with the full weight of an overfed man and finding that she was holding only a repulsive object which looked like a hairy frisbee, hurtled backwards. With great athletic skill, she regained control, narrowly missed three tables, swung round three times like a hammer thrower, hurled the wig into the air, and remained, arm outstretched, a magnificent figure, a Greek athlete in the first ever Olympic games, motionless, as if posing for a vase, while the wig sailed across the flexible multi-purpose function room like a dead chihuahua and landed smack on top of the bluff Graham Wintergreen's bald head. It was the furthest that a hotel manager's wig had ever been thrown onto a bald head by an avant-garde sculptress during a melee in the middle of a beauty contest on a Saturday night since records began.

By the time the in-house security men turned up, nine protestors had been overcome, and it was the work of a moment to pin the other six to the ground. Alderman George Cornwallis, monumental mason and mayor, realizing that it wasn't a terrorist attack, surreptitiously removed all the loose change from his pockets and spread it on the floor. Mr Gilbert Pilgrim retrieved his wig, in great embarrassment, Alderman George Cornwallis picked up the change noisily, and emerged from under the table saying, 'Think I've managed to retrieve it all. Good God! What's happened??' and order was restored.

The police arrived shortly after order was restored, and took the fifteen protestors away. The protestors refused to cooperate, letting their bodies go limp, and had to be carried out. At the suggestion of the duty manager Mr F. Lombardo, who had been conspicuous by his absence until the police arrived, they were removed by a side door to avoid bad publicity. Mr Gilbert Pilgrim, who was wearing his wig again and would never be heard to refer to its brief departure from the top of his head, was not yet up to such clear thinking, but then, as he would tell Mr F. Lombardo later, he'd been 'in the front line'.

Since the protestors were totally limp and inactive, and the police took them with such avuncular kindness, it was surprising that two of the protestors later had ribs broken and one sustained a broken leg. The police said that they went berserk in the Black Marias, and only Paul, Jenny, Elvis, Rita and Ginny Fenwick had serious doubts about their version of events.

How much effect can protests have? It didn't seem that anybody changed their minds that night about the ethics of beauty contests, or of intensive chicken farming, but several waiters and waitresses would never again feel quite the same about their manager, Mr Gilbert Pilgrim.

The night skies still wept for the town's lost innocence. Inside, Rodney Sillitoe returned to the microphone. The lights were dimmed. Everything returned to normal. Well, almost normal. Many people found the behaviour of Rita surprising.

'Ladies and gentlemen,' said Rodney. 'I must apologize for the delay. And I would like to thank all those of you who helped to remove those misguided young people.'

'They weren't misguided,' shouted Rita. 'They were right.'

'Rita!' said Betty and Ted in unison.

'Well, they were,' said Rita quite loudly, but no longer shouting. 'And after all *they* weren't violent. We were.'

'They asked for everything they got,' growled Ted.

'I don't think they were right,' said Rodney. 'However, Rita does have a point about the violence.' Mr Gilbert Pilgrim couldn't stop his fingers from moving up to his wig. 'They were not the initial perpetrators of violence. That is true. And I do have to admit to a sneaking admiration for their courage and passion.'

'Is he going soft too?' groaned Ted, and there were other cries of dissent.

'No, no,' said Rodney. 'Please! My point is this. No violence was intended to us personally, so there's no reason why we should let it spoil our evening, on which many people have spent a lot of money.'

'Hear hear,' exclaimed a drumsticks size controller, and there was laughter.

Rodney introduced, and interviewed, the three remaining finalists. They were Beverley Roberts, Hannah Macpherson, and Glenys Williams of Cambrian Chickens. He asked them how they got their unusual hobbies and ambitions, and many and varied were the replies.

The judges filed out. Both Ginny Fenwick and Amaryllis Thrupp offered helpful arms to Jimmy 'Lino' Parsons, and he availed himself of both, so as not to offend either.

After a few minutes, they filed back in. Edgar Hamilton handed a large sealed envelope to Rodney. The judges took their seats.

The lights were dimmed. The finalists trooped onto the stage in their swimsuits, to yet more applause.

'The three winners will be handed their awards by last year's Miss Frozen Chicken (UK), Karen Parkinson,' said Rodney.

Karen Parkinson entered, smiling radiantly. After a year as title-holder, she even woke up smiling radiantly. She was tall, slim, dark-haired, and was greeting the end of her reign with mixed feelings. It had been fun, but her impending marriage to one of the leading younger insurance agents in Dewsbury would be more fun.

There was generous applause for Karen Parkinson. The five finalists looked extremely nervous and, despite her views on the contest, Rita's heart went out to them. Soon, four of them would return to processing feed, assisting promotion, stripping and trussing dead chickens. This moment should be the highlight of their lives, had been looked forward to as the highlight of their lives, would be looked back on as the highlight of their lives. Yet tonight, as it actually happened, they were miserably sick with nerves.

'I'll introduce the three winners in reverse order,' said Rodney. Slowly, with fumbling fingers, he opened the envelope. Carol Fordingbridge thought her heart would stop. 'Third . . .' He paused. For a few moments he had absolute power, and was corrupted. 'Third . . . Carol Fordingbridge, of Cock-A-Doodle Chickens.'

Carol's heart sank. Her legs were like lead. Third. Useless. Dreams of glamour over, killed in two seconds.

She did her best to look utterly delighted. The other four girls applauded vigorously and smiled radiantly, not yet sure whether to be pleased or disappointed that they hadn't come third.

Karen Parkinson placed the third place sash on Carol, handed her the bronze poussin which would be hers for twelve months, and kissed her demurely on both cheeks.

'Our runner up is . . .' Another pause. More absolute power. '. . . Beverley Roberts, of Happy Valley Poultry.'

Beverley Roberts did her best to look absolutely delighted, when in reality she was bitterly disappointed.

Carol Fordingbridge applauded generously, and smiled radiantly. So did the other three girls, though they weren't yet

266

sure whether to be pleased or disappointed that they hadn't come second.

Karen Parkinson placed the runners-up sash on Beverley Roberts, handed her the silver poussin which would be hers for the next twelve months, and kissed her demurely on both cheeks.

The classless Nigel Thick took many pictures throughout, from all sorts of angles.

'But our winner . . .' said Rodney Sillitoe. '. . . our winner tonight . . . the new Miss Frozen Chicken (UK) is . . . Denise Saltmarsh, of Choice Chicky Chunks Ltd.'

Denise Saltmarsh squealed with delight, relief and, it is to be hoped, but not over-optimistically, anguish at the price that she had paid.

There was generous but not enthusiastic applause at this controversial verdict. Indeed, the applause was mingled with a few groans and even the odd boo. What has happened to standards of public behaviour in this great country of ours?

Hannah Macpherson and Glenys Williams made heroic efforts not to look disappointed, and smiled bravely through gritted rings of confidence.

Karen Parkinson placed the winner's sash on Denise Saltmarsh, crowned her with a hint that she'd have preferred to crown her in a very different sense, handed her the gold poussin which would be hers for the next twelve months, and kissed her *very* demurely on both cheeks.

The male judges had the grace to look embarrassed. Edgar Hamilton, president of the Food Additives Consultancy Council, had suggested that they write their first three choices anonymously. All four men had honoured their promise to Denise Saltmarsh in the confident belief that nobody else could possibly vote for her. They'd been dismayed when she had received four winning votes, especially when the implications dawned on them, and even more so when it dawned on them that the implications were dawning on everybody else. What price anonymity now? They studiously avoided each other's eyes, although in the case of Edgar Hamilton and Alderman George Cornwallis, shame was mixed with pride at being shown to be still capable of it at their ages. The four male judges hurried home as soon as they could. It wasn't clear whether Amaryllis Thrupp realized what had happened, but Ginny Fenwick certainly did. She regarded her earlier description of them as 'a load of wankers' as regrettably inaccurate, even by the standards of the *Argus*.

After the judging was over, there was a communal release of tension. Conversation buzzed. The Crabs began to set up their electronic instruments on the stage.

People began to move around, but nobody moved at the table where Ted and Rita sat with Betty Sillitoe.

Betty was worn out. She'd lived every moment of Rodney's big night. He'd be chatting to all the girls now, bless him. The time to worry about Rodney and attractive young women would be if he ever wasn't seen to be so openly and unashamedly fond of their company. She closed her eyes.

Rita was worrying about Paul and Jenny. Ted said that they'd probably shoved off because they were involved in the protest. He meant this to worry her. She thought it quite likely, and it relieved her. How little he knew her. How incredible their long marriage now seemed! How little he could read her thoughts!

'How on earth could you cry out that they were right? I mean . . . Rita . . . how could you?' said Ted, almost as if he'd read her thoughts about how little he could read her thoughts.

'Because it's true,' said Rita. 'How would you like it if you were described as an ex-company-director, five foot nine, with greying black hair, bloodshot eyes, vital statistics 29–36–5–31?'

Betty opened her eyes.

'What's the five?' said Ted.

'What do you think?'

'Rita! I mean . . . that's extremely personal and very insulting . . . and inaccurate. I mean . . . really!'

'Hasn't it ever occurred to you that maybe a woman's chest measurements are extremely personal too, and she could find them insulting?'

Rita pushed back her chair, and set off towards the bar.

'Oh heck,' said Ted. 'I just don't know what's got into her lately. I don't. Apologize to Rodney for me, will you, Betty?'

'Why don't you do it yourself?' said Betty.

'No chance!' said Ted.

And Ted also went off towards the bar, leaving Betty on her

own. She closed her eyes again.

There was a clunk of machinery. She opened her eyes, suddenly alert. All around her there was a ripple of astonishment and alarm as the flexible, multi-purpose function room demonstrated its flexibility and multiplicity of purpose. Four sections of floor, each with several tables on them, slid towards the wall. Two of the sections stopped, the others continued to swing round. There were shrieks of laughter and excitement from people seated on chairs which, it seemed, must shortly crash into the walls. But they all stopped just in time. A sunken dance floor was now revealed in the middle of the room. There was another clunk, and the dance floor rose until it fitted perfectly with the rest of the floor. There was a round of applause, which subsided somewhat self-consciously as people realized the absurdity of applauding a floor.

Laurence Rodenhurst had worn an expression of studiously lofty indifference as he, Liz, Neville Badger and Simon had slid towards the wall with their drinks. In fact he had frowned at Simon when the wretched boy, not content with drinking Southern Comfort, had let the side down by showing wonder and excitement at these absurd proceedings.

When they were stationary once more, Laurence gave Neville Badger a meaningful look, and indicated Liz.

'I feel like a change of scene,' said Neville, clunking into gear as smoothly as the machinery. 'I don't think I'll be deeply worried if I miss some of the early offerings of The Crabs. Liz, would you like to come and have a drink at the bar?'

'Why not?' said Liz.

'Good idea,' said Simon.

Simon was just about to stand up when Laurence kicked him. 'Ow!' he said. 'Ah! Yes . . . er . . . very good idea. You and Liz have a drink, Neville. Lovely stuff.'

Neville and Liz went off across the as yet unoccupied dance floor, elegant immaculate lawyer and hugely pregnant glamorous granny.

'Sorry about that,' said Laurence, 'but Neville has promised to plead my cause with your mother.'

'Ah!'

'If what your friend Elvis says is true, I must stand a good chance.'

'Yes,' said Simon, without conviction.

Betty Sillitoe bought Rodney a drink, ready for when he returned. He needed it. He deserved it. She might as well buy herself one while she was about it.

Trade was quite slack. This gave the dark, intense Alec Skiddaw a wonderful opportunity.

'He was in this motel with his second wife, who came from Nailsworth, well, I call it motel, it's more a hotel with garages really, I don't see the mystique of motels, me, never have, never will.'

Betty watched Neville Badger and Liz looking for somewhere secluded to sit.

'Well, he hears this dog bark in the very next room – the very next room.'

Betty was wondering why Neville was leading Liz out of the bar, but she dimly realized that some comment was called for. 'Good Lord!' she said.

'Well exactly!' said Alec Skiddaw. 'Because a) pets weren't allowed, which he very well knew, and b) he'd know that bark anywhere. It was his first wife, the dog impressionist from Lowestoft!'

'Good Lord!'

'Precisely. Hard at it in the next room. Doing dog impressions, I mean.'

Rita had come back in. She looked as if she'd been titivating. Who for? Ted? Whoever it was, she was looking round for him.

'Well, the moment he heard her barking, he fell back in love with his first wife.'

It wasn't Ted. She'd spotted Ted and was avoiding him. 'Good Lord!'

'Exactly. You see, things hadn't been too good lately with his second wife.'

Oh! Could it be Neville that Rita was looking for?

'And he decided that things weren't too good with his first wife either, because she only did dog impressions when she'd been on the sauce, which she only did when she wasn't happy.'

And what was Neville doing with Liz? And did Rita know?

'Well, to cut a long story short, next morning, after breakfast, because it was included, so you feel you have to have it, they ran away together. Isn't that wonderful?'

Betty realized that she had been asked if something was wonderful, and she had no idea what. Still, it was presumably wonderful. 'Wonderful!' she said.

Alec Skiddaw beamed, all unwanted protuberances forgotten. He had told the whole of his story. 'Precisely,' he said. 'They're getting remarried. He'll no longer be my ex-brother-in-law.'

'Wonderful,' said Betty Sillitoe.

Neville Badger and Liz were enveloped in a huge sofa in an alcove in the vast foyer.

'I don't want anyone to overhear us,' he explained.

'How intriguing!'

'I had an ulterior motive in asking you out here, Liz.'

'Oh good.'

'What? Er . . . before I embark on the particular matter that I want to raise with you, I must ask you about a different, though by no means entirely unrelated matter.'

'Stop sounding so legal, Neville.'

'Sorry. Er . . . at the horse-racing evening, Laurence made veiled allusion to a matter which I didn't then understand. I later learnt . . . to my considerable . . . as you can imagine . . . that what he was alluding to was remarks made by you, the gist of which, as I understand them, was that you loved me.'

A waiter asked if they wanted anything. The immaculate Neville Badger told him that they didn't.

'As a pure formality, Liz,' he went on, 'embarrassing though I find it, in order to clear the way for the other matter which I mentioned, I have to ask you, did you tell Laurence that you loved me?'

'Yes.'

'You did? But, Liz, why?'

'Because I love you.'

'Good Lord! Good Lord!' Liz gave him a quick kiss. 'Good Lord!'

'To your considerable what?' she asked.

'What?'

'You said that when you realized what Laurence was talking about, this was, in your own words to this court, if I can recall them . . .'

'Liz!'

'Well you're still sounding rather legal, Neville. You said "Laurence mentioned a matter that I didn't understand. I later learnt . . . to my considerable . . . as you can imagine . . ." that I'd said I loved you. To your considerable what? Delight? Horror? Amusement?'

'Amazement.'

Three members of the Worcestershire cricket team entered the foyer and wandered towards the lifts. They looked sad, perhaps because of the vile weather, perhaps because they wished they hadn't been chosen to play in the first ever county match on the town's barely adequate Gasworks Ground, or perhaps because there were no screaming cricket groupies lying in wait.

'Is it really that surprising?' asked Liz. 'I loved you when we were young, Neville.'

'What???'

'Until you met Jane, I thought you loved me.'

'Good Lord!'

'You never suspected?'

'I think I was a pretty immature and stupid young man.' There was a pause, during which the cricketers got into the lift. 'I hoped you might think of denying that.'

'I did think of denying it,' said Liz. 'You almost broke my heart. I sometimes wondered if I married Laurence because he was your friend and I hoped I might still see you. So you see I've at least half loved you for . . . more years than I care to think of.'

'So the reason for your . . .' Neville couldn't think of a sufficiently tactful word, so he just stopped.

'Peccadilloes?' prompted Liz. 'Amours? Sordid liaisons?'

'No! Good Lord, no! Well . . . your . . . er . . . affairs.'

'. . . is that I've been terribly unhappy for many years and only stayed with Laurence because I felt I owed it to the children? Yes.'

'Good Lord! But this is . . .' Again, Neville stopped.

'Dreadful? Wonderful?'

'I don't know. One or the other.'

'So . . . I . . . this is rather delicate, Neville, but I've started, so

I'll finish. Our next contestant is Liz Rodenhurst, whose specialized subject is botched lives.'

'What is rather delicate?'

'Well . . . I know how much you and Jane wanted children . . . happy and fulfilled though you were, I hasten to . . . and I thought, "Well . . . I am about to have a child who has no father." I thought . . . "Well . . . is it meant?"'

'Good Lord! Good Lord! All I can say is . . . good Lord!'

'So it would appear. Anyway, the whole thing astounds you and we should probably forget all about it.'

Four male Japanese tourists entered the foyer and wandered towards the lifts. They were festooned with cameras. They looked sad, perhaps because of the vile weather, perhaps because of the absence of Japanese women or perhaps because they had found nothing worth photographing.

'Now,' said Liz. 'What is this other matter that you want to raise with me?'

'Ah! Well . . . Laurence has asked me to ask you to go back to him. Will you?'

'No.'

'Good. Well, I've done what I promised. No, I haven't. I said I'd plead. Liz, I beg of you . . . think of your marriage vows. Think of your husband, my friend, alone in that draughty great house . . . well, not draughty, I wouldn't want you to think I was ever cold when I . . . think of all the years you've spent together, the memories you share, your children who both love you both. Reconsider this decision. Give Laurence one more chance, I beg of you. Will you do it?'

'No.'

'Good. Marry me, then.'

'Yes. Neville, are you serious?'

'Yes, I . . . I honestly think I am! Good Lord! Good Lord! You see, Liz, I . . . I did at least half love you before I met Jane, although I was too shy and stupid to see that you half loved me, so . . . yes, I honestly think I am. Do you really mean "yes"?'

'Yes.'

'Good Lord!'

They kissed. They were utterly unaware of the tinkling of the piped music and the fountain.

The younger element were happily dancing to the music of The Crabs, which seemed to Laurence to be harsh, repetitive, mechanical, joyless and boring. The group consisted of five tall, pale young men with hollow eyes, gaunt cheeks, tight trousers, and highlights in their hair. Their records were frequently played on Radio Gadd. All their movements were sideways, but despite this gimmick they had yet to break through nationally.

The cynical Elvis Simcock was dancing with Denise Saltmarsh, who was still wearing her winner's sash and crown. Simon Rodenhurst was watching, transfixed with admiration.

The dance ended.

'Thanks,' said Denise Saltmarsh.

Elvis gulped.

'Can I . . . er . . . take you out to dinner some time?' he said.

'Sorry, I'd have liked to, but . . . you know how it is.'

Denise Saltmarsh moved off, and Elvis returned to Simon rather sadly. He realized that he was sadder because he had asked her than because she had refused. He had asked her because she was Miss Frozen Chicken (UK), not because he liked her.

'Fantastic!' said Simon. 'Dancing with Miss Frozen Chicken (UK)!'

Oh Elvis! Is that why you did it? To impress Simon Rodenhurst, of Trellis, Trellis, Openshaw and Finch? Would Jean-Paul Sartre ever have asked Miss Salade Niçoise of 1937 out, just to impress a young estate agent?

'I even asked her out.' Why tell him?

'Amazing! What a nerve!'

'She turned me down. How many women have you had, Simon?'

'Well . . . I haven't counted.'

'As few as that!'

'I'm a professional man in a small town, Elvis. I have to be discreet. Opportunities are rare.'

'Give over! There must be times when you're showing a lady client round a house, you're in the commodious, handsomely proportioned master bedroom with five power points and luxury bathroom en suite, and you're tempted to remove her spacious knickers, fling her on the bed, and make mad, passionate love to her.'

'That sort of thing doesn't happen at Trellis, Trellis, Openshaw and Finch.' Simon sighed. 'I wish I was clever enough not to have to worry about toeing the line.'

'The problem of identity which most people suffer from isn't the trendy one of not knowing who they are, but the much more mundane one of knowing only too well who they are and not liking it,' said Elvis.

'Bit deep for me,' said Simon.

'Exactly!' said Elvis.

The Crabs, who'd been deep in consultation in an effort to pretend that their programme was spontaneous, sidled sideways to their instruments and launched themselves into a number which sounded identical to, but louder than, their previous effort.

'I'm going to take you in hand, Simon,' shouted Elvis. 'I'm going to transform your life. I'm going to open up uncharted seas.'

'Oh dear,' said Simon, but Elvis didn't hear.

Elvis walked away, giving a last glare at The Crabs. They were the kind of talentless apes who gave genuine modern popular music a bad name.

To judge from Laurence's expression, as Neville Badger approached him warily, modern popular music was definitely being given a bad name. Laurence tried to read, on Neville's face, evidence of how well his diplomatic mission had succeeded.

'So you . . . er . . . you had a chat with Liz, did you?' he asked, fighting against the music of The Crabs.

'Yes, I . . . er . . . I did . . . yes.'

'And?'

'I'm afraid things didn't go *entirely* to plan. I did . . . er . . . I do assure you that I did put your case to her very forcibly . . . *very* forcibly. I pleaded . . . begged . . . but . . . to no avail.'

'Oh. Well, thank you, anyway.'

'Not at all. It was a pleasure. Well, not a pleasure. I . . . er . . . I was glad to do it for you.'

'Tell me honestly, Neville, as a friend . . .' Laurence looked away, towards the dancers, as if the answer was really of no great account. '. . . do you think there's any hope?'

'Well . . . as a friend . . . I have to say . . .' Neville Badger also

275

looked away, towards the dancers. '. . . I'm afraid there isn't any hope at all.'

Laurence turned his enigmatic, stiffly smiling gaze back on Neville.

'How can you be so sure?' he asked.

'Well . . . I also have to tell you . . . also as a friend, I do assure you . . . that . . .' Neville forced himself to meet Laurence's gaze. '. . . we're engaged.'

'What???'

'Liz is going to ask you for a divorce, and then she's going to marry me.'

'You bastard!'

'I would like to assure you categorically, Laurence, both as a friend and as a lawyer, that I have satisfied myself thoroughly and completely . . .'

'I bet you have! You swine!'

A spasm of affronted dignity crossed Neville's face. '. . . that I have satisfied myself thoroughly and completely that the breakdown of your marriage to Liz was irrevocable, and that I elicited this information without prejudice, without asking leading questions or influencing her decision in any way.'

'You assured me not three hours ago that you had no knowledge of any relationship between you.'

'I didn't then.'

'And now you're engaged?'

'Yes.'

'And I thought you were my friend!'

Laurence walked off, as angry as Neville had ever seen him.

Neville felt uneasy. He had a vague but pervasive sense of guilt, of betrayal. Oh, Jane, he said silently. I never meant to do this. I wanted to mourn you for ever. He looked up at the ceiling, studded with lights, like a film studio. He tried to conjure up her body, in its finest, tiniest details, the exact length of eyelash, the exact size of thumb. Gone. Replaced by a vague concept of Janeness. He tried to ask it if it approved of his plan to remarry, if it gave him its blessing. It was too diffuse and opaque to answer. Hundreds of miles away, in a flexible multi-purpose function room, people were applauding a fairly untalented group. Here, in the world centre of Janeness, her widower felt sad that he couldn't feel sadder, felt ashamed that he couldn't feel more ashamed, felt a sense of loss at the loss of his sense of loss. There came a vast diffused sadness. Into the sadness stepped a woman, a real woman, alive, precisely defined. She was smiling nervously. It was Rita. He returned the smile with instinctive impeccable manners, and then, feeling guilty because he'd been thinking of Jane, he rewarded her with one of his suavest, warmest, most irresistibly charming smiles.

Encouraged by Neville's smile, Rita said, 'I wondered if we could fix a date for that dinner.'

'Absolutely!' said Neville enthusiastically. 'That sounds a marvellous idea. Let's do that. Rita, I have some news that may be rather a surprise to you. Liz and I are going to be married.'

Rita felt that she died at that moment. Yet there she was, standing there like a lemon, at a table beside a dance floor crowded with chicken executives and guests. She heard herself saying 'What??'

'I thought you'd be surprised! I'm rather surprised myself.'

Rita made a conscious effort to recover her social poise. The old impulse to keep up appearances still had some power.

'Well . . .' she said brightly. 'Congratulations.'

'Thank you,' said Neville. 'Don't mention it to a soul, will you? I'm telling you in the strictest confidence. There's still the little matter of Liz's divorce. But I wanted you to know.'

'Me? Why?'

'I rather like you, Rita.'

Rita closed her eyes. She didn't want to hear any more, and it wasn't possible to close her ears.

'And I rather fancied you rather liked me,' said Neville, imagining that he was being the charming doyen of a town's lawyers, having no idea that he was a wild boar pulling up every flower in Rita's cottage garden with his disgusting snout. 'I thoroughly enjoyed our little dinners together. I felt an air of relaxed, undemanding companionship that I've only ever had before with male friends. Didn't you feel it?'

'Oh yes,' said Rita. 'It was lovely and relaxed and undemanding. I hope you'll both be very happy.'

Rita swung her blue handbag over her shoulder as she set off round the edge of the dance floor. Neville Badger watched her go with astonishment, which turned to realization and horror.

Rita rushed past Elvis and Simon, who were standing together watching the dancing. Elvis realized that something was wrong, and hurried after her. He caught her up by the doors to the bar.

'Mum?' he said. 'What's wrong?'

She turned to face him. There were tears in her eyes. 'I was,' she said.

'You what?'

'I was wrong about something. I've just been put right. So I'm not wrong any more, so everything must be all right. Mustn't it? You're the philosopher.'

'Mum!'

'Your education was a complete waste of money. You're totally inarticulate.'

'No. It's just that . . . I mean . . .'

'"Mum!"'

'Exactly.'

'Do you feel like buying your mother a large drink?'

'Mum!'

Paul was oblivious of all the other people in the bar. Only instinct prevented him from bumping into them as he went in search of the alcohol that would dull his pain. He'd only come back because he couldn't face being on his own. He needed to reduce the burden of his pain by dramatizing it and sharing it around.

There at the bar, standing out against the dim blur which was all he could see of the rest of the room, was the magnificent long hair of Carol Fordingbridge. She was buying drinks. She was no longer wearing her swimsuit, but a pleasant white dress. White! He wanted to blame her. He wrestled with the impulse to say something really insulting. He also wanted to tell her how lovely she was. He wrestled with this impulse too.

In the end, he compromised. 'Hello, Carol,' he said.

She turned towards him.

'Hello, Paul,' she said. 'What's wrong?'

'Jenny's left me. She's taken Thomas.'

'You told her!'

'I had to.'

'You idiot!'

'Did the protest take place?'

'Oh yes. While I was being interviewed.'

'I'm sorry.'

'It was dealt with.'

The result of the stupid competition was no longer of the remotest interest to him. He was deep inside the wreckage of his life, and he didn't need a flight recorder to tell him what had gone wrong. Two things had gone wrong. He'd been born, and he'd met Carol. And yet . . . because he was there, and because she was there, and because he had to say something, he found himself saying, 'Did you win?'

'No,' said Carol Fordingbridge. 'I came third. Denise Saltmarsh won, because she slept with all the judges, and the coloured girl came second, to show they aren't prejudiced.'

Suddenly he did care. All that injustice seemed to be a part of his pain. His pain seemed to be linked to all the misery and injustice in the world.

Elvis and Rita approached the bar counter just as Paul's anger erupted.

'I'm not sorry about the protest,' he shouted. 'I'm glad. The whole thing's been a farce.' His voice became a scream of fury. 'A bloody farce!'

People shrank back. They'd heard of men suddenly going berserk. Alec Skiddaw fingered his incipient boil as if it were the only friend he had.

'What the hell's going on?' said Elvis.

Paul grew calmer. 'The whole evening's been a disgusting mish-mash of corruption and stupidity and decadence that could only be mounted in a society that's so rotten it's disintegrating,' he said.

'Yes, yes, I know that,' said Rita. 'But what's happened?'

'Jenny's left me.' There was no anger now.

'Oh God! No!!' said Rita. 'Why?'

Carol Fordingbridge hurried off with her tray of drinks.

'I slept with Carol Fordingbridge.'

'You didn't!' There was instinctive admiration mixed with Elvis's shock.

'Elvis!' said Rita.

'Well don't get on at me,' said Elvis. 'He did it.'

'And you admire him!' said Rita. 'I think that's even worse.

Philosopher? Huh!'

'Bloody hell!' said Elvis. 'What a family!' He stalked off angrily.

'What a family indeed,' said Rita. 'You'd better come home with me, Paul. Two fools together.'

Ted entered from the flexible, multi-purpose function room.

'Oh God, here's another,' said Rita. She realized that Ted wanted to speak to her, and handed Paul the ticket for her coat. He went off like a zombie.

'Rita!' said Ted.

'Hello.'

'Have you heard . . .' He dropped his voice. '. . . something very secret and confidential? Concerning Neville.'

'It seems so secret and confidential that everybody knows it. And if you gloat I'll knock your block off.'

'Rita! I'm not gloating!' They might have been in the middle of the Sahara for all the awareness they had of their surroundings. 'I'm not gloating. But.'

When she realized that it was one of Ted's utterly final 'buts', Rita said, 'But what?'

'Well . . . I mean . . . I just thought . . . you know . . . I mean, doesn't it? Rather change things.'

'Not much, no. It just means I've made an utter fool of myself as usual.'

'No, but . . . I mean . . . it makes us . . . well . . . free. To try again. Doesn't it?'

'I don't think I want to try again, Ted.'

'Rita!' said Ted. 'Why not? I mean . . . give me one good reason.'

'You're so small-minded. Refusing to talk to Rodney. It's pathetic.'

'After what he did . . .'

'He didn't make you bankrupt. Nothing he's done has actually harmed you. And pretending he doesn't exist wouldn't solve anything even if he had.'

Rita set off towards the cloakroom, which was on the ground floor, just off the foyer. Paul was still queuing.

'Bloody ridiculous!' he said. 'One woman to deal with a hotel this size.'

He sounded angry, but Rita sensed that he was glad of the delay.

It's less painful to be furious about delays at a cloakroom than about having lost one's wife and son.

Rodney Sillitoe had returned. They were trying to watch the dancing without listening to The Crabs, Betty and he. They were tired, but at peace. Too tired to go to the bar. Too much at peace to need to go to the bar.

'Look out,' said Betty. 'Here's Ted.'

Ted plonked himself down beside them. 'It wasn't a bad meal,' he said, 'to say they were catering for a crowd.'

'Quite good,' said Rodney. 'Better than the Angel, anyway.'

There was modest applause as The Crabs reached the end of a mournful dirge of their own composition, entitled 'Everything's Great Except Life'. They scuttled sideways, into a huddle, to decide on their next number.

'You spoke to him!' said Betty.

'Well!' said Ted.

'I'm glad,' said Betty.

There was a pause. Ted had done his bit. He couldn't think of anything else to say. Then it struck him. 'You're both sober!' he said.

'There've been enough problems tonight without our . . . what do you mean?' said Rodney.

'Nothing. I just . . . nothing.'

'Are you suggesting that usually we aren't?'

'No. No!! No, it's just that . . .'

'. . . we usually take it in turns to get drunk?' said Betty.

'Well . . . yes.'

'What *do* you mean, Betty?' said Rodney.

'It's what Rita said earlier.'

'No tact, that woman,' said Ted. 'Never has had.'

The Crabs attacked 'Don't Put the Boot in, Boris', a light-hearted number about a Russian invasion, written by The Crabs. It reminded Ted of something. At first he couldn't think what. Then he remembered. It was like 'Everything's Great Except Life'. But louder.

'Apparently people have the idea that you and I get drunk alternately,' shouted Betty.

'Don't be offended, Rodney,' yelled Ted. 'It's one of your more likeable qualities.'

'No,' shouted Rodney. 'I was working it out. Do you know I think it's true? I think we do.' And he burst into laughter. Betty joined in. Eventually, in spite of himelf, Ted found himself laughing too.

Rita approached. She was carrying her coat. The laughter subsided. She felt that laughter had been subsiding at her approach for almost thirty years.

'I just came to say good night,' she said.

'Oh. Good night, Rita,' said Rodney. 'Thank you for coming.'

'Thank you for inviting me,' said Rita. 'It's been quite a night. Good night, then.'

Ted caught up with her as she edged her way round the dance floor. He followed her into the bar, where it was quieter. 'I'm talking to Rodney again,' he said.

'Talking to Rodney wasn't a qualifying test I was putting you through,' said Rita.

'What do I have to do, Rita?'

'The one thing that's impossible, I'm afraid.' She spoke sadly, gently, regretfully. 'Have behaved up till now differently from what you have.'

'So . . . this is it, then, is it?'

'I really do think so, Ted.'

They had passed right through the bar. A board in front of one of the lifts read 'Out Of Order'. Rita pressed for the other lift.

'Rita?' said Ted. 'Don't get me wrong. This isn't important. But . . . oh heck . . . the house . . .'

'I don't see the problem,' said Rita. 'I've got the house you walked out of. You've got the flat she walked out of.'

'Yes, but . . . not that it matters, but . . . I paid for it. You're living in it.'

'I'll move out soon, don't worry.'

'I don't want you to move out! I want to move in.'

The lift came. They travelled down in the company of an underpaid Portuguese waiter who was carrying a plate of smoked salmon sandwiches, at least half of which hadn't been eaten. They didn't like to discuss personal matters in front of the waiter or the sandwiches.

When they had stepped out into the vast brightness of the tinkling foyer, Ted said, 'Why shouldn't we try again?'

'Oh Ted!' said Rita. 'Do you really want to? Don't you think there must be something better?'

Paul stood by the fountain, patient because he had nowhere better to go.

'Where am I going to find anything better?' said Ted. 'A failed bankrupt with no money.'

'I didn't think you'd failed,' said Rita. 'I thought you were moving laterally into design.'

'I am,' said Ted. 'I am, Rita. But . . . I mean . . . I can't concentrate without a good woman.'

'Find one,' said Rita. 'We're a splendid sex.'

'I won't do anything like that again. I mean it, Rita. I won't.'

'It's too late, Ted.'

'On your own head be it, then.'

'You what?'

'If anything happens to me, Rita. If I stab myself to death with one of my own toasting forks.'

'Don't be silly, Ted,' said Rita. 'Don't say such things.'

'I'm serious,' said Ted. 'Do you really think my life's worth living any more? And if I do, Rita, I'll make sure everyone in this town knows who drove me to it. I mean . . . I will.'

Ted strode back towards the lifts. Rita watched him, wondering. He got into the lift, pressed the button, and stood, staring bleakly, angrily into the vast soft foyer, so carefully designed to blot out all bleakness and anger. At last the lift doors closed slowly and silently. Rita sighed, and joined her son.

As Ted re-entered the bar he glared at the whole assembly, but especially at Liz, and especially at her swollen belly. That was his baby in there.

He ordered a double whisky. The dark, intense Alec Skiddaw hesitated before serving him.

Laurence approached Liz. He avoided looking directly at her, and especially at her swollen belly.

'I'm off now,' he said, 'but I couldn't leave without congratulating you. I understand you're engaged. What splendid news! We're still married, and there's been no talk of a divorce, but these are mere bagatelles. When is Ted's dear one expected?'

'Don't be angry, Laurence.'

'Why on earth not? What an extraordinary remark.'

'You wouldn't really have wanted to bring up my child, would you? You never seemed all that keen on your own.'

'Maybe I wanted a second crack at parenthood. It's possible that one learns from one's mistakes, don't you think?'

'But it may grow up to look like Ted.'

'I don't resent Ted any more. After all, he was just a pawn in your game.'

Liz's breasts, though flattened by the downward pull of her baby, heaved. She went white.

'What *do* you mean?' she said.

'You didn't decide to keep the baby because you wanted Ted's child. You've kept it as an excuse to break with me. You never dreamt I'd make things awkward by accepting it. You kept that baby for Neville.'

Liz was icy, rigid. She just managed to move her dry lips enough to say, 'Are you suggesting I planned all this?'

'How much does a cat plan?' said Laurence. 'Or does it just instinctively behave in such a way that it gets what it wants? Ah! There's your fiancé. I must go and thank him for inviting me. He's a stickler for good manners, and he tried so hard to bring you and me together tonight. He must be devastated by the extent of his failure. I must go and sympathize with him. I've rendered you speechless at last. Goodbye, Liz.'

Liz felt her contractions begin. She was frightened. She needed to be with Neville. She waited for Laurence to finish with him.

She didn't have to wait long. Laurence handed Neville a piece of paper and carried on towards the lifts, raising his right arm in a parody of farewell as he left the Royalty Suite.

'*Thank you for inviting me, you bastard,*' read Neville Badger.

Sixth Do

September:
The Registry Office Wedding

An Indian summer hung over the solid, squat council offices, which housed the social services department, the housing department, the planning department and the registry office. The autumn sunshine was pale, misty and golden, and a warm, gentle breeze wafted the exotic scents of turmeric and fenugreek, cumin, chillies and garam masala, garlic and ginger, cardamom and coriander, saffron, mace and cinnamon, over the unlovely stone-faced municipal fortress at the wrong end of Commercial Street.

Two unlovely stone-faced planning officers emerged from the fortress, eager for their early lunch. They glared at the row of decaying unambitious brick buildings opposite. Piles of old packing cases and yellowing files were visible at the windows of the semi-derelict upper storeys. The planning officers sniffed the rich spicy air and smelt nothing but scope for redevelopment. Nor did they have any eyes for the young couple who were approaching the registry office.

The owner of the good Indian restaurant, at 114 Commercial Street, stood at the door of his dark temple of gastronomy, and stared with a superior air at the daytime activities of the English, whose graceless behaviour in his restaurant he despised so much. He did have eyes for the young couple. Disapproving eyes. His long, equine nostrils curled in contempt for the semi-long-haired young man in the ill-fitting suit, who was accompanied by a beautiful and extremely long-haired young lady. She moved with, for an English girl, a surprising, gentle sexy grace which aroused the owner of the good Indian restaurant. But what a fool the girl was to throw herself away on this abysmal fellow, this graceless Anglo-Saxon young man, who no doubt got himself 'tanked up' and then came into the restaurant at closing time, to be loud and patronizing while he stuffed his crude gut with lovely food which he was quite incapable of appreciating, the clod-hopper! Beautiful English girl, I hate you for your lack of judgement, thought the owner of the good Indian restaurant, where all the dishes were expertly and subtly spiced.

The owner of the bad Indian restaurant, at 110 Commercial Street, stood at the door of his more cheery establishment and beamed at the world with an infectious, gleaming smile. He liked the look of the young couple who were standing on the concrete at the side of the registry office. The young man put a friendly, encouraging hand on the small of the girl's back. These two young people had already had carnal knowledge of each other. Well, that was normal these days. I am happy for you both, thought the owner of the bad Indian restaurant, where all the dishes came with variations of the same fiery, red, gut-churning sauce.

'I knew we'd be early,' said Paul Simcock.

The young couple stood in the sunshine on the concreted area at the side of the building. They were reluctant to enter its gloomy recesses until it was unavoidable.

They found it hard to believe that everyday life, life outside the wedding, could still be continuing. But it was. They saw Larry Benson, of fitted kitchen fame, lock the door of Kitchen Wonderland, at 112 Commercial Street. They saw him walk away from his island of formica, entirely surrounded by curry. He walked wearily, as if soon to be defeated by life, in the direction of the Black Horse where, unbeknown to them, he would meet his lady wife, who was no lady. They saw the tall, handsome Melissa Holdsworthy stride past purposefully. They saw the suave Doctor Spreckley drive by and suddenly lose all his suavity as he caught sight of her. They saw him turn his head just too late to avoid her witheringly contemptuous stare. He had steered well clear of her since he'd heard of her antics at the crowning of Miss Frozen Chicken (UK). They saw the first customers enter the bad Indian restaurant. They saw the owner of the good Indian restaurant give a silent snort of his long nose and close his door upon this hopelessly undiscriminating town. He didn't realize that more people went to the bad restaurant than to his because most English people are so insecure that it's more important for them to feel liked in a restaurant than to get good food.

'Perhaps people are inside,' said Carol Fordingbridge. 'There's a waiting room.'

'I'm not going in there,' said Paul. 'It's like a doctor's waiting room without the magazines.'

'I hate doctors' waiting rooms,' said Carol, who was wearing a pretty, very pale yellow dress which made her look as if she were very nearly a virgin, and might become one some day, if she was careful. 'You look at other people and you don't know whether it's a fatal disease or a pimple on the bum. Plus which, some of them are so infectious, if you aren't ill when you go you will be by the time you leave. I'm talking too much. It's nerves. I'm very nervous.'

'You look lovely today, Carol.'

He kissed her. Her soft, creamy cheeks went ever so slightly pink.

'Thanks,' she said.

'I don't know why I said "today",' he said. 'It makes it sound as if you don't look lovely on other days. And you do. Every day.'

'Thanks,' she said, and she kissed him.

Elvis Simcock arrived at last. He wore a very casual suit on which there was one bright orange stain, a relic of the bad Indian restaurant.

'Sodding cars,' he said. 'Sodding inadequate municipal parking facilities.'

'The great philosopher has spoken,' said Paul.

'Why can't I park a car?' asked Elvis.

'Because philosophers aren't practical men,' said Carol.

'Exactly,' said Paul. 'I don't expect Bertrand Russell could reverse into a parking space. And Jean-Paul Sartre wouldn't have recognized a rawlplug if he'd fallen over it.'

'Bertrand Russell didn't work for Cock-A-Doodle Chickens. Jean-Paul Sartre didn't get a bad third at Keele.'

'Cheer up, Elvis,' said Carol Fordingbridge. 'It's supposed to be a wedding.'

'I'll cheer up when I want to, Carol.'

'Charming!'

The two young men scuffed their heels uneasily. The concreted area was surrounded by municipal flowerbeds, with flowers evenly spaced in rows, like councillors at a meeting. Beside a small side door, there was a notice which stated, 'Please help your council – do not throw confetti'.

'I'll go and see if there's anybody in the waiting room,' said Elvis. 'Anything's better than standing here like lemons.'

'Charming!' said Carol.

Elvis strode off to the main entrance.

'I assume,' said Paul.

'You what?' said Carol.

'I said you look lovely every day. I can't be absolutely certain that's true, because I haven't seen you every day.' He was talking too much. He couldn't help it. He was very nervous. 'It's possible that on all the days I see you, you look lovely, and on all the days I don't see you, you look absolutely hideous, but it's very improbable.'

'You are an idiot.'

'Oh Carol!'

'What?'

'It churns me up when you say nice, affectionate things like "You are an idiot". If it wasn't for my making love to you, I wouldn't have split up with Jenny, and now that I've split up with Jenny and I'm free to make love to you, you go and decide to marry my brother.'

'You don't want me. You still love Jenny. You're coming out with all this nonsense because you're nervous because she's going to be here.'

'Rubbish.'

Elvis returned. 'Nobody,' he said. He kissed his fiancée. 'Was I a bit abrupt earlier?' he said.

'You could say that,' said Paul.

'I'm speaking to Carol,' said Elvis.

'You could say that,' said Carol.

'I'm sorry, love. I'm nervous.'

He kissed her. They clung to each other. Paul smiled broadly, trying not to feel redundant.

'I don't know why they've invited us if it's family only,' said the cynical Elvis Simcock. 'I'm not their family.'

'You are,' said Paul. 'You're my brother. You just about scrape in.'

'I think they must be short of people to invite,' said Carol.

Rita joined them. She was wearing an elegant and expensive trouser suit which revealed the contours of her attractive body as none of her curtain-like dresses ever had. It was fennel-coloured. Her hair was stylishly cut. She looked altogether younger.

'Mum!' said Paul.

'Good God!' said Elvis.

'Thank you very much,' said Rita drily.

'No, but . . . you look amazing!' said Paul.

'You look lovely!' said Elvis.

'Thank you very much,' said Rita drily. There was no doubt about it. She was relishing the situation! Their reactions were amusing her. They felt resentful. 'I suppose I shouldn't be surprised if you're surprised. Listen boys . . . hello, Carol! Congratulations!' Rita kissed Carol Fordingbridge warmly. 'Listen, boys . . .'

'What about me!' said Elvis. 'Aren't you going to congratulate me?'

'It's you I should be congratulating,' said Rita. 'I should be sympathizing with Carol.'

'Mum!'

'Listen, boys,' said Rita. 'I've brought a friend.'

The siren of a passing ambulance carved through the silence of her sons.

'What sort of a friend?' said Paul at last.

'A male sort of a friend,' said Rita.

'What??' said Elvis.

'Thank you very much,' said Rita drily. 'I rang them, and asked if I could bring him, and they seemed delighted. I think they're rather short of guests.'

'Where is he, this male sort of friend?' said Elvis.

'Trying to park,' said his mother. 'It's hell round here. He said it didn't matter if he was late, but I mustn't be, so he dropped me off. I'm glad. It's given me the chance to warn you.'

Her two sons exchanged uneasy glances.

'What do you mean, "warn us"?' said Elvis. 'What's wrong with him?'

'Has he only got one leg or something?' said Paul.

'Nothing's wrong with him,' said Rita. 'I'm delighted to say he's complete in every respect.'

'Mum!' said Paul.

'So what are you warning us about?' enquired Elvis, ever the more intellectually persistent.

'That I have a male friend,' said Rita.

They stared at her blankly.

'So that you won't gawp in astonishment when you see him,' she explained.

They gawped in astonishment.

'Why on earth should we gawp in astonishment?' said Elvis.

'At the idea that your mother could have a "boyfriend".'

They blinked in disapproval at her use of the term 'boyfriend', but Elvis said, 'I think we're a bit more sophisticated than that, Mum.'

'Yes, well,' said Rita, 'we mothers never really believe our children have grown into mature adults, do we?'

'Who is he, Mrs Simcock, your boyfriend?' asked Carol Fordingbridge, who had been finding it difficult to join in these family exchanges.

'You remember that actor they had at the charity horse-racing evening?' said Rita.

It was Elvis who said, 'Harvey Wedgewood????' with four question marks, but it could just as easily have been Paul. They were both gawping again.

'You're both gawping again,' said Carol.

'Shut up, Carol,' said Elvis.

'He invited me to go to his play in London and go backstage.' As Rita talked, shirt-sleeved salesmen peered out of their slowly moving cars, trying to catch a glimpse of the bride. 'It took me weeks to pluck up the courage to go, but in the end I thought . . . well, I've been invited, I'll go. I was shaking. I mean, little provincial me, in an actor's dressing room in the West End! I nearly turned away when I got to the stage door. The man was so off-putting. But I thought, No, Rita. You've come this far. And what does it matter if Harvey doesn't recognize you? Nobody you know need ever know you came here. He did remember me. Straightaway. It turned out to be the best move I ever made in my life.'

There was a brief, appalled silence, as the golden sun streamed down on the concrete. The boys were contemplating Harvey Wedgewood, the actor, as their step-father. Harvey Wedgewood's multi-cratered face beside their mum's. Harvey Wedgewood's boozy breath on her prim cheeks.

'Mum!' said Elvis faintly.

'Oh dear,' said Rita. 'You do sound displeased with me.'

Carol Fordingbridge tried to look interested in the flowerbeds.

'No,' said Elvis. 'It's your life. You're old enough to know your own mind. But.'

'That "but" sounds very like your father. He had a very ominous "but" when he wanted to.' Rita wished she hadn't mentioned their father.

'No! Mum!' said Paul. 'All we mean is . . . I mean . . . isn't he? I mean, he is. A bit old.'

'You're both sounding like your father.'

'Because we feel responsible for you,' said Paul. 'Because we love you. We're delighted to see you get your share of female emancipation, but . . . Elvis is right . . . we'd be a bit happier, for your sake, if it were somebody younger. That's all.'

'Because we love you,' said Elvis.

'And we don't want you marrying somebody and his needing to be looked after all the time,' said Paul.

'And dying and breaking your heart,' said Elvis.

'That's all,' said Paul.

'Because we love you,' said Elvis.

A redhaired, freckled, good-looking man in a good suit and his mid-thirties stepped energetically towards them.

'This is Gerry Lansdown,' said Rita.

Elvis and Paul gawped in astonishment.

'Gerry, this is Elvis, my oldest. Paul, my youngest. And Elvis's fiancée Carol,' said Rita.

'Hello,' said Gerry Lansdown. 'I know this sounds corny, but I've heard so much about you boys, it's nice to meet you at last.'

'You all seem stunned,' said Rita.

'Well . . .' said Paul.

'I was trying to tell them how I met you, Gerry. I got to the bit about going to Harvey's dressing room, and they leapt to conclusions. Gave me the most tremendous ticking off because they thought I was throwing myself away on a geriatric.'

'No, I'm not quite a geriatric yet,' said Gerry Lansdown with a smile, which Elvis and Paul instantly hated. 'I'm a friend of Harvey's son. Your mother and I met in Harvey's dressing room.'

Neville Badger arrived, with two other men. If Neville had seemed immaculate before, it must have been an illusion. Now, dressed for his own wedding, he really was immaculate.

'Hello, all,' he said.

'You look marvellous, Neville,' said Rita.

'Thank you, Rita.' Neville realized that politeness required more of him. 'So do you,' he said. 'Marvellous.' He noticed Rita's appearance for the first time. 'No!' he said. 'You really do! I mean . . .' He stopped, embarrassed.

'This is Gerry Lansdown,' said Rita.

'Good . . .' Still off balance, Neville almost said 'Good Lord!', but managed to amend it rapidly. '. . . to meet you, Gerry. My brother Arthur . . .'

Arthur Badger was slightly older and smaller than Neville, and fractionally less charming and immaculate.

'. . . and his son-in-law Andrew Denton.'

Andrew Denton was in his thirties, worked in banking in Leeds, but wasn't rising quite as rapidly as his father-in-law had hoped.

'Andrew's wife can't be here. A great shame. Rita's boys, Elvis and Paul, and Elvis's . . . er . . .' continued Neville.

'Carol Fordingbridge,' said Carol.

'And Elvis's Carol Fordingbridge,' said Neville. 'Well, here we are, eh? All on parade. Well done. Any . . . er . . . any sign of Simon?'

'Not yet,' said Paul.

'Ah!' said Neville.

'More important, no sign of the lovely bride,' said the almost immaculate Arthur Badger.

Andrew Denton surprised everybody by leaping into life, and choosing as his opening remark, 'She's probably buying bedsocks.' They all stared at him. 'Because she's got cold feet,' he explained. 'Joke!'

Arthur Badger gave his son-in-law a meaningful look. It meant, 'Belt up, will you?'

'I think they must be running late,' said Carol. 'The last lot aren't out yet.'

'It *is* rather like waiting for your turn on a boating lake, isn't it?' said Neville.

A cool breeze gusted briefly, emphasizing the fragility of this late summer. Neville Badger sighed, as if emulating the breeze to the best of his ability, and said, 'Oh dear!'

'Oh dear,' said Rita.

'Oh dear, oh dear, Rita, why the "oh dear"?' said Neville, giving her one of his most irresistible smiles. He felt enormously warm towards her, in gratitude for her production of Gerry Lansdown, which had freed him from the guilt which he'd felt ever since he'd realized that he'd trampled on her feelings.

'No, I was saying "oh dear" because you said "oh dear",' said Rita.

'Did I? Oh dear.'

'The condemned man ate a hearty breakfast,' said Andrew Denton, like an unexpected noon broadside from a ceremonial gun.

'Pardon?' said Neville Badger.

'Joke,' explained Andrew Denton.

'Ah!' said Neville, failing to conceal his mystification.

Arthur Badger gave Andrew Denton a dry look.

The traffic was heavy and slow-moving, and there was still no sign of the bridal limousine. Neville could feel the beginnings of panic. He had to talk. 'I hope I don't feel quite condemned,' he said, 'although I must say that, the way I do feel, if I was council property I probably would be. I just feel most dreadfully nervous. After such a long, idyllic first marriage, I think a second marriage is bound to be nerve-racking. I think these registry places make it rather . . . I don't know . . . and yet our first wedding was so large, so grand, Jane always says it made her feel that she and I were irrelevant. Oh Lord. I really ought to stop talking about her as if she's still alive now, oughtn't I?'

It was clearly a rhetorical question, so nobody answered. Indeed, nobody spoke at all. Andrew Denton wound himself up to fire another joke, but Arthur Badger managed to silence him with a look.

A rather forlorn group of six people emerged from the main entrance and came round to the side door. They carried confetti.

The funny little man with the big ears, who went to all the weddings, hovered about twenty yards away from them.

A young couple came out of the side door. The groom had pink hair. The bride, who was heavily pregnant, had painfully thin legs. The six guests threw confetti. It swirled listlessly round the notice that said 'Please help your council – do not throw confetti'.

'They're so young,' whispered Rita. 'There are so few people. What does life hold for them?'

'We'll never know,' said Elvis, ever the philosophical realist.

'I'd like to know,' said Rita. She went up to the young couple and kissed the astonished bride. She was almost crying. 'I hope you'll both be terribly happy,' she said, with a gulping break in her voice.

'Rita is a most remarkable person,' said Gerry Lansdown to Neville.

'She is indeed,' said Neville Badger. 'She is indeed, Tom.'

'Gerry,' said Gerry.

Rita returned, sniffing and smiling.

'That was wonderful,' said Gerry. 'Very few people could have done that.' He kissed her. Elvis and Paul looked embarrassed.

'Don't be absurd, Gerry,' said Rita. 'And my children are very embarrassed at the idea of you being physical with me.'

'Mum!' said Paul. 'Of course we aren't. We're the emancipated generation.'

'Not quite so emancipated that you're happy for me to be the emancipated generation as well,' said Rita. And she strolled off, arm in arm with Gerry Lansdown, to examine the municipal flowers.

The almost immaculate Arthur Badger led Andrew Denton in the opposite direction.

'Andrew?' he said. 'I know you're always like a boy let out of school when you manage to get out without my daughter, but do you have to keep making your jokes?'

'It's a happy occasion,' said Andrew Denton. 'Surely a touch of humour would be welcome?'

'My point precisely,' said Arthur Badger.

The owner of the good Indian restaurant, still without customers, came to the door to have another look at the English girl who moved her creamy body with an almost Oriental serenity. She had two men with her now! Probably she was as shallow and coarse as the rest of her race. He glared at two shapeless women dragging bags of dirty washing to the launderette, and returned into his empty temple of gastronomy.

'I'm not embarrassed, Carol,' protested Elvis Simcock.

'Oh no!' said Carol Fordingbridge. 'You both are.'

'I'm not,' said Paul. 'It's just that it all seems wrong. Under the circumstances.'

'Life has to go on,' said Elvis.

'What insight your study of philosophy has given you!' said Paul. 'I know life has to go on, you dumbo, but it doesn't for him, does it? I mean . . . what is it? Three months? It's as if they don't care about all that. I mean, if it had been natural causes, it'd be bad enough. But suicide!'

The wedding car pulled up, festooned with ribbons.

Liz's dress was long, elegant, expensive . . . and pink! Nobody had ever seen her in pink. It seemed like a declaration of a new personality. She looked demure.

Jenny wore a middle-class, up-market, black-and-white dress. She looked more like her mother than Paul had ever seen her. He felt that a great chasm had opened up between him and his young wife. He wondered if she meant him to.

Evidently not. Evidently she hadn't been expecting him. She looked thunderstruck.

'You didn't tell me you were inviting Paul,' she said.

'Didn't I, dear?' said her mother. 'Well of course I invited him. He's family.'

The immaculate Neville Badger kissed his bride-to-be shyly. 'You look stunning, my love,' he said.

'You don't look so bad yourself,' she said.

They approached the rest of the gathering, arm in arm. Neville looked gallant.

'Hello, Jenny,' said Paul.

'Hello,' said Jenny coldly, walking past him.

'Rita!' said Liz. 'You came! You look wonderful! No, you really do! What's happened? I mean . . .'

'Liz, Jenny,' said Rita. 'I'd like you to meet my friend Gerry Lansdown.'

'Hello, Gerry,' said Liz, almost managing to hide her surprise as she shook hands with him. A firm, dry handshake. If he had feet of clay, it wasn't evident in his hands.

'I know it's corny,' said Gerry, 'but I've heard so much about you both, it's nice to meet you at last.'

Those who were looking for indications of the faults which Gerry Lansdown must surely possess felt that there could be telling evidence in this remark. He'd said it before. Perhaps he was a bore. It sounded rather glib. Perhaps he was a creep. Perhaps he was a creep and a bore. Time would tell.

'I think we'd better go in,' said Neville. 'We're late.'

Indeed, the funny little man with the big ears had already gone in.

'Sorry,' said Liz. 'The traffic was awful. I really resented it, too. What right had all those people to be on the road as if it was just a normal morning when it's my wedding day? Any sign of Simon?'

'I'm afraid not,' said Neville.

'Oh dear.'

'Come on, then. Best foot forward.'

'Right.'

Neville and Liz led the way towards the main entrance of the council offices. They were preceded up the steps by an embarrassed homeless couple and a very angry, unshaven man with a grudge against the social services.

'Oh dear,' said Liz.

'Oh dear oh dear!' said Neville.

'Oh dear oh dear!' said Liz. 'Why all the "oh dears"? Are you having second thoughts?'

'No! No!! Good heavens, no! No, I was saying "oh dear" because you sighed and said "oh dear".'

'Did I? Oh dear.'

A housing officer, hurrying out before he had to deal with the homeless couple, held the door open for the wedding party with a pained expression, as if to say, 'Please don't worry about knocking a minute and a quarter off my lunch hour. It happens every day.' A spark of humanity seeped through his municipal exterior, as if he'd added, 'Oh, and . . . good luck.'

'Are *you* having second thoughts?' said the immaculate groom, as they adjusted their eyes to the dark entrance lobby.

'No! No!! Good heavens, no!' said Liz. 'No, I suppose I meant "oh dear, Simon hasn't come. Oh dear, the rest of my stuffy family are also boycotting the event. Oh dear, Jenny's still totally hostile to Paul, and, whatever we think of him, he is her husband. Oh dear, what does Rita think she's playing at? and, Oh dear, it's hardly Westminster Abbey, is it?"'

'Oh dear, oh dear,' said Neville Badger. 'What a lot of "oh dears".'

They entered the registry office.

'The restaurant that brings a touch of the Loire Valley to the banks of the Gadd' was how an advertising feature in the *Argus* had described Chez Albert in Moor Street, on its opening eighteen months previously. 'The eponymous Monsieur Albert uses only fresh materials, down to the last pea and chip.' It was unfortunate that a display advertisement on the opposite page should have read 'Tyne-Tees Oven-Ready Chips, suppliers to Chez Albert, wish Monsieur Albert and his restaurant every success.'

Monsieur Albert surveyed his establishment with a critical eye. His hairstyle, his luxuriant gallic moustache, his paunch, his Parisian clothes, all proclaimed his French origins.

The candles were lit on the table laid for eleven, and very pretty it looked. The wedding party hadn't paid the supplement which he'd have required had he closed the restaurant for them. They'd thought it would be more relaxed if they weren't the only people in the restaurant. Well, they were going to be the only people, even though they hadn't paid the supplement. The recession had hit the business lunch trade badly.

When the door opened, Monsieur Albert thought it would be the wedding party or a glassware salesman, but it was a middle-aged couple.

'Good morning,' said the man, who was wearing a crumpled suit. 'Do you have a table for two?'

Monsieur Albert's eyes swept swiftly over his empty restaurant. 'Yes, sir,' he said, 'I sink I can squeeze you in. Can I get you somesing *pour boire* – to drink?'

'Gin and tonic and a whisky and soda, please,' said the man.

'Make them large ones. My wife and I don't see each other very often midday.'

'Vairy good, sir.'

'My husband supplies your chickens,' said the woman, who had platinum hair and badly concealed dark roots.

'Ah!' said Monsieur Albert cautiously. '*Edouard!*' he shouted, clicking his imperious Gallic fingers. '*Edouard* will bring you the menus,' he explained.

Rodney Sillitoe gave a brief, approving glance round the restaurant. It had a tiled floor, red check tablecloths, discreet wall lights, recessed photographs of rural France. An arched wrought-iron screen led to a separate bar area, with smaller tables and soft bench seating. Rodney felt, as he sat in the bar with an affectionate arm round Betty's shoulder, that they could spend a relaxed two hours in this place without hardship.

Then Ted Simcock entered, in evening dress, carrying two enormous menus.

All his life, when he had been in evening dress, Ted had felt that he looked like a head waiter. Now, when he was a head waiter, he felt that he didn't look like one.

He felt that he looked like a prat.

'Good afternoon, sir. Good afternoon, madam. Good God!' he said.

The Gallic Monsieur Albert, pouring the drinks, gave Ted a sharp look.

'Ted!' Rodney's surprise at seeing Ted was as great as Ted's dismay at seeing the Sillitoes. 'What are you doing here?'

'Working.' Ted gave Monsieur Albert a brief glance. 'It's a very good place, and Monsieur Albert's an excellent employer. I'm thoroughly enjoying it.'

'Good,' said Rodney. 'Now what can you recommend, "*Edouard*"?'

Monsieur Albert handed the Sillitoes their drinks while Ted spoke. 'Everything is excellent. Our chef Alphonse started in the household of General de Gaulle and later worked at Maxim's in Paris.' Monsieur Albert returned to the kitchen. Ted's manner changed abruptly. 'All right!' he rasped. 'You were my friend. You couldn't wait to get your hot little hands on my foundry when I went bankrupt. Fair enough. That's life. It's a right sod, is the greed of mankind, but we learn to live with it. But.'

'But what?'

'I mean . . . Rodney! . . . don't you think you've done enough damage without rubbing it in? I mean . . . calling me *"Edouard"*! Really!'

'That was a bit naughty, Rodney,' said Betty Sillitoe, who was over-perfumed as usual.

'I'm very sorry, Ted,' said Rodney. 'I just couldn't resist it. I'm sorry.'

'All right,' said Ted, 'but call me *"Edouard"* once more and I'll kick your ruddy teeth in for you. Or there's the *tête de veau vinaigrette à la mode de Lyon.*' Rodney and Betty Sillitoe were bemused by the swift transition, until they saw Monsieur Albert returning with a small bowl of *crudités* and two dips. 'The *poulet de Bresse, sauce perigordienne*, is very tasty. Or if you fancy a touch of nouvelle cuisine, the lamb's liver with lime and kiwi fruit sauce on a bed of purée of red pepper and watercress with banana garnish has its devotees. Or, for those of a more traditional bent, there's always the *cassoulet Toulousienne avec* I mean it! If I see you with so much as a glint in your eyes . . . that's it!' Monsieur Albert had gone. 'And don't waste time deciding what to have. I mean . . . there's no point. It's all lousy.'

Ted made an angry, almost impressive exit.

Rodney and Betty exchanged dismayed looks, and raised their glasses to each other silently.

'I wish we hadn't come here,' said Betty, after taking a goodly swig of her gin. 'I bet the food *is* lousy.'

'Well, it's quiet anyway,' said Rodney. 'And we're together.'

'I'm a lucky woman. Cheers, love.'

'Cheers, love.' Rodney Sillitoe spluttered and almost choked. '"*Poulet de Bresse, sauce perigordienne*,"' he read. '"Maize-fed French chickens . . ." Those chickens are as French and maize-fed as my arse.'

Ted slipped out of the back door and sat beside her. She smiled. As a result of a lifelong addiction to cake, one of her top front teeth was missing. She was listening to music through her expensive headphones, which she could only afford because Ted bought all their food and drink. From the movements of her body, Ted guessed that she was listening to reggae. He was getting quite good at such deductions. Her off-duty life was one long musical orgy, from which Ted was voluntarily excluded.

He put an arm round her soft, spongy, cake-filled plumpness.

'It's nearly finished,' she said.

He kissed her on the cheek. She gave him a full, luscious, rhythmic musical kiss on the mouth.

They were seated on a step at the back of the kitchen, looking out over a yard whose untidyness would have astonished the customers. There was a jumble of crates, empty catering-size tins of rape seed oil, crumpled boxes of oven-ready chips, catering-size tins of chef's soup of the day, overflowing dustbins and black plastic bags torn open by cats with a taste for rotting remains of *poulet de Bresse, sauce perigordienne*.

'Finished,' said Sandra Pickersgill, who was wearing a traditional nineteenth-century Provençale costume. She took her headphones off.

'Come on in, Sandra,' he said. 'There's two customers arrived.'

'I'm amazed they're doing other dinners when there's a wedding dinner on,' she said.

'Sandra! It's other lunches, and it's a wedding breakfast! I mean . . . love . . . get it right. I told them you were an experienced waitress, who'd worked in sophisticated places. I didn't say you were an unemployed bakery assistant I'd met at the DHSS. I mean . . . did I?' When she'd told him she was an unemployed bakery assistant he'd said, 'I'd like to put a bun in your oven,' and she had run the back of her hand gently over his genitals, right there in the crowded, angry DHSS. He'd hardly been able to believe it. 'So . . . love . . . come on! It's a posh restaurant, is Chez Albert. So . . . you have lunch at dinnertime and dinner at teatime and whatever time you have it, it's a wedding breakfast.'

'Why do things have to be so complicated?'

'So that the ignorant can be identified, and class differences can signify.'

'Isn't that bad?'

''Course it isn't. This is England. I mean . . . it's our heritage.'

'Do we know who the wedding party are?' asked the cake-loving Sandra Pickersgill, who was twenty-four years old.

'No. Monsieur Albert's being right cagey about it.'

'That's another thing gets on my wick.'

'Sandra! I mean . . . really! This is a high-class establishment. Things do not get on your wick. They annoy you.'

'Well, calling Monsieur Albert Monsieur Albert gets on my wick when we all know he's from Gateshead.'

'Sandra! Do you think there'd be a wedding breakfast having lunch here this dinnertime if it was called Bert's Caff or La Petite Auberge de Gateshead?'

'Are you glad you met me, Ted?'

'You know I am, love.'

He kissed her, running his tongue across the jagged edges of her cake-ravaged teeth, cupping in his hands her luscious breasts, which only last night he had playfully referred to as her Macaroon Highlanders. Even their love talk was dominated by cake.

They returned to the kitchen and their duties.

Rodney and Betty Sillitoe were seated at a table for two, as far as possible from the table for eleven. Their candle was lit. Behind them, a Breton onion seller was locked in a perpetual smile.

Elvis Simcock and Carol Fordingbridge made straight for the bar, and didn't see their employer or his wife.

'There's Elvis and Carol,' hissed Betty.

'They said they were going to Neville and Liz's wedding,' said Rodney, craning his neck. His first thought was that they'd been lying. Then he saw the carnation in Elvis's buttonhole. 'My God! The wedding's here!'

'Bang goes our quiet lunch,' said Betty, as Paul followed them.

'Oh my God!' said Rodney. 'Poor Ted!'

Poor Ted came in from the kitchen, with a bottle of red wine which didn't deserve its basket. He saw his two sons, standing by the bar with Carol Fordingbridge. He went rigid with shock, and scurried back to the kitchen.

The kitchen was fairly cluttered, not terribly spacious, moderately clean. It gave an impression halfway between the elegant calm of the restaurant and the squalid chaos of the yard. The ovens and grills gleamed, but the extractor fans were clogged with brown fur.

Ted hurtled in so rapidly that he collided with Sandra, who dropped a pile of plates.

'Bloody hell, Sandra,' said Alphonse, the scruffy young chef from Bootle. 'You made me jump. I've cut me finger on this tin of pâté maison.'

'You're always dropping things, Sandra,' said Ted, with affectionate and deeply unjustified exasperation, since it had been at least half his fault.

'Ooooh! Sounds interesting, Ros,' said Lil Appleyard, the older of the two kitchen assistants. Her husband was an attendant at the art gallery. She could smell a double entendre at five hundred paces.

Ros Pennington, whose husband was a policeman, held up a shrivelled gherkin. 'Reminds me of Fred's on the beach at Brid.,' she said.

'Reminds me of Len's all the year round,' said Lil Appleyard.

Monsieur Albert entered from his office. He stared morosely at Sandra, as she squatted to clear up the broken plates. There was a hole in her tights just above the right knee.

'Never mind, Sandra,' he said, in an accent that owed more to Gateshead than Gaul. 'No need to feel guilty about it.'

'Oh, thank you, Monsieur Albert,' said Sandra.

''Cos I'm stopping it from your wages.'

'Monsieur Albert?' said Ted. 'Who exactly is this wedding party?'

'They demanded secrecy, Ted.'

'Monsieur Albert! My two sons are in there. I mean . . . I need to know who it is!'

'Your sons???' said Sandra.

'Yes, I . . . er . . . I . . . er . . .' said Ted.

'Well, there's no harm in your knowing now, I suppose,' said the Geordie Monsieur Albert. 'It's a Mr Badger marrying a Mrs Rodenhurst.'

'Bloody hell! No wonder you didn't tell me.'

'I didn't tell you because they asked for maximum secrecy because, as I understand it, there has been adverse criticism of them for not waiting longer after Mrs Badger's first husband killed himself with an overdose of anaesthetic in his own dental chair.'

Sandra dropped her broken plates noisily into the bin. Alphonse jumped again, and glared at her.

Ted peered cautiously round the door into the restaurant. He saw Jenny enter, followed by Rita and a redheaded man in his thirties, who had his arm round Rita!! He went pale.

'Oh my God!' he said. 'And what has she got in tow??' He turned to Monsieur Albert. 'I can't go in there,' he said.

The cake-loving Sandra Pickersgill, another pile of plates in her arms, caught the urgency in Ted's voice and turned to look at him.

'You go in there, Ted, or it's your cards for you,' said Monsieur Albert.

Ros Pennington and Lil Appleyard listened, the garnishing for the lobster mayonnaise forgotten.

'Albert!' pleaded Ted. 'Be reasonable! I mean . . . I've had an affair with the bride. I've been left by the bride. The bride and groom are bringing up my baby as their own.'

'Your baby???' said Sandra.

'My wife is in there with some freak whom I assume to be her lover.'

'Wife!' shrieked Sandra. 'Baby! Sons! Oh shit!' she added, as the pile of plates crashed to the floor.

'My two sons are there, plus one son's fiancée, and the other son's estranged wife,' continued Ted. 'None of them know I work here. Well . . . I mean . . . be fair . . . can I go in there and ask them to taste the wine, which I know they know sod all about and they know I know sod all about? I mean . . . can I? I mean . . . it's not on. Is it? I mean!'

Lil Appleyard and Ros Pennington stared at Ted open-mouthed.

'Wife!' said Sandra again, and they all turned to look at her. 'You forgot to tell me you had a wife, and sons, and a baby.'

'Come on. You can discuss this afterwards,' said Monsieur Albert.

'I was going to tell you, love,' said Ted. 'It slipped me mind.'

'Slipped your mind?' The former bakery assistant was incredulous.

'Yes!' said Ted. 'Absolutely! Because it's over. Kaput. Finito. Yesterday's cold custard.'

The mention of food set Monsieur Albert off. 'Silly me!' he said, his irony as heavy as his gâteau. 'I thought this was a restaurant. How could I have been so stupid? It's a group therapy clinic. I realize that now. So why don't you all continue to discuss your problems while I go quietly bankrupt?'

'Honestly,' said Ted. 'Over. Unimportant. That's why I didn't tell you.'

'I can manage without you, Ted,' said Monsieur Albert. 'So, if you aren't prepared to go in there, just leave.'

'Go in and give them hell, whack,' said Alphonse, the scruffy young chef from Bootle. 'Show 'em you don't give a toss.'

'If she's really that unimportant, what does it matter?' said Sandra.

Ros Pennington and Lil Appleyard, the double act with the double meanings, held gherkins suspended in mid-air.

'All right,' said Ted at last. 'To hell with them!'

'Right,' said Monsieur Albert. 'You open the champagne, Ted. I'll go and greet the customers.'

But the customers were destined to wait a little longer. The phone rang, and Monsieur Albert almost forgot to use his French accent as he answered it. It was a booking for three, name of Thoroughgood. The gentleman wanted something special. He waffled on about prodigal daughters and fatted calves. 'You vant veal?' asked the Gallic Monsieur Albert. 'No, no,' said the Reverend J. D. Thoroughgood. 'We're against veal on moral grounds. I spoke figuratively.'

Monsieur Albert groaned. A wedding party was being seriously neglected, and he'd got some berk who was against veal on moral grounds, and spoke figuratively.

'What do you mean, "it slipped your mind"?' persisted Sandra, as Ted wrestled with the champagne. 'You must have remembered you were married when we talked about us getting married?'

'When did we talk about that?' said Ted, alarmed.

'When I told you –' Sandra lowered her voice to a whisper, '– that I'd been sacked from the bakery because me pearls all fell into the mix for this wedding cake, you said to me, "you are the only pearl I want around our wedding cake, my luscious Victoria sponge." I thought that was lovely. I went gooey all over.'

Ted grimaced. It was awful having your love talk quoted back at you in cold blood. He vowed never to use cake imagery again.

Elvis, Carol Fordingbridge, Paul, Andrew Denton, Arthur

Badger, Jenny, Rita and Gerry Lansdown were standing in a purposeless huddle by the bar counter. Behind the bar there was a photograph of a French bar counter, manned by a burly character in striped jersey and beret. Nobody was manning the bar of Chez Albert.

At last, Liz and Neville Badger made their entrance. There was a communal 'Aaaah' of welcome.

'Well, we've done it,' said Liz.

'Congratulations,' said Rita.

'Thank you. I think we ought to congratulate you too,' said Liz. 'You seem to have made quite a catch.'

'I'll second that,' said Gerry Lansdown, and there was forced laughter, which didn't quite drown the loud bang from the kitchen.

'Either that's a bottle of champagne being opened, or the chef's shot himself,' said Paul.

'Don't mention suicide,' whispered Carol Fordingbridge.

Paul went scarlet.

'Isn't that the Sillitoes over there?' said Neville Badger.

'They've seen us,' hissed Betty Sillitoe.

'We'll have to congratulate them,' mouthed Rodney.

'It'll look as if we're angling to be invited,' whispered Betty.

'We can't not. That'll look as if we're upset because we weren't invited.'

'Oh Lord.' Betty waved and called out a cheerful 'hello'.

'Hello,' echoed Rodney, craning his neck.

The wedding party turned *en* as much *masse* as they could muster.

Betty and Rodney raised their glasses.

'Congratulations,' they cried.

'Thank you,' said Neville and Liz Badger.

'They must be having lunch here,' mouthed Liz.

'Surely not? Won't they be waiting for a plane to Istanbul?' said Andrew Denton.

The almost immaculate Arthur Badger glared at his son-in-law.

'Joke,' explained Andrew Denton.

'Well, we did decide that as we were a small party it might be more relaxing if there were other customers,' said Neville.

'Yes, but I never thought there'd only be two other customers, we'd know them both, and they'd be lifelong specialists at getting drunk in public,' said Liz.

There was another bang from the kitchen.

'What's going on in there?' said Neville. 'Where is everybody? I heard this place was very good. Apparently the eponymous M'*sieu Albère* . . .' His French accent was immaculate. No uncompromising flat Yorkshire 'Monsieur Albert' for him. '. . . was the manager of Maxim's in Paris, and his chef, Alphonse, is said to be the illegitimate son of General de Gaulle.'

'Don't mention illegitimate children,' whispered Liz, just loud enough for Rita to hear.

'Did you arrange for two vegetarian meals, Uncle Neville?' said Jenny.

'Oh Lord!' said Neville Badger. 'I forgot.'

'Uncle Neville isn't Uncle Neville any more, Jenny,' said Liz. 'He's your father now.'

'Yes . . . well . . .' said Jenny, and she wandered off to examine the cobbled arcaded square of an idyllic stone town high above the valley of the Dordogne.

'Oh Lord,' said Liz.

Monsieur Albert bustled in, Gallic to his fingertips once more.

'Sir! *Madame*! Greetings and congratulations,' he said. 'I am devastated that you wait. I am desolated lest you feel neglected. *Edouard*, 'e will be 'ere any moment with your *champagne*.'

'Nice-looking town,' said Paul.

'Oh, please don't leave Carol,' said Jenny. 'I'm sure she was whispering lovely things in your ear.'

'Carol is engaged to Elvis.'

'Do you expect me to be sorry for you?'

'Jenny! I'm lost without you. Some days I haven't even got the heart to read the *Guardian*'s foreign news. I'm turning back into the slob I was before I met you.'

'I repeat . . . do you expect me to be sorry for you?' said Jenny.

The Gallic Monsieur Albert made a tactful exit as Ted entered with a tray of eleven glasses, filled with champagne.

'Ah!' said Neville. He saw that it was Ted. 'Oh!' he added.

'Good Lord!' said Liz.

'Ted!' said Rita.

'Dad!' said Paul.

Ted smiled bravely, and held the tray out towards Neville.

'Would you like to taste the wine?' he said. He had to force himself not to say 'sir'. He was damned if he'd say 'sir' to anybody, in front of Rita and that freckled ape she had in tow.

'Well, I . . . I'm sure it's . . .' The immaculate Neville Badger frowned, not because Ted hadn't said 'sir', which he too would have found embarrassing, but because he regarded it as a grave social solecism to ask the host to taste the wine at a wedding breakfast. But he couldn't humiliate Ted by refusing. 'Yes . . . right,' he said. He took a glass of champagne and tasted it. 'Very good!'

'Madam?' said Ted to Liz.

'Thank you, Ted,' said Liz, taking a glass and meeting the eyes of her former lover.

'May I take this opportunity of wishing *Madame* the lasting happiness that has so far eluded her?' said Ted.

'Thank you, Ted,' said Liz coldly.

Ted turned to Rita.

'Well . . . this is a surprise,' she said.

'It certainly is, madam,' said Ted, glancing at Gerry.

'This is Gerry Lansdown. Gerry, this is my husband,' said Rita.

'Ah!' said Gerry Lansdown.

Ted looked suspiciously at Gerry Lansdown as he offered him the champagne. He hadn't liked the sound of that 'ah'. It had sounded like an unexploded social bomb, as if Gerry had meant, 'Ah! No wonder you weren't prepared to have him back. I see in him all the character defects you've been telling me about with such relish these last weeks.'

He moved on to Jenny.

'Thanks, Ted,' said Jenny in a low voice. 'Though I don't feel much like it.'

'Still worried because half the world is starving?'

'No. I mean, I am, obviously, but no, I was just thinking how sad I am about the way everything's turned out.'

She touched Ted's arm, sympathetically, and he moved on

hastily with his tray.

'Is this a permanent post, Dad?' said Elvis.

'Elvis! Of course it isn't! I mean . . . really! No! It's just a fill-in while I develop my portfolio.'

'Your portfolio?' said Paul.

'My designs. My toasting forks et cetera. Personalized coal scuttles and what-have-you. My portfolio.' There was one glass left over. 'Oh, are we only ten?' he said. 'I thought there were eleven.'

'Simon hasn't come,' said Liz.

'Ah!' said Ted. Oh, versatile monosyllable! Ted's 'ah!' was faintly insulting, as if he'd meant, 'Ah! Well, I'm not surprised, under the callous and entirely distasteful circumstances of your characteristically self-centred decision to remarry so soon after driving your husband to his tragic end,' but he hadn't made it sound insulting enough for Liz to be able to accuse him of being insulting, so she had to content herself with giving him a cool look, which would serve as a response to his 'ah!' if he had meant what he hoped she realized he had meant, but which if he hadn't meant anything specifically insulting could well have been just one more of the cool looks which she'd been giving him ever since he'd appeared.

'Would you like a glass?' said Neville.

'Oh! Thank you very much, sir,' said Ted. He was concentrating so hard on sounding sufficiently surprised at the offer of the drink which he had been expecting for so long that he let a 'sir' slip out. He closed his eyes momentarily in disgust at his carelessness. 'Well, here's to your happiness,' he said.

They toasted Neville and Liz Badger. Then there was a moment's embarrassed silence, during which Ted didn't know whether to stay on as a guest or leave as a head waiter.

'We can't not offer them a glass of champagne,' whispered Neville to Liz. He turned to Ted. 'Waiter? Er . . . Ted?' he said. 'Could you get two more glasses?'

'Certainly, s . . .' Ted bit back the 'sir' almost in time. He felt slightly insulted but also rather relieved at becoming a head waiter again. But he was less than halfway to the kitchen when Neville commanded 'Wait!' He returned. Neville was saying, in a low voice, 'If we ask them to have a drink we'll have to ask them to eat with us. I mean, we can't just send them off back to their table.'

'Oh Lord,' said Liz wearily.

'I think they're discussing whether to ask us to join them,' said Betty Sillitoe in a low voice. 'Don't look round,' she hissed, as Rodney began to crane his neck.

'Well, don't you stare at them,' he said.

'I can't·never look in their direction,' she said. 'That'd look totally unnatural.'

'Oh Lord!' said Rodney Sillitoe, the big wheel behind Cock-A-Doodle Chickens, none of which were French or maize-fed.

'Ted? Could you ask M'sieu Albère if I could have a word?' said Neville Badger.

When Monsieur Albert came to have a word, Neville took him to one side and asked if he had any other bookings for lunch.

'No, sir,' said Monsieur Albert. 'Usually we are vairy busy, but today . . .' He gave a very French shrug. ' . . . people make ze most of ze last sunshinings and Thursday, he is, 'ow you say? . . . a leetle bit quiet, and . . .'

'There's no need to justify yourself,' said Neville. 'I'm not suggesting your restaurant's a flop.'

Monsieur Albert gave Neville a sharp look.

'I'm sorry,' said Neville. 'I'm on edge. It's my wedding. What . . . what would you charge me to close the restaurant this lunchtime? Bearing in mind that you have no bookings.'

'Well, sir . . . people might arrive . . . and I lose custom. It must cost you . . . a hundred pounds.'

'You French drive a hard bargain. I'll give you fifty.'

Monsieur Albert knew that he must accept. It would be pure profit and, in truth, there was little likelihood of any more custom. But for decency's sake he pretended to reflect deeply on the matter before saying, 'All right. Eet ees . . . 'ow you say? . . . done!'

'And Mr and Mrs Sillitoe will join us as our guests.'

'Vairy good, sir.'

Neville approached Rodney and Betty, while Monsieur Albert turned the 'Open' sign to 'Closed'.

'Liz and I would be absolutely delighted if you'd join us for lunch,' said Neville.

'Oh!' said Rodney.

'What a surprise!' said Betty.

'Well . . . yes . . . thank you,' said Rodney.

Ted entered with a tray on which there were two glasses of champagne and an opened bottle.

'Sir? Madam?' he said to the Sillitoes, just as they joined the other guests in the bar. 'As it's such a special occasion, will you break the habits of a lifetime and indulge yourselves in a drink?'

'Thank you, *Edouard*,' said Betty icily.

'Er . . . while I remember, wai . . . *Edou* . . . Ted,' said Neville. 'I'm afraid I forgot to ask, but could we have two vegetarian meals?'

'Three,' said Rita.

'Ah!' said Ted. (Another gem, meaning, 'So the man's a vegetarian. He's probably also a hypochondriac and a suppressed homosexual and is almost certainly seeking a mother substitute in attaching himself to Rita.') He turned to Gerry Lansdown, finding it hard to conceal his satisfaction. 'You're a vegetarian.' It was a statement, not a question, and a statement expressed in the tone in which other men might have said, 'I see! You interfere with small boys in public lavatories.' Judge then of Ted's amazement and dismay when Gerry said, 'No. Morally, I feel I should be, but I'm afraid I'm too weak. I'm a founder member of the real men don't eat quiche brigade.'

'I'm the vegetarian,' said Rita.

'Good God! Rita! I mean . . .' Ted realized that neither as estranged husband nor as head waiter did he have the right to criticize Rita's eating habits. 'Er . . . three vegetarian meals,' he said. 'Right. It is rather short notice, and . . . let's be honest . . . Frenchmen and vegetarians are virtually contradictions in terms, but I'll see what Alphonse can rustle up.'

Ted hurried out.

'I'm awfully sorry, Rita,' said Neville. 'We had no idea.'

'Absolutely not!' said Liz.

'I believe you,' said Rita. 'I imagine his appearance must have been quite as embarrassing for you on your wedding day as it was for me.'

'What very nice wallpaper this place has,' said Betty hastily.

'Doesn't it?' said Rodney. 'I noticed that.'

Ted leant wearily against the large table in the middle of the kitchen. Alphonse, the scruffy young chef from Bootle, stared at him as if he couldn't believe that he'd just been asked, at this short notice, to prepare three vegetarian meals. Lil Appleyard and Ros Pennington, the double act with the double meanings, were putting the finishing touches to the salad garnishings for the lobster mayonnaise. Nobody had ever yet commented on the way they formed tiny vegetable genitalia with an injudicious juxtaposition of two radishes and a gherkin.

'Oh dear oh dear,' said Ted.

The cake-loving Sandra Pickersgill looked at him accusingly. 'You said I was all that mattered,' she said.

'Sexually,' said Ted. 'Emotionally. But.' He took a handful of cress and began to chew mechanically. Lil Appleyard gave him a dirty look.

'Take your hands off my garnishings,' she said.

'Oooh!' said Ros Pennington. 'You dirty beast.'

'But what?' said Sandra.

'What?' said Ted.

'You said "but",' said Sandra. 'But what?'

'There's my two boys in there,' said Ted. 'They still mean a lot to me. She doesn't.'

'Oh no?' said Sandra. 'I saw the way you looked at her bit of stuff. You're jealous.'

Alphonse dropped six eggs into a saucepan contemptuously, as if blaming them for not being lobsters.

'Sandra! I'm not! Love! I'm not! But!' Ted spread out his arms, appealing for moral support from Lil Appleyard and Ros Pennington. An error! There was to be no support from that quarter. Or from Alphonse. Suddenly they were all so deeply involved in their preparations for the wedding feast that they didn't even seem to be listening to these exchanges. But Ted knew that they were riveted. Sandra waited patiently for him to continue. He continued. 'Rita was a good wife. She was a good mother. She kept a good home. I mean . . . she did. I mean . . . I don't like to see her gallivanting around. Spending time in London. Letting herself be used by that young whippersnapper. I mean . . . would you, in my position? Right. You wouldn't. So.'

'How do you know he's using her?'

'Sandra! She's more than ten years older than him!'

'You're more than twenty years older than me. I'm not using you.'

'That's different.'

'Are you using me?'

All these questions were exhausting him. He slumped into a chair in the corner. Sandra looked down on him. She was carrying a tray, with four portions of lobster mayonnaise on it.

'No, love!' he said.

He stuck his left hand up her nineteenth-century Provençale costume. The fingers of his right hand explored the hole in her twentieth-century tights. She shrieked and dropped the tray. Three of the plates broke, and four portions of lobster mayonnaise were scattered across the tiled floor. Monsieur Albert entered like twelve vultures which have spotted a corpse.

'Sandra!' he said. 'You'll be paying me by the end of the week!'

'It wasn't her fault,' said Ted, as he helped Sandra rescue what she could of the four starters. 'Not this time. It was mine. I mean . . . you can't take it out of her wages if it wasn't her fault, can you?'

'I can, if I want to. You're all non-union,' said the Geordie Monsieur Albert. 'But I won't.'

'Thanks.'

'I'll take it out of *your* wages instead.'

In the bar, over the champagne, two separate efforts were being made, by two different generations, to bridge some of the gaps that had developed between the Rodenhurst and Simcock families.

In both instances, the initiative was being taken by the Simcock representative.

Rita led Liz away from the group to a corner of the bar, beside a photograph of one of the smaller châteaux of the Loire.

Liz raised her eyebrows as she waited for Rita to speak.

'I want to apologize,' said Rita. 'I didn't come here to make bitchy remarks like that.'

'Why did you come here? To show off your conquest? To let us all see how far you've travelled?'

'Oh Lord,' said Rita. 'Perhaps I did. I hoped I'd come as a gesture of . . . I don't know . . . goodwill. Reconciliation . . .

after all our families have been through.'

'That's certainly why we invited you. I mean . . . let's face it
. . . our families are still linked by marriage.'

'What do you mean, "Let's face it."?' Rita looked round as she
spoke. Paul was talking to Jenny. 'Don't you want Paul and Jenny
to get together again?'

'Of course I do. They've got a baby.'

Rita felt a sharp longing to see little Thomas again. They grew
so fast.

'Ah!' she said. 'You wouldn't want them to if they didn't have a
baby?'

'Conversation's impossible if you examine every word under a
microscope, Rita,' said Liz. 'I hope Paul and Jenny get together
again. I hoped you and I could strike up some kind of friendship
against all the odds.'

'What do you mean . . . "against all the odds"?'

'Rita! No microscopes!' Liz realized with a shock that there was
humour in Rita's eyes, that Rita had found it funny, not hurtful,
when she'd said 'Against all the odds'. She was disconcerted. This
wasn't the atmosphere in which she expected conversations
between Rodenhursts and Simcocks to be conducted. 'All I meant
was,' she said, conscious that it was a bit lame, 'who'd have
thought that you and I could ever be friends?'

'Nobody in the old days,' said Rita. 'But things have changed.
You need all the friends you can get.'

Their eyes met. Each held the look firmly. Who would have
given way first, or would they have stared at each other for all
eternity, if Ted hadn't approached, with more champagne, and
chucked a conversational stone onto their frozen village pond?

'Making friends? How touching!' he said.

The stone bounced. The ice cracked, but it didn't break.

The ageless peace of the old stone hill town above the Dordogne
formed the backcloth to Paul's efforts to restore his relationship
with Jenny.

'You don't really want to live on your own, do you?' he said. 'It
must be hard work bringing up a baby on your own.'

'Two babies.'

'Well, that's all the more reason to . . . two babies??'

'I'm pregnant.'

'Jenny!'

Paul put a hand out, to touch his wife with the deep love that surged through him. She wriggled to get free of his touch, at exactly the moment when it occurred to him that it might not be his baby, and he withdrew his hand as fast as he could.

'Ironical, isn't it?' she said. 'I must have conceived the night before the Crowning of Miss Frozen Chicken (UK).'

It was his! How could he ever have doubted it? She wasn't . . . she wasn't like him! Oh God!

She couldn't see that he was thinking these things. He couldn't see that she was wondering about the old man who was crossing the square in the photograph. Was he still alive? What was he doing at this moment? How strange for him to be so unaware that he was immortalized in this restaurant in northern England. It seemed an insult to the dignity of his life to use him as picturesque local colour.

'The night before I found out that while I was in the maternity hospital you were having it off with the runner-up.'

'Jenny! It doesn't help to exaggerate.'

'You weren't having it off?'

'She wasn't the runner-up. She came third.'

The doorbell rang, and there was a rattling and banging on the locked door of the restaurant. Monsieur Albert rushed out with his sternest, most Gallic face. If it was those kids again . . .

'We're closed,' he called out.

'I'm invited,' shouted the young man outside.

'It's Simon!' said Liz.

Simon Rodenhurst, of Trellis, Trellis, Openshaw and Finch, was well dressed in his usual rather anonymous way. He blinked and smiled nervously at the assembled guests.

Liz kissed him. 'Simon!' she said. 'You've come!'

'Yes,' he said. 'I've come. I've . . . er . . . I've compromised. I wanted to show you I disapprove . . .' Liz flinched. '. . . but I also wanted to show that I still love you.' Liz touched his arm. Monsieur Albert locked the door, and Ted approached with a glass of champagne. Simon Rodenhurst stared at him in astonishment. 'Thanks,' he said feebly. 'Yes,' he continued to his mother. 'So I decided to come to one and not the other. Then I decided that the ceremony was really the official wedding, so to show my disapproval that's what I should stay away from, and the breakfast's the really personal thing, so to show my love that's what I should come to. Besides, I don't like registry offices and I'm starving. Well, I hope I haven't missed too much of the fun.'

'Oh Simon!' His mother began to cry. Simon was astounded. He had never seen her cry before, not even at his father's funeral.

Liz had understood that Neville was going to arrange the seating for the wedding breakfast. This was probably because he'd said 'I'll arrange the seating for the wedding breakfast'. Judge then of her astonishment when he made no attempt to do so. The guests drifted towards the table. She gave Neville a meaningful look, but its meaning escaped him. People sat exactly where they liked, or, if they were among the last to arrive at the table, exactly where they didn't like.

'I thought you were going to arrange where people sat,' she said.

'I forgot,' said Neville. 'Anyway, it's all worked out all right, hasn't it? Anybody unhappy?'

Everyone shook their heads.

'You see,' said Neville. 'Everybody's perfectly happy.'

Liz forebore to point out that it wasn't possible to say, 'No. I'm extremely unhappy. I hate the people I'm sitting next to.'

'It couldn't have worked out better if we'd planned it all,' beamed Neville.

Neville sat at one end of the table. On his left, along the wall, with their backs to a huge photograph of the wide, shallow, stony river Loire, sat Gerry Lansdown, Rita, Carol Fordingbridge, Elvis, Simon and Jenny. Liz sat at the other end. On her left were Rodney and Betty Sillitoe, Arthur Badger, Paul, and Andrew Denton. If one started at Rodney, it went man, woman, man, man, man, man, man, woman, woman, man, man, woman, woman. Hopeless. Liz felt that it was quite wrong that Rita should sit next to Gerry, Elvis next to Carol, and Rodney beside Betty. Couples should be split up and made to be sociable, otherwise they might just as well be at home. It was also wrong that Jenny should be beside Simon, and appalling that Simon should be next to Elvis. And it seemed almost deliberately perverse that Paul and Jenny, the one couple who *should* be next to each other, because they were estranged and should therefore be made to be sociable, were separated by the length and width of the table.

Apart from these criticisms, she was totally happy with the seating arrangements.

Monsieur Albert entered with a huge tray, resplendent with ten portions of lobster mayonnaise. Sandra followed with a smaller tray, and three portions of egg mayonnaise. Ted brought up the rear with the chablis.

Monsieur Albert placed a dish in front of Liz, beaming with self-satisfaction. He waited, as if expecting lavish praise and astonishment.

'Thank you,' said Liz coolly.

'Ah!' said Neville, as Ted approached him with the chablis. 'Good man!'

Ted didn't exactly relish being addressed as 'Good man!' by Neville, but he bore it stoically. He was almost beyond social suffering on his own behalf. His main concern was for Sandra.

Sandra moved stiffly and nervously round the table under Ted's discouragingly encouraging eye. After what Lil Appleyard and Ros Pennington had said, she couldn't bring herself to look at the twenty-six round red radishes and the thirteen sad shrivelled gherkins that topped the garnishings.

Nobody else had realized that there were thirteen at table, but it worried Sandra dreadfully.

Miraculously, there were no disasters.

'Chef, 'e apologizes if ze egg, he is slightly of ze lukewarm,' said the Gallic Monsieur Albert. ''e was not given much noticings.'

Neville smiled apologetically at Liz.

Paul had been particularly unfortunate over the seating arrangements. Not only was he seated between Arthur Badger and Andrew Denton, but every time he looked across the table he could see his mother making a fool of herself with Gerry Lansdown. Mutton dressed as lamb was bad enough, but mutton dressed as lamb and falling in love with another lamb, that was going too far. He munched his lukewarm eggs morosely. If he wasn't going to be able to go back to Jenny, he'd a good mind to become a meat-eating, fish-guzzling slob again.

Jenny said, 'Doesn't it worry you that they scream when they're boiled alive?' to Rodney, and Paul called down the table, 'Thanks to you, Jenny, two fluffy yellow chicks have been aborted,' but apart from that the conversation was well suited to the occasion, and Andrew Denton enjoyed his lobster so much, being happily oblivious that it had recently been sliding across the kitchen floor, that he didn't make a single joke throughout the whole first course.

Ted replenished their glasses with the pale yellow chablis most punctiliously. He caught a look of surprised approval on Liz's face as he carefully gave Rodney and Betty Sillitoe rather less than their due. He was also less than generous to Gerry Lansdown and Rita. 'It has a certain flinty integrity, doesn't it, sir?' he said icily to Gerry, investing the 'sir' with a light coating of irony. Gerry sipped his wine reflectively, and said, 'I hate to take issue with an expert, but I think it has a rather flighty insouciance. I find that most of the wines from the southern end of that particular vineyard, near the railway bridge, do have a slightly roguish character,' and Ted moved on hurriedly.

People were cracking lobster limbs long after the last lukewarm egg had disappeared. The vegetarians felt superior but hungry.

Monsieur Albert carved the chateaubriand himself. It was crisp outside, and juicily red inside. Ted neatly divided the mushroom omelette into three portions.

'Chef, 'e is desolate that it is for ze vegetarians once again ze egg,' said Monsieur Albert. 'If 'e 'as only 'ad more time, what a wonderful creation 'e will 'ave been making for you.'

Neville smiled apologetically at Liz.

There were seven separate vegetables. Sandra served them, and there was only one unfortunate contretemps, and even this could have been worse, since braised fennel matched Rita's trouser suit perfectly.

'I grew twenty-three vegetables last year,' said Andrew Denton.

'Very good!' said Paul morosely. The beef smelt magnificent. The mushrooms were tinned, and the omelette was rubbery.

'Seventeen peas and six beans,' said Andrew Denton. 'Joke.'

Ted poured a tiny drop of the Gevrey-Chambertin. Neville examined it against the light, sniffed it, and said it was excellent.

Ted left most of the glasses less than half full, so that the wine could breathe. He gave Liz a defiant glare as he filled Rodney's and Betty's glasses almost to the brim. He made no comment on the wine to Gerry Lansdown.

Liz asked Rodney if he had seen the revealing and degrading photographs of the Crowning of Miss Frozen Chicken (UK) in the colour supplement of the . . . er . . . she couldn't remember which one. They were all the same, weren't they? They had accompanied an article about the degrading awfulness of beauty contests, which had been sandwiched between a feature on Europe's last stretch of untouristy coastline and how to get there, and a tirade against the cheap sneers made about our royal family in the foreign press, with all the cheap sneers reprinted in full. He told her that he had seen them, and would like to wring Barry Precious's neck, if he could trace him. She asked him if he had seen the series of nude studies of Denise Saltmarsh doing very strange things with chickens, which had appeared in the porno-graphic magazine *Slime*, or so she had been told, as of course she hadn't seen them. He told her that he had seen them, and would like to wring Nigel Thick's neck, if he hadn't left Marwoods of Moor Street and gone to London. 'Oh dear,' she said, as if the thought had suddenly occurred to her. 'I do hope this isn't an embarrassing subject for you.'

Carol Fordingbridge told Rita how Denise Saltmarsh had been stripped of her title as well as her clothes, so that Beverley Roberts was now Miss Frozen Chicken (UK) and Carol was now second, which was just as useless as being third. Rita didn't bother to launch herself into her views on female dignity, partly because it wasn't an appropriate time but mainly because she was conscious that Gerry was trying to get her attention. Gerry was trying to get her attention partly because Andrew Denton was telling him jokes, but mainly because he had a very important question to put to Rita. But Rita couldn't wriggle free from her conversation with Carol Fordingbridge as long as Carol seemed so eager to talk to her because Elvis, her intermittently negligent fiancé, was busy listening to the whispered confessions of Simon, which were irritating Liz enormously, partly because it's rude to whisper at table, but mainly because she couldn't hear them.

'You remember you were talking about all the opportunities I must get, showing beautiful women round houses, of making mad, passionate love to them, and I said that sort of thing isn't done at Trellis, Trellis, Openshaw and Finch,' Simon was saying.

'Yes.'

'Well, it's not quite as much not done as it used to be not done.' There was no mistaking the pride, coyly though it was expressed, that throbbed in the young estate agent's veins.

'Congratulations, Simon. Tell me more,' said the cynical Elvis Simcock. 'I know you're dying to.'

'Not at all!' Simon Rodenhurst was as loftily indignant as it's possible to be in an undertone. 'I always think men who boast of their sexual exploits are pathetic.'

'Fair enough,' said Elvis. 'Good point.'

'She's a married woman,' said Simon. 'Very attractive. She went to look at this house, said her husband wanted to move, but she didn't, but she had to go through the motions to please him. She said he was a bit of a drip, and her life was dreadfully dull. Even I could see she was making advances to me.'

'So you ripped up your specifications, said, "Darling, forget the handsome proportions, the charming southerly aspect over the well-stocked garden," and flung her on the spacious, convenient bed and had her there and then.'

'Good Lord, no! That would have been professionally unethical. It was someone else's house.' Simon looked round the table anxiously. Elvis wasn't sure whether he was worried that he might be overheard or worried that he might not be. 'I took her to my flat.'

'Who is this mystery woman?'

'Elvis! This is a small town. She's a married woman. Credit me with a little common sense and discretion.'

'Sorry.'

Sandra cleared the dirty plates. Paul wondered morosely whether the dessert would be egg pudding. It wasn't.

'Better than losseroles, eh?' said Andrew Denton.

'You what?' said Paul blankly.

'These are profiteroles.'

Oh, Jenny! thought Paul. I want you so much.

'Profiteroles are better than losseroles.'

I need you so much, thought Paul.

'Joke.'

I love you so much, thought Paul. He realized that Andrew Denton had been speaking. 'What?' he said.

'Joke.'

'Ah.'

He laughed.

'Elvis?' said Simon, still warm with the glow of the confessional.

'Yes?' said intensive chicken farming's leading young thinker cautiously, warned by something in Simon's tone.

'I . . . er . . . this isn't easy, but . . . you and I . . .'

'Oh my God! I think you're going to say something nice to me.'

'Exactly. Oh Lord, I wish I wasn't so Anglo-Saxon. It shouldn't be that difficult to say "Elvis. I'm so glad I met you."'

'Well . . . thanks, Simon. I've met worse twits myself. Not many, but some.'

'You've changed me, you see. If it wasn't for you, I'd never have had the courage to get anywhere with Judy.'

'Judy!'

'Oh Lord.' Simon Rodenhurst looked round the table anxiously, and this time he definitely hoped that he hadn't been overheard. 'I'm no good at this sort of thing.'

It was almost three o'clock on a sunny autumn afternoon. The weather seemed to be holding up pretty well in the Loire Valley too. The little group in front of the huge photograph of the river bed, in the otherwise deserted restaurant, were mellowed by good food and wine. Simon turned to talk to his young sister. How lovely she was. How fond he was of her. How well, he felt, they had always got on. Squabbles, rows, fights, whole weeks when they had refused to speak to each other, these had merely been light fluffy clouds in the perpetual sunshine of their youth.

When she saw that Simon was talking to Jenny, Carol Fordingbridge grabbed the opportunity of having a few words with her fiancé. They discussed their honeymoon, and what they would do on it. One ambition was to stand naked in the Mediterranean, with their hands round each other's bums and a ripe fig in their two mouths, and to chew the fig until their lips met. Some of their other plans were of a rather more sensuous nature.

And so, like a ripple through a pack of cards, Simon's turning to talk to Jenny had its repercussions throughout the group. Rita no longer had to talk to Carol. Gerry was therefore able to put his question to her.

'Will you marry me, Rita?' he asked.

Rita was astounded. She was pretty astounded by her answer

too. Expecting to hear herself say, 'Yes, of course I will, my darling' she found herself saying, 'You're just saying that because you've had a few drinks and you're infected by the romantic mood of the wedding.'

'No,' said Gerry Lansdown. 'The drink may have helped me pluck up courage, but I decided to ask you days ago.'

'I'm married.'

'Get divorced.'

'I'm more than ten years older than you.'

'Hardly what I'd expected, but you can't plan love.'

'I've two grown-up sons.'

'Don't you want to marry me?'

Rita thought hard. She thought quickly. After all, there's a limit to how long you can decently pause before answering a question of that nature.

'No, Gerry,' she said, looking straight into his pale blue eyes. 'Quite honestly I don't think I do.'

Neville Badger, unable to talk to Gerry Lansdown, had a choice between his own company and that of Andrew Denton. No contest! He began to think about Jane.

With his belly full of beef and burgundy, and his heart full of warmth and love for all women, but especially Judy and Jenny, in the early afternoon of that autumn day, Simon Rodenhurst felt that he must sort out his young sister's life for her. 'Go back to Paul,' he urged. 'I mean, he's not the first or the last married person to have a fling.'

'We built our marriage on an edifice of total trust which was an essential part of our whole philosophy of existence.'

'Phew!'

'I know. It's very easy to laugh at us.'

Simon hesitated, then decided that he owed it to her to persist.

'I wouldn't laugh at you if you could laugh at yourselves,' he said.

'Yes, but you've got to try to live your life with some ideals and standards, haven't you?' said Jenny.

'Yes, and if you fail, maybe you ought to try harder next time, rather than just give up.'

'That's not easy.'

'I'm aware of that, but . . .' He knew he was sounding pompous.

Well, his dignity was less important than Jenny's happiness. He gritted his teeth and continued. '. . . nothing worthwhile ever is easy, is it?' he said. 'I didn't find that easy to say,' he added, 'but . . .'

'. . . nothing worthwhile ever is easy, is it?' said Jenny, and they both laughed. 'You know, you've improved recently, Simon,' she said.

'That's one of those awful remarks that sound like a compliment and are really an insult, like "you look smart!", suggesting that for twenty-five years you've looked as if you've just crawled through a hedge,' said Simon.

'No. What I mean is . . . you've suddenly grown up.'

'At last, do you mean?' said Simon. 'Is that the implication?'

'Oh God,' said Jenny. 'Did I sound awfully patronizing?'

'Dreadfully.'

'Oh Lord.' She gave a rather forced, uncertain little laugh. 'You see,' she said. 'I am laughing at myself a little.'

Suddenly Jane was there, all around Neville, and the pain of it was shocking. He looked down the table at Liz, whom he had known for so long, who was so beautiful, as lovely perhaps as Jane, and he saw a total stranger. He needed to be on his own. He rushed out. He dimly saw Jane's alarmed face. No, Liz's alarmed face. Oh God. He locked himself in a cubicle in the gents' toilet. It was the only course of action he could think of in which his movements would not need explaining.

Perhaps he had noticed Ted's wet bottom at the charity horse-racing evening, or perhaps he expected somebody to lie full length on the tiled floor and peer under the door to check up on him. Or perhaps he dropped his trousers from force of habit.

There, in that undignified position, with his pants and trousers round his ankles, the immaculate Neville Badger called out to his former wife.

With the profiteroles Ted had served *premier cru* Sauternes. Neville Badger had done things in style. What a pity that he was sitting in the lavatory, communing with his dead wife, and couldn't immediately enjoy the vintage port which was served with the cheese. Ted was careful to fill the glasses of Rodney and

Betty Sillitoe to the brim.

'Thank you, Ted,' said Rodney. 'It's funny,' he said to Betty, 'how it took Ted and Rita to realize that we take it in turns to get drunk when we go to dos.'

'Absolutely,' said Betty. 'Absolutely absolutely.'

'You realize why we take it in turns to get drunk at dos, don't you?'

'So that there's somebody sober to drive home.'

'I think there's more to it than that. I think one of us stays sober instinctively to protect the one they love from making fools of themselves or herselves which they may very well do if drunk and have. Because we love each other so much.'

'We do, don't we? Over thirty years and we still love each other.'

'But the driving's important, too. I mean, take today. I can . . . not get drunk, because I'm not . . . but have a bit too much, knowing you're driving.'

'I thought you were driving.'

'What?'

'Oh dear. I think the system's broken down,' said Betty. 'Because, because I thought you were driving, I've had . . . well, not too much too much, but a bit too much. I mean, I wouldn't describe myself as drunk exactly. More . . .'

'. . . totally plastered.'

'Yes.'

Rodney and Betty Sillitoe roared with laughter.

Everybody looked at them.

Ted permitted himself a slight smile, then gave a last glare in Gerry Lansdown's direction, and returned to the kitchen.

'You *are* jealous,' said Sandra. She took an uneaten profiterole from the top of a pile of dirty dessert plates, popped it into her mouth, and added, with her mouth full, 'You keep looking at them.'

Alphonse, the scruffy young chef from Bootle, had set off for his meagre lodgings on his motorbike, to sleep for two hours in a tiny, dank bedroom which smelt of petrol, chips and semen. Lil Appleyard and Ros Pennington were clearing up and washing up. In the pocket of Ros Pennington's apron there was a shrivelled gherkin. It would be greeted with roars when she produced it in the Crown and Walnut that evening.

'Sandra!' said Ted. 'I do not keep looking at them. I am not jealous. I mean . . . I'm not!'

Sandra hesitated, then took the remains of another profiterole. Ted frowned. Her love of cake and buns bordered on the obsessive. She even backed Chelsea and Dundee on the pools each week. One day, if he wasn't careful, her buxom charms, the delicious amplitude of her catering-size breasts and bottom, would degenerate into mere vastness.

'Sandra!' he said. 'Don't eat the leftovers. It's disgusting. It's unhygienic. You can catch things off used cake.'

'Your eyes hardly left them,' she said.

'Sandra!' he said. 'I am not jealous! I mean . . . love . . . I'm not. It's over. I wouldn't have her back if she came to me on bended knee.'

'Some chance of that. She's got a new feller.'

'Sandra! You're so naïve sometimes. Rita's using him. To make me jealous. Because she wants me back. She *is*.'

'I thought you said *he* was using her.'

Lil Appleyard and Ros Pennington waited breathlessly for Ted's reply.

'They're using each other,' he said.

'Well that's all right then, isn't it?' said Sandra.

'That's what I'm telling you!' Ted was almost shouting now.

'Well why go on about it, then?'

'It's you who's going on about it,' he cried through gritted teeth. 'Oh God! Sandra!'

He swept out to the restaurant.

Tears were streaming down Neville Badger's face, and his lips moved silently as he spoke to his dead wife.

'Oh, Jane,' he was saying. 'I didn't want this to happen. I didn't want a new life. I didn't want the agony to end. Forgive me.'

'Are you all right?'

He jumped, and almost justified his presence in the cubicle. Then his heart slowed again. It was a male voice, quite unlike Jane's.

326

'Fine, Arthur. Andrew told me a joke that I found rather indigestible.'

The almost immaculate Arthur Badger laughed and returned to the restaurant.

Neville Badger, elegant doyen of the town's legal community, blew his nose, pulled his trousers up, pulled the chain from force of habit, left the cubicle, washed his face, couldn't find any towels, tried using the hand dryer, got a repulsive faceful of hot air, and summoned up the strength to return to his wedding breakfast and his new wife.

Ted was taking orders for brandies and liqueurs. Liz tried to prevent him from asking the Sillitoes, but he didn't seem to see her frantic but discreet signals.

Liz asked Neville if he was all right. He frowned, as if she'd committed a social solecism by almost mentioning a natural function, common to all, whose existence in the world was completely ignored by polite society. Liz smiled uncertainly at him. He gave her a cool, unsmiling look which terrified her. Then, at last, unnaturally, with difficulty, he smiled.

Rita and Gerry were deep in private conversation again. Neville thought this rather rude. It was also extremely inconvenient. It meant he'd have to talk to Andrew Denton. So he listened, discreetly, to their conversation, hoping that he would find some suitable peg on which to hang his interruption. He was horrified to hear Rita say, 'I'm not saying I don't love you. I'm saying I don't want to marry you.' He sighed, wished that he wasn't a gentleman, and turned to talk to Andrew Denton.

'What do you want to do?' said Gerry, no longer overheard by Neville.

Rita's reply was barely audible even to Gerry. 'Live together,' she said.

'You really are determined to throw off your conventional past, aren't you?'

'I don't think there's anything terribly unconventional about two consenting adults living together these days,' said Rita. 'I'm just not sure I can throw off my past enough to do something as bold as marry you.'

Three fourth-form boys from the Abbey School, in their straw hats and smug blue blazers, pressed their noses against the windows of Chez Albert, made loud raspberries, and ran off, laughing. Is there any hope left for the human race? thought Paul, with that angry contempt which people so often feel for a stage of life which they have not long left.

Gerry Lansdown didn't even notice the boys. 'It's a little awkward, Rita,' he said. 'In my position.'

'You mean I might lose you votes?'

'Well, I wouldn't put it as crudely as that, but, yes, it is true that a politician can't really afford to have a private life that isn't blameless.'

'You're prospective Liberal candidate for Hindhead, not shadow foreign secretary.'

'Rita!'

'I mean does the word Liberal really mean anything to you?'

'Are you asking me to quote my election manifesto?'

'Gerry!'

Rita felt that they were on the verge of their first row, here in public, at a wedding breakfast. Ted would witness it. She didn't want to give him the satisfaction.

'I'm only saying I'd prefer to marry you,' said Gerry. 'Of course I'll live with you if you won't marry me.'

'Oh, Gerry, I'm so happy.' Rita began to cry. She hurried from the table. Liz raised her eyes at Gerry. He smiled reassuringly. Liz felt a pang of disappointment.

Ted, approaching with a tray of brandies and liqueurs, interrupted Rita before she could leave the room.

'Rita!' he said. 'You're crying! What has he done to you?'

'We're going to live together.'

'I knew it! He's an unprincipled swine!'

Rita blew her nose. 'Give up, Ted,' she said. 'Our marriage is over.'

'Oh no! No!' said Ted. 'No! I know that, Rita! No, I was just thinking of you. I just don't want you to be unhappy, that's all.'

'I'm not. Oh God, so why am I crying?' She turned to look back at the wedding party. Only Gerry appeared to be aware that she was talking to Ted, though Liz's lack of interest struck her as suspicious. Gerry half rose, asking her in mime whether she wanted to be rescued. She shook her head, tried to smile reassuringly, and turned to Ted. 'Shouldn't you be serving those liqueurs?' she asked. 'Elvis'll die if he doesn't get his green chartreuse.'

'Rita! You can't see it because you're besotted,' said Ted, absurd in his evening dress in the middle of the afternoon. 'He'll use you and when he's finished with you . . .' Sandra entered with coffee. Ted changed his tone abruptly. '. . . would you like a liqueur?'

'Thank you,' said Rita, giving Sandra a sharp glance. 'I'll take this one.' She took a liqueur at random. It was Andrew Denton's Cointreau, as it chanced. 'Cheers!' She raised the little glass of almost colourless liquid, sipped, and grimaced.

'Rita!' said Ted. 'You don't drink liqueurs, and that was ordered.'

'I do now, and you can pour another one.'

'Rita! Listen!' Ted went behind the bar to pour another liqueur. He put the tray on the counter. Rita went through the wrought-iron arch into the bar area and perched herself on a bar stool, a thing she had never done in her life, a position she had always felt was only adopted by fast, loose women. Twenty-five years of married life faced each other across the counter of the deserted bar. Exactly behind Ted, and slightly above him, the French barman also stared at her. 'Listen,' repeated Ted. 'You can't see it because you're besotted. But . . . I mean . . . be honest, Rita. He'll use you and when he's finished with you he'll cast you aside like a clapped-out old car sponge that's losing its fluff.'

'Thank you for that flattering image.'

'Oh no! No! Rita! Love! I didn't mean I'd ever think of you as a . . .' He couldn't bring himself to repeat it.

Rita could. '. . . clapped-out old car sponge that's losing its fluff.'

'Absolutely. I mean, who could?'

'Except him?'

'Exactly. Now you're beginning to see it!'

Ted put the replacement Cointreau on the tray, and picked the tray up.

'It was my idea that we should live together,' said Rita quietly, looking over Ted's head to the French barman.

Ted put the tray down again. 'Rita!' he said. 'Are you seriously telling me that you suggested living in sin?'

'No. Hindhead. The Liberals believe you must build the political power base on local foundations.'

'Liberals?'

Rita wished that Ted could have found something more original to resemble at that moment than a bewildered cod. But she also began to feel sorry for him. 'Gerry is prospective Liberal candidate for Hindhead,' she explained.

'Ah!' Ted briefly permitted himself a simper of satisfaction at this 'ah!'. It was a good one, one of his best. It meant 'Ah! He's a politician. I always knew there was something wrong with him. And this explains quite a lot about *your* behaviour.' He couldn't resist the temptation of expanding on his theme, in case Rita hadn't understood all the nuances implicit in his 'ah!'. 'No wonder you're going all cranky,' he said.

'Cranky?'

'Vegetarian. Feminist. Caring about animals and the poor and Bolivia and things. Cranky.'

'He wants to marry me.'

Ted looked as though he'd been bashed over the head with a bewildered cod. 'Well . . .' he said. 'Good. Good. I'm glad he's serious. Good. But.'

There was a long pause. 'What do you mean . . . "but"?' Rita was forced to say at last.

'Well . . . I mean . . . what do you know about him? Where did you meet him?'

'In Harvey Wedgewood's dressing room. Then we ran into each other at a CND rally.'

'I knew it! He's a bloody freak!' Ted had a terrible thought. 'Rita! What were you doing there?'

'I don't want to go into the nuclear debate now,' said Rita, 'but even if you aren't a unilateralist it's clear to me that cruise missiles are an appallingly risky option which only make military sense if you consider them not as a defensive weapon but in the context of the West adopting a policy of limited nuclear response, whereby we'd respond to a conventional attack by being the first to use nuclear weapons, and that is totally unacceptable to me. I wouldn't want to live in a country that had taken such a step or to participate in any victory it might bring. Mind you, I'm beginning to think I am a unilateralist because I believe it's obscene to spend

330

so much on defending ourselves when there's such need elsewhere in the world. I'm not actually sure a society as selfish as that is worth saving.'

'I'm glad you don't want to go into the nuclear debate now,' said Ted weakly. 'I suppose you got all that from him.'

'Of course! Mere woman that I am, I am incapable of independent thought!'

'Rita! Love! I didn't mean that! I mean . . . I didn't. I just meant . . . he's a politician. He's pumping you with propaganda.' Ted sneered in the general direction of Gerry Lansdown, through the wrought-iron screen.

'You shouldn't believe all you read in the Tory papers, Ted,' said Rita. 'Those CND rallies are attended by a lot of respectable people of all ages from many walks of life. Ordinary people like me.'

'Ordinary? I'm beginning to wonder if you are ordinary any more.'

'Thank you.'

'It wasn't a compliment! All right, I'll excuse you, it's your bodily chemistry, but what's his excuse?'

'What??? My bodily chemistry??' And I'd begun to feel sorry for him, thought Rita.

'Come on, Rita. I mean . . . be honest. It is, isn't it?' Ted mouthed the offending words, even though they were alone in the bar. 'The change.'

Rita felt her cheeks going red. It wasn't the pink spots. It was anger. Splendid, fierce anger. She didn't care if he did mistake it for a hot flush.

'How dare you??'

'Rita. People'll hear. What *will* they think? I mean . . . keep it casual.'

Rita smiled. In a bright, casual voice, she said, 'You prejudiced, bigoted, blinkered, chauvinistic, rude, small-minded sod.'

'Rita!!!'

'Ted! People! Casual!'

'Yes, but . . . I mean . . . look, OK, he's not a freak. Fair enough. But.'

'Again, I'm forced to ask "but what?"'

'He's a Liberal namby-pamby. Middle of the road. Always

sitting on fences.'

'A minute ago he was pumping me full of fiery radical convictions. Now he's sitting on fences. You can't have it both ways. Unless you mean he's sitting on fences around American air bases.'

'Rita!'

Sandra returned towards the kitchen. She gave them a look. Rita didn't see her. Ted gave Sandra a determinedly casual look. Rita looked round to see the object of his determinedly casual look, but she had gone.

'I mean,' said Ted. 'I mean . . . do you? Know anything about him? He could be a con man.'

'He's been adopted by the Liberals.'

'It's been known, Rita. What do you personally know about him?'

'He played rugby for Rosslyn Park. He's a good cricketer. He loves opera. His father's a headmaster. His mother's a J.P. His brother's a doctor. I've met them all. Gerry owns a small but successful micro-chip factory in Godalming.'

'Good!' said Ted after a pause. 'Good! Well . . . good. I mean . . . he sounds all right. I'm glad, Rita.' He paused, then resumed, as if he took her silence for disagreement. 'I am! I mean . . . I am!'

'Is there anybody in your life, Ted?' she asked.

'Yes. Yes, I'm glad to say there is. Very much so, in fact. Yes. Sexual and emotional fulfilment have crossed the Simcock threshold.'

'I'm glad, Ted. Would you like to tell me about her?'

There was a crash of plates from the kitchen.

'Not a lot, no.'

Ted didn't like the look in Rita's eye. Did she suspect about Sandra? Well, if she did, she did. What did it matter now? Why not admit it? Because he couldn't. He found himself saying, 'She's . . . er . . . a bit of a public figure in this town. I mean . . . discretion, eh?'

'I understand,' said Rita. Did she? 'Well, I'm glad there is somebody, Ted. You'll be anxious to get the divorce through as quickly as I am, then.'

Rita moved off, leaving Ted flabbergasted. He pulled himself together and hurried over with the brandies and liqueurs. He gave

Liz a big smile as he handed Rodney and Betty Sillitoe their drinks.

Betty raised her glass to Rodney, but he didn't respond.

'It's the skeleton at the feast,' he said. 'It's the spectre in the cupboard.'

'Pardon?' said Betty, puzzled. 'What is?'

'My chickens. Can you reconcile your kindly husband with the cruel beast who keeps living creatures cooped up in misery?'

'I must admit. Sometimes at night I dream I'm like that. Cooped up. Awful.'

'We've had a good innings,' said Rodney. 'We've got a bit set by. What say we go off and do it?'

'Do what?'

'Set my chickens free.'

Betty had a vision of hundreds of chicken trussers, all built like Beverley Roberts, singing 'Set My Chickens Free' in marvellous, full-throated unison as they busily untrussed chickens. The vision faded in the face of Rodney's intensity.

'Are you serious?' she said.

'Never been less serious in my life.'

'It would be rather nice.'

Rodney stood up. 'Er . . . Betty and I have work to do,' he announced, 'back at work, where I work. So . . . er . . .'

Betty Sillitoe, who was over-emotional as usual, stood up, lurching only slightly. 'Thank you very much for inviting us,' she said. 'Well, not inviting us exactly. Seeing us there and thinking "Oh Lord, have to . . ."'

'Betty!'

'". . . have to invite them now," but you did, that's the point, and thank you.'

Rodney and Betty were swaying like poplars in a gale. Liz gave Neville an urgent stare, and he awoke to his responsibilities with a start.

'You can't drive like that,' he said, hurrying over to them.

'I won't,' said Rodney. 'I'll get a taxi. Here. My key cars.' He handed his car keys to Neville Badger with great solemnity, as if fulfilling his part in some traditional ceremony. 'There. Proof. Taxi. Work to do. Come on, Betty.'

Liz took Betty by the arm, Neville took Rodney, and they

steered the Sillitoes to the door as fast as they could without provoking resistance.

'Thank you very much,' said Rodney. 'Betty didn't mean . . .' He turned to the other guests. 'Goodbye, each,' he said. 'Where was I? Oh yes. I would like you to know that I do not agree with Betty.'

Liz felt it safer to make no reply. She rattled the door frantically, but it was locked.

'Don't agree with me what?' said Betty.

'I think Liz genuinely loves him.'

'Rodney!'

'No. Please. It's got to be said. I do. I don't think she's calculated the whole caboosh down to the last thingummy.'

Monsieur Albert hurried into the restaurant, wreathed in Gallic charm. Liz asked him if he could order a taxi. He understood that this was not a theoretical question about his competence, but a concrete request. He intimated that he would comply with it, and asked why they didn't wait for it in the restaurant. Neville answered with a discreet movement of his head towards the Sillitoes, and Monsieur Albert drove a tank through his discretion by saying, 'Ah! Of course, sir!' The Sillitoes gave each other meaningful looks, Monsieur Albert executed a few swift, flamboyant, continental gestures, and what had been locked was open.

'I'm sorry,' said Betty to Liz, as she lurched through the door.

'Well, you shouldn't have said it,' said Rodney. 'But then you're drunk.'

'I know,' said Betty. 'So am I.'

They snaked across Moor Street, which was one-way westwards, and stood in the sunshine, waiting for the taxi. The sunshine was painfully bright after the gloom of the north-facing restaurant. The Sillitoes blinked like owls caught in a car's headlights. Wayne Oldroyd, Nigel Thick's pasty-faced replacement at Marwoods, watched them with amusement. He would never change his name or become famous. A badly maintained bright yellow corporation bus howled smokily up the gentle hill that led from the Flannerly Roundabout and the placid autumnal Gadd towards the abbey church. The owner of the Chinese takeaway took himself away to the betting shop, and a young despatch rider overtook the bus, thus taking the lead, in the seething excitement of his mind, in the Isle of Man TT. Neville Badger shook his head slowly, as if amazed that life outside Chez Albert was continuing at all.

At last the taxi came. Neville and Liz breathed a sigh of relief as it sped the big wheel and his overdressed wife off towards Cock-A-Doodle Chickens.

'She was drunk,' said Neville.

Liz felt that it would have been better if he'd said nothing.

The party broke up, stretched their legs, formed little groups. Andrew Denton took the opportunity to approach Simon Rodenhurst. 'Excuse me?' he said.

'Why, what have you done?' asked Simon, who was slightly drunk. 'Joke.'

'Are you the Mr Rodenhurst of whom my wife speaks so warmly?' said Andrew Denton.

Simon suddenly felt slightly sober. 'I beg your pardon?' he said.

'Are you Simon Rodenhurst, of Trellis, Trellis, Openshaw and Finch?'

'Yes,' admitted Simon cautiously.

'You showed my wife Judy round a house in Swaledale Crescent the other week. She said you were most obliging.'

'Well, I . . . tried.'

'And succeeded, from the sound of it! Though I'm afraid the time you spent with her was utterly wasted.'

'Not at all, I do assure you. I mean . . . it happens in business. You've found somewhere else, have you?'

'We've decided to stay in Otley. We like the schools, you see.'

'Ah!'

'That's why she can't be here today. She's having a bad day. After many years of trying, we're expecting a happy event.'

'Oh! Well . . . congratulations.'

'Thank you. It's a great relief for me, as the doctors suspected I might be sterile.'

'Well . . . what do doctors know?' Simon sat down abruptly.

'Absolutely. You're right there. Are you feeling all right?'

'Fine,' said Simon. 'Yes, I . . . I just feel a little sick.'

335

'You'll make a fortune if *you're* pregnant,' said Andrew Denton. 'Joke.'

Andrew Denton moved off. Slowly, Simon dared to hope that his comments had been innocent, and he didn't suspect.

Elvis Simcock approached. He looked concerned.

'Are you all right?' he asked.

'I wish I'd never met you,' said Simon Rodenhurst, of Trellis, Trellis, Openshaw and Finch.

The Geordie Monsieur Albert asked Ted to enter his little office. It was covered in bills and paper. It had a roll-top desk and a table with a green leather top. On the wall there was a calendar from Frodshams the Friendly Frozen Food Folk. It had a picture of a nude young lady. On the desk there was a calendar from the Gadd Valley Garage. It had a picture of the Gadd Valley Garage.

'I've been watching you, Ted,' said Monsieur Albert. 'You've coped well under great personal pressure. Just as, when we're busy, you've coped well under great professional pressure. Are you happy in your work?'

'Well, I can't exactly say being a head waiter was my burning ambition. Especially when I've only got one waitress under me.'

Ted thought about Sandra under him. Increasingly, as he grew older, his moments of greatest sexual feeling were ill timed. He felt a sharp spasm of desire for her. He longed to take a walk through the black forest of his beloved gâteau. Oh God! No more cake imagery, please! Oh God, he'd missed what Monsieur Albert was saying.

'Sorry,' he said. 'I missed that.'

'I said, you have an impressive capacity for shutting out personal considerations and concentrating on your work,' said the Geordie Monsieur Albert.

'Ah.'

'How would you like to go into partnership?'

Ted gawped.

'I need a partner,' said Monsieur Albert. 'I want to expand. I've already found a site for *Chez Edouard*.'

'*Chez Edouard*! I'm not a restauranteur, Monsieur Albert. I don't want to open a restaurant called *Chez Edouard*. I want to be a freelance designer of toasting forks, fire irons and assorted useful household objects of similar ilk.'

'Going well, is it?'

Ted didn't reply. Monsieur Albert smiled and offered him a large cigar. He took it. Monsieur Albert lit it with a flourish. Ted coughed.

'I'll think about it,' he said, between splutters.

'I'm adequately funded.'

Ted had often wondered how Monsieur Albert had got his capital. He couldn't miss this cue. 'How did you manage to become "adequately funded"?' he asked.

'Simple. With tips. Tips from generous customers. Tips from financiers about where to invest those tips.' Ted gawped. He couldn't believe you could build a fortune out of tips. 'I worked for eleven years in a fashionable Italian restaurant in London,' explained Monsieur Albert. 'Full of famous people. Terry Wogan. Des O'Connor. Dame Peggy Ashcroft. Ian Botham. Professor A. J. Ayer. General Dayan. Michael Heseltine. Frank Carson. Joan Sutherland. Good tippers. It's surprising how much you can make if you aren't strictly honest about sharing out. Why this imitation of a mentally retarded newt?'

'Those photos in the Angel . . .' Ted began.

'The owner died. The restaurant was closed. Nobody seemed to want them. I got a very good price from the Angel.'

Cigar smoke eddied around the little office. Ted coughed. Monsieur Albert also coughed, but his was a social cough, a prelude to the broaching of a delicate subject.

'Just one thing,' he said. 'Sandra.'

'Sandra?'

'Sandra. Are you . . . er . . .?'

'That's my business, isn't it?'

'Not if you join my business.'

'Ah!'

'Precisely. So . . . I repeat . . . are you . . . er . . .?'

'Yes. We are . . . er . . .'

'One thing we will be, Ted, is classy. We may not be good, that isn't important, people are pig-ignorant about food, but we will be classy. Therefore, I'm afraid, if you're my partner, no Sandra.'

Ted felt angry and insulted. He disliked Monsieur Albert intensely, both in his Geordie and his Gallic guise. He felt angry

337

for Sandra, too. Damn it, she was human. Flesh and blood. A little too much flesh but, if she could be weaned off the cake, who knew? But he also felt cautious enough not to show that he was feeling angry and insulted. And he felt ashamed of himself for feeling cautious. And he felt that he was feeling too much. It was getting stifling in the little office. He was sweating. He found himself looking at the nude girl in the Frodshams the Friendly Frozen Food Folk calendar. Cigar smoke wisped around her pubic hair. He turned hurriedly to the Gadd Valley Garage.

Monsieur Albert was smiling. 'Think about it,' he said.

It didn't take Rita long, after the happy couple had returned, to negotiate a little private chat with Liz.

'I'm sorry for what I said,' she said. 'I bear no grudge any more.'

'Thank you, Rita,' said Liz. 'I hope you and Gerry'll be very happy.'

'Thank you very much.'

'You're wondering if I mean that.'

They were standing beside the remains of the meal. Sandra Pickersgill was clearing away. Twice, Rita threw her thoughtful glances. Sandra felt that Rita knew.

'These things are hard to tell,' said Rita. 'I think I choose to believe that you mean it.'

'Oh good,' said Liz. 'You don't think I'm a total bitch, then?'

'That's a very strong word, Liz. Total.'

Liz gave Rita a long, cool look, then laughed.

'Your friend Betty thinks I've planned it all,' she said.

'What do you think?' said Rita.

'I think . . . you're absolutely right, I don't think I really know . . . can one know about oneself, do you think, let alone about other people? . . . I think maybe I did plan it without really knowing. I do think I love Neville, though. People think we should have waited longer, but our hearts couldn't wait. Nothing could bring Laurence back, and I find that I don't believe he's there, watching, anywhere. So, why pretend? I feel we're getting too old for pretence.'

'I feel that too.'

'And the sooner we got married, we felt, the better for little Joscelyn. The young are more important than the dead.'

'How is he?'

'Blooming. Neville's as proud of him as if he was his own.'

'He . . . er . . . he doesn't . . . er . . .?'

'Oh, come on, Rita. No more pretence. No more evasion. Say what I know you're thinking.'

Simon was approaching, desperate to latch onto somebody's conversation and avoid the risk of another confrontation with Andrew Denton.

'He doesn't look like Ted, does he?' said Rita.

'Oh dear,' said Liz. 'I'm very much afraid he does. A tiny, pink, dribbling, almost bald Ted.'

'The mind boggles,' said Rita.

Simon turned away, and had to sit down again. His mind was boggling, too. Supposing, one day, Arthur Denton noticed that his baby was a miniature, bald, dribbling version of the estate agent he had met at Liz and Neville's wedding.

Elvis and Paul were bearing down on Rita. 'My God!' she said. 'This looks like a deputation.'

'I'll leave you to it,' said Liz, and she moved off to see if Simon was all right.

'Mum?' said Elvis. 'Can we have a word?'

'You think I'm making a fool of myself with Gerry.'

'Well . . . we've nothing against him as a person,' conceded Elvis.

'Which he is,' said Rita. 'As you'd know. Being a philosopher.'

'He seems quite nice, as far as that goes,' said Paul. 'But . . . he's so young, Mum. We're thinking of you.'

'Because we love you,' said Elvis.

'He is young,' said their mother. 'And I'm so old.'

'No! Of course not,' said Elvis. 'You aren't old. But . . . I mean . . . he is young . . . isn't he?'

'Oh yes. Terribly. He's so young and Harvey's so old.'

'All we mean is, Mum,' said Paul, 'it's all very well now, but will he still love you when you're . . .'

'. . . old and wrinkled?'

'No!'

'Oh dear,' said Rita. 'I wonder what reason you'd find to disapprove if I was marrying somebody of exactly my own age.'

'Mum!' said Paul.

'Marrying???' said Elvis.

'You've talked me into it,' said Rita. 'I'm marrying Gerry. He doesn't know yet.' She clapped her hands together. 'Ladies and gentlemen,' she shouted.

Silence fell quite rapidly. Rita stood with her back to the table where they had eaten. The others gathered round. Simon still looked pale, and took care not to be too near Andrew Denton.

'Ladies and gentlemen,' said Rita. 'I think we'd all like to thank Neville and Liz for inviting us to this very enjoyable wedding, and for giving us such a lovely do, we all like a bit of a do, and this was no exception, and I'm sure we'd all like to wish them every possible happiness.'

'Hear hear,' said Gerry Lansdown, and there was warm applause.

Monsieur Albert scurried in, sensing an approaching compliment. Ted and Sandra followed more slowly.

'I think we ought to thank Monsieur Albert and his staff for the excellent meal and service,' said Rita.

'Hear hear,' said Gerry, and there was warm applause.

Monsieur Albert beamed. Sandra tried to put her arm round Ted, and he fended it off angrily.

'You sound as if you're in the House of Commons already, Gerry,' said Rita. 'I wonder how I'll enjoy being an MP's wife.'

'Rita!' said Gerry.

'Yes,' said Rita. 'As soon as my divorce comes through, ladies and gentlemen, I'm going to marry Gerry.'

There were murmurs of surprise and delight. Nobody looked more surprised, and also more delighted, than Gerry Lansdown. Paul and Elvis looked chagrined. Jenny seemed thrilled. Ted looked astounded, and definitely not delighted. Sandra gave him a look that was as dry as a rock cake, and he rapidly managed to look fairly delighted.

The little gathering broke up again, and congratulations were offered to the happy couple. Paul went through to the bar and examined the little stone town above the Dordogne, where the white-haired old man was still crossing the road.

He was damned if he'd approach Jenny again, and risk another snub. Ever. Oh God! What right had that old man to cross that road so happily? What right had the mellow, arcaded town to be so beautiful? What was the point of love, if it made you hate?

'Paul?'

She had come to him. He almost stopped breathing. He turned slowly, trying to look calm and aloof, trying to hide his thumping heart.

'I'm glad for your mother,' she said.

'Oh yes. So am I.' Once he had promised never to lie. What had life done to him? What had he done to himself?

'And Carol's marrying Elvis. It's all a bit overwhelming.'

'Yes. Yes, it is.' His heart was racing. What could these overtures mean? 'I'm glad.' That at least wasn't a lie. But that was the one she doubted.

'Are you?' she said.

'Of course I am. Why shouldn't I be? Carol never meant anything to me.'

'Ah!'

'I mean, in *that* way. I mean, I like her as a person. As Elvis's fiancée. But not in . . . you know . . . that way.'

'Ah.'

The silence between them was probably quite brief. To Paul it seemed endless.

'Quite a day all round,' he said feebly, at last.

'Yes.'

'A brief escape from the world's problems.'

More silent seconds slipped slowly by. They stood as motionless as the white-haired old man. Was Jenny waiting for him to say something, something which he might never be able to say, if he didn't say it now. He hesitated, preparing his approach. It was important that he should be at his most seductive. His whole life might depend on it. 'I mean,' he began at last, 'in the context of religious wars, terrorism, imprisonment without trial, deeply divisive and unjust social and financial policies, famine, racial oppression, the destruction of the environment, the increasing gap between rich and poor, the imminence of the nuclear holocaust, and the ruthless, violent and totally unjustified suppression by both superpowers of the freedom of political choice in Afghanistan and Nicaragua . . .' She was nodding her agreement. He felt that he'd done it. '. . . in the context of all that, one silly one-night fling doesn't seem that important, does it?' he said. 'I mean, Amnesty International wouldn't bother with it.'

'Perhaps with the world like it is, it's all the more important not to do these things,' said Jenny.

He swallowed, hoped she couldn't see his leaping Adam's apple. 'I'd never do anything like that again,' he said.

'Yes, but don't you see?' wailed Jenny angrily. 'I'd never ever be sure ever again, would I?'

'I'd make you sure. I'd never leave your side ever again. I'd be a perfect husband.'

The seconds dragged by. He longed to be able to see into her brain. Looking at a person, standing there, it was impossible to understand how things could go on, at all, in brains.

'We may as well give it a try, then,' she said.

The beribboned limousine stood waiting. Neville and Liz Badger emerged into the afternoon shade, followed by Rita, Gerry Lansdown, Simon, Paul, Jenny, Elvis, Carol Fordingbridge, Andrew Denton, Arthur Badger and Monsieur Albert.

Jenny kissed Liz and Neville. Paul kissed Liz. Rita kissed Liz and Neville. Simon kissed Liz. Liz and Neville got into the car. Paul kissed Jenny. Rita kissed Gerry.

'No point in being left out,' said Elvis gruffly, and he kissed Carol.

The car drove off, unencumbered by old tins. The guests and Monsieur Albert waved.

Arthur Badger turned to Monsieur Albert, and thanked him with a prolonged volley of almost immaculate French. 'Merci, monsieur,' said Monsieur Albert, trying to look as if he'd understood.

'Goodbye,' said Andrew Denton to Simon. 'Don't show my wife round any more houses.'

'I won't,' said Simon Rodenhurst with feeling.

'I believe we'll be happy,' said Neville Badger, hoping that his words would make him feel happier.

The limousine slid smoothly up Moor Street into Tannergate, turned right, and passed the heavily scaffolded abbey church, where less than fourteen months ago Jenny had married Paul.

'Good. I hope we will, too,' said the second Mrs Badger.

'Jane thinks so, too.'

'Oh Neville!'

'Oh, I know she's dead, but, you see, I do still feel that she's with me. I can't help that.'

They swung down Westgate, past the heavily scaffolded frontage of the Angel Hotel. Liz remained silent. Neville wondered if she was upset.

'Perhaps I shouldn't have mentioned it,' he said, 'but I don't want to have secrets from you.'

Liz patted his hand, but didn't look at him.

'Well,' she said. 'I don't suppose you'd have married me if she didn't approve.'

'Happy?' said Gerry Lansdown, as they sped south towards Hindhead and his potential supporters.

'What a question,' said Rita.

'Listen with me,' pleaded the cake-loving Sandra Pickersgill.

'All right,' said Ted.

The sun was streaming into the yard, helping to rot the food in the bins and plastic bags. Soon they'd go home. Ted didn't want to. He wasn't feeling up to what Sandra would expect of him.

Sandra removed her headphones. Two bars of what sounded to Ted like cacophonous rubbish rang out. A rat scurried away, terrified. The music stopped.

'We've got an urgent report from our motoring unit,' boomed Dave-Boy Yarnold, the popular Radio Gadd disc jockey. 'It's for drivers heading towards Langstone-on-Gadd and Ecclesedge. The B6879 to Langstone-on-Gadd and Ecclesedge is covered in chickens just below Upper Mill. That's right. I said chickens! Apparently they've escaped from a battery chicken farm and are running around all over the place. So drive those lorries carefully, or you may end up with an instant cock au van.'

'That's Rodney,' said Ted. 'He's done it!'

He thought that the next record sounded quite nice. Sandra switched it off in disgust.

'Cheer up, Ted,' she said, putting her arm round him. 'It's a happy day.'

'Is it? It wasn't happy for her ex-husband.'

'No . . . well . . .'

'Poor Laurence. Nobody ever thought he felt anything.'

'Well, there you are. That's it.'

'What?'

'Life. You never know what people are thinking inside those heads.'

A mangy grey cat entered the yard. Ted threw a catering-size tin of meadow-fresh mushrooms at it, and it fled.

He hoped Sandra didn't know what he was thinking, inside his head. He was thinking that he just didn't know what to think.

'Don't be morbid,' she said. 'Don't think about him. Everything else has turned out right well.'

'Has it?'

''Course it has. I mean the happy couple are happy, obviously, and so are your Elvis and Carol. And it's worked out really well for your Paul and Jenny. It's even worked out for the chickens.'

'Has it?'

''Course it has. Freedom's important. I think so, anyroad.'

'I'm not sure if it is for chickens.'

Sandra hesitated before continuing. An autumn wasp hovered around them. Ted swatted it angrily. Why should it pick on them, in this cornucopia of decay? It floated lazily away, drunk on fermenting food. Sandra found the courage to continue.

'It's happy for Rita and Gerry, too,' she said. 'It is, Ted. Face it. It is.'

'I just don't see it, Sandra,' he said. 'I'm sorry, but . . . I mean . . . I don't.'

'You don't see it because you never appreciated what you had till you didn't have it.'

'All right, but . . . I mean . . . whichever way you look at it, love . . . I mean, it is. Isn't it? Ridiculous.'

'Love is ridiculous.'

'Yes.'

Sandra slid her left leg across his legs, and kissed his cheek. Her breath had the sweet stickiness of a wasp's breakfast.

'A year ago you might have said it's ridiculous if somebody had said you'd be a head waiter and you'd spend the rest of your life with a sacked bakery assistant you met at the DHSS,' she said. 'But it isn't ridiculous, is it?'

'No. Of course it isn't.'

'Well, cheer up, then,' she said. She placed her left hand gently on his crotch. 'Don't you love me?'

'Sandra! Love! What a question! Of course I do!' He kissed her gently. 'Madly!' he said. 'Deliriously! Totally!' He kissed her again, much more enthusiastically, running his tongue round the gap in her top teeth. Then, slowly, he withdrew from the embrace. 'But,' he said.

8